Amos and the Cosmos

A Rollicking Journey through
America's Heart and Soul

by Alan Schwartz

iUniverse, Inc.
New York Bloomington

Amos and the Cosmos
A Rollicking Journey through America's Heart and Soul

iUniverse books may be ordered through booksellers or by contacting:

iUniverse
1663 Liberty Drive
Bloomington, IN 47403
www.iuniverse.com
1-800-Authors (1-800-288-4677)

ISBN: 978-1-4401-9000-1 (sc)
ISBN: 978-1-4401-8998-2 (dj)
ISBN: 978-1-4401-8999-9 (ebk)

Printed in the United States of America

iUniverse rev. date: 03/23/2010

To B.K.S., T.S., A.S., and the rest…

Praise for Amos Boris Lardowitz's *From African Princess to American Slave: A Love Story:*

"Amos Boris Lardowitz, American historian and dealer in rare manuscripts, and partner in the publishing firm of Lardowitz and Fink, based in Manhattan, New York, has snared the literary prize of the twentieth century for his book *From African Princess to American Slave: A Love Story*. The pristine handwritten prose and poetry of the young slave Rebecca during America's Civil War has come alive for all Americans. At first, with no knowledge of English, and then a budding poet, exploring her world of horror and pain and momentary beauty ... she discovers love, forbidden love, expressed with softness and tenderness, hopelessness and despair ... the love of her white slave master ... plantation owner. The coup for Mr. Lardowitz, in the direct face of the probable ridicule of his peers, was to intersperse Rebecca's spontaneous prose with *his* descriptions of her feelings and the realities of her surroundings. Somehow Mr. Lardowitz has succeeded where he should not have ... taking a literary license usually frowned upon ... as if he took Rebecca's handwritten words and added his own touches of reality ... her own breath becomes his ... in unison ...

"How Mr. Lardowitz has accomplished this literary feat is beyond this writer ... No matter ... This is a love story ... It is alive ... a full 120 years beyond its passing."

—Excerpt of cover story from *Time*, June 3, 1984

"1984 has come, feared and dreaded in 1949 on the publication of the novel of the same name by George Orwell—but instead of 'freedom is slavery' ... slavery becomes freedom for the love poet Rebecca ... and accolades go to Amos Lardowitz for his literary masterpiece."

—*The New Yorker*, August 7, 1984

"It is rare ... and the committee thought long and hard, but Rebecca stole the hearts of the American people ... and she spoke to us more than a hundred years ago. Our decision to offer a special Pulitzer Prize for Poetry will probably not happen for another hundred years."

—Excerpt from Pulitzer Prize Board press release, 1985

"Amos Boris Lardowitz, American author, has exposed the true soul of America for the entire world to see. To publish the Black on White love poems of a kidnapped princess, sold into slavery, gives hope to the international community that America is coming to grips with its past."

—Special mention, the Nobel Committee,
Stockholm, Sweden, 1987

"A man-child of enormous curiosity … ethical curiosity … and love for his America … an America that may not exist at all without the likes of Amos Boris Lardowitz."

—Allen Ginsberg, July 4, 1986

O beautiful, for spacious skies,
For amber waves of grain,
For purple mountain majesties
Above the fruited plain!
America! America!
God shed his grace on thee,
And crown thy good with brotherhood,
From sea to shining sea!

O beautiful, for patriot dream
That sees beyond the years,
Thine alabaster cities gleam
Undimmed by human tears!
America! America!
God mend thine ev'ry flaw,
Confirm thy soul in self control,
Thy liberty in law!

Katharine Lee Bates, 1859—1929

Preface

In publishing my memoirs I suppose I run the risk of ridicule, especially among the movers and shakers of my world, the literary world. As a shy young person I never thought I would be writing about myself, let alone publishing the story of my life, but I am.

In publishing the phenomenally successful poems and prose of the slave Rebecca, *From African Princess to American Slave: A Love Story,* in 1984, I know I took a risk, one that I have only now revealed. Rebecca was my Jewish dad's grandmother. This fact is the catalyst that created the need to illuminate a journey—an American journey that led to the discovery of my American heritage.

My story is about my ancestry, my personal history. It is as well a story about my America and was initiated by a sort of quixotic quest to find the meaning behind an old picture from my family. My curiosity and passionate interest in America were born to me as well as my inner uncertainty that causes me to always question and search for some truth in the universe.

As I grew in size and age, I seemed to be trying to connect everybody in my life and ultimately the world to my story. As I questioned the world, I wondered where it would lead, and as I look back on my completed journey (at least to this point in my life), I wonder how many of us have the same story: a story of interconnected lives of people from history—people who may not look like you or me and people who may not have acted like you or me. And as I think now in the broadest sense, I wonder whether, if I hadn't pursued my story, my life and others close to me would even know each other or possibly even exist.

My journey never would have happened without my mentor and dearest friend, Ben. He introduced me to the "Cosmos" and the aura of creativity that encompasses it, and because of it he helped me find my American family.

And well beyond my immediate family I have discovered that humankind is a quilt whose interwoven threads consist of all of us—and when you trace just one small thread at the frayed end, you will find that

Maybe it was a mistake. Maybe the person who wrote the inscription stopped in the middle of Henrietta's last name and didn't know how to spell it and just plain quit. Maybe the person didn't know her last name was Lardowitz, which was our family name. It was strange—a mystery to me.

I was always a curious boy, although it was rare for me to seek help or to have my questions answered. I would go deeper and deeper into my own head to figure things out. I spent a lot of time with my own thoughts.

Normally, I would have continued to mull it over in my head for a few months, but I was beginning to develop an obsession with this, so I decided to bite the bullet and ask Dad. It was his family after all.

Dad was a quiet person, but he would answer any question completely and straightforwardly.

"Dad … about my aunt Henrietta?"

"Yes, Amos."

"What was her last name?"

"Amos, she was my sister."

"So, I guess she was a Lardowitz."

For some reason, as with all questions to Dad, I couldn't bring myself to follow up. That was the end of it for the moment.

I went to the attic often after that. I would sit and smell the wood and snoop around old clothes and old magazines that Mom and Dad had saved. And again, as if under a spell, I would pull out of the box *My sister, Henrietta Lardy.* Each time I would run my hands over the picture and across the back of it, as if rewriting *Henrietta Lardy.*

Then one day, as I sat doing the same thing while the steady sound of rain beat the roof, my fingers took me to the bottom of the back of the picture as if I were being controlled by a Ouija board. There appeared, as if it hadn't been there before, very faintly on the margin, the handwritten words *Your brother, Hardy.*

I awakened suddenly, in the dead of night, with the words *Hardy Lardy* on my lips.

The words would float around in my head at first, one after another. They started, every night, as silent words spoken with my eyes closed. That seemed to go on for an hour. Then my mouth would open slightly, a crack, and I would very softly utter the words out loud in the dark, "Hardy Lardy, Hardy Lardy," at first without moving my lips. Then I would open my mouth wide and exaggerate the sounds. They were so perfect, floating and then rolling off my tongue and out into space, into the quiet night. I would accentuate the first syllables and then the second: "HARdy LARdy, HarDY LarDY."

It seemed to go on, every night, for six months as soon as I hit the pillow and the lights were out. I was just fifteen years old, and I abruptly stopped dreaming of girls.

It was always "Hardy Lardy."

Little did I know then, in 1955, that that moment in time would be the thread that would weave the fabric of my life together.

The Early Years

MY DAD'S NAME is Har Phillip Lardowitz. I was told that his family was from Europe. They were turn-of-the-century immigrants. He never really talked about them like Mom did with her family, who also were turn-of-the-century immigrants. Actually, Mom came to America with her mother and father when she was three years old. I thought Dad's first name was possibly Russian or Polish or some other European name. I never asked, really. Mom always called him Phillip or "dear." Dad was a physician. I have seen letters addressed to him as H. Phillip Lardowitz, MD. I also knew Dad had a sister, Henrietta. I never knew Dad's family. His parents died before I was born and so did his sister.

I am Amos Boris Lardowitz, or, as I was formally known in school, Amos B. Lardowitz. I was named for my mother's grandfather and grand-uncle. As usual in the Jewish tradition, you would be named only for the dead, nobody living. As Jews became more modern, I guess, they wanted to have more choices, for I knew many Jewish friends who were named with just the first letter of their relatives. My great-grandfather was named Amos, and my great-grand-uncle was Boris.

My mother called me Amie (pronounced Amy—like the girl's name) throughout my whole life, although occasionally I would hear, from downstairs, a loud and crisp "Amos Boris Lardowitz" in even cadence. *Oh boy, I burned the potholder!*

In high school my friends called me A.B. Unfortunately, it sounded like Abie. Dad called me Amos all the time.

My mom was the historian in my family, but the family history was always her family history. She never spoke of Dad's family and Dad didn't either. Actually, rarely did Dad speak compared to Mom. When he did speak, he did so sparely, and it was concise and to the point. He said what needed to be said and it was consistent, maybe because he was a doctor.

It appeared that Mom was always orchestrating our family and our activities. And when she spoke of her relatives, they were members of her orchestra also.

"Grandpa Morris [her father] carried Bea [her sister] like a kitten in a blanket."

"Grandma Bessie [her mother] would cook that boiled chicken [her favorite meal] in a broth filled with herbs; I never did find out what they were."

It seemed that all history was Jewish and obviously all family was Mom's. It also seemed that all Jewish history began on the day her family landed in America, around 1900. There was never talk of Europe or wherever they came from. Our Jewish life was centered on our synagogue and her brothers and sisters, all of whom lived within ten miles of us in New York.

When my sister, Susan, first met her future husband, he worked in a bank. I would hear Mom talk to her friends on the telephone. "Susan is going out with a Jewish banker."(He was a teller.)

Fortunately for my mom and Susan, Alvin did become a banker. He was promoted to a vice president eventually, eight years later.

"Jewish banker," I would think—I wonder, if Susan had met a Christian banker, Mom would have announced that Susan was dating a "Christian banker." Somehow a Jewish banker sounded more powerful. "Christian banker" evoked to me a person who worked in a bank that was in a church. Or as my weird mind would always think, a person named Christian Banker. And Mom would say, "Susan is dating Christian Banker."

Christian Banker, I would think—a cool name: Christian Banker III, no less. He probably played varsity football for Mamaroneck High School. He was also a National Honor Society student and president of his junior class.

Amos Boris Lardowitz, I would think—he took some pictures for the high school yearbook.

This was the daydreaming Amos Boris Lardowitz. I dreamt only of an American history. From the days of my youth, in the forties, I dreamt of Joe DiMaggio and the Yankees. As I became a teenager, I was absorbed by the American Civil War and anything that was American. From the moment I saw "Daughters of the American Revolution" in print, I wanted to become a member. In fact, when I was twelve, in 1952, I wrote them, and they responded, asking me to provide proof of my heritage. I bought *American Heritage* magazine and kept it under my bed and read the same issue for thirty straight days. On Saturdays, I would peruse old bookstores and buy Civil War–era newspapers and books. I would stop by every historical marker and read it three times and walk around all soldier statues seven times. There was so much American history in America. But alas, our family history seemed to stop at 1900—it wasn't even considered antique in 1953.

I was born in the Bronx Hospital on January 1, 1940. Amos Boris Lardowitz, son of Helen and Har Phillip Lardowitz, younger brother (by four years) of Susan Lardowitz (no middle name; girls didn't have a middle name). I was born in a good year, at the beginning of a decade, and on the first day of the year, so it would be easier to measure my age and accomplishments. I was not the first baby of the year in the Bronx Hospital, but my family did get a pair of knitted woolen baby slippers with the year 1940 crocheted in (which are now sitting in an old box with a family of baby squirrels inside). I was told that Dad moved the family to our new and larger apartment from one section of the Bronx to another on my birth—Americans moving up.

In the forties, my world was New York City. Its capital to me was Manhattan. From my earliest recollection, I can remember being shuttled on day trips to Manhattan on Saturdays with a teacher and other schoolkids. The Museum of Natural History. Central Park. The Empire State Building. I can still remember the smells of hot lunches, especially the soups, at the Museum of Natural History. Everything was really big. The movies were big. The theater was big. The seats were big. I guess I was small. It was the beginning of my American consciousness. My American heroes were gods. Most of them walked with their legs wide apart, like they hurt, and always with a grunt here and there. Most of them were accompanied by a musical jingle with each step. It must have been the spurs—but I never knew what they were for. Most of them carried a wide belt with shiny bullets slanted always to one side with a holster filled with my American icon, the silver six-shooter. When I saw one who appeared to be one of my American heroes without a belt and gun, I would not trust him—he must have been a teacher or something. Gary Cooper and Randolph Scott and Amos Boris Lardowitz always rode together.

There was the future also, and he was called Flash Gordon. He was always running gracefully through a doorway, pointing and directing everyone to an escape. His enemies were always foreign to me: Ming—the Merciless, no less—a mixture of Oriental and evil. Today, I would name my cat Ming. Every episode would end in near disaster. But the next week Flash was always there again—but only on Saturdays in the movie theater, of course—saving an American world from the evil Ming.

We would occasionally drive across the Brooklyn Bridge to Brooklyn, and my father would playfully say we were entering enemy territory. Consequently I always brought my toy six-shooter and laid it under the back window, looking backward and upward as the bridge passed behind me. The flickering across my eyes from the passing rapid shadows was like a surreal movie. I would look up at the cables for hiding Nazis or Japs. Manhattan was my world—my country. The Bronx was not my real home. I owned the Empire State Building. It was the center of my universe. And when King Kong was being pursued to his destiny, he found the Empire State Building just like I did.

My life in the forties was my shiny six-shooter and my bicycle and the wonderland produced by the occasional serious snowfall in the Bronx. Life was also the summer, before air-conditioning. From the time I can remember, we schlepped by car to the country, Dad, Mom, Susan, and me. For eight weeks we went. Dad would only take us up and then go back home and work, and come and visit every other weekend. We swam in a small pond where I once exposed myself to a girl, at eight years old, under water. I learned how to play baseball, how to swim, and how to act; we performed plays in a barn once monthly. We also had performers come once a month. I remember a magician calling me up on stage. He sat me in a chair, took an egg from his pocket, and announced to the audience that he was going to push the egg right through the top of my head and have it come out of my mouth. He palmed the egg and started pounding my head, once, twice, three times. He then squeezed my jaw with his hand over my mouth, and out popped the egg. In the same split second, I heard his whisper in my ear, "Tell them it came out of your mouth." I was dazed.

I walked off the stage thinking the egg had come out of my mouth. Oh, the naiveté of youth.

I always remember the smells and the look of late summer. It was the time in late August when we would head back home to the Bronx. The air was warm and soft, and the light was hazy. When we walked into our apartment, the smell was new all over again. Mom would have covered all the furniture in white sheets. There was a musty smell that existed only on the day we arrived home. To this day, that smell is endearing. Years later, I wondered if Dad lived in white sheets for the whole summer.

I remember going with Dad to pick up our new 1949 Dodge. It was a four-door sedan. I was so excited. I remember playing in the backseats before he drove it off the dealership lot. It was like a house. I could go out the back doors. On the way home, I was sitting in the front passenger seat when suddenly I felt a jolt and heard a screech. I felt myself flying forward. Instantaneously, as I was moving forward, a long, large arm from my left came across my body, and I recoiled back into my seat. It was Dad's arm preventing me from hitting the dashboard. At that point and for years after, I realized how small I was, or how big Dad was. This was my first seat belt experience. It was also the last year of a small childhood lived, for 1949 was ending, and the start of a new decade was beginning—to help measure my life with.

When I was a little older, about ten, Dad would take me to his office on Saturdays. He was a general practitioner, as mostly all doctors were in the forties and fifties. Dad delivered all of my cousins, but of course, he didn't deliver Susan and me. I always remember Dad as the tallest person in a group. Actually he was probably six feet, but he was relatively thin with long, straight arms and had perfect posture (not like me), so he appeared taller than he was.

Dad's office was in Lower Manhattan, on the East Side, not far from Chinatown in a mostly Jewish neighborhood, which was closely bordered by Italians and Poles. His office was on the ground floor in a renovated store. It had a second floor, and a third that he didn't use. The second floor had two rooms. One was a storage room and the other was his personal office. He had a large desk that was darkly stained and a wooden office chair on wheels. The desk was filled with cubbyholes. It seemed to me that it was enormous. It was always stuffed with papers. The desk surface was also piled up with magazines and papers and medical records. A black telephone sat on the corner of the desk, and the only light was an overhead ceiling globe. Dad worked every Saturday except during the summer when he took every other weekend to visit with us in the country.

Dad went to the synagogue every Saturday morning at seven. He then came home at eight fifteen and made sure I was ready to go to the office. I was always excited Friday night when Dad announced that he was taking me to the office the next day. I didn't sleep well because of my excitement. It seemed that I was always awake when he left for the synagogue, eagerly awaiting his return and thinking of spending the day with him.

We always arrived from the Bronx at nine fifteen. No one was there. The first thing he said to me upon arrival was "Amos, go upstairs." There I would play, mostly sitting in his big chair. I would hear the door buzzer at about nine thirty. The buzzer was sharp and annoying. Then the door opened, and I could hear, "Good morning, Dr. Lardowitz."

"Good morning, Sadie." And his first patient arrived.

Roughly one hour later, I would hear Dad's even footsteps come up the stairs. "Let me sit down, Amos." He would write and write and write while I looked out the window at the tenements and people and cars below. Then the buzzer, and then Dad would lean his head and speak as loudly as I have ever heard him speak, "I'll be right down, Mrs. Nosonowitz."

"What?"

"I'll be right down, Mrs. Nosonowitz."

"What?"—until Dad just got up and walked downstairs.

Occasionally, Dad would leave his stethoscope on the desk with his rubber mallet. I would play doctor. I would put the hearing piece on the desk and listen for sounds. I never failed to hear thumping sounds every time I tried it. I was convinced that the desk had a heart. I would also hammer my knees for ten minutes, until I couldn't walk. I remember Dad once asking what was wrong with me—and I just mumbled.

Dad had a nurse, but she didn't work on Saturdays. Her name was Ethel, and she was fat. Occasionally, I came during the week when there was a school vacation. Dad would tolerate me downstairs only when Ethel was there. On the ground floor, there was an examination room, an x-ray room, and a room full of drugs. It all smelled like alcohol. When I was downstairs, it seemed that I was never able to get out of the way of Nurse Ethel. "Excuse me, Amos." "I'm sorry, Amos." "Watch yourself, Amos."

When Dad talked to his patients, whether they were sitting or standing, he looked like a statue, tall and graceful. The one sound that sticks in my head is the "argggggh," produced by a patient with a tongue depressor gagging her. Dad's patients were mostly older women. He must have seen children, especially on Saturday, but I probably blocked out the crying by singing into one of his stethoscopes with the earpieces in my ears. It seemed that all of his adult patients were infirm, stooped over, and with misshapen bodies, but their eyes seemed to open wide when they saw me. "Amos! And how are you?" Many times, I would suffer a sore cheek or butt from the inevitable pinch.

"This will hurt only a little." I think I heard that expression in my dreams, ad nauseam. I don't know if it really only hurt a little, because everybody thought it hurt a lot. It seemed everyone got penicillin, the wonder drug of the forties. I got penicillin. Susan got penicillin. All my cousins got penicillin. Whenever I was home from school with a fever, Mom would call Dad and ask him to bring home a penicillin shot. I dreaded the shot. Those days, I dreaded Dad coming home. I hoped that he had an emergency and would stay really late in the hospital or something. I had a conflict, because I hoped my fever would be gone by the time Dad came home. But then again, I think I liked staying home from school more than I disliked penicillin shots, for I was sick a lot. First the smell of alcohol, and then the "Roll over, Amos"—and then the only time that my butt would tighten so much, then the scream, cut short by the split-second jab. My mind must have said, "It's over?"

I also remember Mom's alcohol rubs when I got a fever. She would undress me completely and take a washcloth and wet it with alcohol. She started at my toes and methodically massaged me up my limbs and right into the top of my head. It was a wonderful feeling and well worth the penicillin shot.

Dad also made house calls. When he occasionally brought me along, it seemed that everybody was delighted. I would sit in the parlor, not hearing much, while Dad was in the kitchen examining his patient. At each home, the old ladies would ask me if I wanted anything and Dad would always say, "You could give Amos some milk and cookies." I remember one Saturday vomiting profusely at home after making the rounds. Dad realized that I had had one gallon of milk and eighteen cookies.

Memories, memories—mostly noneventful memories. My memory of Dad in those years was of a methodical and even-tempered man who did the same thing every day: helped people.

It was early spring 1952, and I was in my room after dinner with the door open. I heard Mom say, "It has three bedrooms and a finished basement."

"Yes, Helen, and it's in a real neighborhood of houses—a real suburb." One word I didn't understand. I heard "subub," or something like that. I was a shy boy, and often if I didn't understand something, I kept it to myself—a pattern that would obviously be repeated and repeated. For weeks, I kept saying the word over and over.

When I was in the fourth grade, Mrs. Krause came to our class and asked all the students if they would be interested in playing a musical instrument so that we could be in the fourth-grade orchestra. I raised my hand but I wasn't sure why. She showed us instruments and suggested to each one of us—for reasons I still don't understand—which one would be good for us to play. She said, "Amos, you play the clarinet." We were taught the basics. I believe there were three other kids in other classes who were taught the clarinet. I remember practicing in school a lot, and in my room at home. It must have been two months later, after we had all played a simple program as an orchestra, that Mrs. Krause singled out all the kids playing the same instrument. She then asked each kid in a semicircle to perform. I was the third out of four kids in the clarinet group. I did my scales. Mrs. Krause said, "What?" after I had finished. She proceeded to grab my instrument and loosened the reed, turned it around, and put it back in the mouthpiece. She said, "Here, play."A musical sound actually emerged from my instrument. For six weeks I had played this instrument. For six weeks my sound had been nothing like the other sounds. For six weeks I knew that my sound was different, but I'd never said anything. This experience became a metaphor for my life—I knew that my sound was different, but I couldn't do anything about it.

I think I understood that our family was moving to a new house somewhere—but they never told me, so I never asked. But I did walk into Susan's room one night and say, "Susan, you're a subub."

She said, "Shut up, Amos."

Then one day, Mom ran her hand through my hair and around my face and said, "Amie, how would you like to live in a house?"

"Where, Mom?"

"In the suburbs."

"Where, Mom?"

"In the suburbs, in Westchester County."

"Where is that, Mom?"

"About fifteen miles from here, in the country."

"What about my friend Stephen? Is he moving?"

"No, Amie, you'll make new friends."

I got away without asking what the word *suburb* meant, but I was very unhappy. I went back to my room and cried.

When the whole family went in the car, I always sat in the right backseat, Susan, the left, and Mom in the passenger seat; Dad, of course, drove. I always wanted to look at Dad's face while he was driving, and I wouldn't see him from the seat right behind him. It seemed that Susan never looked around inside the car. She always brought a book and kept her head down and the pages open. I tried that once, and Dad had to stop the car and I threw up on somebody's lawn two times.

The fateful day finally arrived. Mom had announced to Susan and me twice at breakfast that on the coming Sunday we would see our new house. Mom and Dad must have gone at least two times alone, because Susan and I were sent by ourselves, two times, to play at Aunt Bea and Uncle Carl's apartment with our cousins.

Mom had two brothers and two sisters; Sam, Morris, Bea, and Sadie. We had nine cousins between the four families; Stanley, Robert, Jules, Carol, Lilly, Richard, Janice, Estelle, and Henry. They all lived in the Bronx.

About once monthly, we would all gather as a family at one of the sister's or brother's homes. It was a madhouse. I was always late for school on the Monday morning after a Sunday visit because I couldn't get up. I was so tired from the day before. All the cousins would be on the floor and all the adults would be sitting in chairs or on the sofas. Everyone would be talking at once. There were always the simultaneous smells of pot roast, kugel, coffee, and Uncle Carl's cigar in the air.

My favorite cousin was Janice. I think I had a crush on her. She was two years older than I was. Occasionally, when I looked up from playing blocks, all I could see were flying hands and arms. Everyone waved their arms when they talked—everyone except Dad. He always sat in a dining room chair, straight up, with his hands clasped together on the dining room table. When he talked, it was in the same tone as when he was speaking to his patients, even and clear, quiet but firm. It seemed that at least every thirty minutes I needed to find Dad and just look at him for two seconds. He was the still photo amid old-time movies.

As well, I couldn't do without my mother's touch or her softness and her hugs, the way she ran her hand through my hair, the way she ran her hand over my face, the way she called me Amie. My mom was small—five foot two—with hazel eyes and almost brown red hair. I remember the monthly smell when I came home from school. Mom was in the bathroom with her head under the sink—henna. It smelled like wet, dark dirt. I didn't know at this time in my life that henna made her hair color what it was. I thought she was actually washing dirt out of her hair.

I really needed Dad. I needed to see him standing up tall and straight. I needed the only way he ever touched me, resting his hand on my shoulder when he talked to me.

We all got into the car, me on my favorite side. It was a sunny day, a Sunday. I felt very excited. We drove up the Bronx River Parkway, which I know today is the oldest highway in America. Dad always let me carry our box camera. It was a Kodak. It was simple. I kept the camera in my lap like it was a gun I needed for protection. I didn't bring my six-shooter—maybe I felt we were not going into enemy territory. The trip took less than an hour. I deliberately let myself daydream. I felt like I was an early trailblazer who was about to discover some western land, and maybe Indians. I occasionally wondered what the heck Susan was thinking of while I was fantasizing. I actually fantasized what she would be fantasizing. I think that on this trip I imagined myself as Susan in a covered wagon holding a stuffed rag doll with a bonnet over her head, peeking out the back. Suddenly, Indians attacked the wagon and Susan fell out and was whisked up from the ground (Raggedy Ann and all) by an Indian on a paint horse—then I was back. *Girls: what the heck do they think about anyway*—and was it ever important?

The air started to smell different. It was late May and there were a lot of fragrances. But the air seemed to be different from that of the Bronx and the country. It was definitely different from Manhattan. Manhattan air was good. There was diesel gas and cigarette smoke. There was perfume and garlic. It was great. But this smell wasn't all bad. It was not the city, and not the country. I guess it was the "sububs." The whole trip was on the Bronx River Parkway. It was gently winding, with parklike views and beautiful trees. Then suddenly, Dad said, "I turn here, right, Helen?"

"Yes, dear."

Small tree-lined streets and little old houses, fairly close together. We drove through a few blocks like this, up and down little hills. "Here it is, kids, the white house with the green shutters." At this point, I half lost it. I expected that we were moving in right then and there. *Holy shit!* I must have regained myself when Mom said, "Amie, Susan, now be nice to the lady. She has to leave her house in two months." *Two months. A reprieve!*

We all got out of the car. It was sort of creepy, but exciting. The house was a small three-story box colonial with a roof over the front door. There was a two-car garage in the back of the driveway that was separate from the house. There really was no walkway to the house. We walked up the driveway and then across some flagstones and up the wooden stairs. There we stood, I think back now, like the homeless four looking for a place to sleep. Dad rang the bell. An old lady opened the door. "Dr. Lardovitz, velcome. This must be Mrs. Lardovitz, and you two must be Zuzan and Amos."

Dad said, "This is Mrs. Kudlich."

"I vill show you through the houze." We proceeded to walk through the living room, dining room, and kitchen, and on to the upstairs. There were three bedrooms, a big one and two medium ones.

"Amie, this will be your room," Mom said at the smaller of the two medium ones. This room was bigger than my room in the Bronx. There was also a third floor, but we didn't go up there. We then went outside and around back. There was a covered porch outside the dining room and a small green lawn bordered by hedges and what looked like other houses behind them. So this must be the "sububs," I thought—so far, not bad. I didn't see any other kids on this block. Actually, I didn't think beyond this initial visit. My excitement must have disappeared. I really had no feeling. Maybe I was blocking out this traumatic event. We left the house and Mom said, "We're moving here in mid-August." On the way back home, I was stunned. I didn't have anything on my mind, which was very unusual. I think this was the only case of near depression that I have ever had in my life. I had never been a depressed person. My mind was always too active and curious to allow any depression in. I've been sad and melancholy, though—and actually, melancholy was almost a relief whenever my overactive mind had been too overactive.

Home, sweet home—my Bronx. Suddenly the Bronx became my Bronx, for weeks. I guess I was in early mourning or something. *My friends*—that was sad. I really had only one friend, Stephen. I wanted him to move with me. I cried for a minute every night for two weeks, and then it suddenly stopped. Suddenly, I stopped thinking about the trauma of moving, probably because the last day of school was the next day. Summer was freedom. Summer was fun. Summer was warm. Summer was actually hell. Moving was hell. The summer of 1952 was different. I couldn't follow my beloved Yankees. I couldn't go to any home games. The contents of every drawer and closet in our apartment were taken out and neatly stacked in almost every square foot of floor space.

"Stephen, Amos, go outside ... Watch it ... Don't break the porcelain."

What was the porcelain doing on the floor? *We have no room to put our army of little soldiers. We can't have a war without room on the floor!*

The fateful day must have come when Mom opened the door to what appeared to be a bunch of smelly thugs, reeking of cigarette smoke and body odor. They certainly had no respect for me, and little for Susan. We were in the way all the time. Mom was aware of my toys, my soldiers, my games, because she packed them herself and told me not to worry about them. "Amie, when you get to your new room, all your stuff will be there," she said. I daydreamed that these guys were sent to empty the remaining apartment and search out the Nazi map that led one to the hidden store of gold bullion.

August 15, 1952, the last day. The meeting of Lee and Grant at Appomattox—to sign over the deed and exchange keys.

Actually, there was a distinct coziness that I could not measure but that surely I felt. The whole family was in this together. This time the wagon train was truly headed west (really north) into unknown territory—but into a new land of opportunity.

Especially in my early years, it is obvious that incidents in American history have been metaphors for my life, and this move was monumental in its historic significance.

Living in a house seemed so different. The first night, I couldn't get used to not having neighbors above, below, and to the right and left of our ceilings and walls. When I was downstairs and heard footsteps and a door close, I thought strangers were upstairs. I began to realize that I could yell at Susan more and play my radio louder.

I didn't seem to have much time to enjoy the rest of the summer, because I woke up in the morning of our third sleepover to what I thought was an earthquake, but was Susan shaking my bed violently and yelling into my ear, "Amos, wake up. Mom is having a family meeting downstairs in ten minutes."

There I was, bleary eyed amid the clutter of boxes, sitting at the kitchen table with Mom, Dad, and Susan.

"OK, family. Do you like your new house?"

"Yes, Mom ..."

"Uh huh, Mommy ..." (That was me.)

Then Mom proceeded to tell us about our new schools. Susan was to go to the high school, and I was going into seventh grade in the lower school. We would still take the bus. She had two folders, one with Susan's name on it and one with my name on it. She took out Susan's and proceeded to show her where her school was and what the rules and regulations were, and told her they would visit the school the next day.

She looked at my folder and said, "Amie, you're going to be a bar mitzvah in four months, so I want you to be sure to go out of your way to meet Jewish friends at school."

I don't know why that bothered me at the moment. Well, maybe I do know. There Susan sat, smug faced, with a slight sarcastic grin on her puss, staring at me.

When we lived in the Bronx, I went to Hebrew school two days a week after school, and my circle of friends were certainly Jewish, as well as my bevy of cousins. So I guess the Bronx was a safe Jewish haven, free of the Gentile riffraff.

But we had moved to the "sububs," where I guess it was not safe to be Jewish unless you were with other Jews. I was thinking that it probably made sense if you thought of it that way. Obviously, I was not going to cry or have a panic attack, so I had to provide some rationale in my head.

Then it hit me about the bar mitzvah. Girls were not bar mitzvahed in our religious circle. Even if they were, it would be called a bat mitzvah, and when my older cousins were bar mitzvahed, all the adults stressed that "Today, you are a man"—which I guess definitely ruled Susan out. So it was my deal and my problem, and my hard work.

"Amie, I know that four months is not a long time to study your haphtarah, but you know we didn't want to start at our synagogue in the Bronx, so we waited, honey."

Oh shit, not only a new school, but a new synagogue. Suddenly the "sububs" were really becoming evil—probably, I thought, it's just what they were all along.

The last few weeks before school were a whirlwind, I remember. Off to the new synagogue, off to the new school, off to the new dentist, off to the new market to help Mom with the groceries. There was no other life anymore like the one I had cherished in the Bronx. There was no Stephen to play war with. There were no trips into the city for now. I'd lost my centering, I thought. Looking back on this, I find it really strange that a pre-teenage adolescent could ever feel centered, but this was the growing Amos Boris Lardowitz—life experiences happening.

There was a park within walking distance of our new home. It was adjacent to the Bronx River Parkway and had a playing field for baseball and football. I met one Jewish friend at the synagogue when Mom took me over there to introduce me. He actually lived on the next block and invited me to come down to the field to play touch football. There I met a few kids who turned into more kids—boys and girls. I don't think I was ever as popular with boys and girls as at this moment in my life, sixth through eighth grade, before high school. I'm not sure if Mom really knew, but I had two girlfriends right off the bat. They were sisters—and they were Irish. In fact, most of my friends at that time were not Jewish, although I certainly had a small group of Jewish boy friends I had met at the synagogue. All my girlfriends were shiksas—non-Jewish girls—in other words, off limits to little Jewish boys.

My life in the suburbs gradually became comfortable. In fact, it seemed that almost suddenly and without difficulty, I understood that there was no word *subub* and that the suburbs were actually not evil—well, mostly not evil. There was a period of time during my bar mitzvah studies that I felt (and all my other Hebrew class friends felt) that Cantor Krickstein was evil. We also had a rabbi, but he seemed to have no personality. The cantor was the one giving our bar mitzvah class and teaching us the difficult intonations of singing the Torah, which was the integral part of our manhood exercise. Cantor Krickstein had a big mouth and big teeth and mostly big bad breath. He also had a strange malady. Strings of saliva would start to attach and form like rubber bands from his upper teeth to his lower ones, while he sang. They would dance in rhythm, coiling and stretching up and down, up and down. Not one boy in the class could keep from staring at Cantor Krickstein's mouth while he sang or even talked. There was an evil obsession going on—a mesmerizing curse that wiped out our Hebrew memory during our studies. Cantor Krickstein actually complained to our parents that this particular group was the worst he had ever taught and that we must be stupid or something. In actuality, our group of six was held hostage to a strange natural phenomenon that we dubbed in private, and swore secrecy from all—"the dancing spit."

It was a tough time during that ritual to manhood, for age thirteen in the Jewish religion is the beginning of manhood. It must have meant something eons ago since all Jewish teachings are based on practical lessons in living, but it certainly seemed silly in modern times that a snot-nosed, hyperactive, adolescent thirteen-year-old child could become a real man.

My bar mitzvah was well attended. I was just about able to control my mind over "the dancing spit." The six made a pact to get through the ritual by using a form of mind control: do not look at Cantor Krickstein at all! My whole family came as well as our old friends and neighbors from the Bronx, and some of our new friends. Dad was very proud of me. Mom was proud of me—Susan was indifferent. Looking back on this confirmation, it seems incongruous that our large Jewish family was all Mom's. I don't remember questioning this or even thinking about it. Dad was my dad and always by my side, it seemed during these early years. And, well, Mom was Mom and she came with the whole bundle.

Dad continued to take me down to Manhattan on Saturdays. I was growing up, and I felt my interests in American history started to become more focused on specific interests and pursuits. I stopped staying all day in Dad's office upstairs and started to become more curious and brave about my Manhattan. I had a paper route at home where I delivered the daily paper to adjacent neighborhoods and made some money. I also received money from my relatives for my bar mitzvah, and Mom allowed me to use half of it for my developing interests. Generally, during the fifties, young men received fountain pens for their bar mitzvah if they didn't receive money. I believe I got three hundred dollars and fourteen fountain pens: hence the well-known colloquial expression at the time, "Today, you are a fountain pen."

I began to explore the subways. I loved the smell wafting out of the grates in the sidewalk from the subway. I loved the sound of the distant rumble, getting louder and louder, shaking my body as it passed below me and sped away. I felt secure being rolled around on the seats, listening to the rhythmic click-clack of the wheels across the separations in the tracks. Sometimes I would take the subway uptown and then stay at the same station and take it downtown, and then uptown and then downtown, spending only a quarter. When I came back to Dad's office, ready to go home with him by car, he would say, "What did you do today, Amos?"

When I did my ride-only day, I would say, "Nothin', Dad."

One day, I got out on Fourth Avenue, below Canal Street, and discovered the street of old booksellers. This was my place. The stores were lined up one after another, with sidewalks filled with tables and tables of old books, maps, and so on. Inside, the stores were humongous, with stacks and stacks of books, and sections of maps and manuscripts, all categorized by topic: the Civil War, the American Revolution, Literature, Mysteries. I was mystified by the varied collections. The smell of old paper and glue was a high to me. I was enchanted by some original titles, like Horace Greeley's *American Rebellion* 1868. Prices were cheap. There really was no interest at that time in antique books. Books printed in 1823 priced out the same as a novel from 1933, often less than a dollar. I began my collection of Civil War books, preferring those written during or just after, as well as those written just before. Dad was mildly curious about my hobby. Mom was more direct: "Amie, why do you want old books? You can read old books in the library. All the books are old there. And actually, what's wrong with reading the Torah? It's the oldest book of all."

Susan of course, and as usual, thought I was becoming a derelict or something. "Amos, you're crazy! Just keep them away from my room."

The pre-adult Amos Boris Lardowitz was narrowing his life to two interests: pursuing and collecting Civil War memorabilia and pursuing and collecting Gentile girlfriends (albeit just necking with them). For some strange reason I kept distancing myself from any relationships with Jewish girls.

My excitement was in my trips to Manhattan, and I started to make them on my own via a combination of bus and subway rides. I remember my first day alone, on a weekday. There was no school because of a teacher conference, and I spontaneously headed down into my Manhattan. What an experience. This was not a Saturday. I had gone with Dad, Mom, and Susan to the city during the week, but my first time alone on a workday was phenomenal. The subway station was a bustle and hustle of adults moving and positioning themselves, 98 percent of them men. It was like a high to me. Everyone seemed to be just a shell almost aimlessly careening from one place to another. Each one of them carried a folded newspaper tucked under his armpit. Each one of them was wearing a fedora hat. Each one of them had a long flannel-like coat. Each one of them wore gray.

This was the dawn of the American science fiction movie (as well as the Japanese Godzilla). My first trips to the city, like this, began to be imprinted on my memory as scenes from these black-and-white films. There was no particular plot. These were just automatons controlled by the invaders from Mars. They were planted, one by one, to interact with us normal Americans. Once they sat on the subway, they immediately crisply unfolded their newspapers (which were really antennas) and buried their quasi heads in them. Then we normal and American-born humans would sit down next to them only to have our mind and memory slowly erased and replaced (not all at once but over many subway rides) by the aimless thoughts of these programmed creatures from another planet. They didn't use mind control on American women—American women were meant to keep their minds, a mixture of home and family thoughts and of wild romance (and you never knew which you would get). There I would stand, waiting for the train. There I would sit, in the train. I was different. *They have no control over me.* They were gray. I was bright and colorful. I would never buy a newspaper and bury my head. It's what they wanted from me. There were these newspaper stands positioned strategically throughout the city. The guys inside these tiny spaceships were gross and ugly. They hawked at you to suck you in to take these antennas of doom—not me. I would continue to ride my subway and find a way to combat this creeping terror.

Amos Boris Lardowitz will not succumb.

Each time I climbed the last stair on my last train to my Manhattan destination, I breathed the fresh air of escape. I had made it. They hadn't gotten me. I was free again to smell the diesel gas and garlic and urine from the homeless. It took me two years to finally even buy a stick of gum from a newspaper kiosk.

In one of the bookstores, I happened upon a collection of original handwritten letters from the Civil War era. I was fascinated. This was real history. As I read each word, I could feel the pen on paper as it made its symbol. I could see the hand write the words. I could imagine the room in which the letter was written, and I could see the person who wrote their thoughts. My interests in American history were strangely magnified by the true handwritten letters, signed at the bottom by the person of old who had exposed their thoughts for perpetuity. With my savings and paper route, I started to amass a small collection of pre–Civil War letters, from 1850 to 1860. They were not even priced according to content. They were generally bundled as two to four letters from the same person. Most of them were sold in a much larger estate sale of books and household furniture and belongings by the person or family to whom the letters were written. They were inexpensive, and some were historically fascinating. One example was a gem of a letter describing the writer's experience of hearing a speech given by aspiring presidential candidate Abraham Lincoln. I felt that I too was there. I also amassed a collection of Civil War–era newspapers such as *Harpers Weekly* and the *New York Times.* I would read the papers as someone of that era would. The print was always very small, but I read everything, including the advertising.

I became known to the sellers on that block of Fourth Avenue, and was even consulted when other collectors had questions about authenticity or content or the quality of the letters. I remember being really proud when a bookseller asked me to sell my election letter to a buyer. He offered me $35 for an item that had cost me $1.50 three months before. Selling this letter would be like giving up a new puppy I'd been given, and I anguished about it for two weeks. But something was pushing me, and I brought the letter down one day. As thirty-five dollars in cash was placed in my right hand and the letter was passed to the buyer on my left, I felt a rush of excitement that would prove to be the motivation for a career in historical manuscripts.

So went this indoctrination of growing up and forming ideas and pursuits of life. This time period, from age fourteen to my fifteenth year, culminated in the consolidation of the early years of Amos Boris Lardowitz into his discovery years—for the fall of 1955 was soon upon me, and my strange and mysterious discovery in the attic was about to happen and begin to envelop me.

Post-Discovery

I WAS ENTERING MY third year of high school and becoming more responsible and feeling less of an adolescent, but my life changed after that moment in the attic in the fall of 1955. My mind became fixated on that photo and its inscription, and I was still plagued by the paralysis of indecision. I had already talked to Dad, and I wouldn't talk to Mom about it. Thinking back now, I was only being who I am: a curious person and a romantic of the heart who needed to have a deep secret with which to inspire my life.

The beat of rock and roll became an infectious inspiration to me, and I started to take guitar lessons with a teacher from our high school. I must have taken three lessons and couldn't stomach any more with her. I remember right after the last lesson just sitting in my room with my new cheap acoustic guitar and moving my fingers all over the fret board until suddenly at one in the morning a sound emerged that was incredibly rhythmic to me. It must have been a blues or rock-and-roll riff that I stumbled upon. From that moment on, I became self-taught, innovating riffs and melodies of the newly hip rock revolution. I was enchanted with rock ballads, the slower undulating melodies with the plaintive romantic lyrics. My guitar would prove to be a good friend for years to come.

My collections continued, and I actually made some money trading historical letters. I began to purchase up and bought valuable editions like an original newspaper printed at the time of President Lincoln's assassination describing the terrible deed, as well as a signed letter from Secretary of State William Henry Seward. There were always more valuable and interesting materials to find, such as an original letter from Lincoln, but I was a novice and used my own earnings only to purchase additional stuff.

Reading the letters of the day, when there were no other means of real communication, including telephone and television and computers, made me realize how the written word really expressed a person's inner feelings in earlier centuries. Many people were isolated and could not travel easily by the limited means of transportation, and it required a focused effort to express their feelings on paper. Life was certainly more basic and primitive, and required concerted efforts to get basic needs for food and shelter met. My mind and heart delved into the past, and I felt that I was very different from my friends and high school classmates.

The culture of high school started to become strange to me. Instead of jumping in and joining, I was progressively zoning out into my narrow interests. The fifties were cool, with my friends starting to drive and going to drive-in movies and developing cliques of friends and chasing down the girls, but I seemed to lose my pre-adolescent charm with the opposite sex, and my bevy of girlfriends seemed not to know who I was anymore.

For a brief period I envied the life of my classmates, especially the football players and class officers, but it didn't last long. Mom was insistent that I become a good student in high school and go to Cornell, since two of my older cousins were there studying premed. And good student I became. My interests in American history and my new interests in historical manuscripts and music seemed to catapult my learning focus, but I don't think I ever lost my personality and my absurd view of the world, even though I was finally becoming more of a man.

Susan met Alvin. Boy, was he a nerd. Alvin, of course, worked in a bank. He was skinny and wore thick-rim black glasses. They were always falling down his nose. The first time I met him was the first time Susan brought him to the house. He drove a small green Nash Rambler. It sat in the street in front of the house like a little puppy waiting for its master. He was four years older than Susan, who was four years older than me. He came from an Orthodox Jewish family and made a good attempt at being an Orthodox Jew. Mom loved it. Dad was his usual understated self, subtly nodding his approval.

Alvin was relatively clumsy, and when he was answering questions about his family (asked by Mrs. Lardowitz), his ears became increasingly red just before he talked. Then they abruptly became white when his glasses slipped down his nose and he pushed them back up with the index finger of his right hand. Right then and there he reminded me of the angelfish in my fish tank. Especially when I was younger, I would coax the little thing up next to the glass and then snap my finger, only to scare him and see all his stripes disappear. I desperately wanted to try this on Alvin—snap my finger right on the tip of his nose—and almost could not stifle a deep laugh while I was sitting there in the living room like a good brother and son.

Orthodox Jews—God, it's hard enough to be a Jew for me, I thought. Alvin had found his Jewish mate (albeit not Orthodox, but he would make her one), and I couldn't even go out with a Jewish girl. I started to think as I was sitting there that the only times I had a passion for Jewish girls was in the synagogue and on high holy days. There all the thirteen- and fourteen-year-olds sat, dressed like little women, with makeup. They were bored and seemed to look around distractedly. So was I. This was like a French foreign film, shot in grainy color with church music hauntingly played (in a synagogue) as the two lovers (in their minds) caught each other's glance and then looked away for fear that their parents (and the evil Cantor Krickstein) would single them out and banish them to their aunt's country estate—never to have experienced the only love they would ever have in their life. Then the service was over—then the fantasy was over—then I didn't want Jewish girls anymore. It was obvious that forbidden fruit was attractive, and certainly grabbing and kissing a girl in the synagogue on high holy days was forbidden—but once eaten, it was only fruit. And I guess that is what I thought about any relationship with a Jewish girl. "It's only fruit," and I was not a big fruit eater … "Amie, eat the fruit, it's good for you," my mom always said.

Susan was not curious, and I don't think Alvin was either. This was probably good for them, for their life would be very complex, with two separate sets of dishes, no mixing of meat and dairy, eating only kosher foods, and never driving or working on Saturday, the holy day. They would have ritual after ritual; their kids would go to a special Orthodox school, and they all would attend the Orthodox synagogue (which was not ours) often.

Alvin's father was a clothier. He had three stores in Brooklyn. They were all called Rabinowitz Clothiers, and they made fine handmade suits. Susan would go from Susan Lardowitz to Susan Rabinowitz—just a few letters away, and not a great stretch.

Their wedding took place in Brooklyn at a kosher catering firm that also had a chapel. It was on the second floor, and you could see out to the elevated train. Mom was very involved and very happy about the upgrading of her daughter to a finer brand of Judaism. Alvin's family was large like ours, although he had many relatives on both sides. I really believe that a good time was had by all. Everything went well that cold December day in 1955.

Susan and Alvin eventually had three children, two girls and a boy. There was Sydney, Morris, and Clara. Clara was the youngest. She was small and rotund and just like her maternal grandmother, my mother. Even at just five years of age she would admonish me and say, "Uncle Amie, why do you read old books? You can buy new ones." Morris was the middle one and just like Alvin. He was a nerd, and I was nowhere near his radar no matter what I did. Sydney was the oldest. She was tall and attractive and very feminine. Her physical build was like Dad's. Sydney was just like me. She saw absurdity in many things and had a creative mind and curiosity about life. Even as a little child she would come into my room and ask me if she could hold and read the old letters and newspapers I collected. Then, instead of reading them, she would bring them up to her face and smell them as if they were flowers. She seemed to take joy in everything that gave me joy. In time she would become my closest confidant and friend.

Susan didn't go to college and Mom never seemed to push her to advance her education. I think that all along, the family had hoped Susan would find a man like Alvin. She would also not work, for keeping a kosher home and raising a kosher family was a real job by itself.

Three weeks after Susan's wedding, I turned sixteen and Mom and Dad took Susan, Alvin, and me to a fancy kosher restaurant in Manhattan to celebrate my birthday. I guess they wanted to honor my love for Manhattan and to show off their new, more classy Jewish paraphernalia. Susan was still living at home until Alvin could find a suitable apartment in Brooklyn for the two of them. Alvin was still also living with his parents. The restaurant certainly was classy. It was on Park Avenue and was richly appointed, and the waiters wore tuxedos—but our waiter was like a

Borscht Belt comedian. When Susan requested only one matzo ball in her soup (she obviously was trying to impress her new husband by watching her weight), our waiter said, "Young lady, do you want to be responsible for a lonely matzo ball sitting in the kitchen alone?" Then he left and came back. "Have you ever seen matzo ball tears?" Etc. etc., ad nauseum.

Sitting at dinner with my family on my sixteenth birthday, I was beginning to feel very comfortable. In one month I would probably be getting my driver's license. And most of all, my Manhattan was yielding its trove of treasures to me. My life was filled with promise—and there were secrets yet to be discovered.

Ben's Den

It seemed to be just a slice out of the adjacent Fourth Avenue bookseller stores. I noticed it because of the 78-rpm records stacked in a box on a card table on the sidewalk, outside the store. In the window was a half-suspended acoustic Martin guitar. Peering into the space, I could see walls and tables of records, in boxes. The store was barely eight feet wide. On the window in six-inch letters was Ben's Den, and below that, off center, in four-inch letters was Music and Rare and Used Books. I was attracted by the guitar, a Martin, the best and first manufacturer of American guitars. The door was open, and I could smell a combination of cigarette smoke and stale sweet perfume wafting out. I could just make out a figure in the back of the store. He seemed to be sitting on a stool and had a cigarette dangling from his lower lip. The late-afternoon sun was making it difficult for me to see everything clearly inside.

I had never noticed this store sandwiched between the large and deep used bookstores surrounding it. It's possible that the store had never been open on the Saturdays I had come before. It's possible that the card table had never been on the sidewalk before, and it's also possible that the Martin had been newly hung in the window.

I turned to continue my walk down Fourth Avenue, and suddenly, as if awakened from a daydream I heard, "Hey, kid, you play?" At first, I didn't know where the voice had come from. Then awakened, I looked inside, and walking toward me was the figure I had seen on the stool. "You play?"

"Play what?"

"Guitar."

"Yeah."

"You like Martins?"

"Yeah, who doesn't?"

That's all it took. He reached up, stepped into the window and unhooked the Martin, thrust a handshake in my direction, and said, "Ben, Kid."

He was about my height. He looked to be in his mid-thirties. He had wavy black hair, moderately cut, with a very small rubber band or something holding a wisp of hair directly in the back of his head. I thought he was quite a handsome guy. He had what looked like a two-day beard and was wearing a very loose knitted sweater with deep pockets and crumpled papers hanging out of them. Of course, he talked with the dangling cigarette dancing on his lips with every word. The ash threatened to jump to the floor at all times, but never left the end of the cigarette. It was mesmerizing.

He proceeded to tune that Martin in what appeared to be one minute. His fingers flowed over the six strings, checking the tone, and it was done. I thought this was cool. He then played a short rhythmic rift, bending strings and fingerpicking as he went along. Then just as suddenly, he thrust the Martin toward me, and said, "Play, Kid."

Elvis Presley's "That's All Right" was released in 1954 on the Southern Sun Records, and I had been working on the chords and lyrics and practicing singing it. It was the spring of 1956, and Elvis had just released the first RCA songs that made him famous, including "Blue Suede Shoes" and "Hound Dog." I was singing the song in my own voice and hadn't tried to mimic Elvis's unique style. I was really excited to play this Martin and didn't feel nervous.

Well, that's all right Mama, that's all right for you, that's all right, Mama, it's any way you do … that's all right, that's all right, Mama … it's any way you do …

"Oh, Presley, the Southern white boy with the Negro heart," Ben said. "You got a Negro heart too?" he then said abruptly.

I was somewhat stunned and said, "I dunno, should I?" (It was quite stupid to say … but I couldn't come up with anything else so fast.)

"'That's All Right' was written by Big Boy, Big Boy Crudup. I was there when he wrote it. He's a buddy of mine. He's still trying to get paid for the song. You know, he'll never get a dime. He's not the One."

"What do you mean, he's not the One?" I asked.

"Kid, he could be the One. He's not asking for fame. He's doing what he does, but I got a feeling he'll just disappear into the Cosmos like ninety-nine percent of the earthlings. You know the Cosmos giveth and taketh, Kid," he said, almost like a prophet, I thought. "But you know, this kid, Elvis, even though he's being exploited and corrupted, he'll be the One, I betcha—but not for his whole life. He'll be pulled apart."

"Really?" I think I said stupidly.

"Kid, Jackie Robinson's the One. Tennessee Williams is the One. They don't try. They do. They could be manipulated but they don't care. They just pull the creativity out of the Cosmos. Fame is no goal. Money is no goal. You just do because it's in you—or it's not. You can't force it. Kid, you could lose it in a minute if you're not yourself." While he was saying this, I was wondering what the hell "the One" and the "Cosmos" were—but fortunately, I kept my eyes glued on Ben's face and nodded in agreement.

Just as abruptly as he had started this conversation about "the One and the Cosmos" he shifted gears and reached for the Martin (it was hard for me to let go) and said to me, "Kid, you live in the neighborhood?"

"No," I replied. "But I come here often."

"For what?" he said.

"I collect old books."

"What kind?"

"I'm interested in American Civil War books and letters and manuscripts of that time."

"OK, Kid, you come back and I'll show you the only American literature worthwhile, and you can play the Martin too."

"Yes, I would like that," I said, blushing. And with that short ending, he took the Martin. I gave him kind of an embarrassing wave of my hand and backed out of the store. He didn't look back at me as I left.

Oh my God, that was great! I thought. What a contrast between this guy and his life, and my life in high school. He seemed so cool—so detached and confident. I wanted to circle the block and come back right away—but even I was smart enough to know that would be stupid.

Sometimes I didn't know what made me crazy for something, but he seemed to be everything I would want to be. He owned his turf. He knew his turf, and he knew exactly what he wanted you to know about him and his world. My time in that store was no more than twenty minutes—yet its memory was to be embedded permanently in my life.

All week long I was obsessing about when to go back. I had actually forgotten to look at his store hours, so I was in a state of panic about his possibly not being there when I made a trip into Manhattan. I couldn't take a chance on another Saturday, and I didn't want to wait that long, so I got an idea. I was going to play hooky. What the hell, I was a sophomore. I was a good student, and I rarely missed a day in high school (not like my early years). Just don't tell anyone. Do it once and don't mention it to Mom and Dad and especially Susan. Great, I thought.

The Monday after that weekend I woke up like I was planning a bank robbery and this was the perfect day to do it. I wanted to pick a day when I didn't have too much work in school. I must not have had any discipline, because I couldn't wait two days. On Wednesday I decided it was right. I wasn't sure what I was going to do with my books. I figured I would have to hide them somewhere and pick them up later in the day. Also, suppose someone saw me, some classmate or maybe a teacher (God forbid) or the mother of a friend. Anyway, I still had to go, and I decided that if I was seen, I would say I had an appointment with a skin doctor in Manhattan that my mother had arranged (see, pimples are good for something).

Oh, what a great day it was on that Wednesday—and for the first time I had complete control of my life. Wow, life is great, I thought. I was doing what I wanted to and when I wanted to. I took only a notebook and stuffed it with old papers like it was my schoolbook and then stuffed the whole thing in a trash receptacle adjacent to the bus stop.

My heart was pounding on that sunny morning as I mounted the stairs on Fourth Avenue and briskly walked toward Ben's store. I could see from the angle of my approach that the store was open. I was really excited. As I turned to enter the store, I remember smelling the perfume I thought I'd smelled when I went initially, except it seemed fresh.

Oh God—on the stool I had seen Ben on was a woman. She was thin, and her body was kind of leaning in a feminine way, with her legs crossed down to her feet. She had wavy layered blonde hair that seemed to have brown in it also and was just about shoulder length. Her face was soft and white and she wore a hint of red lipstick. She was wearing the same sweater I thought Ben had been wearing, but it was really a smaller version of the same one. She wore Capri-like pants and her ankles were exposed. Her shoes were wisps of a thing and looked like ballet slippers.

How did I see all this in the split moment that I walked into the store? I don't know. It was probably because she was strikingly beautiful—then it was back to reality and my disappointment that Ben wasn't here.

"Excuse me, is Ben around?" I said cavalierly.

"He's out." She didn't even lift her head up.

"Is he coming back soon?" OK—pretty good.

"Probably."

All right, next could be dozens of responses—like "I'll wait" or "I won't wait" or "I'll be back too" or "I'd like to see some records" or "Never mind" or . . .

"Who are you?" she said, waking me from my trance.

"Amos," I said limply.

"Oh, Kid, Ben talked to me about you. I'm Zelda. Ben's out chasing down an original draft of a Tennessee Williams. He's like a tiger: once he gets into his predator mode, you'd better watch out."

I was shocked that she knew of me, but I laughed spontaneously at her remark, and that immediately broke the ice.

"Why don't you look around? Actually he said he'd be here at eleven—it's already eleven thirty."

"Thanks," I said, relieved.

I spent the next fifteen or so minutes browsing the store while at least one eye was fixated on Zelda. While I looked around, I noticed that she was writing. There were shelves and shelves of 78-rpm records in the front part of the store. I carefully pulled out four or five and looked at them. They seemed to be early blues or jazz records, with names I didn't know. I gradually moved into the back room, which I had not seen when I was with Ben before. Out of Zelda's sight, I felt bolder. The back room was about the size of the front one, but it had only books on the shelves, wall to wall. They seemed to be used but not antique. It seemed all of them were from the twentieth century and looked like novels. There were also what appeared to be manuscripts and/or letters in folders on one wall. I didn't want to pull them out for fear of damaging them, but they seemed like handwritten notes or letters. I was in another world when suddenly I heard from the other room, "Hey, Zel, I snared it." It was Ben. He then saw me in the back room and said, "Hey, Kid!" He seemed even more attractive and buoyant to me. "Welcome back, Kid," he almost sang.

I could see that he was ecstatic or something. I came back into the front of the store and listened while he said to Zelda, "Brando wanted me to have it. Williams gave him this revised script of *Streetcar* and told him to burn it. It was right after the opening of *Streetcar* in 1947. Imagine, Brando kept it."

"Great, Ben," said Zelda.

"Believe me—in five years Tom's going to be happy to see it again," Ben said.

What was he talking about? I thought. I found out later but didn't ask then. Brando was Marlon Brando. He had acted in the Broadway hit production of *A Streetcar Named Desire,* written by Tennessee Williams, in 1947. It won a Pulitzer Prize for Drama in 1948, and Tom was Williams's real first name—Thomas.

"OK, kids, lunch is on me," Ben suddenly announced. I looked at him like maybe he wanted me to go home, or there was someone other than me in the store with Zelda—but he grabbed my arm with one hand and store keys from his desk with the other, and said, "Let's lock this little vault up."

He held on to my arm as we walked out the store and up Fourth Avenue with the afternoon sun on the left side of our faces. He walked briskly and started to keep cadence with my step, and just as suddenly I felt Zelda's arm hooking into mine. What a feeling this was—WOW!!! I had this strange feeling that the sunlight was following only us, and that everyone was looking as we walked.

We crossed the street and walked another block, and Ben turned in to a coffee shop on the corner. He went right to a window seat and we all sat down. The sun was shining right onto our table and warming me comfortably. "Betty, coffee for all," he said. I had never drunk coffee up to this point in my life, but the smell was like an aphrodisiac, and you could see the vapors dancing out as she brought us three cups. There we sat, I think now, on top of the world—and it wasn't even my world. We had an aura of confidence and sureness, and a smell of hash brown potatoes and bacon wafted around us.

"BLT for Zelda and me—and you, Kid?"

"Yes, BLT sounds good to me," I joined in.

Ben seemed really excited. His face had a permanent smile, and he looked even more cool and handsome. I was sitting at the aisle seat with Ben at the window, and Zelda was sitting opposite me. It was here that I first was mesmerized by her blue eyes—sexy blue eyes. When she talked, she was all feminine and clear. I was embarrassed to even look at her.

"So, Kid, you're back so soon." (Oh boy … I guess I hadn't been too cool about my desires.)

"Well, I was in the neighborhood." (Not cool.)

"Kid, there is so much bullshit in this world—purity is a rarity," Ben said, almost in response, I thought, to my white lie. "You have to trust yourself and who you are and not be concerned if your beat is different from the rest of the world." I momentarily started to think of my clarinet experience and how my sound was different but then was sharply corrected by my music teacher. How can I maintain my own beat? I thought.

Once again, I was startled out of a momentary trance when Zelda said, "Kid, Ben tells me you're a book collector."

"Yeah, I'm interested in American history, especially the Civil War era."

"Why war?" Zelda said simply.

This was the first time in my sixteen years of life that I think I was being asked honestly about my interests, and it was quite a trip. At first, I didn't know what to say. Then, it came out. "The Civil War was a turning point in our country. There was such turmoil and tragedy. I think there's a fascination with the conflict of brother against brother, and the future of America in doubt."

"Yeah, OK, but war is not unique to America. The world has been consumed by war. It's a destiny—eons of strife," replied Zelda.

"I guess so," I answered sheepishly. Then I added almost defensively, "I have a really deep interest in the past and what people were thinking and how they lived. I also collect old letters and manuscripts."

"Aha," piped in Ben loudly. "Okay, Kid"—he emphasized the letter *k*—"now you're on to something." He knew about my letters on the first day but I guess it was time to make his point. "The written word—the written thought. There's no bullshit there. You want the truth? You can see the truth in a written word or sentence. Even the idiots in this world—the movers and shakers who manipulate others—have to come clean. If you can find their private thoughts, you've got them!"

I really think I understood Ben. My feelings when I read the letters I have collected have told me the same thing, I thought. I always felt that I could actually know what the person writing the letter was thinking about. I think this was what Ben was referring to—except, of course, I think he was on to something far more cerebral than I was.

The conversation drifted rapidly away from me, and Ben and Zelda talked about Marlon Brando and his resistance to becoming an insider in Hollywood. Then the conversation just stopped, and we continued eating our BLT sandwiches and drinking coffee. I was feeling really relaxed with Ben and Zelda, and then there was a sudden "OK, trio—time to split. Hey, Kid, come back to the shop and play your Martin before you go."

The coffee shop experience was a moment in my life that will never be repeated. I was just sixteen and becoming my own self when I saw my future and my life in this moment with Ben and Zelda. I don't think it was because I would become them. It was because I felt that *they* were part of *me* and I could be myself. But like all monumental defining moments in one's life, growth doesn't happen without some pain. I was dogged by my own adolescent interest in war. "Why war?" would echo in my mind for years to come, and I would have to come to grips with my early life and my American boyhood.

Ben and Zelda became my friends—on their turf, of course. I tried to get to Ben as often as I could, and I always spent time in Ben's Den before or after perusing the booksellers. From the coffee shop experience on, I didn't buy any more Civil War books, but I kept buying letters from that time. I guess this was my unconscious attempt to challenge my own interests and beliefs. I didn't really analyze it, but I think it brought me closer to Ben and Zelda. Ben would have me sit in the store while he went "hunting" for his manuscripts and books. The store was generally quiet. I don't think he made much money from these retail sales, but I guessed that he dealt in rare goods. I would play the Martin almost without stop. What a joy. Sitting on Ben and Zelda's stool and playing and watching the active street life, people of all types passing in front of me, and cars and trucks beyond them—the noise of the garbage and delivery truck, and the smell of the city. I was home.

Ben and I did talk about our mutual feelings about words on paper and how they gave away the person writing them. He complimented me on my awareness and told me it was an art to read manuscripts and study the great ones of literature. He reinforced in me the notion that all creativity has existed before and that it all lives in the Cosmos, where anyone can just "grab it" and make it their own. He encouraged my interest in such a narrow field and seemed to be honestly enthused when I found a soldier's

Civil War letter to his family even though he knew I was seemingly interested only in the war. He wanted me to practice reading their minds, to read their hearts and to be in their bodies at the time they revealed inner secrets.

I saw Zelda only once more in the next two months that I traveled to the city while I was still in the tenth grade. She stopped in when I was minding the shop and Ben was out. I had a real crush on her. It was great. All I needed to do was to think about her. I didn't need to see her.

The end of my sophomore year was approaching, and Ben asked me what I was going to do with myself for the summer. I was now driving. I was making some money buying and selling letters. I really didn't have a social life at school. My life had become Ben and Zelda.

Mom and Dad knew about my trips to Manhattan to buy and sell letters. They also knew about Ben and Zelda, although they'd gotten a much abbreviated description of our relationship and its meaning to me. I desperately wanted to spend my summer in the city. I was sixteen going on seventeen and my grades were still good. I had my sights set on Cornell and was in a position academically to go there. I knew the liberal arts college was expensive, but Mom and Dad had said long ago that they would pay for my college. I felt that my grades and studies were important to them and therefore to me. I felt that I was still very different from my friends, but I still kept my family close to my heart.

I wanted to work for Ben but I really didn't want to ask him for money. I was going down about once a week, mostly after school, and was getting progressively quieter at Ben's Den because I felt I needed to do something to make more money. I was in conflict.

One afternoon, I was sitting in the back room and Ben was in the front of the store when I heard him call me. "Hey, Kid."

"Yeah, Ben."

"Come here."

"Yeah, Ben."

"I want you to do something for me. I want you to read a novel for me and then I want you to read some notes and letters written by William Faulkner."

"Really, Ben?"

"Yeah, I want you to read Faulkner's *Intruder in the Dust*. It was written in 1948. I came across some notes on that book as well as a rambling, revealing letter that he wrote to his nephew about the story. It's about a black farmer who is accused of killing a white man. It would be good if you knew the book. I want you to write a piece in my *Literary Journal* about it. I want to pay you a big buck for it."

Ben was sole editor and publisher of *The Literary Journal*, a quarterly newsletter dedicated to American twentieth-century novelists and playwrights and poets. I'm sure he read me "like a book" and knew the inner me. *Intruder in the Dust* was Faulkner's tribute to Southern blacks and how they were treated by their Southern white brethren. I'm sure Ben knew it would be a subject close to my "Great Rebellion" heart, and I truly believe he thought I was capable of an insightful analysis of Faulkner's mind. And oh my God! A big buck was a hundred dollars! I also believe he was my guardian, an angel capable of entering my thoughts and moving me forward through my life.

At that moment, I knew Ben wanted me around, even if he would just be creating something to pay me for. In reality, though, he was nurturing me to help me reach my potential in life.

Right after he told me of my job, he said, "Kid, before you do this, I want you to do an exercise for me. I want you to get into the mind of Vincent Van Gogh. I want you to read two letters he wrote to his brother Theo, and then I want you to go to the Met and find *Starry Night,* and then I want you to get up really close to the painting. I want you to see each brushstroke. I want you to picture in your mind's eye the moment he made that stroke. Grab it from the Cosmos, Kid. And then I want you to do that with the whole painting, and then step back and then step forward until you have seen the whole damn thing from every position in the room where it hangs. After you've completed this, I want you to come back here and within three hours I want you to write a critique of that painting in a hundred words or less. Don't get too heady—got it?"

Oh boy … I'm getting more ensnarled, I thought. I started putting together in my head my "plan of action" since I was still in school and had to do this within the time I had in Manhattan. In my mind, I traced a plan that would take me to the New York Public Library to look for the letters and then to the Met to see the painting, and then back to Ben's back room to write.

I found it really exciting. I thought of myself as a military courier or spy who would surreptitiously try to discover the clues in the letters so I could decipher the code hidden in the painting.

This first exercise, putting my thoughts to paper, was the beginning of the unleashing of the writer in me. My mind was always working. My thoughts, since I can remember, were always circling around in my head, always trying to find a way out. Writing would prove to be a way out for me—as I'm sure it was for the myriad of souls trapped by their own minds. Reading others' thoughts was also the way to expand your own universe by "getting into their head," as Ben would always say.

The Van Gogh exercise was quite time consuming. Initially, I was not sure why I should read two letters, not one, and not more than two, and what it would mean to my interpretation.

I did realize by myself that I needed to humanize and personify Vincent Van Gogh to the point that I saw the vulnerability and realness in him. Well, two letters were good enough, and I picked out two that I felt were quite personal. With my feelings fresh, I scrambled off to the Met. This part of the exercise was like an out-of-body experience, for I actually homed in on what I was doing and really felt the hand stroke the canvas with the brush, and I thought I heard the sound it made. The colors, especially, jumped out when I got up close. It was something else, because after a half hour or so of this intensity, I couldn't turn my back on the painting at all! I just kept backing out of the large room it was in until I could turn the corner and barely see it.

I don't even remember now what I wrote, but to this day I know it was OK, for I was there. I was in Van Gogh's studio. I do remember one thing that Ben said to me about this exercise. He said my use of the word *turmoil* twice was quite significant and that I truly must have had an out-of-body experience.

"Kid, did you know that V. painted *Starry Night* in an asylum in Saint-Remy?"

"No, Ben."

"Yes you did. You were there. You pulled it right out of the Cosmos."

Ben never had me analyze another painting after this experience, although he would often include the expression "writers, musicians, sports heroes, and painters" when he talked of "the One" and "the Cosmos."

It took me about a month to complete my first paying literary job, my byline on a piece about a William Faulkner book in Ben's *The Literary Journal*. Looking back on this, I realize that Ben was quite amazing, because the literary giants he took on were alive and kicking, and many of them were cranky eccentrics. William Faulkner received a Nobel Prize in Literature in 1949, and here I was, being thrown into the literary world by Ben just for fun. He really didn't give a crap about his reputation. He was always pushing the envelope—in this case using a teenager to analyze a Nobel Laureate.

I told Mom the white lie that Ben had hired me for the summer (he never said that—but he had given me one paying job). I was determined to be around Ben's Den all summer and somehow, through Ben or my dealing in letters, I would make some additional money. I just told Mom that Ben wanted me to work five days a week and that I could pick my days but that I may have to stay in the city overnight (great story).

School finished, I started coming in regularly according to my fabricated story. I was feeling more comfortable until Ben abruptly announced that the edition of the journal with my piece in it was to be sent out the next day. I got really nervous. Mostly, I was minding the store when one day as I was putting the mail where Ben had told me to put it, I noticed two typewritten letters with this name and address:

Amos Boris Lardowitz
The Literary Journal
425 Fourth Avenue
New York City, NY

Unbelievable. What did I do now?

Ben came back and looked through his mail and noticed the letters. He opened them and laughed his "snicker laugh." "Two of my most heady patrons. They each wrote long letters in response to your treatise on Faulkner, Kid."

I read the letters. These guys really took my article seriously! Ben said, "You did it, Kid. You've joined the world of the written word. You're hired."

"What do you mean, Ben?" I asked incongruously.

"You're hired. Kid Lardowitz. Editor, *The Literary Journal.*"

I was officially hired as editor of *The Literary Journal.* My job was to arrange the articles that Ben wanted in the four-page paper and to proofread its contents, and to shorten or embellish the contents to enhance its readability. Ben offered me twenty-five dollars weekly plus lunch. He wanted me in the store five days out of seven through the week before my twelfth-grade year started. After that, he would give me a job throughout the year two days a week, any days. For this he would pay me ten dollars weekly plus lunch. My job would be the same, but if I had nothing to do, I would "mind the store," as Ben put it.

Yippee!!!!!! I was on cloud nine. I felt that nobody I knew in my class, or of my age, could be as happy as I was going to be that next year.

The first month of my new permanent (albeit part-time) job was serendipity personified. I was in awe over my new mentor and in love with his wife (or woman—he would not tell me if they were married). Jack Kerouac and Allen Ginsberg were routine telephone callers. Often, I would be taking a message from Kerouac to Fink (Ben's last name). At times, I would be listening in the front of the store while Ben, in an admonishing voice, said, "Jack, Beat Man, you're out of your mind!"

It was the summer of 1956, and there was a new movement in the literary world: Beat poets and writers. Allen Ginsberg's poem "Howl" was just about to be performed in San Francisco, and Jack Kerouac's book *On the Road* was being edited and finalized for publication in 1957. These guys were a crazy bunch of freewheeling, free-thinking intellectuals, and their doings would eventually be instrumental in spawning the beatniks, hippies, drug culture, and rhythm and blues.

Ben asked me one hot summer day to stay over at his house in the Village over the next weekend because there was a book fair on Fourth Avenue all day Saturday and Sunday. I was ecstatic once more.

I packed a small bag that Friday. We took a cab to Ben and Zelda's apartment in Greenwich Village.

They lived on Perry Street, a quarter block off Bleecker Street right in the heart of the Village—the coolest place in New York City. Their apartment was in the back of a small courtyard. The building was an old early-nineteenth-century brick complex of three units surrounding this small and charming courtyard. They lived on the second floor in a walkup, a two-bedroom apartment with two bathrooms and large old windows that looked out over the roofs of the Village eastward and slightly north. You could see in the distance the top half of the Empire State Building—my childhood shrine.

That weekend would prove to be the most memorable in my young maturing life.

Friday night we ate some leftovers and headed for bed early. I was up at five thirty and waiting for Ben. We spent the whole day in the store. The street was bustling with activity. I had never seen so many people on that block or in the store. We sold records and books and had lots of conversations. Ben was a walking encyclopedia of music and literature. Zelda stopped by for about fifteen minutes.

We arrived home after our subway ride at eight and Ben announced that we were "out for eats, drink, and talk" for the rest of the evening.

Zelda, Ben, and I left the apartment about ten and walked down Bleecker Street for three blocks, turned on Christopher Street, and made an abrupt stop. Ben extended his arm to me to head down a flight of stairs. Once down, we entered a smoky bar with a small stage that had a microphone and three stools on it. There were about a dozen or so small round tables of four with café-type chairs. The bar itself was a rich, deep mahogany with a glistening mirror behind it and colorful bottles of liquor in front of it reflecting light from the subtle spots surrounding the subterranean place.

Ben extended his hand to a table and we three sat down. Zelda looked beautiful. She was wearing a silk blouse that seemed to slither every time she moved her body even slightly. Her blue eyes were bright and piercing. She was so feminine. We sat for about two minutes quietly and then Ben looked up as two men walked into the room. "Jack … Gins … over here," he said casually.

One of the two grabbed a chair from another table and they both sat down. They were very different from each other. One was large, with a big face, big glasses, and the most hair I had ever seen on a person. He looked like a clown. The other was thin and had short hair, and I thought he was quite handsome, although ordinary looking. Each one of them reached over one at a time and kissed Zelda on both cheeks, and then Ben said, "Jack Kerouac … Allen Ginsberg … Kid," and looked at me.

"Amos …," Zelda said, almost interrupting the *id* in *Kid.*

"Cool," said one.

"A writer?" said the other (I don't remember who said what).

"Of sorts … He's definitely a reader," Ben said.

Then the conversation abruptly veered toward Zelda.

"Zel, I read your last short—now you're on to something … Long live femininity," laughed Allen Ginsberg as his belly shook.

Zelda smiled slyly and said, "You creeps, you think the movement is all about men, don't you?" (She looked *so* luscious as she seemed to land some sort of punch on the hairy one.)

"OK, guys—you two are in enough trouble," Ben piped in rapidly, and then he continued, "Jack, writing on a roll of toilet paper. That's a new one. Gins, you'd better be prepared to defend your obscene material."

In Jack Kerouac's case, Ben was referring to the soon-to-be published *On the Road,* which was written on a continuous roll of teletype paper (he was kidding about the toilet paper). In Allen Ginsberg's case, Ben was referring to the recently written poem "Howl," in which Ginsberg makes oddball homosexual references. Ben always knew how to keep control of the conversation. He was a master of confidence—and a true charmer.

The three of them, just about in unison, burst out laughing as Zelda smiled. Then just as suddenly, Ben lifted his arm, looked over to the bar, snapped his fingers, and said, "Kevin, give these men their libations."

And so went the next hour and a half—eating, drinking, and being merry. They were all over the place—laughing and discussing their adventures and reciting line after line from memory of the stuff they were working on.

Sometime just past midnight three Negro musicians walked through the crowd of about thirty people in the bar and mounted the stage. It appeared that they were about to perform. Kerouac and Ginsberg looked at each other and Ginsberg said, "Time to split, my dear friends. We have an interview tomorrow morning, together, at the ungodly hour of nine." They got up, blew a kiss to Zelda, and headed out the door and up the stairs into the Village night.

"Crazy, and I love it," Ben said as he put an arm around Zelda.

One of the three musicians brushed past the chair Ben was sitting in and looked down. "Benny, you're here, man."

Ben looked up and grabbed his arm and squeezed it as he said, "Wouldn't miss you, Elmore."

The musician was Elmore James, a blues composer and singer who would be credited with the invention of the slide guitar. He was playing an acoustic guitar with a pianist and saxophonist, and when he started up, it sent me through the roof with joy. I had never seen the slide. He had a tube over his pinky finger and used it when he was changing chords in the blues progression. It was rhythmic with a great bluesy rock-and-roll feel. The songs that blew me away were "Dust My Broom" and "The Sky Is Falling."

He played a set, climbed down from the small stage, pulled up a chair, and sat at our table. He had short, cropped hair and looked to be under forty years old, possibly older than Ben.

"How is Big Boy?" Ben asked him.

"He doin' okay. We are all comin' together to cause a big ruckus in Bolivar County down in the Delta on the Thanksgiving."

"Who's coming?" asked Ben.

"Big Boy, Mississippi John, Son House, Sunny Boy ... and who knows who."

"El, you have to let me know when, OK?" said Ben excitedly.

Elmore played another set that had everybody in the place hooting and yelling. It was great. We left the bar about four in the morning. I felt spent but completely relaxed. On our short walk back to the apartment, I could still feel the energy of the Village—people were going everywhere, heading home.

We opened the store at noon that Sunday. The street was still full of people, and I was thoroughly exhausted. I'm not sure how I got through that weekend, but I considered it the best time I had ever had.

I took that Monday off, and when I arrived in Manhattan at the store on Tuesday, Ben was already there. "Kid, read this, and this," and he handed me a book and a long manuscript. One was a prepublication copy of *On the Road* and the other was the poem "Howl." He motioned to the back room as if to say, "Get in there and don't come back until you're finished"—and get in there I did.

It was terrible. Initially I started with "Howl." I worked really hard to read the poem and try to understand it word by word, as I would with a letter written by someone to someone else. I got through about thirty lines and almost vomited. I decided then to just read the whole poem really fast—as fast as my mind could read it without comprehension. After I was through, I needed to close my eyes for about five minutes. All I could think of were words bouncing off of words, and short spurts of descriptive text crashing into the following words, bursting into the next, and on and on—all in the most infantile manner—until it all ended abruptly in a massive word wreck.

At least "Howl" was a relatively short exercise. *On the Road* was a freakin' book! I read about a quarter of the rambling narrative of breathing, living, and moving across the country. I realize we had sat for a few hours and laughed like idiots over the trash Jack and Allen were throwing out—but publishing this shit? I was only sixteen and naïve as hell, but Ben had better straighten me out on what to expect in *his* literary world, I thought.

Ben didn't mention the book or poem that day—I guess he knew I was about to need a head amputation.

Wednesday was a quiet day, and both Ben and I were in the store. He motioned me to the back room and said, "OK, Kid, talk to me." I knew he was provoking me into some sort of literary jousting. I just didn't know where to begin.

"Uh, Ben ... I never read anything like this ...," I stuttered.

"Stream of consciousness, Kid ... stream of consciousness."

"But Ben, what does it mean?"

"You know, Kid, when you read your Civil War letters—many times you're reading someone's prepared thoughts ... things that they want you to know or hear. You're not getting the rest of their brain waves ... waves we all have ... thoughts we all have ... that are careening off the inside of your skull and want to make you crazy ... fears ... paranoia ... wishes ... hopes. Life is full of ambiguities and we all have them."

"But Ben, is this literature?"

"It sure is—if you have the guts to write it!"

And that was that.

Up to this point, I didn't know if Ben ever wrote. I assumed he did, but he never showed me anything. Also, I was really curious what Zelda was writing about. I knew that at some point in the near future I would have to engage Ben in this conversation.

The summer was winding down and Mom wanted me to spend at least the week before my senior year of high school at home. Susan had long gone to her Orthodox haven and was talking babies with Mom all the time.

I was playing guitar at home, learning and singing the blues. I couldn't get out of my mind the jam that might happen in the Mississippi Delta. Could Ben really be going? The way his eyes lit up told me he wanted to go. I desperately wanted to be there if Ben went.

I started my senior year, and the intensity I'd been feeling in the summer was winding down. I was preparing to apply to Cornell. My grades were good enough. I was in a foggy transition, for I was kind of looking back at my life with Ben and Zelda and at the same time nervously looking forward to college.

I applied to Cornell in mid-September, about the time Mom started talking about where we were having our annual Thanksgiving family get-together. Generally, it rotated among Mom's sisters and brothers. This was a different year, she said, because Susan was no longer in the house and this would be my last year at home. She seemed almost sad at the realization that her kids had finally grown up and I would be the last to fly the coop soon.

I really wanted to tell her right away. I knew Dad would probably not make much of a scene, although he would probably look at me with his well-educated medical eyes and say something like, "Amos, you know we always have Thanksgiving with our family …" And then he would probably look over to Mom as if to say, "OK, Helen, time to skewer him with the sword of guilt."

First I needed to see if Ben was really going. The next day in the city I asked Ben immediately. He told me he had already confirmed with Elmore that the jam was on and where it was, and that it was to be on Thanksgiving Day. I pleaded with him to take me. I said I was off from school and it would be an incredible life experience. Ben told me to ask my parents.

"Mom … Ben invited me for Thanksgiving."

"Amie, what do you mean?"

"Ben invited me for Thanksgiving dinner."

"Where … at his family's?"

"No, in Mississippi …"

"What's Mississippi? No one lives in Mississippi." (She meant no Jews.)

"Amos, you know we always have Thanksgiving with our family," Dad said as he looked over to Mom. (I told you so!)

"That's a horrible place … Do you know what's happening to the Negroes there, Amos?"

And then began my civil rights awareness—for until this moment, I was oblivious to race and the issues of discrimination in that day's America, although I had seen it on the news. My interests were in the Civil War, which was all about race and slavery, but I had never translated the problem into 1950s New York. In fact, in my early years in the Bronx, I had never even met a black kid in school. In the suburbs, my circle of friends never included black kids. There were a number in high school, but I was homed in on my own interests. I was certainly acutely aware of the turmoil and tragedy of the slavery issue as an amateur historian, though.

Rosa Parks had refused to sit in the back of the bus in Montgomery, Alabama, on December 1, 1955, barely nine months before. In May 1955, NAACP activist Reverend George Wesley Lee was murdered in Mississippi, as was activist Lamar Smith in August. Even more horrible, a fourteen-year-old Negro boy, Emmett Till, visiting from Chicago, was lynched in the Mississippi Delta town of Drew, in Sunflower County, in that month in 1955. That whole year in Montgomery, Alabama, Martin Luther King was leading the Montgomery Bus Boycott.

"But Mom, I'm only going down there to visit people and listen to music."

"Negro people and Negro music?" she queried.

"Yeah, Mom, you know my interest in the blues."

With that last statement, Mom just made a strange disgusted grunt and turned and walked away. Dad looked at me and said, "Amos, you really upset your mother," and put his arm on my shoulder.

And so it went on that cloudy September day in 1956, in the house of the Lardowitz family in the suburbs of New York.

I could not shake my desire to go with Ben to the Delta. Mom became herself, but I didn't hear her talk about Thanksgiving. Up to this point in my life I had never really fought my family's wishes (except for outright not telling them I'd played hooky that one day, to see Ben). This would prove to be a watershed for me. The year before, in 1955, I had seen *Rebel Without a Cause*, the film with James Dean. He was killed in a sports car accident that same year and immediately became a cult figure.

For the next week, I started turning my shirt collar up like James Dean. I tried to walk like him. I thought of myself with Natalie Wood, holding her tenderly. I spoke in short teenage talk, and when I was alone in my room, I would look in the mirror and make believe I was yelling back at my parents to "Leave me alone!!!!!!"

I'm not sure what my parents thought of me the next two weeks, for they didn't say anything about my transformation. I was going to go and that was it, I thought to myself. Would I have to lie? How could I? Obviously, Mom would not give me a choice. I would have to be at Thanksgiving dinner.

The only thing I could do was insist that I wanted to go, and that I would make it up to my family somehow. My God, I was only sixteen. How could I be such a rebel?

"Yes, hello, Mrs. Rabinowitz, this is Mrs. Lardowitz," Mom said into the telephone. That is how my mom and Alvin's mom addressed each other. I think it was sort of a respect thing, but I am not sure. It may have been a sparring sort of thing—the Conservative Jew mom versus the Orthodox Jew mom. At any rate, they were very considerate of each other.

"Thanksgiving dinner? Actually that would be very nice. How many are coming? Yes, certainly, our family is getting that way too. Kids growing up, I guess."

She didn't know that I overheard her conversation. It seemed that in a heartbeat Mom had accepted an invitation to the Rabinowitzes for Thanksgiving dinner, probably to notch another Orthodox coup that she could brag about to her friends and family. But it also seemed that maybe someone or another was not going to be there. Alvin had a brother and a sister—aha, an opening!

"So are we going to Bea's house for Thanksgiving, Mom?" I said the next day. (Cool.)

"No, Amie, actually, we have been invited to the Rabinowitzes for a real Orthodox kosher meal," she said proudly.

"Who's coming?" I said slyly (cool times two).

"Uh, mostly everyone ...," she replied hesitantly.

"Alvin's brother and sister?" I said. Mom would never lie to me. She told me early in life that lying was like not being true to yourself. It is something I have carried through my whole life. To get around lying, I obviously would just not say anything—like in that hooky thing. But if pushed, the Lardowitz clan would have to 'fess up.

"Alvin's sister is visiting a friend in Chicago," she 'fessed up.

"Mom ... please can I go with Ben? He's a good friend and would take care of me. You know that." Ben and Zelda, on their way upstate one day, had stopped spontaneously at our house. Mom and Dad were there. Ben was his gracious and charming self, and they had stayed for coffee.

"Amie, my Amie ... you always seem to be a little offbeat ... my Amie."

Mom had never analyzed me up to this point in my life. It seemed so strange for her to say that, but her words were soft, and her concern and love were written all over her face.

I knew I was going to the Delta.

I could not contain my inner excitement. At the same time I was completing my application to Cornell, and it seemed to be, momentarily, a distant priority, although I was told my acceptance was almost certain.

I studied a map of the United States and saw that our trip would take us through New Jersey, Pennsylvania, Maryland, Washington, D.C., Virginia, North Carolina, South Carolina, Georgia, Alabama, and into Mississippi. We were going by train. We would take a direct train to Richmond, with major stops in Philadelphia and Washington. The next leg would be from Richmond to Columbia, South Carolina, and into Atlanta. We would have a short wait and then ride to Montgomery, Alabama, and then into Jackson, Mississippi. From there we would take a bus two hundred miles to a small town right in the Delta, in Bolivar County. We would not have a sleeper. It was cheaper. We would sit straight up. The train trip would be twenty-four hours and thirteen hundred miles, and then the bus ride would be about five hours. How great!! I knew everything about the South from my studies of the Civil War. There was so much history. Almost every town and city had a battle associated with it. We would have to leave Tuesday night, November 20, to arrive by early Thanksgiving morning. We would then leave again to come back home on Saturday morning and arrive in New York City, at Grand Central Station, about ten at night, when I would take the last train to Crestwood and then walk home. The trip was a full seven weeks away, and already I couldn't wait.

I was still going in to Manhattan to work for Ben two days a week. Mostly, I practiced my guitar. Ben was quite busy cataloging his books and records. He was doing his complete inventory and said he would always shoot for the week before Thanksgiving to finish. Then he would generally lie low, or travel for about ten days and return to the store two weeks before the Christmas holidays, for sales picked up then.

I thought of nothing else but our trip to the Delta.

Delta Bound

It was a rainy and cool early morning that Tuesday, November 20, 1956. I was already packed, with one small, old suitcase that Mom filled with a few days' worth of clothes, my toothbrush and toothpaste, and hairbrush. I was up at five thirty. I couldn't sleep any longer, I was so excited. I remember Dad coming into my room about six in the morning and touching me under the covers and mumbling something like "Be safe." I still had to go to school that day, but we were to be let out at noon. I left for school at my usual time, around seven thirty, and Mom went to the door with me, ran her fingers through my hair, and said, "Amie, I love you ..."

After school I took the bus to the subway and arrived at Ben's store about three. We were going to leave from the store. It was closed with a sign on it. I had my key and went inside to wait for Ben. I sat quietly in the store daydreaming about the biggest trip I had ever taken and what kind of experience I was going to have. I pictured myself as a little speck moving farther and farther away from New York City into territories that were not discovered yet. I had never felt this type of experience before, a coziness of anonymity, disappearing into cultures I had never witnessed.

Grand Central Station was filled with men in hats and coats with nighttime newspapers. Ben and I boarded our first train. We seemed to be the only people looking like us, not businessmen. The car was not half bad, I thought, with relatively comfortable seats. Somewhere about two hours into our trip, at a station, I heard an announcement asking everyone going on to Washington with connection to Richmond to please move forward a number of cars—and move forward we did. The cars were different, a little more basic and noisy and uncomfortable. I would daydream often on this trip, Ben allowing me whenever possible a window seat. There I would sit with my head against the glass, looking out unfocused at the rapidly disappearing sights, and at the same time seeing my own reflection in the window glass. The stop at Washington, D.C., was about fifteen minutes. I would have loved to get off the train to see all the historical sights I had studied, but I had finally hit my overexcitement wall. I just sat stupefied until I was abruptly jolted by some train coupling or uncoupling and the scratchy announcement once more: "Move forward to Richmond, please"—and move forward we did. Oh boy … Our trip was getting more and more uncomfortable. This car was really old. The seats were really hard. The noise was really loud—oh well, so be it.

Somewhere in the deep night of travel oblivion once more I was awakened by the scratchiest and most-ear piercing announcement: "Richmond, Virginia … Richmond, Virginia … twenty-minute stopover … twenty-minute stopover …"

I rolled off the seat and into Ben's lap, and he laughed out loud. "Kid, you up? Get off the train … take a walk … get your sea legs." I stumbled through the car, careening off the corners of the seats until I finally could walk straight enough to almost fall down the three stairs out of the railway car. There I stood, in what appeared to be a smaller version of the Grand Central Station terminal. The building seemed pretty old and historic. My mind started to work, and I was thinking of Richmond's fate in the Civil War, being burned to the ground by Grant. I felt history here. I was getting excited—and then I realized I needed to take a leak. Looking around, I saw that it was really late and there were not a lot of people milling about. I thought I noticed a guy going into a men's room. I followed him in and went directly to a urinal. Half consciously, I noticed that it was really smelly and dirty. As I was peeing, I heard this easy, deep laugh to my right. I turned my head and saw this old Negro man peeing two stalls over. He had a gray stubble beard and a broad smile. "Young fella, you need to look around more when you travel down here," he said with a smooth southern drawl. At first, I wasn't sure what he meant. Then he continued in a more mumbled way, "If the world was filled with young like you, maybe we wouldn't need two urinals." He pronounced urinals urine-alls. And then he laughed even louder, flushed his urinal, and walked out. I was stunned and not sure what had taken place. I walked out of the bathroom and looked around. I looked up, and above the entrance was a sign that said COLORED.

Whites only, colored, whites only, colored ... and on and on ... seemed to go on in my brain on the same beat and with the same rhythm of the wheels click-clacking across the track separations. I had no thoughts with this mantra. It just went on and on, dulling my uninformed mind for hours and hours and hours.

That moment of recognition—an old Negro man, I'm sure with a lot more life experience than a teenager, musing about racial segregation—would stay in my mind the whole Delta trip. The deeper we got into the South, the more I saw WHITES ONLY, COLORED ONLY on water fountains, waiting rooms, cafés, and restaurants. As our railroad trip meandered deeper into more rural areas, the Negroes who boarded seemed to move to a small area in the back of the car. In fact, I remember, between Columbia, South Carolina, and Montgomery, Alabama, I overheard an old Negro woman ask the conductor where the "colored car" was.

As usual, whenever I had an epiphany about anything, I kept it to myself. I didn't engage Ben about my personal shock at seeing blatant segregation, possibly because I felt I should have known, and it would be embarrassing for me. One thing I admired about Ben was his directness and acceptance. He was always so self-assured and confident. If he could make something happen, he would do it. If he couldn't, it was off his radar.

Ben did talk to me just before we pulled into Montgomery. "Kid, this is the time to cool yourself ... focus in on what we are here for and picture it in your mind. Keep to yourself and don't talk to anyone. If asked, we are visiting relatives for Thanksgiving." The Montgomery, Alabama, station seemed different. There were a lot more people and a lot more police officers. I also noticed about a half dozen police cars with flashing lights on the periphery of the station. Ben grabbed my arm and said softly as we pulled in that we were staying in our seats until we left.

"Jackson, Missssisssipppiii, next ... and last stop" (repeated three times). I could hardly contain my excitement. The air became progressively warmer, and the cars had no air-conditioning. We were able to open our window to a certain level. For the first time in my life, I felt that I was in an exotic place, for I could smell and feel the difference in the air. It felt like what I would expect in the tropics. I could hear sounds that were different also. The birds were different, and there were insect sounds everywhere. It looked like we were going to pull into Jackson about six thirty that Wednesday evening. Ben told me we had about forty-five minutes to catch the bus to Bolívar County and that the bus station was just a short walk from the train terminal. Ben then told me, I believe for the first time, the name of the town we were going to: Mound Bayou, "the oldest Negro town in America founded by Negroes," he said.

We got our things together as we pulled into Jackson and headed out of the train and into the terminal. What an experience! I felt like a real world traveler, coming from civilization into an exotic and unexplored new land. Once again, I could smell the difference, as if I were in the subtropics. We walked to the bus station, where Ben was going to get us two tickets to Cleveland, Mississippi; the bus did not stop at Mound Bayou. I heard Ben talking with the ticket agent about how close we could get to Mound Bayou. I heard the ticket agent say, "Why would you want to go to Mound Bayou?" but I didn't hear what Ben said in response. He must have given him some good reason, because it seemed that the ticket agent was trying to get us there. Ben walked away from the window with two tickets to Cleveland, Mississippi. He then told me that close to Merigold, right after Cleveland, we were going to ask the bus driver to let us out on the highway, and then we would walk the three miles to Mound Bayou.

The bus was really old and dilapidated, and all the seats had tears in them. It was very noisy. There must have been about twenty people on the bus, with a few Negroes in the back. The ride was bumpy and uneven, but it was strangely comfortable, massaging our bodies this way and that way, seemingly to smooth out the stiffness in us produced by the long train ride.

Once more, I felt my heartbeat increase with excitement as we got closer to our destination. It was nightfall, and it seemed I could see practically nothing outside the bus that was not lit by its headlights. We must be going through rural area after rural area, I thought. I must have momentarily nodded off when I was jolted by Ben jumping off his seat and running to the front of the bus. He then signaled me to hurry up. It was obvious we were being tossed out within the next few seconds.

Man, there we were, about midnight, standing in the middle of a road with no streetlamps, and certainly no traffic. Ben again used a hand wave to move me in the direction we should be walking. It must have taken about forty-five minutes as we meandered off the main road to an unpaved dirt road with one streetlamp and small clapboard-style houses on either side of the street. "Mound Bayou, my friend," said Ben as he raised his hand as if making a presentation. My God, Ben had never, ever called me anything but "Kid" right up to this point in our relationship. Looking back, I think he was proud that I was sharing this very special part of his life experience with him.

We must have been standing there for about a minute, and I was waiting for Ben to signal me to some house where we must be staying, when I was momentarily blinded by the headlights of a car coming right around the bend on this rural road. I thought it was going too fast and did not see us, because it screeched to a halt within two feet in front of us. I then noticed that it was a police car. A large burly-looking policeman got out of the car and stood right in front of us. The headlights and flashing red police lights on top of the car were almost blinding.

"What y'all doin' here and where y'all stayin'?" he growled.

"We're here for a Thanksgiving dinner and a spiritual," said Ben confidently.

"Let me tell y'all ..." He removed his glasses and continued, "You and the niggas better be doin' just that ...," and he turned his head to me with a stare that I had never seen before and that I will remember my whole life. His eyes were filled with hate—hate that to this day I cannot understand.

"I knew they were following us," Ben said. "This is a very difficult time ... but things will happen after the turmoil that will change our little world for good." It seemed that this was one of the rare moments when Ben would talk about the collective world and its fate instead of just every individual's "bullshit" in the world.

The police car made a U-turn and peeled out in the direction from which it had come. My whole body was shaking with fear. Ben noticed and broke the ice with "It's party time, Kid, follow me."

Ben knocked on the door of a two-story white clapboard house with a rickety, ripped screen door. I could hear within the house voices that I thought belonged to excited little kids. The door opened and a woman shrieked with joy as she wrapped her arms in a wide sweep around Ben's body. "Ben, you made it!" she screamed. I could see two small kids hiding behind her skirt. "Little Bo, Big Bo ... come on out and see Ben."

Two heads peered out from behind her, belonging to two little boys, one older than the other, with wide smiles and large white teeth. "Who's that, Mama?" the little one said as he pointed toward me.

"Who is that, Ben?" said the mother.

"Kid, introduce yourself," Ben said.

"Hi, I'm Amos ... and I'm so happy to be here," I gushed. The little boy could not take his big brown eyes off me, it seemed. I guessed that he was about five or six years old. The other child seemed to be a few years older.

Lucy Brooks was Elmore James's kind of common-law wife, and Little Bo and Big Bo I guess were his kids. We sat down for a short late-night supper in the kitchen of Lucy's house. All the time, I could see out of the corner of my eye Little Bo just staring at me with a half smile. Lucy told us that the boys, as she called them, were coming together in two trucks with all their instruments, and would probably arrive within the next hour. They were going to put themselves up at the Baptist church where the whole town was going to have Thanksgiving.

Lucy's house was very simple and there was not a whole lot of furniture. She explained that there were only three electrical outlets and two lamps, the electricity in town not being able to support more. There was a small coal stove that Lucy used to heat water for baths and cooking, and we had to use an outhouse, for the old bathroom wasn't working now.

Ben and I settled into a third, very small, bedroom with two very uncomfortable cots. We both were exhausted, and I don't even remember saying anything to Ben before I fell asleep.

I awoke to the sound of a resident rooster very early in the morning. To my surprise, on the far end of my bed, all curled up, was Little Bo. I must have felt his small body all night long, and I guessed that he had plopped himself like a puppy at my feet as soon as I fell asleep. As I got up, I could smell eggs and grits, which were new to me.

At breakfast, I started up a conversation with the kids, asking Little Bo how he got his name. Little Bo just responded, "Tuesday." I asked him again and he said "Tuesday" again. I thought he was playing games with me until Big Bo interceded and said, "We were both born on Tuesday." Then Lucy announced that BoBo is an African name for a child born on Tuesday, and that because both of her kids were born on Tuesday, she'd split BoBo into the two Bo's. Then boldly, I asked if they had another name also. Lucy said Little Bo was Willie, named for Willie Brown, a Delta bluesman, and

Big Bo was named Robert, for Robert Johnson, the most famous of all Delta bluesmen.

Ben said he wanted to go over to the church and raise hell with his friends by pouring cold water all over them. Everyone laughed at what appeared to be Ben's silly joke, until he got up and grabbed the largest bucket he saw in the kitchen and proceeded to fill it with water. Everyone stopped laughing except Little Bo. He was squirming in his seat as he chuckled and chuckled, and then he said, "Can I go?" and away we went.

As we crossed the street of this really small town, I noticed around the bend a police car along the side of the road with nobody in it. Ben noticed that I had seen it and said, "They think they're trying to keep us honest. What could they be afraid of, Kid?" he seemed to ask rhetorically.

The Baptist church was also the town's meetinghouse. There was a chapel with about six pews and a community room with a small stage. I believe this was also the kids' school because there was a blackboard and a bulletin board with math lessons on it.

Little Bo grabbed my hand, and the three of us walked inside the community room. There in this open room sprawled six men, sleeping on the floor on blankets and makeshift beds. Ben immediately, like he was watering flowers, ran around the room and poured water over each one of these unsuspecting guys. What a ruckus ensued! Little Bo was laughing hard as these guys each jumped up in shock. "What the …" "Holy shit …" "Hey, man, what you doin'?"

"Hey you, white ass …," yelled Elmore (the rest of the guys I didn't know yet). Then he proceeded to burst into laughter and one by one, all the black dudes followed suit.

And there they were: Elmore James, Big Boy Crudup, Howlin' Wolf, Mississippi John Hurt, Son House, and Sunny Boy Williamson—all friends of Ben Fink.

Within the hour, the room was like Grand Central Station. Townsfolk were setting up folding tables and chairs. Womenfolk were setting the tables with plastic dinnerware and placing little vases of wildflowers. There were more little kids, boys and girls, playing jacks and jumping rope in the room. The musicians were unloading their instruments and tuning them and talking music. I started to smell really good cooked food about two in the afternoon. Ben was talking to everyone; he seemed to know other people in the town too. Over the background voices of kids and adults you could hear the blues harmonica of Howlin' Wolf setting a cool beat along with the occasional blues riff of the other guitarists. I walked over to the food table. I found out what okra, collard greens, and black-eye peas were. I sneaked a taste of Hoppin' John, which is black-eye peas, rice, and ham hock. There was swamp cabbage! And sweet potatoes, and corn and beans. There was rabbit, deep-fried chicken, and pork. There was corn bread, biscuits, corn pone, and hush puppies. For dessert there was peach pie, apple pie, rhubarb pie, and sweet potato pie. But there was no turkey! And I found out that there was plenty of corn whiskey, only it wasn't in the community room—it was outside in the musicians' trucks, and they certainly took a lot of breaks outside. There were plenty of hand-rolled cigarettes, but somehow everyone knew not to smoke inside the "house of the Lord," for that is what Anna Mae said.

I found out who Anna Mae was very abruptly when she came into the room and suddenly everyone stopped talking. She was quite a striking and imposing figure. She was large and wore a big tent-size floral dress. She also wore a pink Easter-like hat. Anna Mae was obviously the matriarch in Mound Bayou because everyone seemed to be subservient to her—and she made sure they were. "There will be no smokin', drinkin', or cussin' in the house of the Lord," she said as she looked toward the six musicians. I thought to myself, What did we come here for? until I saw Howlin' Wolf turn his head away and chuckle—and then I knew there would eventually be a "ruckus."

Late afternoon came and there must have been about sixty men, women, and children, although there were more women and children than men.

Anna Mae stood straight and tall and announced that we were to say the Lord's Prayer.

Dinner was fantastic. I ate more than I think I had ever eaten at one sitting. After dinner, the kids dispersed outside and the women started to clear the mess. I felt so at home in this strange and different culture, although the more I thought about it, the more it seemed no different from our own wild and wooly Jewish family get-togethers.

It was getting near eight in the evening and was already dark outside. The blues guys were getting antsy, I thought. Anna Mae was still a force in the room, and most everyone was still hanging around. "Sing to the Lord, my friends, sing to the Lord ...," she announced loudly. She then looked up to the bluesmen with a staring eye and said, "You sinners ... show us your redemption ..." Almost like on cue they all stood up straight as Anna Mae began in a strong and beautiful voice:

Ohhhhhh ... Oh ... What a friend we have in Jesus

All our sins and grief to bear

What a privilege to carry

Everything to God in prayer.

Howlin' Wolf leaned his body far forward, placed his harmonica in his mouth, and cupped his hands around the instrument, accompanying Anna Mae with a soft, twirly kind of sound. About the same time, Mississippi John sat down at the drum set and, with brushes, softly massaged the cymbal drums.

Everyone in the room seemed to change—their bodies seeming to float from side to side, and their hands softly clapping in unison to the hymn. Even the children moved their bodies in a slow matching rhythm. People started to also look up, and out of the crowd I heard "Hallelujah" from one side of the room, and then another "Hallelujah" from the other side of the room.

Oh, what peace we often forfeit

Oh, what needless pain we bear

All because we do not carry

Everything to God in prayer.

On the second verse Elmore picked up his guitar, and when Anna Mae finished a sentence and took a breath, he fingered a melodic slide all the way up the neck, fading it out as she started another line.

Can we find a friend so faithful

Who will all our sorrows share

Jesus knows our every weakness

Take it to the Lord in prayer.

And Son House, Sonny Boy, and Big Boy leaned their heads closer to one another and hummed harmonically, letting their guitars and bass guitars swing gently, hanging from their necks unplayed.

Anna Mae started clapping in unison to her singing, and slowly, it seemed, increased the beat, the hymn becoming faster. Suddenly then, she changed rhythm and started very slowly another gospel hymn:

No ... body knows the trouble I've seen ... No ... body knows ... the trouble I've seen ... se ... eee ... eee ... eeen

Noooooo ... body knows but Jesus ...

Sonny Boy started to accompany on the piano, rolling his fingers across the keys, and she repeated it three times very slowly and soulfully.

Sometimes I'm up … Sometimes I'm down …

The crowd started to clap and sing "Nobody Knows" rapidly, and continuously, in succession without stop while Anna Mae continued and increased her beat.

Oh yes, Lord … Sometimes I'm almost to the ground … And the beat became faster and faster with everyone clapping and singing "Nobody Knows" continuously right through Anna Mae's singing, which lasted about half an hour.

It was infectious and spirited, with everybody gyrating and moving from side to side. There was a unison that I cannot describe—the whole group of children and adults became one in spirit. I had never felt rhythm like this. I felt goose bumps as I clapped along.

Anna Mae bowed her head as she was finishing and sang a "Hallelujah" that must have lasted two minutes and hit every high and low note in the scale. As her lips uttered the last sound, there was not a movement in the room; everyone had their heads bowed. As I lifted my head, tears welled up in my eyes—tears that I could not control, that rolled out of both my eyes, down my cheeks, and to the floor. It was truly the first spiritual experience that I had felt—one that would remain with me my whole life.

Anna Mae lifted her head, stood tall and straight, and turned and walked right out of the room. I felt she had done what she was supposed to do—bless the room, bless the house of the Lord, and bless its people. I think she knew the blues were coming—the basic and human blues, the blues of everyday life and strife, the drinking and smoking and cussing blues—and at least she had given it a chance for a pure start.

"Sing it, you black sinner, sing it," yelled Sonny Boy to Big Boy.

And with a smile from ear to ear, Big Boy started up:

Wellllllll, that's all right, Mama, that's all right, Mama, it's any way you do …

"Swivel them hips … just like the Elvis boy, Crudup … Swivel them hips," yelled Howlin' Wolf. The whole band started in singing and playing and mimicking Elvis Presley's hip gyrations. It was hilarious. Everyone was laughing and almost on the floor—what a scene. Here they were, the literal inventors of rock and roll—and here was Big Boy Crudup singing his own song that Presley had usurped and he was copying Elvis's style.

It was ludicrous, I thought. But such was life, and such was the world at that time.

The children and women started filtering out about ten thirty, leaving about twenty of us and the musicians. And then the band played on well into the night, punctuated by trips to the outside for corn whiskey and cigarettes. As time went on, the trips became stumbles and the playing became a "ruckus"—which was exactly what Elmore had said was goin' down on the Delta on Thanksgiving. There were a couple of firsts for Amos Boris Lardowitz: smokin' and drinkin'—and sick and drunk. Luckily, the vomiting ended about five thirty in the morning when I stumbled into my cot and almost crushed Little Bo at my feet—but he only smiled.

Friday until about two in the afternoon must have been a blur, for that's how long I slept, with the occasional tickle of my feet from the mischievous Little Bo.

It was a warm day, and people were milling about on the rural dirt main street. The police car was gone and there seemed to have been no incidents relating to race. I saw each of the blues guys, and we gave high fives and clasped our hands together as we did it—a cementing bond of our experience and respect for each other. I'm not sure why they included me in their club, but in my heart I knew we had all shared a most wonderful experience.

I never did see those guys again.

Elmore James died in 1963 after his third heart attack. While John Lennon is playing the slide guitar on the Beatles' "For You Blue," George Harrison says, "Go, Johnny, go … Elmore James got nothin' on this baby." Jimi Hendrix, the Allman Brothers, and Stevie Ray Vaughn were great admirers.

Sonny Boy Williamson II died in 1965. He toured with the Yardbirds and the Animals in England, and his song "Eyesight to the Blind" was used in *Tommy,* the rock opera by the Who.

Mississippi John Hurt died in 1966. His "Stack-O-Lee" was probably the earliest recording of that popular song. He recorded as early as 1928 with more songs with the blues in them than you could shake a stick at.

Howlin' Wolf died in 1976. His songs have been covered by Cream, the Rolling Stones, Jimi Hendrix, and Led Zeppelin. Eric Clapton and Steve Winwood played on his album.

Big Boy Crudup died in 1974. He was, of course, labeled the "Father of Rock and Roll" and had at least three songs covered by Elvis Presley.

Son House died in 1988. He played alongside Robert Johnson and toured the United States and Europe extensively. He played the Newport and New York and American folk festivals.

They were all born in Mississippi.

The trip back home was like a grainy black-and-white movie that flickered across my eyes and kept me in sort of a semi-trance.

Ben did not talk to me much about the jam in the Delta. Of course, he knew how profound that experience was for me. Ben was smart and intuitive and always received whatever he needed from any experience he observed or witnessed, and he knew it had changed my life.

I woke up Monday morning about five thirty. I had to go back to school that day. There was something floating around in my head that I had to write down, and as I wrote it, I actually sang it with melody:

Gonna lay me down in the bosom of my Lord,
Gonna lay me down in the bosom of my Lord
Gonna lay me down today.
Oh Lord, can you hear me today? Oh Lord, can you hear me today?
Can you tell me that Righteousness is on the way?

And that was it—I had written a Negro spiritual in my sleep. That also was the first thing that I had ever written, deeply expressed, from the inside of my being. I was embarrassed to tell Ben because it was a Negro spiritual—and why would I have any reason to feel this … and to write it?

Zel

I WAS STILL GOING to Ben's about two days a week during my senior year of high school. Even with all the new experiences and my—I hoped—pending acceptance to Cornell, I was still plagued by my discovery in the attic and my doubts about something in my family.

I felt that I knew Ben well enough to at least talk to him about it and get his advice.

“”Ben, I think I have real problems about doubts I have in my life,” I said abruptly.

“Okay, Kid, what could be your problem?” he said nonchalantly.

“I don't know … I think I have a secret in my family's roots that I need to find out about. My mind seems to drift off into the past…especially America's past… and look for things …,” I said, feeling kind of insecure.

“OK, Kid. So what?” said Ben.

“But it really bugs me, and I feel ambivalent about a lot of things relating to it, being Jewish and such.” I rambled and continued, not knowing why I was opening myself up to all my seemingly adolescent hang-ups.

Ben interrupted me and said, “Kid, you're a great reader and observer and a good writer … so write, man. You don't need to go searching for things inside yourself … it's a waste of time.”

“Yeah, Ben,” I replied dejectedly.

“Look, use your mind's stream of consciousness … Write it. Don't search for it. You own it … You own every one of your thoughts and doubts. Get in the back room now and write me four lines of what is in you … now!" ordered Ben.

My God, what was I thinking? I look back now and realize I was only sixteen years old and yet I was already in angst to discover the undiscovered—to reveal the unrevealed.

I sat and stared up to the shelves of books and manuscripts like they should be helping me or telling me something. I must have sat silent for about ten minutes, and then, as if I wasn't directing the pencil, I wrote my first word: *History.*

History … what are you? America? My America? Why are you? Are you me? Living and breathing in the centuries before … What matters … the door? The stool that I sit on? Am I a Jew or a stool? I am explorer … adventurer … romantic … guilt ridden … in love … cascading down a mountain of culture and heritage only to look up and climb again—breaking my fingernails … I exist only on paper.

I could see Ben's eyes scan left to right as he quickly read my four lines of gibberish. He had one of his half snickers on his lips. "OK, What's this Jewish thing, Kid?" he queried.

Uh oh, here we go, I thought. "I don't know, it seems to be an underlying theme in my life. I'm looking for things away from my Jewish roots. After all, I am Jewish and I come from a Jewish family … and …"

Ben cut me right off then. "So what? I'm Jewish—and if it's guilt you're talking about, *I* don't have any. I am me, and who I am, and I behave the way I want to behave."

What???? Ben is Jewish? … I never even thought of him as Jewish. He seemed to be beyond being anything but Ben. Holy shit!

"And so is Zel, for that matter … She's beyond anything—she's existential."

Holy, holy shit! Zelda is Jewish … It can't be … She's beautiful and sexy … and I'm in love with her … forbidden fruit that's not forbidden … although she is ten years older than me … Oh my God, there I am in a disjointed stream of consciousness.

"Kid, you look like you've had a stroke or heart attack or something. Talk to me, man."

I was speechless.

Looking back now, I realize that I was still growing up and not mature yet, and I certainly hadn't felt all the deep emotions that come with advancing life experiences. It was actually a good thing to separate from

Ben at this point, for I was going away to college and needed to grow and learn. But I was in love with Zelda, and she would always be the love I could not have—the real love, not a fantasy, but a real person who moved and talked and had the most beautiful sexy blue eyes—and she was Jewish.

"Ben! I got into Cornell!" I said excitedly, the second week of February, 1957, as I ran into the store and saw him. Zelda was there also, and they both jumped up excitedly and hugged me together. We were like in a bear dance—three people jumping in unison with arms around each other. They were sincerely excited for me. "OK, Kid, now you can come back and teach us a thing or two," said Ben almost humbly (not too humbly—for Ben was far too confident to be really humble).

We went out to the coffee shop. It felt like the day we'd gone there when Ben had snared that manuscript—except now it was me who had captured the prize, me who was the One. It really was a nice momentary feeling of happiness and success, the moment all young people have when they pass their driver's test and when they get into the college of their choice.

I never did get over loving Zelda, but being the romantic that Amos Boris Lardowitz was, it wasn't a bad thing—it probably was a really good thing. It kept me vulnerable and emotional my whole life—and it certainly kept me searching.

College Bound

My parents drove me up to Cornell University for orientation in August 1957. Cornell sits in the Finger Lakes region just above Cayuga Lake, in Ithaca, New York. The drive from the metropolitan New York area takes one through farmland and small rural towns, where the culture is definitely "upstate," rural physically and culturally. It could not be any more different from Manhattan.

Ithaca was a "townie" city then, with local retail and local trades. It sat in the valley at the banks of Cayuga Lake and looked up at the natural stone spires and granite buildings that made up Cornell.

Once up on the "Hill," the environment changed. There was an aura of culture and intelligence that only an Ivy League school could have.

The campus was big and laid out according to the individual schools within the university itself. There was the Engineering Campus, the Arts Quad, the Architecture Campus, and so on. The buildings foretold the learning inside of them, being generally massive and made of stone. They ranged in age from Victorian in style, Cornell being founded in 1868, to the modern glass and steel of the mid-twentieth century. Fantastic gorges cut through streets along the hill. They were magnificent with flowing waterfalls meandering down to Lake Cayuga. Only later did I find out that they were great jumping places for the suicide prone.

The view looked down and consisted of the valley and the picturesque lake that was Cayuga. If you looked very carefully into the distance on the lake, you could often see the pencil-thin silhouette of the crew boats racing: the Cornell crew.

Late summer was always beautiful to me. The sounds of the cicadas and the smell of the drying leaves on the trees were very special.

We had a map that gave us directions to the boys' freshman dorms. Of course, we drove through campus first and to the orientation building, a large pillar-less hall called Barton Hall. We picked up a large package of papers and proceeded to the freshman dorms loaded with three suitcases, a duffel bag, and my guitar case.

There they were, what appeared to be numerous rectangular buildings constructed of cinder block, with very small windows neatly spaced on the two-floor structure—it was a damn prison, I thought. Right then and there, my bubble burst and I felt trapped. I noticed then that the freshman dorms were down the hill somewhat from the main campus and had no view at all. I also noticed that the hill was very long and steep. I reminded myself that freshmen could not have cars (not that I would have gotten one anyway). *Oh boy!*

My dad and I started schlepping my belongings up the stairs and to the second floor to find my room in Dorm 4. The only saving grace was that my experience was being simultaneously repeated by dozens of families—boys and men moving goods. My room was small, with one window and two single beds on either side, and two small desks and one closet built in. There was no bathroom. The only bathroom on each floor was at the end of the hall and had three toilets and two showers. *Oh great, there goes my privacy*. My roommate did not show up that day. We settled me in, and Dad and Mom and I had an early dinner in the cafeteria in Willard Straight Hall, "the Straight." The tough day was over.

Life can throw you some curves. It can make you feel uncomfortable and insecure. It can make you want to cry—and cry I did, on the first night in the dorm, without a television, without a radio, without my room at home—and without my parents. It was amazing; just a few months before, I had been an adult. I had worked at Ben's Den and met literary giants. I had been to the Delta and was part of a "ruckus" with the greats of the blues. I was a literary editor and a collector and dealer in manuscripts. But I returned to being the child of my parents, and this new adventure made me feel insecure. Late at night, actually early the next morning, I opened my guitar case and played my guitar—and all started to feel better.

I was enrolled in the School of Arts and Sciences. My major was American history and my minor was American literature, thanks to Ben.

My courses included math and biology and English and gym. My legs became strong from the hikes up the "little" hill to classes that seemed to be all in different buildings and required running to make it on time. I also enrolled in the ROTC program, the Reserve Officers' Training Corps. My interest in everything American took me to this elective two-year officer training class. That conversation with Zelda and Ben about war had had quite an effect on me, but my separation from Ben threw me back to my fascination with the military, and enrolling in the ROTC was an attempt to clarify my feelings about it.

I began to enjoy college. I felt protected, challenged, and excited by the vibration of the learning environment. Of course, American history was my life, and the structured classes only made me feel more secure. I enjoyed math and English as well. My music carried me everywhere. In the dorm, and out on the hill, I would fingerpick new melodies of my own that I was working on. I would also play folklike songs that were already developing a commercial audience.

The talk in classes was all intellect, the talk in the Straight student union building was mostly intellect, but the talk in the boys' dorms was no intellect. First-year social life was like what you would imagine taking place with adolescent subhuman primates—a lot of sniffing and posturing.

There were essentially no meaningful boy-girl relationships as a freshman. Talk was only of raiding the girls' dorms and demanding panties and bras. Talk was of attacking the small girls' colleges that lay a distance from mighty Cornell on a Saturday night. Talk was of climbing down the hill to Ithaca and attacking the small townie bars, with the bimbo girls who sat on bar stools waiting for a pickup, and scoring. It was mostly talk with the very infrequent buzz that some lucky, dumb freshman dormie in Dorm 3 scored in Cazenovia College last night, or made out with a townie in her car behind the Slurp and Burp Bar. After all, anyway, this was the sexually deprived fifties. Mamie Eisenhower with her odd hairdo was the pin-up queen. But the fifties were ending very soon, and Marilyn Monroe was almost here. Anyone lucky enough to have in their possession her beautiful naked body on a red background was a mega-lottery winner—actually, anyone lucky enough to have seen that photo was blessed.

My social life was very strange. I certainly was becoming more mature, and I certainly did want to go out with girls, but I still was chasing the goyim, or non-Jewish people.

I was convinced that there was a conspiracy against Amos Boris Lardowitz dating anyone, especially Gentile girls, because whenever I was either fixed up or arranged a date with anyone, the date never materialized—vapor girls. I remember going to a freshman sorority for an arranged blind date (with a straight-hair blonde) and the greeter at the desk, who was always a student, said, "Yes … may I help you?"

"I'm here for a date with Jane. I'm Amos," I said.

"Stay here, I'll be right back," she said.

"OK," I said.

She came back. "Jane's not here," she said.

"But I have a date with her," I said.

"Are you sure it's tonight? She's not here," she said. *See … vapor girls … That probably was Jane … She needed to check me out … went back to her friends and decided she didn't want to go out with me—girls are so cruel!*

I wasn't a bad-looking kid. I was always told that I had beautiful, expressive eyes and beautiful, wavy hair—especially by my mother. I'm convinced that my nature was to be a romantic, and romantics are generally hopeless—like "hopeless romantic." The expression *hopeless romantic* is a great combined usage of two words that are synergistic with each other. (He was a *hopeless romantic.*) Anyway, it is more fulfilling and romantic to dream, isn't it?

My school interests were kind of competing: American history and American literature. I really owed my developing interests in American lit to Ben and Zelda. They had opened my eyes and heart to the minds and hearts of the creative writers coming out of America. But I still had this deep fascination with the Civil War and the turmoil during those defining moments of our country's history. So, the Reserve Officers' Training Corps was a real way for me to experience firsthand the training, life, and mind of the soldier.

I was about one month into my ROTC course, which was one class per semester for four semesters. I remember the day that the thirty of us who were in this particular class section were standing, in uniform, out on the field next to Barton Hall. Our instructor, who was an upperclassman and already committed to military service after college, was lecturing us, for the first time, on the mental strength and good judgment of the developing soldier. He growled, "Let's do a little lesson in judgment, you jugheads." He then moved about twenty yards away from us and said, "A grenade was just thrown right here," and he pointed straight down to the ground. "It's going to go off in ten seconds. In four seconds I want each of you to react … … … … … … … NOW!!!!" he screamed.

I'm not sure what happened next, but seconds later I found myself belly flopped on the spot where the grenade was supposed to be, covering the area like a blanket. The next thing I heard was "YOU IDIOT! The million pieces of what is left of your body and ammunition clip is now being imbedded into what were your buddies! Get up!" I got up and turned to see twenty-nine other students in a crouch covering their heads and bodies with their arms about fifty yards away. (Uh oh, I guess I must have had poor judgment.)

I sheepishly walked back to where everyone else was. The instructor then announced, "Dismissed, soldiers!"

I began walking off the field to get my books and noticed that three other students were laughing and approaching me from behind. One of them said, "Really cool, Lardowitz," possibly in an admiring way, I thought, but I really could not believe it.

"Yeah, you've got a hero's heart, man," said another.

"Stupid, but really inventive," said the third.

They all started to slap me on the back simultaneously and grab me around my neck in a mock-choking way, all the while walking off the field and laughing hilariously. One of them said, "OK, soldiers, off to the Straight for some R-and-R and coffee."

I didn't know these guys, but they seemed to know one another. I was getting the drift that they were all in the same fraternity together. It really was fun, and I felt comfortable with them. They did most of the talking, about funny things that had happened to each of them. About an hour had passed when one of them asked me if I was Israeli. I said no and asked why. He replied that I seemed to have a Jewish name and a military mind, so I must have come from Israel, where they breed ferocious fighters. I laughed and said no, I was from the Bronx. "What's the Bronx?" said one.

"Hey, stupid, the Bronx is in Manhattan ... idiot," said another. Then I really laughed out loud. Another joined me and we were really making a "ruckus," for everyone in the cafeteria was looking disapprovingly at us.

"Are you really Jewish?" one queried me.

"Yes, born and bred," I responded.

"I never met a Jewish person before," he replied. The others seemed to shake their heads like they were trying to remember whether they had ever met a Jew.

There was silence for about twenty seconds and then one said, "The Israelis mainly came from Europe, where they were Jews. They came back to Palestine to claim their homeland. You know, they are great military strategists. Last year's invasion of the Sinai Peninsula was unbelievable." He seemed to be the most knowledgeable of the three guys and more thoughtful, I thought. His name was Robert Armstrong. The other guys introduced themselves as Edward Hitchings and Donald Koslowski.

Robb, as he introduced himself, came from Michigan. He came from a long line of men who had served or were serving in the Army. Ed lived in Ohio near Cleveland. Don came from the Pennsylvania coal country.

"Amos, you know we call each other by our nicknames. What's yours?" said Robb. I wasn't sure what he meant. I was certainly not going to tell him Amie. I supposed that I could use A.B., which was my high school nickname, but that was high school—I'm in college now, I thought. I must have been deep in thought, for Robb interrupted me and said, "I'm 'Army,' Ed uses 'Hitch,' and Don is 'Turk'; they all relate to some military meaning … Hey, I think you're 'Ammo,'" and they all started laughing.

"Yeah, Ammo for Amos," said Hitch.

"Yeah, Ammo for blowing yourself up out there on the field," said Turk.

"Army, Hitch, Turk, and Ammo. All right … the Four Horsemen," said Army spontaneously as he looked around the table and everyone, including me, smiled.

The moment after Army announced the Four Horsemen and our eyes connected, time seemed to stop for me. There were many people in the Straight cafeteria, but there seemed to be a light shining down on the four of us—as if we were on a stage and everyone else was a dark shadow that could not be identified. The sound also changed. I heard a soft, continuous buzzing over the distant conversation of the people around us. And just as suddenly, I seemed to awake out of the trance when Army said, "I'm off, hey, next week."

We all got up, I more slowly, and we appeared to head off in four different directions. When I think back on this moment, I can almost see the feeling I had. I see the large open cafeteria from above, with many people sitting in small groups, and four individuals standing simultaneously and moving at right angles to each other: the Four Horsemen off to the four corners of the globe to meet their adventurous destinies individually—yet to come back and be one again soon.

That night, as I lay awake at midnight, I felt a comfort in my thoughts, something different from my excitement in meeting Ben. I felt my whole body pounding as I lay in anticipation of an adventure, as if I were a warrior.

I was very buoyant and smiling softly in my classes the next morning. On my walk across the crowded Arts Quad at a quarter to ten to get to my lit class, I literally bumped into a guy, and it was Hitch. We both laughed as he said, "Hey, Ammo," the first time I was called by my new nickname.

"Hey, Hitch," I replied in rapid fire.

"Where you headed to, Ammo?"

"To lit."

"You have a break after that?"

"Yeah, about one hour."

"Meet you at the Straight—front hall."

"Yeah, great."

Hitch and I sat down for an early lunch. He asked me about my major and interests. I told him about my interest in American history. I didn't mention literature. He asked me what I was going to do beyond my bachelor's; interestingly, I thought, this was the first time I'd been confronted with that question on campus. Mom and Dad had never actually said they wanted me to be a doctor, but Mom certainly had mentioned my two cousins in premed. Dad would never discuss my career like that; it just wasn't in him.

"I don't know yet," I said after the rambling thoughts in my head stopped.

"I'm going to law school—Cornell Law," Hitch blurted out, almost like he had asked me only because he wanted the stage to talk about himself. "On to law school, then general counsel, then CFO, then CEO," he continued.

Wow, that was a mouthful, I thought. "Where, Hitch?"

"The largest growing conglomerate I can find, man," he said excitedly. I laughed. He then abruptly changed the subject. "Hey, man, you get into a fraternity?"

"No, I didn't rush," I said.

My time with Ben and Zelda had done something to me. When our freshman class was being rushed by the fifty-odd fraternities at Cornell, I just felt beyond the process. It seemed so superficial. I was still savoring this rewarding adult experience and just couldn't bring myself to get excited about any fraternity life at that time, so needless to say, I was passed up. Who knows if this would have changed with time? I just didn't want to take part in that ritual hazing process at that moment.

"You know, Army, Turk, and I got into the same house," he said beamingly. "It's a jock house, man," he continued.

Fraternities at Cornell in 1957 were a reflection of society at that time—almost blatant discrimination was the rule. There were a few Jewish fraternities—two for the nebbish Jew, and one for the cool, handsome Jew. There were egghead fraternities, and a very small number would take in many foreign students from foreign lands. But there were many whites-only WASP fraternities. It probably really didn't matter what your religion was, as long as you were not Jewish. It just mattered what you looked like and what you did or appeared to do. So I guessed that Hitch, Army, and Turk had got into a Gentile, whites-only house, and I was correct.

But interestingly enough, I was flattered by their interest in me. Here I was, sitting with one of them in the Straight cafeteria, and he was interested in me. I knew my interests in the military made me who I was with them, and I liked it. There was a competing picture in my mind: Zel's soft face and her question "Why war?" that became fuzzier and more distant as the picture of the Four Horsemen's heads replaced it. I was enjoying myself for who I was at that moment.

That's all Hitch and I talked about. Just as we got up, I said, "Oh, by the way, what does *Hitch* stand for in military talk?"

"A hitch, man, like a tour of duty in the army," he said.

"OK, how about Turk?" I asked.

"You'd better ask him yourself, Ammo—only Turk can tell you," he said, suddenly serious. "He's told only two people—Army and me," he added.

I left the Straight thinking first about Hitch. He wasn't like me really. I liked him and he was sure of himself, like Ben, but he had an agenda in life, a superficial agenda, related to monetary success that was not on my radar and certainly was not the real motivation for any of Ben's life pursuits. For me personally, he didn't seem vulnerable enough. He didn't seem to see the rest of the world through others' eyes, although he was a likeable person.

My mind drifted to Turk and what Hitch had said about him. Of the three of them, Turk, I felt, was more like me. I could see in his eyes secrets, vulnerable secrets that lay deep within him, even though he also had a tough outer persona that he liked to show. I wondered what could be the origin of Turk's name—maybe someday I could ask him.

Army was a pleasant person and very quietly sure of himself. He told me that his grandfather was a one-star general and his dad was still an active colonel in the army. His uncle was in the military also. They all served or were serving in the army, and they all had gone to Ivy League schools to get an education first. I felt very proud to know Army. I would have loved to fantasize about being Robert Armstrong awhile back. Since I had met Ben and Zelda and traveled down South, though, my heart had opened up to the maladies of my America and the inconsistencies in the world. I may have passed the point of being the totally secure, unquestioning patriot, I thought.

At the end of one ROTC class, Army said, "Hey, guys, let's make Friday night a Four Horsemen night. It's off to Zincks at 2200 hours for all the beer we can drink." My other two buddies nodded enthusiastically, and I shook my head in agreement, although I may have had reservations.

There we sat, at a table for four, and finished a pitcher in about fifteen minutes. "It's the Four Horsemen of war," snarled Hitch.

"Yeah, man," said Turk.

"Buddies in the trenches," yelled Army.

I didn't say anything because my heart was pounding, but I finally let go and said, "All for one and one for all" and raised my glass, spilling half my beer on Turk.

He said, "I'll drink to that." Another pitcher came and we all seemed to be slurring our speech. As we rambled on, things got really quiet and I noticed that Army and Hitch were disappearing under the table.

As I sat staring into space, I heard right next to me, in almost a child's voice, "Mama, Mama, it's OK, wake up … Mama." I turned my head and it was Turk talking almost in a stupor. He then said, "Turk is here to help you, Mama, Turk is here," his voice stronger and more assertive. Amazingly, I could see tears running down his face as he said, "Daddy, Turk is here. Turk is here." He started to sob uncontrollably.

Instinctively, I cupped both my hands around his head, held him straight up, got really close to him, and said, "It's OK, Turk … it's OK … I'm here … Ammo is here." This went on for about three long minutes as our other buddies seemed to be in la-la space.

Suddenly, as quickly as it began, Turk said, "I'm OK … I'm OK."

My sleep that night was in fits and starts—I was quite restless. What had happened with Turk was very disturbing to me. Over the next few days, I really tried to search Turk out one on one. I reached him by phone and asked him if he wanted to go to the Straight for lunch on Wednesday.

"Turk, man, you know I don't want to be nosy, but what went on the other night?" I said as I fiddled with my tuna sandwich.

"Thanks for what you did. I don't know many people who would jump in that way. I'm kind of embarrassed," he said with open and trusting eyes. "I don't know—there is something in my childhood around and after my dad's death. He was killed in 1943 when I was three years old. My pop went to war in 1941. He really wanted to serve his new country—he was a new immigrant about seven years before. He had followed one of his relatives to America from Poland and started to work in the coal mines. My uncle told me he was very patriotic and just enlisted in the infantry with two kids and a wife. I don't know, Ammo, every once in a while, especially if I drink, I get this fuzzy image of me as a child with my mother ... and I feel I want to save her ... and I'm Turk and I want to save her, man ... I'm Turk. I've called myself Turk since I was a young child. My mom and Patricia, my sister who lives with my mom, forbid me from using *Turk* in the house. She calls me Donny ... My mom never remarried and Patricia hasn't married either ..."

As he kept saying *Turk,* his whole demeanor changed as if he bulked up and became stronger, like a bodybuilder. It was a literal transformation. I could see then the difference between Don and Turk. When Turk became Don, he was softer and his eyes were more open and seemed more vulnerable. When Turk appeared, like the first time I had met him and was with him, he was more focused and his eyes were narrower; he seemed less accessible and single- minded and strong.

Turk's mystery was on my mind all the time. It replaced the occasional return to my own secret in the attic of my home. Since college had started, thoughts of my family had taken a backseat to my new adventures anyway, but Turk's mystery simultaneously brought forward my own mystery. They would both float around in my head for weeks to come and then spontaneously disappear with the rigors and business of my new college life.

Army, Hitch, and Turk invited me to their fraternity for the once-monthly Saturday night rock-and-roll party. It was obvious that they had to clear this permanent invitation with their upper-class fraternity-mates. I guess I was their new fraternity mascot, because when I came and saw any of their housemates, they would yell out, "Hey, Ammo, great to see you." It really put a new light on my life—one I had dreamed about as a child. Here I was, "Ammo"—military guy, schmoozing with Gentile jocks who thought I was cool. I'm sure they didn't know I was Jewish.

I became really close to those guys into the second semester of my freshman year at Cornell. For a period of time I was feeling the dream of the kid I was.

I got an idea that I would get some of my Civil War soldier letters from the field and read them in a ritual we would have once a month. I would read one letter under candlelight as if I were the soldier writing the letter to my family.

There we sat over a pitcher of beer as I read my first letter …

Camp Dickinson near Fort Lyon Alexandria, Va. Oct 6, 1861

Dear Lola,

Our hopes have been realized, your little note has reached the 27th and to say it was received with pleasure would be no name for it … … … … … … … … … … … … I cannot write. There is a funeral in an adjoining camp and as the band is playing it seems as though I could hear the voice of prayer mingled in the melody. Tis majestic, it seems as if I was going along to keep him (the dead) company to heaven. In the delirium of the moment, I forget the words. "Between me and thee there is a great gulf fixed and the absence of fortune's bliss." Hark! Tis heavenly! I wish you could hear it. I have heard music in hundreds of churches but never, no never, has anything carried me away as the music of this band.

"Ever of thee I'm fondly dreaming." I have been requested to burn all my letters and know that I may not bring any home. This is the first I have received and will carry it close to my heart. I became a soldier and my fate is unknown. Please keep me in your heart and I would be pleased if you respond again.

Sam Brockett

The second month, after I had read a new letter, Army said softly, "A pact is being made tonight … by the individual Four Horsemen and the Four Horsemen as one … If our country fights a war, we will enlist together as one … and one together"—and he reached out his open hand on the table and each one of us placed our hands over his.

There was always a distant feeling that this was not me—not the Amos inside: the major part of college life, as a freshman, becomes a pact with three other buddies to serve in the armed forces and fight a war.

At this junction of my growing maturity, my dreams and values would certainly begin to collide. Thinking back, I knew that my destiny lay in allowing my inner flow to reach its ending point—and so I went along, with an inner excitement, trepidation, and pounding heart.

As my first year ended, I grew more physically. I was also stronger, for I worked out with my buddies. I studied hard and spent most of my time with the Four Horsemen. Girls were secondary. We dated, but we never strayed further than the Four Horsemen as one.

I thought of Ben and Zelda often. My life with them was like a dream. I visited Ben twice during school breaks and worked for him ten days at vacation time, five days at two separate times.

Since I was taking American literature, my connection with Ben was still strong. We always discussed what I was reading. He gave me great insight into the author's intentions, and I always trusted him.

I went out with Ben and Zelda a few nights during the year. I still had my deep crush on Zel. I felt at that time that I always would. It was like a secure piece of my emotional being that I could always count on. It would be hidden in a place I could always find, a feeling I could summon at any time: my unreachable love for Zel.

My first year ended on a high note. My relationship with Ben was buoyed by my studies in American lit, and my personal adventure with my bosom buddies was still quite high.

I came home to a job with Ben for the summer and the excitement of being an uncle to my first niece, Sydney. She was born June 17, 1958, and was adorable from the start. Mom was in heaven, and I could see that Dad was very happy. Alvin was moving up in the world of banking.

Ben encouraged me to take more risks in my editor's job, and he had me review a few new novels by new writers. He also gave me more time to buy letters for myself, and I became fixated on Civil War soldier letters from the field, which were the only letters I would purchase.

I listened to a lot of music that summer of 1958; rock and roll was booming. I played a lot of music also, mostly the blues. My trip to the Delta had transformed me in many ways; the most profound was my identification with Negro America and its plight, and my love for the blues.

I was living at home while I worked for Ben during the summer, and traveled by bus and subway to the city. My naiveté seemed to disappear; my knowledge of the city and my confidence grew, and the vignettes of my life continued to appear every once in a while to remind me of the special turning points in my life—like the coffee shop experience with Ben and Zelda.

Mom's Metamorphosis

I REMEMBER THE DAY vividly—August 15, 1958, when I was working in the store and the phone rang.

"Amos, Mom is in the hospital in Bellevue—she collapsed," cried Susan.

"Where ... what happened?" I said in a panicked voice.

"Dad said he's not sure ... but it could be a stroke," she responded.

"Oh my God."

Time stopped for me. My curiosity and my growth and my interests were not mine anymore. It was the first time in my young growing life that a major catastrophe had cut my lifeline short. I would not know how to feel an experience like this until I experienced it suddenly and without notice or expectation.

I must have scribbled a note to Ben and put it on the window and closed the store. I really don't remember. I also don't remember my dash to Bellevue Hospital. I only remember entering through the emergency room doors and the squeak of my shoes every time I moved my feet in panic. Who to ask? Where to go?

The hospital was so strange to me—it was not my world. As a kid, my dad's office was a sanctuary, but as I grew up, I felt more distant from the world of alcohol and needles, and I realized I had never been to a hospital.

A nurse must have seen my panicked face—the face, I suspect, of a child searching for its mother, a child lost, a mother lying somewhere injured or hurt.

"Can I help you?" she said.

"My mom's in the hospital. She had a stroke or something. My dad could be here. He's Dr. Lardowitz," I said rapidly.

"Oh my … Surely you must be Amos," she tried to assure me. "Come with me."

By her voice I could not tell if my mom was alive or not. She was helping me—but was she preparing me? Was she taking me to a place to tell me my mom had died? *Oh God, no … Mom, I need you … I don't want to lose you … You can't lose your mother. Can you? Where is Dad? Where is Susan?*

We walked through corridor after corridor, and then through a doorway and walked rapidly up the stairs. The nurse didn't say anything else to me. I was frightened and felt like my life was over. Suddenly she stopped, and with an open hand she ushered me into a room. There was Dad! He was with another doctor. He turned to me and with a tired look on his face said, "Amos, please sit down outside the door for a minute."

I just sat outside the room with my head cupped in my hands and my elbows on my knees, collapsed in spirit and thought. I felt so small. I felt so useless. I don't know how long I had sat there until, on my shoulder, I felt Dad's hand pressing down on me.

"Dad, where's Mom?" I cried.

"Amos, she's down the hall in intensive care. She's unconscious now. We don't know how much damage there is, but we do know that she suffered a stroke. Time will tell. Twenty-four hours will tell a lot." He said this all very steadily.

"Oh, Dad … is she going to be all right?"

"We'll see, Amos."

I was confused. Was he my dad, or was he a doctor telling me about my mom? Looking back, I think that he was both and that he was comforting me. I will always remember that moment.

Dad slowly walked with me down the hall. He placed his hand on my shoulder again as we turned in to the room Mom was in.

There she lay, quietly, with a strange, contorted look on her face. Her left arm was crossed over her chest, and the fingers of her left hand were curled like she was making a fist.

"Amos, you can talk to her. She's asleep but she will hear you," Dad said.

"Mom … Mom … hi … it's Amie," I said childishly. "Mom … it's me."

She did not respond, but I was with her and that felt more comforting.

There I sat, in her room all night. Susan, I think, could not bear to see her like this, so she didn't come down to the hospital, although she must have called three times during the night.

Dad stayed also, but he slept in another room and came with a nurse two times overnight.

Our family had stopped being at this time. We were on hold—on hold until the fate and destiny of the small Lardowitz family was determined by some unknown force or being.

I was in a strange state all night. I felt drugged, half awake, half asleep. When my eyes opened, I could see a blurred vision of my mom in bed; then I slept, then I awoke.

A strange bright light caught my half-closed left eye, and I shut it out with a reflex of my hand. I then opened both eyes, and in the blindness of the sun I knew that it was morning.

Mom was lying in the same position, and Dad and a nurse were over her. I could not hear what they were saying because they were whispering to each other. Dad turned to me, and I could see that he was worried and tired and looked older than his fifty-six years.

"Amos, no change yet. Let's hope for the best," and he once again put his hand on my shoulder. He then walked out of the room with the nurse.

I was so dejected. I must have dozed off in passive acceptance of my family's fate. I jumped up to a sound. It came from Mom's bed! I ran over to her and said, "Mom … it's Amie … Can you hear me?"

"Amie … my little Amie," I heard in a strange garbled voice with no movement of Mom's lips.

"Mom … it's me." I was so excited. I ran outside and looked down the corridor to find Dad. I must have yelled his name, for he came running, probably thinking something terrible had happened to Mom. Then Dad could understand what I had said—that Mom had talked.

We both heard her say, "Amie ... my Amie" with closed lips—but when she uttered the words, her left lip was curled down as though in a snarl.

"Amos, that's a wonderful sign," Dad said with a half smile that lit up his face.

We called Susan, who seemed relieved. Then Dad told me that Mom's ability to speak was very important, especially so soon after her stroke. Of course, he said, her partial paralysis would remain, and we didn't know what her eventual recovery would be like.

That horrible day was over. It had barely been twenty-four hours, and I had lived through something I certainly had not experienced before—a teenager's terror over the perceived or real sudden death of a parent.

I spent every day, all day, at Mom's bedside. That was all I did for seven days straight. Mom started to lift her head and open her eyes. She started to use other words in partial sentences like "Susan and baby ... at home?" or "Brothers and sisters ... here?" On the eighth day I was exhausted and arrived later in the morning.

The nurse was in Mom's room and asked me out into the hall. In a half whisper, as if Mom would hear, she said, "We will get her a kosher meal. I'll arrange for it."

"What did you say?" I said.

"A kosher meal," she repeated.

I was told that Mom had lifted her head and in a clearly pronounced, complete sentence said, "I want kosher meals while I am in the hospital." She then lay her head back down and went to sleep.

The nurse was amazed, she said. Dad was at his office, so he hadn't seen it, and no other doctor was there. About twenty minutes later, Mom had lifted her head and said the exact same thing. The nurse said this was real progress and that she had to let Dr. Lardowitz know.

Here I was thinking, What's going on? Mom's brain is scrambled. Maybe she thinks she's kosher now. I'm certainly not going to tell the nurse. *She isn't going to tell Dad, is she?* Maybe they'll think she got crazy from the stroke and put her away, I thought.

I saw Dad and asked him if she was OK, and he said that her ability to speak a complete sentence was a vast improvement. As usual, I could not bring myself to ask Dad a question like why she wanted kosher meals—and he didn't give an explanation.

In the afternoon, the nurses raised Mom's bed and she was actually sitting up, although she couldn't move the left side of her body and it seemed that the left side of her face looked different from the right. She talked more, although in less perfect sentences and with that little curled lip like a snarl on the left side.

I was amazed. The first meal I saw Mom eat I heard the nurse's aide say, "Here's your first kosher meal, Mrs. Lardowitz."

Mom continued to improve. I was there when she was helped up to actually walk. I was scared, and it seemed almost pathetic because they had to hold up the left side of her body. She had brightness in her being, though. I felt that she was a good patient, and I could see that she didn't want to worry me, because she would ask me in short sentences how I was doing. She also talked a lot about Sydney and how she was doing. Susan came to the hospital a few times, without the baby since they were not allowed. Susan seemed very affected and nervous about Mom. It was very difficult for her, I thought.

Eventually Mom could walk with a cane. She actually looked like a little old man, but she was not pathetic anymore. She was able to move her left arm more and more each day, and her face became more normal, although the little snarl on her left lip was still there when she talked. Mom was going to get physical therapy to help her continue to improve. It was also fortunate that Mom was a righty, because the stroke affected only the left side of her body, and she could actually write with her right hand.

All of this took place in the hospital. The time for me to go back to school was getting closer. This catastrophe had lasted about two and a half weeks, and I needed to go back in a few days.

Dad told me not to worry and that Mom would be getting out of the hospital in a few days. He said the hospital had arranged for an aide to help her during the day.

I visited Susan and Alvin before I went back to school. They had a very nice apartment in Brooklyn. Sydney's room was beautiful. I could see that Susan gave great thought to the coziness and comfort of her family. Of course, Sydney was barely two and a half months old and still slept in Susan and Alvin's room in a crib.

I could see that Susan was seriously affected by Mom's stroke. She was more nervous than her normal self. I learned that it was common for a woman to have postpartum depression just after giving birth, and I think Susan had this. I know that she was very close to Mom and that Mom's illness and subsequent vulnerability, at the same time Susan needed her mother for her newborn and for her depression, would take awhile for Susan to recover from.

I arrived at Cornell for my second year. I felt different; possibly I was just preoccupied. My Four Horsemen buddies got together within the first week of classes. I seemed to be the only one with a family crisis. They were all sincerely concerned but voiced optimism that my mom would make a full recovery.

I remember my first call to Mom from school.

"Mom … you well?"

"Amie … honey, I'm fine. The schvartza is here helping me."

I didn't realize that Mom's aide was a Negro. *Schvartza* was kind of a colloquial Yiddish word for a black person and I guess could be mildly degrading. Generally, Jewish people have been very tolerant as a whole and as individuals, but many times they've been judgmental.

"Mom, can she hear you? Don't call her a schvartza. What's her name?"

"Jemima."

Oh hell, like the pancake syrup Aunt Jemima? She was on the pancake syrup bottle with a kerchief, like the old-style black mamas. Oh boy, a rotund Negro lady stereotype saying Uncle Tom things. This won't be great for the progressive Lardowitz family.

I had become pretty sensitive to issues concerning civil rights and Negroes by now. My experiences in the South and the turmoil in the civil rights movement in America were going on at that very moment.

"Is she helping you the way you like?" I said, trying to be more normal in my response.

"Yes, honey. She's here five days during the week and we get along really well," Mom said brightly.

I ended the phone call with an "I've got to see this for myself" attitude and decided I could take the next Friday after my ten o'clock lit class was over and get home before Jemima left. I had already decided I would try to come home most weekends if I could, for a while. I still didn't have a car, but many people headed toward the city on Friday and came back on Sunday, and they posted ride-sharing notices on the Straight bulletin board.

I arrived to a strange sight—Mom with a cane, hobbling around the house, rearranging the whole kitchen, showing her Negro aide how to arrange the dishes, utensils, and food for a kosher kitchen.

"Mom, what are you doing?" (As if I didn't know.)

"I'm setting up milchig and fleishedik" (the separation of dairy from meat in the kitchen).

"Mom, when did you become kosher?" I said bravely.

"Amie, I was always kosher," she responded without hesitation.

I could not say more. Did she pull a number on her family? Was she planning this all along and just slyly announced it during her stroke? Or had she truly had an epiphany during her stroke—like a divine intervention from above?

At any rate, I could just hear her next phone call with Mrs. Rabinowitz. "Hello, Mrs. Rabinowitz, it is Mrs. Lardowitz—also with a kosher home."

Or maybe she was even smarter and wanted to please Susan and Alvin and ease their worry about her. This way she could have Sydney over more and cook for the kosher contingent of our extended family. Whatever it was, it was weird, for it seemed to happen as her first complete sentence nine days after her stroke. She was a very clever woman, so I am guessing that it was all of the above and it would only seem to help our family—it was brilliant.

What a pair these two were. Mom with her cane, using it as a sword to make a point, or sticking me with it to make another point, or using it to move objects, for it gave her more length.

And there was Jemima. She wasn't the size of Aunt Jemima on the pancake syrup bottle—she was two-thirds the size but still rotund. She did have her hair up in a bun and with a kerchief over it, though, and she wore a long skirt with an apron over the top.

She had a beautiful smile and became instantly familiar with me. I was walking through the kitchen with everything out on the table and reached for a bowl I didn't remember seeing before. "Scat … scat," she barked. I was startled. No one had ever said *scat* to me before. But this word would chase me around my own home for months to come—*scat … scat*. She also called me Amie. No one but my mom called me Amie. Actually, I felt quite comfortable with Jemima, and she and Mom became friends over the next few months.

I came home most weekends to help Mom since Jemima worked only during the week.

God in heaven—we became a kosher home. Mom just did it and that was that. I learned to be careful with the rules and regulations of separating dishes and meat and dairy and being sure that anything I bought was truly marked kosher.

I studied at home on the weekends, and my whole college life seemed to be changing. Just months before, I was becoming a soldier—going through the indoctrination and basic training. At that time, my mind was mired in the military and my friends were brothers in blood—all for one and one for all. I was still in the ROTC class and my buddies were close, but the intensity was diluted because of my distractions at home.

I met a fellow in one of my classes who was talking to another student about sailing. He had a sailboat on Cayuga Lake, a twenty-six-foot sloop. His family was from the Finger Lakes. Initially, I wasn't sure why I was interested, but I engaged him about his boat and sailing. I guess I was looking for some other diversion to take my mind off the unusual and difficult couple of months before. He asked me if I wanted to go out with him one day, fall sailing being the best time. I found out later that people who sail love to take others out to share the feeling that turns them on.

It was a wonderful three hours the next Wednesday afternoon. It was just him and me, and he showed me the essentials of the rigging and the concept of "ready about" and "sailing into the wind." While I was out with him I had no other thoughts on my mind except the boat slicing through the water on its own quiet power, the soothing gurgling of water against the hull, and the sound of the wind against the sail.

What a joy. He said I was a natural. He told me that if you are in love with the experience instantly, you will be a sailor your whole life. It gave me real peace to hear that, for sailing would become a part of my life.

We went out as often as we could. He said having one mate was a godsend to a sailor because you could then go under all kinds of conditions and work as a crew together. He said I was his first "first mate."

We sailed late into the fall. Ithaca gets really cold in the winter, but this particular late fall he was able to keep his boat in the water through the second week of December. I learned a lot that two-plus months and became really good at sailing the boat by myself with him just observing. It was a wonderful feeling, and I was really looking forward to putting the boat back in the water in the spring.

In school, I became closer to Turk than my other Four Horsemen buddies. Seeing him always brought me back to the place of my own secrets in life—my discovery, my unfinished quest—or my quest yet to begin.

Mostly, if we were not talking military talk, Turk was Donny. It seemed strange, but none of his other buddies called him that. He seemed to call me Amos most of the time.

Both of us opted for the two-year ROTC program; Hitch also. Army was going the full distance, the four-year training that would prepare him for an officer's commission upon graduating Cornell. The last two years of training were military tactics and war training.

Mom got better and better, although she was left with a slight snarl of her lower left lip after she spoke. She continued to use her cane, but I don't think she really needed it for anything but to use as a weapon.

Jemima continued to work for Mom even after Dad felt she could be alone. They were a great couple and good friends, and since Mom's house was more complex because of the newly added kosher dimension, Jemima being there helped a lot.

Susan was over often with Sydney, and I believe Mom's having a kosher home helped her. I think that Susan's strength was sapped permanently by Mom's stroke and vulnerability, though, especially coming at the time Susan really needed her mother.

My nineteenth birthday came and went without much fanfare, what with our new Sydney and Mom's recovery. I really didn't mind much because I felt that I was growing up and was only sidetracked by Mom's stroke. My attention to school and my own interests was starting to return.

Babatunde

BABATUNDE OGUNDE—SELF-CONFIDENT, SLICK, assured. He was black, with short, cropped hair and a crisp, confident voice. He had a Nigerian accent and you knew right away he wasn't an ordinary American black man. He always wore a sport jacket and a crisply ironed shirt without a tie but with cufflinks. He wore slacks, and his shoes were loafers with hard leather heels and soles. When he walked, you could hear the click-clack cadence of his step—like a fine-tuned African drum skin. His laugh was always deep and sincere but with a mild sarcasm. He exuded confidence.

I really met Babatunde indirectly through my course textbooks. As we were getting our courses together for my second year at Cornell, the buzz was around about half-price new course books through some guy on campus. Books were expensive and they ate into our personal party money, so it was a no-brainer to check it out. In the fall of 1959, I gave my book list and cash to a friend of mine and he passed it on to the source. In two days I received my course books for the semester from my friend. I saved seventy-five dollars. That whole year, my sophomore, I got my course books from Babatunde, whom I still had not met. I assumed that he worked for the Campus Book Store and could get books wholesale.

One day in early spring, at the beginning of the second semester, my friend who had arranged the book purchase deal with Babatunde and I were walking to the Straight cafeteria for something to eat when we literally bumped into Babatunde talking to two other guys just outside on the steps. There the five of us were. I was introduced to Babatunde, and with a sly smile he said, "Hey A-Moes," like he had known me forever, but pronouncing my name like no one had ever done before.

The conversation continued almost round robin, about school and such. The talk was of calculus, and I noticed that one guy was stuttering "ca ca ca ca ca ... ... culus" about every other sentence. I also noticed that Babatunde, who was almost opposite me, was looking straight into this guy's eyes as he stuttered, with a ferocity, it seemed, of a poised lion about to pounce.

Then a normal sentence—then a long stut ... t ... tt ... ered word. Suddenly, in the middle of a stutter, Babatunde sharply looked at the guy and said, "Cut that shit out, man!"

Unbelievable! In the split second after that admonishment, the guy completed the word. I had never witnessed such an event. Such chutzpah. Such balls. Almost within two or three seconds, Babatunde turned to me and said, "Hey, A-Moes, I'm giving a dance party at my apartment Saturday night. Bring a woman. Ten o'clock. One twelve Thurston, man."

I was dazed as my other friend and I continued our journey into the Straight for something to eat.

One morning in high school, in the tenth grade and in our homeroom seats, I had leaned over to ask Joel Berkowitz something about a math assignment. As I got closer to his face, he said sharply, "Goddamn, Amos, don't you brush your teeth in the morning? Your breath stinks!"

It had hit me like a brick. Given my personality and how I take things in general, and who I am, I said, "I'm sorry. I must have an upset stomach. I think I brushed my teeth."

I always take the responsibility. I always accept the blame. I have never taken the whip to others. I would never bite back sharply or respond in that fashion.

After the stuttering incident with Babatunde, my mind was filled with similar life incidents, and how I would act or respond: "Actually, Joel, I grabbed some litter in my cat's litter box, just after he urinated, and slugged it down. I did it on purpose. I just wanted to gross you out."

I really wanted to go to Babatunde's on Saturday night. I wrangled a date with a girl with straight blonde hair who was in my English class. I knew she knew how to dance. I was relatively comfortable on the dance floor, so it was easy to ask her to come along.

Babatunde's apartment was dark and lit up only with candles that I could see from the street. I could hear the rhythmic beat of drum music as we approached his apartment. As we entered, I could tell the music was African and very mesmerizing. There must have been almost fifty people in the four-room apartment, a mixture of guys and gals and different nationalities. Almost immediately, Sally and I started dancing. In the periphery of my vision I could see Babatunde dancing with a girl. I could see him inch over to me gradually, and over the music he cupped my ear and said, "Hey A-Moes, I could take your white woman away from you in a minute—ha ha." He then proceeded to change partners. He was a great dancer. He had all the moves of an African rhythm maker. The record was over, and he uttered another sly laugh and walked away from us to other people.

The whole next week I thought of Babatunde. He was the first black man I had met who seemed different. I guessed it was because he was not an American. His confidence floored me. I felt excited by his presence. Certainly Ben had the same confidence, I thought—he gave no bullshit and he took no bullshit. Ben was always the same person, unprejudiced and fair, although he challenged and provoked authority in his own way.

My thoughts would float around comparing the two of them, their differences and similarities—and why I was attracted to Babatunde.

It came to me gradually that the reason was definitely related to Babatunde being a black man. I thought that if he were an American Negro, he would never be this way. There was a tension between races that was palpable. I wondered how I would feel if I were black. Then I thought, suppose people could see a label on my forehead that said "Jew" and I walked around campus, and any interaction I had was associated with my cultural being, my religion, so to speak.

Well, the reasons Babatunde was who he was are probably more complex than my analysis. Babatunde was a Nigerian, not an American. He was a person from another country, actually, where everyone is the same color. He was also who he was because of his unique personality, his awareness of the world.

Babatunde's party was the first time I heard what I thought was original African music. I was instantly attracted to the rhythm and the beat and the excitement. I'm sure there was a time line in my head connecting the American blues with its primordial parent in Africa. I sought Ben out and asked him about African music. Ben told me he had many records and was surprised I had not already made the connection to my beloved blues. He practically ordered me to the store on my next visit and told me, "Get your education" in that telephone call.

I was completely shocked to see Babatunde walk into my political science class two weeks into the semester, which was one week after his party. I was sitting about two-thirds of the way back in a small auditorium-like lecture room with fixed seats. There were a few seats open one row up and to the right of me. He caught my eye and winked. He grabbed the seat closest to me and looked down at me again with a sly smile.

When class was over, I hoped he would wait for me. As we all filed out of the auditorium, I could see Babatunde slowing up and turning to me.

"Hey, A-Moes, how are you, man?"

"Good, Babatunde," I said.

"You free, man?"

"What?" I replied like I didn't really understand him.

"Free, man, like for a cup of java."

"Oh yeah ... I've got forty-five minutes."

There he sat, directly opposite me, with his arms on the table surrounding his coffee and a pastry, looking directly into my eyes.

"You Americans ... you need an infusion of confidence, man," he said slowly and evenly.

"What do you mean, Babatunde?" I think I said naively.

"You think the world needs you ... but you really need the acceptance of the world, my A-Moes," he said flatly.

I realized later in my relationship with Babatunde that he must have singled me out. He must have seen who I was—my vulnerability, my curiosity, my doubts. I'm sure he wanted to provoke me—like with the dancing incident. I am sure he wanted to connect to me as a black Nigerian to an American. As I thought about it, I could not picture at all being from another country, coming to America and observing it. At that moment in my life, I could not see America from another's eyes except my own. What would it look like to me?

Inside of me, though, my curiosity was really breeding a revolution—a revolution of changing values and responsibilities and recognizing rights and wrongs. I had always had no choice but to think about things—thoughts held power over me. It was the direction of those thoughts that would very gradually become clearer to me as my young mind continued to mature.

We sat for an hour that morning as Babatunde talked about Afro beat music after I asked him about it. He provoked me only in the moment we sat down, and that was it. I actually didn't mind the provocations, for it was why I had been attracted to him in the first place. I was really looking forward to having him as a friend.

I thought about my ROTC buddies, my Horsemen brothers—especially Donny. I nixed altogether asking Donny to join Babatunde and me for lunch. I knew Donny would not understand Babatunde, especially his provocative attitude about America. I thought Donny would relate to Babatunde as an American Negro and would be angry because of Babatunde's personality and perceived arrogance. Yet I felt close to Donny, my buddy, my Turk. Why am I the bridge to this gap? I thought. I really didn't understand at this moment in my life.

The same night, I had a dream. I seemed to be on two lands, very different from each other, separated by a deep gorge, with one leg on each cliff edge, trying to keep my balance so as not to fall into the chasm's abyss.

My Civil War soldier letter reading continued the next month with Turk, Hitch, and Army. I tried to read the letter with the same intensity, like the soldier in the field: afraid, excited, questioning. I felt a profound sadness welling up inside as I continued to read.

... the thundering of cannon, the whistling of bullets. The sharp report of small arms. Cannon balls tearing the earth and everything in their course. The bursting of shells finding destruction and death in every direction ... some crying for water and others begging to be carried off the field, some sending their last word to their friends, others praying and still others cursing their fate. Together with the shrieks and moans of the dying which could be heard above the din of battle with the mangled corpses of the dead littering the field. Misery, yet you hear the shrill command of the officers, and the men rush to obey apparently unconscious of the scene around them ... Sam P. Brockett, 27th Reg N.Y.S.V. Washington, D.C., July 26, 1861

But the tears did not flow—they stayed inside of me.

I found solace in sailing most of the spring semester of 1959. The few hours when I shared the water with my sailing buddy and his boat cleared my head of the tumultuous thoughts I had been carrying. Everything mixed together, including Mom's illness, took my innocence away that year.

On spring break, I went down to Ben's to "get my education" in African music. Ben and I sat for about four hours one Saturday afternoon as he played African records and lectured me on the origins of the blues.

The natural rhythms and tribal songs were carried by the slaves to their eventual homes on plantations. In the fields, in order to maintain some sense of dignity and be able to make it through the day, they would sing these songs and rhythms in a call-and-response fashion. I had seen and heard the gospel call and response in the Delta that Thanksgiving a few years earlier. These field songs would become the first gospel songs, since many of the slaves were Christians already through conversion by their masters. Slaves embraced Christianity for their own purpose, even though the slave owners felt they were truly converting them. The slaves generally identified with the Old Testament and the stories of Moses and persecution; it gave them hope for themselves. Their chants and pleadings eventually gave birth to the "spiritual" or gospel songs. Out of the gospel songs, the blues were born.

I felt so close to this music and its people, and I began listening to and learning more original African songs.

Babatunde and I would drive into Ithaca once a week and eat in a townie restaurant. After dinner we would come back to his apartment and he would take out his djun djun drum, an original African drum. Djun djuns are made of a solid piece of carved-out wood with a goatskin drum skin. Babatunde would play without music. The rhythms were infectious to me. When he played, his face seemed to light up like I had never seen before. He had this open smile and wide bright eyes. I felt I could see into his soul when he was playing, and he seemed different from the provoking and often irreverent person I had initially met.

Babatunde told me how important music and rhythm were in West African culture. On our second night he said to me with a sly smile, "A-Moes, I think that you are ready. You have the heart of a Yoruba." He went into the next room, came out with what appeared to be a smaller version of his djun djun, and said, "Here, man ... it is yours ... Play through your soul. You are my brother, A-Moes."

I could not believe he had done that. It was such a special experience for me. I have always had rhythm in my heart and music in my blood, and my trip to the Delta and subsequent experiences had just reinforced it.

Here we were—my new Nigerian friend and his new Jewish kid from the Bronx friend. I actually played that drum as if it had been mine all along. I felt as if I was playing off the rhythms of Babatunde and his roots and culture. We must have played together for more than an hour, me following his lead as he changed beats or rhythm. Our bodies were wet with sweat when we finished, and I felt a meditative peace come over me.

We sprawled out on the living room rug, lying on large pillows. I had this curious fascination with Babatunde and the culture of Africa. I remember asking him about Nigeria and what it was like.

"A-Moes, Nigeria is very old … many tribes … many cultures … and much colonization, from the Dutch and Portuguese to the French. Everyone wanted a piece of paradise. On top of this, our people were sold to the colonials for a life of enslavement … Everyone to blame, my friend … everyone.

"Your America, A-Moes, doesn't know sacrifice. It doesn't know pride … Its pride is built on material things. Africa, my friend, is built on the soul's pride."

Babatunde spoke in an ethereal way, almost philosophical in nature, and I think I understood him. America in 1959 was coming to grips with its dark past—reluctantly so. America seemed to me a dichotomy, a contradiction almost, of both hope and despair. But it lacked spontaneity, like I think Babatunde was talking about. It was not the spontaneity of spirit—of life, of song and music—that was the African people. And it certainly was the most puzzling thing, I thought, that the enslaved of America were the most spirited.

I was interested to know if Babtunde thought about whether any of his relatives were descendants of slaves from Nigeria.

"A-Moes, don't you think that I do? You Americans think only to the tip of your nose. There is much beyond that, my friend."

I knew that when Babatunde used the term *you Americans* he wasn't talking to me personally but to our country as a collective entity. It was actually very refreshing, I thought, to hear a non-American talk about America—and I was beginning to see how big our world was and that it did not end at the borders of our country.

At the end of this second evening, Babatunde pulled a record from his collection and handed it to me. The album was called *Olatunji, Drums of Passion*.

"A-Moes, this is my friend Baba Olatunji. This record will be released in a few months. There were only ten initial copies and Baba gave one to me. He is my brother, man—my spiritual brother. We were brought up in the same region. I have known this man since I was eight years old, A-Moes. He came to America to study at Morehouse College in Atlanta. He came to America as a musician and brought the essence of Africa with him to spread its wealth to others. Man, he was at Radio City Music Hall last year for seven weeks presenting his African drum fantasy with the symphony orchestra."

I do remember Ben talking about this performance. He and Zelda had gone. Ben had told me this guy was real.

"I want you to meet him, A-Moes. He is in Harlem now, man. You come with me, hey?"

"Babatunde, my friend ... I can't wait."

I had never been to Harlem, believe it or not. And believe it or not, Harlem was in Manhattan—but not my Manhattan. My Manhattan was from Central Park and south into the Bowery and to the southern tip. My dad's office was in Lower Manhattan. Early on, when I drove from the Bronx with my dad into Lower Manhattan, we would pass 125th Street and what was considered the center of Harlem, but it had no meaning for me. Later when we moved north into the suburbs, only about ten miles outside New York City, I would take the elevated train from the tip of the north Bronx and it would pass through Harlem and make local stops there. It was at that point in my life that I became aware of what a different culture Harlem was. Of course, any reasonable mom would say, "Be careful when you take the trains—don't get off at 125th Street by accident." And of course, my absurd mind would always fantasize about what would happen if I suddenly and mistakenly got off the train at Harlem.

Possibly, I thought, I would be instantly electrocuted. Or then again, I may not be able to breathe, for the air was different. Then again, I may be shot instantly and killed, for I would be the only white person ever to set foot on the train platform at 125th Street, and it would not be tolerated. And probably, that last fantasy of mine was the reality of my mom's thinking—for all Jewish and other white middle-class mothers felt that all Negroes were dangerous. And this comes from the northern states—the supposed bastion of racial tolerance!

At any rate, even at the earliest age, I could not come to grips with this type of prejudice—let alone the outright segregation that existed in the South at this time in the fifties.

My trip to the Delta was my coming-of-age ritual and it would be ingrained in me forever, but here I was again, taking new risks and pursuing new adventures.

I remember the day, in late spring in 1959, when I had come home for a long weekend. I received a call from Babatunde.

"Hey, A-Moes, man. He's here. Baba Olatunji … in Harlem, man. We go tomorrow. I will give you the directions, man, and you will meet us for a jam. OK? And bring your djun djun."

I felt excitement running through me. Whenever I came home I always brought my guitar and my new gift, my djun drum. Great, I thought. And then, Oh boy—I've got to get there, I'm sure by train, and with my drum under my arm … and I've got to get through Mom's whining and unfortunately Jemima's also because she stayed this weekend.

"Amie, honey, really … can't your new friend come here and you play music?"

"Amie, what you doin'? Harlem? Boy, you don't need to go there—they aren't your people. Even my people moved away uptown to Yonkers."

And on and on—one after the other—the whitey and the blacky.

But I was getting used to this and had plenty of experience with my inaugural escape to the Delta, so I just played the game until they wore themselves out and both gave me a hug as I walked out the door, djun djun under arm, toward the unknown realm of Harlemland.

My destination was 131st Street just off Lenox Avenue. I needed to get off the train at 125th Street and walk the few blocks up.

As I sat on the elevated train, rocking back and forth, as I had done for countless rides into Manhattan, my mind drifted, as it often had, and suddenly I was jolted into reality when I heard, "125th Street … next stop … Harlem … 125th Street."

I jumped up in a reflex action as the train screeched to a jolting halt at 125th Street. A strange thing then happened—the car just seemed to empty of color in a split second. All the Negroes ran out and the whites stayed, probably like it had happened countless times before my previously blind eyes. And man, I was out of there also.

I can remember people staring at me, but I'm not sure whether it was because I was white or because I was carrying an African drum under my arm. No one confronted me, but I certainly felt out of place. The streets seemed dirtier and the stores more schlocky and the whole environment more dingy—a prescient presentation of what would be called the "ghetto" in the next decade.

I found Lenox Avenue and walked up to 131st Street and turned in to a row of dilapidated attached brick town houses. There were plenty of little kids running around and sitting on the stoops. There were also young black men everywhere. I'm sure I heard someone say, "Hey whitey—what you doin' here?" but I sped up, found the house, and climbed past a few little kids and up to the third floor. As I climbed I began hearing the beat of drums, and it got me excited.

I knocked on the door of number 314, but nobody came to open it up. As I was taught, I just kept standing there as the beat of multiple drums permeated around and through the thin walls and door. I don't know how long I stood there, but something changed inside of me, and I actually just tried the door to see if it was open. Sure enough it opened, and I walked into an apartment filled with people.

"A-Moes, you're here," yelled Babatunde from the other side of the room. He came to me and shook my hand exuberantly and said, "Baba … meet my friend A-Moes." It seemed like such a sincere intro to me, and I felt shy.

The brightest and happiest man I have ever met greeted me with a strong earthquake-like handshake. "Well … well … Amos … Welcome to Yorubaland, my friend."

Baba Olatunji was a special spirit, a man infused with enthusiasm for life and the confidence that all people can grow spiritually. He was of course a musician, but his music was music that spoke from the soul and to the world. This party was rocking, although I could really tell the Africans from the Americans. There was a joy within and on the faces of the people from Africa. I could see that there were black American musicians and other black Americans, but they were missing an emotion, a zest for life that I knew even then should live within the black soul but was missing in my American black brothers. I thought back on Mound Bayou and the happiness of its families but realized that Mound Bayou was a completely segregated and isolated town whose people made their own life—and here in the unforgiving and competitive biracial cities the toll of discrimination and oppression could be too much to bear for many.

Baba's energy permeated the whole apartment as he played his djembe drum in the center of a group of African drummers who played off of him. There were three women, obviously African, who sang along, I'm sure in the Yoruba language. Each song was different, with unique rhythms and chanting. I could see the Americans in the background trying to keep up with the accomplished musicians. Babatunde joined in and signaled to me to "beat my drum," and I shyly joined the group.

I was in heaven. We played for two solid hours, Baba taking us from one song into another with his infectious smile and enthusiasm. And when we stopped, I could see the faces of everyone in the room almost looking like they had been purified in spirit. I felt as if we were all one person with many faces. I felt close to everyone, and I was the only white person there. I could see that the Americans had changed. I could see, I think, the whole inside of them as they discovered their primordial ancestry.

Baba sat on the floor and started to talk about his upbringing in a small fishing and farming village on the coast of Nigeria in West Africa. Baba talked about the rich cultural heritage of family and village. He spoke of the responsibilities everyone shared to be sure even the littlest person had role models. Baba spoke of the rhythm of the Yoruba language and how that rhythm was the soul of their life. We must have sat for another hour while Baba spun parable after parable. It truly was an experience of a lifetime, and I could see how all who were present would have their inner lives changed forever by a man bringing to them only what had been lying dormant for so long within.

There were aromas floating through the air as we finished, smells I had never experienced. It was the food of West Africa and Nigeria—peanut stew and jollof rice and Nigerian avocado salad and spinach. There was lovely Nigerian color sweet cake and *obe ata* (pepper soup) and *amala* (yams). I felt as if I had been transported to a place where I was no longer me. I felt connected to a larger consciousness—a community consciousness. I was utterly joyful. I remember at the moment bringing back the memory of my Mound Bayou experience. Only afterward would I try to meld the two experiences into one, but ultimately they represented two cultures that were once one—and the divide that existed between them would never close.

As I sat cross-legged on the floor with all the smiling and laughing faces, I turned my head, and kneeling down to me was Baba. With his most extraordinary smile and white teeth glistening, he said, "Amos … you must come to my village … you must see my home."

Why me? I thought as he moved on. Later I realized he must have seen deep joy in my face and heart.

I spent a great deal of time with Babatunde in the next few months. Our shared interests were music and culture. Babatunde was my door to the outer world of different cultures as Ben was my door to my inner world. He opened up a vista I had never imagined existed. I believe America was probably the largest and most productive melting pot in the world. But then again, our own peculiar brand of the American melting pot made it difficult to appreciate the myriad diversity of the rest of the world. For some reason related to my own DNA, my appetite for discovery of my American relationship to the rest of the world was insatiable. To myself, I was alone. I saw no one in my circle of life who had this nagging desire to fantasize or to explore the life thread that made all us humans actually the same.

Heading into the summer of 1960, I noticed a change in Babatunde. He started to confide in me his concern over the serious political situation in Nigeria. Nigeria was a British colony, and the British had divided it into political areas that suited their colonialism but did not address the hundreds of culturally diverse tribes and the culturally distinct areas that had existed previously. As with all forced rule, the natural ebb and flow of compromise was suppressed. The year 1960 was when the boiling pot flowed over for the Nigerian people, for they declared their independence. This was the start of a process in which the Nigerian people would have to find themselves as one governing country consisting of hundreds of tribal groups. Eventually, as one could predict, a civil war would be looming in the future. Unfortunately, Babatunde came from a politically connected Yoruba family tribe and turmoil was brewing. Sadly, he felt he had to leave Cornell and go back home.

I felt deep sadness over the loss of my dear friend. But I had other strange feelings also. I felt the parallel feeling of civil war and the wrenching disruption it causes for people and a society. And I knew this feeling quite well, for the American Civil War was my life's study.

My junior year was winding down, and I had felt closer to myself than ever before. I felt bad for Babatunde, for the swagger and confidence that attracted me to him were suppressed by the present urgency of life. He was my dear friend, and I knew he would be gone in a month or two and I would possibly never see him again.

"A-Moes ... I will be back. We are brothers, man," he said with his usual confidence over a cup of coffee at the Straight one morning.

"Yeah, man, no ocean or strife will separate our connection," I said with bluster. "I'm coming with you. I'll stay for the summer," I said, surprising even myself.

"A-Moes, what are you saying? You want to enter a world you have never seen and experienced—one that I even dread right now?"

"So what ... Baba invited me to his village ... You are my brother, so Nigeria is my home also."

"You are crazy, man ... You need to finish school. You need to be here."

"I will. I want to go with you. I want to see your home. I'll come back for my senior year."

"A-Moes ... my black brother," Babtunde said as he clasped my hand firmly.

I remember calling Ben that day and telling him I was traveling to Africa this summer. Ben was truly enthusiastic for me. "The cradle, Kid ... the cradle of emotion and spirit ..."

Ben had been to Ghana and Kenya to record original music with a producer friend. He had spent two months traveling to small villages to get "the essence ... the sound."

In one way I guess I had grown up, for years before I would have anguished over telling Mom and she would need to be the first—for if she wouldn't approve, I possibly wouldn't have gone. It wasn't like I needed the money since I had saved enough from my manuscript dealings—but I needed to speak to Mom.

"I don't understand, Amie—Africa? Do you mean a zoo, like Wild African Park or something?"

"No, Mom—Africa, like the continent." And then my poor attempt at a joke with Mom ..."Yes, Mom, I know there are possibly no Jews there."

"What are you saying, Amie? Don't you know the Sephardic Jews are Africans? What's the matter with you, honey? You don't know where the Jews are?"

And we both laughed.

Babatunde wanted to finish his third year. It was perfect for both of us. We would leave one week after exams ended. I figured that I could stay over four weeks and still have at least a month at home before my senior year.

I felt the anticipation of traveling to my first foreign country and Africa to boot—and on top of this of flying in a jet plane for the first time. I think my excitement helped Babatunde in his transitional state. He had many friends and a rich network of cultural contacts in America. In the short time he was here he had laid a foundation that would last a lifetime. I realized during this time that if all went well, he would be back. America needed him. I needed him.

On one of my phone calls to Mom from school after our conversation, she announced that she and Jemima were going to take me to Gimbels to buy me a valise for my trip to Africa. I felt where this was going: control. I knew Mom had been too easy with this thing—she hadn't schlepped me shopping with her since I was about eleven years old.

In all my trips to Manhattan and my love of the adventure in finding things, I couldn't stand department stores. They were alien to me. But Mom was a whiz at this. Maybe that's where I got my spirit of discovery and adventure, for she could smell a bargain as soon as she glided through the revolving door. Seven floors of merchandise had no chance with this hunter—she nailed what she wanted in no time at all. The only good thing about our trips to Gimbels and Macy's and S. Klein on the Square was that we traveled to Manhattan.

I found those stores so strange. They were the only environment in which intermittent chimes would ring in undecipherable codes. There would be bell-like strings of code that rang throughout the store summoning the strange middle-age sales ladies to a place of unknown destination, possibly to be programmed by the secret S. Klein or Gimbels international security police. These ladies all seemed to have a few things in common: They all had glasses on a string dangling from their necks. They all had their hair up in a bun with strange skewers holding it up. They were all chewing gum. They all had nametags glued to their chests. They all made the most intolerable scratchy, tortuous sounds when they slid hangers on poles back and forth and back and forth. And they all smelled the same: a nauseating mixture of stale perfume and gum. It was not the smell of my Manhattan that I loved so well—my diesel fuel and garlic. *Oh well …*

"Our son needs a valise. He's going to Africa," said my mother to the salesperson in the luggage department of Gimbels, with me in the center flanked by her and Jemima. *How many ways can I be embarrassed by Mom? And I'm almost twenty-one ...*

The lady cocked her head and seemed to scan the three of us. I swear I could hear her thoughts: *This is a first ... Wait till I tell Murray ... He'll die laughing.*

And that was that, although the nearly four hours—yes, four hours—of deliberate shopping for my trip did yield the snappiest mini-wardrobe and most functional toiletries I'm sure anyone would ever carry on a jet-plane trip to Nigeria.

In 1960, my mom felt that traveling in a jet plane was the most sophisticated thing anyone could ever do. I'm sure a lot of people felt that way at the time. When Mom found out that our flight went to Paris and then from Paris to Lagos, her eyes really lit up. I'm sure she got a lot of mileage out of this with Mrs. Rabinowitz and all her *mishbukka*. I'm sure this had figured into her relatively easy compliance when I told her I was going. She was going to really do well with this.

Well, we got off on June 3, 1960, leaving from New York City's Idlewild Airport. We flew on Pan Am's American Clipper, a Boeing 707. It was sleek and new and all shiny. I felt so important. This was the way to travel. Everyone was dressed up. Men wore jackets and most wore ties, and the women wore skirts or dresses. The stewardesses—yes, only stewardesses, no men—all looked like they were fashion models, tall and thin. The pilot and co-pilot greeted us at the gangway, and they were truly handsome, and I'm sure not Jewish (Chuck Baxter and Jack Lane III). We were treated like we were special. "Could I get you a drink, sir?" "Would you like chicken or fish?" Certainly not like when I made my trips back home from school: "Eat what I made you, Amie."

Our flight to Paris needed to make a fuel stop in Gander, Newfoundland, announced one of the stewardesses over the loudspeaker. And then we were off.

Babatunde was cool. I could see that he was a world traveler—after all, he did travel the world to get to Cornell. But also he was at ease and comfortable in conversation with strangers, and obviously very direct and often confrontational in a positive way. I also noticed that the stewardesses and other passengers seemed to treat him differently. He appeared to be from another country, not America, and possibly a diplomat. And once more I had thoughts about the Negroes in America at this time. If they thought he was an American Negro, he would not be treated so well.

Paris. We needed to stay over one night in Paris. Babatunde told me he had spent a summer in Paris when his uncle was an envoy to the Nigerian attaché. He told me I would love Paris. He said it was very sensual and I should come back. I thought I understood what he meant. But at this moment in my life my love interests had taken a backseat to my inner explorations.

Off again—unfortunately with a bloated belly and cramps. Flying started to become physically uncomfortable, although I gave the airs of a seasoned world jet-setter to everyone with whom I made eye contact. Maybe everyone else felt the same way. I don't think Babatunde experienced any discomfort, though. His whole demeanor changed as he talked only about his family and the political and cultural situation in Nigeria and the rest of Africa.

Babatunde's family had always been in public service, he told me, and it was going to be a serious time for him as soon as he arrived home.

Fresh with jet lag and a large hangover from the two additional cocktails that I could not refuse from the prettiest eyes on the plane from Paris to Lagos, we arrived.

We traveled by bus from the airport to the city where we were going to stay—Lagos. Babatunde told me he felt a different vibration from his city of Lagos. He said it was the "taste of independence." Lagos was to be the capital of the new Nigeria, and there seemed to be a palpable excitement.

Most of his family was living within or on the outskirts of the city. Babatunde was going to stay with his brother, and they had room for me. In the first few days I met Babatunde's brother, one of two sisters, and his mother. Babatunde's father was on a trip for an extended time, drumming up support for his place in the new ministry. Every one of Babatunde's family welcomed me with an open heart and a wide smile. They were well educated and very conversational, and by their sincere laughter I could tell they were of the same genes.

Lagos was a growing and busy city with developing high-rise buildings. The city had a colonial British flavor, but you could tell it was Africa. I felt refreshed by the fact that I was the "person of color" wherever I went. Obviously, the city had many Caucasian people, especially Brits, but they were very much in the minority. And certainly I was traveling in the circle of the native folks. I momentarily questioned why I felt so comfortable in a foreign land, but I soon realized that it was because of my lifelong desire to explore the intricacies of our human gene pool.

Being around so many bright and educated black people only reinforced my heartache over the apparent difference between them and my American Negro brothers. Here I was, in a sea of black color and feeling secure in a culture that was not my own.

I walked the city streets by myself often since Babatunde and his brother had to take many day trips to other districts to help their father's political aspirations. This two-week period in my life was another first that I will always cherish. It was a time that I felt very alone yet secure. I felt no pressure from anywhere—I was an observer and a participant.

I decided even before I went to Nigeria to travel by myself to the sparser coast east of Lagos. This was where Baba was brought up, this was where the fishing and farming villages were, and this was where the more traditional and more rural Yoruba people lived.

The two weeks I spent within the city and with Babatunde and his family were wonderful. I felt this was my transitional time with my dear friend, a time that allowed both of us to say goodbye for a while and to have many good memories to bring back when we needed them.

My bus ride to the country was something else. The bus must have been twenty-five years old, and it shook around like a washing machine going through all the different cycles at once. The weather was muggy and hot, and the roads were unpaved. Dust flew in the open windows, swirled around, and then exited, only to come back in again through the whole six-hour trip. My seatmates changed at almost every stop—there were more than two dozen. And a few times I had to have conversation with a crate of colorful chickens or something like them, and once with a monkey on a very long string that took a liking to my shoelaces—but only untied.

The landscape was flat and mostly rural the whole trip, with shack-like houses dotting the horizon. I could see that this was farming country, but it appeared to be subsistence—meaning just enough to feed the family living within.

As we continued, I could actually smell the seawater and tell that we were close to the coast, the Gulf of Guinea. The more isolated farmhouses were disappearing, and we were passing small villages consisting of five to ten houses in clusters. They appeared to be fishing villages. I realized that we were close to Adijo, the village I was going to.

We seemed to be following what appeared to be electricity poles as we wound and wound our way on a two-way dusty, hard-packed dirt road.

Every time we passed another bus coming in the opposite direction, I could hear a collective mumble as the buses came closer to each other. It culminated in a collective chorus of roars when the buses were opposite each other. At first, I just watched, but it didn't take too long for me to follow suit, for it was a fun thing. I felt as if I was back at Cornell on Scholkopf Field watching the Big Red football team with everybody collectively cheering at the top of their lungs.

Baba had written a letter to the head of the village to expect a visitor from America. I must have been pretty brave, because how could I be sure that anyone had actually received it? But to know Baba, I felt, was to know his village—and I expected the same.

Well, this was it. The bus driver obviously spoke English and announced to his horde in a shrill voice, "Ajido … Ajido … Meke … Latho …" Two other people got off the bus with me. There were kids everywhere and a few adults. I didn't see any cars.

"Mr. A-Moes? Mr. A-Moes?" I heard from a young man coming toward me.

"Yes."

"Welcome … welcome, my friend. I am Kehinde."

Kehinde was about my age, had a wonderful smile, and was quite talkative. He told me he had been appointed by the village chief to be my "servant" and to stay with me all the time. He told me right away that his name meant "the one who lagged behind" and that it originally meant he was the second of twins and took a long time to be born. He also said his trait had haunted him all his life, for every adult in the village would try to cleanse him of this "lateness" by various methods. The chief had told him with a laugh that lagging behind would be a good trait for his duty with me, since he could walk a few feet behind me.

The village consisted of clusters of small homes made of mud blocks with mostly thatched roofs. There was an occasional corrugated metal roof, which Kehinde told me meant it was a special house. I was to stay with Kehinde for the two weeks I was there. He lived in his father's house in a separate room.

I found out in a relatively short time that the Yoruba culture was a proud and complex one. Respect for individuals and family was very important. And the Yoruba language reflected the hierarchy.

Kehinde came from a relatively small family. I was properly introduced to his brother and sister, and his mother and father. His dad was a fisherman and Kehinde was his apprentice. Kehinde's family belonged to a larger clan of people spread throughout this small village. The clan is very important in the Yoruba culture. People in a clan believe they share one common remote ancestor.

I noticed that Kehinde and his father and some other people I met had the same small decorative scars on their forehead. Kehinde told me that people of the same clan often identify themselves with scarification that is similar. The clan is really a "super family" and owns rights to the land that their members farm.

Kehinde's young brother was apprenticing with one of his uncles as a farmer. His sister was becoming a potter like her mother. About once a week, there was a local market where mostly everyone sold their goods. Kehinde and I walked about four miles to get to the market. It consisted of many open tents with vegetable stands, smoked meat and fish stands, and crafts such as pottery and woven fabric. Everything was locally made. People were milling around everywhere. It seemed that there were more women than men trading here. Kehinde told me that generally men did the farming and fishing, and women did the craft making and trading, but it wasn't written in stone.

I was introduced to Kehinde's uncle, who Kehinde said was a rich man. He had a high position in the clan as well. Upon an introduction to this man's wife, Kehinde introduced her as my uncle's "senior wife." As we left, I whispered to Kehinde, "Don't tell me there is a junior wife."

"Yes, A-Moes, there is one—and my uncle is looking into another one to keep the junior one happy."

Well, I learned that polygamy was common among the Yoruba tribes. It was very structured, and a man could have more than one wife only if he was rich and older, since they all lived within his house and he had to provide a dowry to his wife's family to marry her.

I was really impressed with the respect that people gave each other here. It was reflected in the quality of their life. Almost everything came from the land and sea, and the culture was a constantly renewing one.

Kehinde's family worshipped one of the traditional Yoruba deities. There were hundreds, but they all related to the natural world and the beauty of it.

Babatunde's family was Christian. Of course, as I had found out earlier, the Europeans who colonized the area brought their religion. But there seemed to be a mixture of Christianity, Islam, and native spiritual religion among the Yoruba and other tribes of Africa.

I discovered that among various villages there were wandering drummers and that they were respected by the chiefs and villagers. Once monthly, there was a spiritual gathering, always accompanied by many drummers and chanting. Men and women sang at the same time, but they sang different tunes. It was a very beautiful sight, with many colorful dresses and head coverings. I attended one of these gatherings, and once more I felt the joy in the rhythm of their life. It was really a very simplistic scene, but it reached deep within my spiritual heart. They also seemed very happy to see someone from across the "great waters."

I learned from Kehinde and others that the whole village was involved in the upbringing of a child. They seemed to teach economic and educational independence, but not social independence. I could see how this cultural approach nurtured the spirit of the young and gave them confidence in life as they grew.

I fished with Kehinde and his dad. I even tried my hand at pottery with Kehinde's mom and sister. They could only laugh hysterically as the rapidly turning clay flew all over my face.

I met Baba's extended family and they were all I had expected.

It was a full and revealing two weeks, and a time that seemed to span the "great waters" and the two separate cultures. My reverse bus ride was uneventful, and I spent my last two days with Babatunde. We talked about Cornell and our life in New York.

I felt pretty much fulfilled looking out my window at thirty thousand feet, envisioning myself once more as a small speck moving across the map of our world, eventually to plop down in my familiar surroundings.

I don't think I ever had a hug so encompassing as the one my mom gave me on seeing me again after my trip. I know it was a relief for her to see me home safely. But once again, she shocked me. Thinking I must have spent time with the Sephardic Jews she said, "Did any of them keep kosher?"

Growing Inward

MY LAST TWO years at Cornell were probably the most formative years of my life. I traveled to a distant and alluring Africa, and I felt I had finally become an adult, albeit a young one. I had all the ingredients surrounding me that eventually formed the soup that would become my being.

I guess *soup* might seem to be a strange metaphor for describing one's life maturity, but it fits me. My soup would become a complex one, starting with a simple broth, as all chefs start with, and then adding flavors and textures in the form of herbs and spices and vegetables that become the finished product. And in tasting my finished soup, each mouthful would be different, possibly containing a small or larger broth with a different combination of vegetables in each spoonful.

The vegetable soup metaphor is certainly more appetizing to me than a meat or fish soup, since I would then have to say I was a lamb stew or a clam chowder and describe myself in terms of the main ingredient (and I can't really identify with a Cape Cod clam). And for the vegetables, well, I wouldn't want to call myself a Brussels sprout—but then again vegetables are cooked together, each of them lending a flavor and nuance to each other, and it then all becomes a sort of dance of the senses as you give oohs and aahs to the chef for his wonderful and unique creation, telling him you have never tasted anything like this before—and even if you did, you wouldn't tell him—and if it wasn't any good, you still wouldn't say it. *There goes Amos Boris Lardowitz in an uncontrolled stream of consciousness.*

I must have been born with the desire to seek what has occurred in the past, especially the American past—my America's history. Obviously, history in itself is collective and cannot be changed. You can analyze it and you can ask "what if," but it stands like the monument it is—all stone and immovable. Certainly my main fixation on war stands as a collective entity, although it was made up of individual events that had taken place in an earlier era that we often tend to romanticize.

History really forgets the individual. There are stories about individuals in history, but they are stories, and unless you are privy to a recorded conversation or can read a revealing correspondence, you can only guess what an individual's psyche was up to.

As a child, playing war was my start, possibly as it is with many children in America. It's a simple strategy to develop one's eventual being. You control your destiny, your enemy's destiny, and the outcome. You can kill and get killed as many times as you want. For me, though, my interests in the war conflicts of my America's past gradually became individualized rather than collective. Gradually war and history became very personal to me. I wanted to be there and feel what a soldier felt: the possible fear, the possible physical pain. My search for the written word was my attempt to feel a person's thoughts, and a printed reproduction of a manuscript either photocopied or typed in a book was not enough. I needed to feel the paper and touch the words that became sentences that the hand produced—which would give me the insight into a person's 150-year-old soul.

I brought this part of my being to my college studies. This was who I was without learning, without studying.

I also brought, in infancy, a new part of me, the part Ben and Zelda nurtured: the awareness of the novelists' and poets' written word and the musicians' rhythms of their hearts.

Ben's lesson on Van Gogh was one I would cherish my whole life, for it showed me how acutely aware one can be to share a moment of creativity, in this case the hand behind *Starry Night*. It was especially poignant that Vincent Van Gogh was destitute and unloved and unrecognized as he put his soul to canvas. And yet it is so meaningful, because that is exactly the point. I wasn't sent to look at a famous painting hanging in a famous museum. I was sent to feel the artist—to be with him at his moment of unrecognized creativity. Yet, at this same exact moment in time, in 1888, there may have been a thousand creative painters putting their hand to canvas—yet seventy-two years later in 1960 we had deified only one. And through Ben I was beginning to learn that there was a Cosmos of creativity that is tapped by all those who extend their being to paint, write, perform, and otherwise create artistry. I discovered through Ben and Zelda, and my own deep thoughts, that it really didn't matter who the painter or novelist was or actually what he was thinking or why he wrote what he wrote. If the novelist was really writing what was deeply inside of him, I didn't need to analyze or place any historical perspective on his work—it would stand alone with just the words connected to each other. I could actually begin to find that essence by diving deep within the painting, or character in a novel, or line in a poem—and grab it right out of the Cosmos of creativity itself. So I really didn't need to "study" Vincent Van Gogh at all, Ben really showed me; all I needed to do was open myself up to his moment in time in 1888. And in another reality, that was what I was attempting to do with my Civil War letters, on my own. At some point in my readings, I no longer had to understand or analyze—I became part and parcel of the moment.

I had also learned from Ben that being "the One" was not the point. The famous painting, or the applauded novel, has nothing to do with the "Cosmos of Creativity," as Ben would write it, for within the Cosmos there exists all creativity, and putting an artificial earthly stamp on it does nothing to enhance its essence. And that was why Ben was who he was—an irreverent and bluntly honest observer and participant in the folly of human activity.

What made Ben special also was the surety of his being and his empathy for what was real in life. I'm sure he was born with this. I learned from him fast what was bullshit and what was not, and I could see this more easily in my literature and history classes. As I sat in class and listened to professors and read assignments and studied them and heard all the analysis spouted by those who dictated what we should learn from what, I could tell the bullshit from the real.

I began to trust my maturity during these formative upper-class years. The collective analysis became the individual being who breathed through the paper. Events, both fiction and nonfiction, became the backdrop to what would ultimately become most important to me—the empathy to feel through senses that may not be sight, sound, or taste. My inner sense was developing—my cosmic sense that opened up the deeper universe.

My reading became easier because I could feel the essence of the page and therefore read faster. Ben was a genius at reading. I guess I could define him as a speed reader, but he really used his extraordinary sense to scan a page, a story, a novel, or a letter and empathize in a heartbeat with the essence of the work. He used senses that I was unaware existed, and it was those senses that I was actually developing in 1960 and 1961.

Real discovery lay ahead of me in my life, and what I was growing into would be the resource that would enable me to delve into my own personal Cosmos. I still had plenty of insecurity and uncertainty (not like Ben), but that was who Amos was, and I would not want to be anyone else—and because of who I was, there would be adventures and instances that would unfold that I would look back at and say I had possibly made a mistake or an error in judgment. But then again, I would not advise a younger self or stranger otherwise—for life would take turns on its own, and control it we can't. My role was to take the ride.

Graduation Muses

GRADUATION—BEN HAD BEEN preparing me intermittently, my whole senior year, to not be attached to my graduation at Cornell.

Ben did not attend my high school graduation, and in fact, I was not much interested in the ceremonial bullshit either. I also did not go to the high school prom. Dad and Mom had a party for me at home and invited all our relatives. My excitement was focused on college and the maturing experiences that had occurred already.

But that was high school. *God, this is college*. I seemed to be wrestling all senior year with my own feelings about leaving Cornell and going on to something else. Mom was definitely disappointed that I was not applying to medical school. Dad of course had not offered any advice and consequently had not put any pressure on me. But my Jewish mom—well, she was a Jewish mom, and I guess it went with the degree. From the beginning of my junior year, Mom would badger me about applying to medical schools. In fact, Jemima did the exact same thing and with the exact same intonations that she apparently had learned from Mom.

Fall semester 1959, my junior year:

"Amie, honey ... are you looking into medical colleges?" (Mom)

"Amie, boy ... are you looking into medical schools?" (Jemima)

Spring semester 1959:

"Amie, honey ... what medical colleges are you applying to next year?" (Mom)

"Amie, boy … what medical schools are you applying to next year?" (Jemima)

Summer 1959:

"Amie … I have not heard you talk about the medical colleges you're applying to—so nu?" (Mom)

"Amie … what's up with the medical schools—so nu?" (Jemima)

Fall semester 1960, my senior year:

"Amie … it's obvious you're not applying to medical school. So you're not going to be a doctor? Oh God in heaven, it's such a mitzvah to be a doctor—what a shame." (Mom)

"Amie … it looks like you're not going to medical school. You'd be such a mitzvah as a doctor—what a shame." (Jemima)

Great, I've got two Jewish mothers … one white … one black!

Well, that was that, and they eventually stopped talking at me about medical school.

My Four Horsemen buddies were absolutely taken in by all the superficial trappings associated with our pending graduation. Ben, in his discussions, really taught me the dangers of this ritual.

I remember an incident during the party after my bar mitzvah. I can't tell you how many of my adult male relatives shook my hand that day and said to me, "Today, Amos, you are a man."

Well, I must have believed it, for I stole one of Uncle Carl's cigars out of his coat pocket that was hanging on a chair, and found a book of matches on an adjacent table, and locked myself in the nearest coat closet and started to light up the cigar. *Well, I am a man.*

What took place next was absurd, for Uncle Morris must have smelled the smoke and tried to open the door, and I must have mumbled something for him to know that it was me in the closet smoking a cigar. And then the standoff began. I heard Uncle Morris call Uncle Carl and then Uncle Carl called Uncle Sam and then Uncle Sam called Uncle Irving. There it was—me on one side of the door and all my uncles on the other side. I guess I finally began to believe what my uncles were yelling to me on the other side—that even though I was now a man, I was not old enough to smoke a cigar, for I got sick and vomited on Aunt Bea's fur coat—and that was not a good thing to do.

I guess the aforementioned could be a metaphor for my college graduation: don't believe what they're telling you. All societies, I guess, have their rituals and expectations, and life doesn't always behave the way your commencement speaker says it should. The beat of my drum was always different, and I guess unknown forces guided me to a person like Ben—and he seemed to live outside the boundaries of life expectations.

So there I was, ambivalent as usual, wanting to party and feel the same way as my Horsemen buddies and also to simultaneously be aloof to the pull of the crowd.

I handled it, and I guess I did all right. Of course, my family was very important to me, and even though I didn't meet Mom's initial expectations, Jewish mothers *are* very smart and bend with the times, for she still had enormous pride in my accomplishments. And as I learned through my whole life with Mom, mothers will always hold on to you any way they can—and with the original umbilical cord that connected the two of you from the beginning.

In my mind, I have a few contrasting snapshots that remain of that graduation day in June 1961. One was the picture that Army's dad took of the four buddies, huddled together, arms over arms, with wide smiles holding up our diplomas. Army's family was big. Nobody came in uniform, but all the men looked military with short, cropped haircuts. The women were well dressed and handsome as well. Hitch's family was smaller and a little less dressed up but they were all smiles and handshakes, almost like salesmen. Donny's family consisted only of Mary, his mother, and Patricia, his sister. They seemed so uncomfortable and out of place and sad in a strange way. I felt as if they were the black-and-white photo amid the other colorful pictures.

Army had received his commission already as a second lieutenant and was going to report immediately after graduation. Hitch had been accepted to NYU Law School and was working on Wall Street for the summer. Donny was unsure of what he was going to do and decided to go home to Pennsylvania coal country and get a job somewhere.

There was my family: exuberant and happy, except of course for Dad, who had a nice smile all the time but was otherwise reserved. All my uncles and aunts were there as well. Susan and Alvin seemed happy for me. Susan was pregnant with Morris at the time. But the light of my eyes was Sydney. She was dressed up like a little lady and less than a month short of her third birthday. I loved that little girl. She seemed to have a joyous connection with me. I remember holding her hand as we walked everywhere on campus.

And then there were Ben and Zelda. My memory of them that day was like a wisp of a moment—an exciting moment. I could not believe they had actually come to Ithaca to see me graduate. But in reality, Ben came to give me the Martin guitar I had cherished and played only in the store. I remember him and Zelda waiting patiently just outside the circle of family activity for a quiet moment and then both of them walking me arm in arm to Ben's car, where he pulled out the Martin.

"Here, Kid, take this with you wherever you go … Never leave it behind," he said.

I now know that he wanted me to always have my inner creativity at my side. He wanted me to always be aware of the different rhythm within my soul.

And then there was my Zel. It's funny but when I talked of Ben and Zelda, it was always "Zelda." When I talked of Zelda alone, it was always "Zel." I guess that was how I kept a part of her for myself. My memory of her that day is as though we were in a foreign film filled with romantic nuances. Zel seemed to slink softly through the light air everywhere she went. Anything she wore was always sensual to me, and it seemed to catch the wind even when there seemed not to be any. I always could see her blue eyes no matter how far away I was from her. I remember that just after Ben handed me the Martin, Zel grabbed my arm and put her soft face up to my cheek and kissed it, saying, "Love you, Amos." I know she meant the soft and reliable love of a deep friend, and my romantic heart accepted that love from Zel.

I felt my connection to Babatunde was strong even though he was not physically present and did not graduate. He was the first foreign person I had ever met in my life and he connected me back to my America and its roots. I missed my momentary time with Baba Olatunje and his entourage. He seemed to signify purity of purpose to me, and he truly was a servant of the world through music and peace.

My direction after graduation was uncertain. I felt pulled in the many directions that were part of my being. Was I going to continue my business in historical manuscripts and letters? Was I going to go on to more schooling or on to a job in a publishing company? Was I going to pursue the secrets within my family and go on a quest, or was I going to be swept up by my compulsively rash pact with my three buddies and go to war?

When thinking of the latter, I often felt trepidation, but I knew I would somehow have to try to work out the childhood fantasies that kept hold of me.

If graduations are useful, it is because they are moments in time by which to measure your life. They are the true points in time that allow you to assess your being and look at yourself from a distance.

And certainly, that's what Amos Boris Lardowitz was up to.

Coming Home

I CAME BACK HOME after graduation. It was the summer of 1961, and I was twenty-one years old and felt free and comfortable with myself even though I was not clear on getting a "job." Mom wanted me to be home at least for the summer. I think she wanted to hold on to the last of her children as long as she could. Jemima still lived with Mom during the week. She went home on weekends to Yonkers, where I knew her life was nothing like it was with us at our home. They seemed to be better and better friends, and I really think Jemima lived a dual life: a kosher canasta- and mahjong-playing suburbanite during the week and a tired inner-city mother and grandmother and all-around matriarch of an extended family of ne'er-do-wells on the weekends.

I got my old room back, and Jemima was living in Susan's room. Dad was really fond of Jemima. When he came home after a busy day at the office, I could see the light in his eyes when he said hello to the two women in his life. Of course, he was very proper but I envisioned his thoughts as such: "Well, hello, my two wives! Don't you two look stunning together. OK, gals, what did you cook for your weary husband? And who's going to rub my back and who's going to give me a foot massage after dinner?"

The year 1961 was one of stark contrasts to me. My favorite comic rag, the absurd *MAD Magazine,* had the year on its cover in March, announcing it was the first upside-down year and there wouldn't be another until 6009. John F. Kennedy had been elected president. He was a handsome young man with a beautiful wife, and he energized me with his talk of the Peace Corps. His counterpart in Russia was Nikita Khrushchev, a fat and rude scary man who had banged his shoe on his desk at the General Assembly of the United Nations the year before.

There were civil rights protests and confrontations in April and May in Mississippi and Alabama—and the seemingly benign-looking Adolf Eichmann was standing trial in a business suit in a courtroom in Jerusalem for ordering the deaths of millions of Jews.

I decided after about two weeks of doing nothing but playing "my" Martin that I wanted to look for a small apartment in Manhattan and then possibly look for some freelance work as an editor in a publishing house. Ben was talking to me about this and thought I should ease in to the "real" world, which he generally called the "bullshit" world. He thought I should continue to pursue my manuscript and historical-letter business and widen my horizons beyond the Civil War. Ben was somewhat like Dad in not directing me toward any specific career but being satisfied just to nurture my growing maturity. Of course, they really were not like each other at all. Dad was a proper and conservative religious Jewish doctor who did the same thing day after day—and Ben ... well, Ben was Ben, and I could not and would not want to place him in a box anywhere on this planet.

I never had a car. Ben and Zelda kept a car in a warehouse on Fulton Street in Lower Manhattan. They obviously were real city people and rarely used it. It was a '53 Chevy convertible. It really was cool, with whitewall tires and tons of chrome, and it was ruby red. Ben kept it pristine except for the slight fish smell it had from being next door to a Fulton Street fish processor. When Ben and Zelda drove up to Cornell for my graduation, they took the convertible. I remember seeing them from a distance, sitting in it with the roof down at the curb a few hundred feet away from the big field where all the grads and their families were hugging and schmoozing. Boy, what a sight—Ben with his black curly locks and small ponytail and Zel with her shimmering medium-length blondish hair cascading down her long, exposed soft neck. Nobody but nobody of the thousands of people at Cornell that day looked like Ben and Zelda. The amazing thing is that they never copied style or mentioned style—they just were it.

After the two-week respite, I started to travel to the city by train daily and spend my time at Ben's, helping him out and getting a feel for what I wanted to do. I had plenty of time even at Ben's to pursue the other book dealers for new material to buy and sell. They all knew I was in the city and literally next door, so it was easy to get my business done. I kind of hung around for the next few months, flowing easily from home to Ben's. It really was a nice feeling, one I had never had. For the first time in my life, the transitional Labor Day had passed, summer to fall, without a beat in my mind. What a feeling! There was no obligation or requirement for me to go and prepare for school. I was free mentally and physically to just be and not pursue, or to pursue according to my heart's whim.

I placed a small ad in the *New York Times* classifieds under the heading "Letters and Manuscripts Wanted." It cost a small fortune, but I felt it was important to try to stand on my own at least a little. I listed my full name without a business title and the Ben's Den address and phone number.

I remember the moment when I was sitting at Ben's stool minding the store and got the phone call.

"Mr. Lardowitz, please."

"This is he … Who's calling?"

"Mrs. Adrienne Hubbard."

"Can I help you, Mrs. Hubbard?"

"Yes, I have a letter I would like you to look at."

"Certainly, Mrs. Hubbard, who is it from?"

"Abraham Lincoln."

"*The* Abraham Lincoln?"

"I guess so …"

"How long is it … and is it signed?"

"Two pages … and yes."

"Where did you get it?"

"It was sent to my grandfather."

I could feel my mouth watering as I asked her where she lived and how far away she was from Manhattan. She lived in upstate New York and said she didn't drive, but I figured it certainly was worth the drive to go up to see her and look at the letter.

"Do you want me to appraise it?"

"No … I want to sell it."

I had learned from the professional dealers that you ask how much someone wants for a letter rather than offering a price range first.

"I want to sell it for a hundred dollars." My mouth watered again.

I figured it was a two-hour drive. Ben always said I could borrow Rita (the ruby red Chevy) for any reason, and I really felt confident at that moment. I decided not to tell Ben what I was doing, and I knew he wouldn't ask. I had the thrill of the chase in my being. I wanted this all by myself until I'd "snared" it, and then I could bring it to Ben.

My schedule was open, so I decided to go that coming Friday. I had it all figured out that I would return with the letter late Friday afternoon and go out with Ben and Zelda to dinner afterward to celebrate.

The drive was quite pleasant, and I arrived a bit early to the rather sleepy town. Well, there she was, a real farm woman in a long skirt and apron with swept-back hair in a small farmhouse just outside Patterson, New York. She welcomed me into the house and went straight away to a secretary-type desk and opened the top with a small key, pulling out of a cubbyhole a two-page letter, each page about five inches wide by six inches long.

And there it was: a letter to a Colonel Hackett. I read it kind of quickly because I was so excited. Lincoln was questioning something about the pending battle of Antietam, which was the deadliest battle of the Civil War and had the most losses of life in one day of any war in American history. Twenty-three thousand Americans lost their lives. The battle took place September 17, 1862, and this letter had been written September 3. I don't think I had seen or read anything in print before about any correspondence that Lincoln had with questions like these.

The paper felt real. The ink looked real and the signature seemed real. My heart was pounding, but I felt obligated to say, "You sure you want to sell this, Mrs. Hubbard?"

"Yes, Mr. Lardowitz," she said with sad brown eyes.

I couldn't help myself. I peeled off two hundred-dollar bills and handed both to her, saying, "Please, Mrs. Hubbard, take an additional hundred dollars."

She had a sweet, humble smile as she said, "Oh no, Mr. Lardowitz," but I pushed the bills into her palm and closed her hand on the money.

Well, that was it. I had brought a clear acetate folder and slipped the two-page letter into it carefully. I don't know what possessed me, but I hugged her as I was leaving and said, "Good luck, Mrs. Hubbard" and saw her wave to me as I drove away with the top down.

When I got out of sight, I spontaneously looked straight up into the sky and yelled loudly, "Yippee!"

I felt really cool driving back to Manhattan. *Well, today I am a man. A real man.* I had snared a Lincoln worth a few thousand dollars and possibly shedding new light on history. I drove right to the garage and put the top up. Rita and I had made the journey together and returned in pristine condition.

I literally jogged all the way up to Fourth Avenue, trying to make it before Ben closed the shop at five o'clock on this glorious Friday.

"I snared a Lincoln letter, Ben," I said, still breathing heavily as I turned in to the open door of the store. I handed Ben the folder so that he could see it. He seemed to scan the whole two-page letter very quickly.

"Uh huh, Mother Hubbard."

"What … did I tell you about her?"

"No … the Mother Hubbard Gang, Kid."

"What do you mean?" I said with more than a tinge of self-doubt.

"Kid Lardowitz—you've been fleeced by the Mother Hubbard Gang."

"What!?" I said incredulously.

"Kid—come on—yeah, the paper's real. It's easy to get vintage blank paper. The ink and pen are real. It's easy to write with an old pen. And the handwriting appears real. But Kid, it's slow and deliberate, not free flowing like it should be—a real handwriting. Look at the Lincoln signature."

Oh shit … I should have known that. I do know that! My eyes and heart had fooled me.

"She's a crook?" I blurted.

"She's a crook and so are the twenty other crooks who work with her."

"But she looked like a real sweet old lady."

"Kid, she's an actor. There are about five Mother Hubbards—and they're all under fifty … Makeup, Kid—makeup."

I couldn't bring myself to tell Ben that I had given her another hundred dollars. *What an idiot I am.*

"Kid, they work the whole U.S. It's been four years since they worked New York. I heard they were just in San Fran selling Renoirs from an attic. You can be sure they had a busy week—probably had about five appointments today with various fraudulent antiquities."

"But they're so bold."

"Come on—nobody who is in the business and makes this faux pas would ever want to go back or call the police. It's an embarrassment. So the dealer is out a hundred bucks." *Oh shit … it's two hundred.* "And you notice she won't give you a phone number. She knows who's coming … someone who hasn't dealt with the Mother Hubbards before. Kid, that was a rented empty house with only two rooms dressed up. You're probably the last con of the week. That house is empty again now, and they're off to ... maybe Boston—who knows."

Oh shit ... oh God. I've lost my virginity (which shouldn't have been half bad if that were literally true).

So there it was—I had finally crawled up to the big time. See, I wanted to be a real dealer so I had put a real ad in a really respected newspaper, and look what had happened to me. I'd been stalked by a sophisticated gang of thieves, I thought. Ben said they really had nothing to lose since they made their calls from a pay phone, and a dealer who was savvy just backed away from the temptation.

There were plenty of hints that I should have backed off, but my drive for the capture was too great; it wasn't even the money as much as the prestige of getting a Lincoln letter directly from the family.

My God ... there goes my cool Friday night with Ben and Zelda.

This lesson was a lesson in greed for me. It was a lesson in wanting to possess material things to the point of blinding my natural instincts and knowledge. I knew the letter was a fake as soon as I took the time to look at it. But my greed had taken over. So be it. I just grew up again.

About two months later I realized once again that it was all about earthly fame and possessions. Sure, it was a historical letter from one of the most famous people in history, but still it was Lincoln manipulated by the masses. It was all about money and who has the most toys. I realized that I had never sat with this letter initially to pull Abraham Lincoln out of the Cosmos and see him thinking as he wrote. If I had used this knowledge, I would have handed it back to her and said, "I'm sorry Mrs. Hubbard—it's a fake."

Ben insisted that I frame the letter and that it be the first wall hanging in my new apartment.

I found a great sublet on West Fourth near Bank Street, about six blocks away from Ben and Zelda's place on Perry in the Village, at the end of August. It was a "walk down"—a subterranean studio with a narrow window that gave me not a bird's-eye view but a mole's-eye view of every New Yorker's feet passing my place.

I moved by myself. I wanted to. Dad and Mom and Jemima wanted to schlep all my stuff, but I kind of felt silly moving to the greatest place on earth—Greenwich Village—with my black nanny and Jewish mommy and daddy. *Suppose someone should see me?*

Dad lent me his car on a Saturday afternoon, and I moved all my small personal belongings. Mom gave me blankets and pillows, and I slept on the floor without any furniture for the next two weeks while I intermittently searched secondhand stores for a bed and chest of drawers and an easy chair.

I was in heaven in New York City and the Village. There was a palpable excitement all around me. I felt creativity in the air. I honestly felt that the center of the Cosmos of Creativity that Ben talked about was in Greenwich Village at this time and that I was taking it all in. It was going to be my fuel for the rest of my life—my creative fuel.

Week by week, I got piece by piece until my small subterranean lair was furnished comfortably. Ben had given me the names of three major publishing houses in New York City, and he advised me how to present my resume so that I could work as a freelance editor for specific genres of books. He suggested that I list my expertise as nonfiction historical American works and historical American novels. I prepared a resume and forwarded it to the three houses.

Lo and behold, I got an interview and then a job at one of the publishing companies. They were interested in having me work on new historical novels by one of their prolific writers. She had written mostly contemporary work and was now embarking on American historical love novels. Oh boy, the stuff was horrible. But my job was to be sure that at least the historical time line and characters were accurate in description and spelling. The book had no heart, and certainly nothing in it came from the Cosmos, I thought. But it was work for the moment and would actually bring in some bacon.

For my momentary literary joy I was writing poetry in the form of song lyrics and putting it to music for my guitar. I spent as much time as I could with Ben at his shop and gradually got back to pursuing the other book dealers for historical manuscripts and letters, although I became quite cautious and had much lower expectations for success.

My greatest time was the nighttime. The Village was alive at night, and I generally joined Ben and Zelda for a late-night get-together in the bar on Christopher Street where I had first met Elmore James, Jack Kerouac, and Allen Ginsberg.

The bar was nondescript and not easy to find even when you went looking for it. Of course it was ten steps down and hidden away. The only sign on it was eight by thirty-six inches, hanging at the top of the last stair, and said MANNY'S UNDERWEAR FACTORY.

I was introduced to Manny Malone one late fall evening. He was behind the bar serving. Manny, I found out, was a dear friend of Ben's. He was about the same age and only a tad shorter, with the same small ponytail, but his hair was straight and swept back. He had a great smile with a separation between his two front teeth and bright brown eyes. Manny was cool. Ben told me that before he opened the bar, Manny was walking near his neighborhood in Brooklyn past a closed and deserted factory building that had been an underwear factory. It was actually named Manny's Underwear Factory. The sign was over a side door. Manny just ripped it off and announced to his girl Fanny that he was going to place it over the new bar he was going to open in the Village. Manny was a standup comic first and then an actor in experimental theater. He decided that everything was "bullshit" and wanted to just provide a sanctuary and incubator for the "real" people in New York.

Over the top shelf of drinks facing the bar stools and behind the bar was a sign that said NOBODY IS ANYBODY AT THE UNDERWEAR. It was Manny's statement that whoever came in to the Underwear was entitled to be equal to anyone else. There was also a smaller sign below it that said NO GAWKING.

The Underwear would become a place where the famous and known could come and be left alone—and if famous or known people came to be looked at, Manny would actually kick them out. One smaller sign below the small stage said NO WANNABES. I noticed that Ben and Zelda felt really comfortable here.

I met Fanny one night. She was an attractive woman about Zel's age, and her best friend. She was a little smaller than Zel and had shorter black hair. I noticed that when Fanny was with Zelda, their whole persona changed. They seemed like little mischievous girls and not the sexy women they were. Fanny was a poet and writer like Zel.

Once a week Zelda and Fanny would announce "Rita's night out" and they would take Rita, top down, to some destination like Jones Beach or City Island. They had a ball of a time, it seemed. I noticed that Manny and Fanny and Ben and Zelda had real trusting relationships. When the girls were out and I sat with Ben at his table and Manny sat down to "shoot the breeze," they didn't seem to get testosterone laden. They were real men like the girls were real women, I thought. I admired both their relationships.

Manny could tell funny stories to the point of belly laughs. He was a real cutup. One "stupid" gossip columnist in the city had mentioned in her column that the Underwear was a place to spot "celebs" in the Village. Well, Manny said, this got around the whole country really fast, and at least once a week there would be "aliens descending," as he called them. Manny would try different schemes to "scram the aliens" fast. This time he had hung a small sign next to the entry that said PLEASE DON'T FEED THE RATS. WE ARE TRYING TO ELIMINATE THEM. Fanny had made a fake rat tail out of gray fabric, and when Manny saw this obviously gawking touristy couple descend, he turned away from them quickly and hung the tail between the space in his front teeth. He then feigned surprise as he saw them and, with the tail swinging between his teeth, said with a lisp, "Damn it, Fanny. I almoth caught the rascal. He got away but I think I ripped hith tail off." The woman fainted. An ambulance was called, and Manny said he was sure she had the experience of her lifetime.

Gradually, Manny said, the publicity faded and the Underwear became the watering hole it was supposed to be.

The highlight of my first year and a half in New York was my nights out at the Underwear with Ben and Manny and occasionally Zelda and Fanny. I seemed to be working on two books at once and would do most of the work from my studio. I was also buying and selling American historical letters and manuscripts, which brought in some extra money. Ben would give me a call and just say, "Underwear at nine" and then hang up. I knew to be there. That's where I met Joseph Heller that year. He had just published *Catch 22*, and he was a hell of a crazy guy. He was vibrant and filled with irreverence and quite witty. I find it amazing that the title of his book has become a household phrase and is listed in the dictionary and used regularly by people today.

I remember the night I walked downstairs and found Marlon Brando sitting with Ben. He was a stirring kind of guy. You hung on every word of his. He could carry any conversation and was much attuned to human rights. Brando definitely seemed like the outsider even then.

I had drinks one night with William Faulkner and Ben. By this time Faulkner was a very recognized figure in America. In fact he would die of a heart attack only months after I saw him. Faulkner was suave and smart and had a kind of sophisticated southern drawl. What a drinker, though!

I also shared drinks and food with Ernie Kovacs, the zany actor and comedian, and heard the seminal Bob Dylan in his maiden tryouts at New York clubs. Dylan played a number of times at the Underwear.

The people who came to the Underwear were real and honest, and Manny and Ben would not have it any other way. This experience helped to build my trust in honest creativity. Ben was a great charmer and an easy conversationalist, and if he chided any of his creative buddies, it was to "humanize them and bring them down to earth," he said. He was an orchestra leader and brought out the essence in the world.

I was privy to so much in the creative world over the next two years in New York City. It was what I had dreamed about as a kid but was able to experience as an adult. I don't think my career was going anywhere, but I felt as if I was in post-graduate learning—learning about life and the world through the experiences of a dynamic city filled with people like me but in various stages of their life.

My inner concern about the injustices toward Negro America still haunted me during this time. In June 1963, in Jackson, Mississippi, where I had been during my Delta trip, Medgar Evers, an NAACP official, was shot to death outside his home. It was a ruthless murder and shocked the country. Martin Luther King was becoming a formidable leader of the civil rights movement and organized a march on Washington in August. I decided I would go, and went with a car full of people I had met in New York during that year. I remember his "I Have a Dream" speech vividly. My dearest friends at the Underwear, including Ben and Zelda, were of course sympathetic people who didn't have a prejudiced bone in their body, yet they were not activists, and I would never have expected them to be.

I really didn't feel any pressure from my parents to have to justify the lack of decision concerning my future. I thought it was odd that Mom and Jemima and possibly Susan didn't push me for a timetable for advancement or even for marriage and children.

At the occasional large family gatherings with my uncles and aunts and cousins I could overhear Mom describe what Amos was doing with his life. She might start with "Amie is living by himself in Manhattan," and if she got an "Oh, nice," she'd stop right there and not give out any more info about my life. If that didn't work and she got a "So what is he doing there?" she might say something like "He's an editor." If that didn't work she would ratchet it up a notch and say, "He's a publishing editor," and if she really needed to impress, she would say, "He's a publisher."

Oh Mom, come on! So be it—at least she wasn't nudging me.

Donny and I talked every three or four months. He was still kind of lost, but he was working in the regional office of a large mining company near home. I felt bad for him since he generally seemed empty of spirit. Hitch was in New York City. We got together once and it was like oil and water, although we liked each other. He was high on the money world that was also New York City, not the creative world like me. He was focused in his quest to climb the corporate ladder to the top and stand on the heap below him. We actually had a nice dinner in a trendy Manhattan restaurant uptown on Madison Avenue and laughed about our college days. It was an OK evening, but I felt that my life had gone much further than his single-minded aspiration. We agreed to keep in touch.

I remember the moment that I looked at the return name on the envelope and blanked out momentarily on who Capt. Robert Armstrong was—and then a moment later I blurted out, "Army!" It was the first time since graduation that I had heard from Army.

I opened Army's letter:

1 Sep 1963
Capt. Robert Armstrong
First Calvary 5th Reg
Saigon, Vietnam

Fellow Horsemen:

Greetings to all from Saigon, Vietnam.

Hope all is well.

Your brother Army, keeper of the pact, is putting my three buddies in the trenches on notice for big happenings here in Southeast Asia. I cannot say the word but be put on notice for action.

Respectfully,

Robert Armstrong, Captain, U.S. Army Special Forces

Saigon? Vietnam? It seemed far away and not on my radar. Obviously, Army was talking about war and was in this letter giving notice about our pact in college.

It seemed strange, but I initially chuckled when I read the letter. Then I felt trepidation and excitement creeping in from the past.

It was only two days later, and I had completely forgotten about the letter. I was lying in bed reading about ten thirty in the evening when the telephone rang.

"Ammo—it's Turk, man."

"Donny?"

"Ammo—did you get the letter?" Donny's whole persona was different from all the times I had spoken to him since school. He was upbeat, and I could almost see his piercing eyes through the phone.

"Yeah, Turk."

"Is it time, man? Are you ready?"

"Are you kidding? Is there a war on?"

"I did some reading, Ammo. Army's telling us there's going to be a war in Vietnam—a confrontation. A big one, man—a big one."

"Really?"

"Can you picture how long this letter traveled, man, and where it came from to get to our houses, Ammo? Do you think there's a jungle there, and lions and tigers? Do you think Army has ridden an elephant through the jungle, Ammo?"

He talked like a child. I kind of "yessed" Donny, for I felt really good for him and his exuberance for life. I remember mostly just listening that night after our initial conversation. I know I didn't share his excitement except for the joy it brought him. He was a dear friend, and I felt close to him and wanted him to be happy.

"I can't wait for the next letter, Ammo—can you?"

"No, Turk."

Donny's call to me after Army's letter deeply affected me starting the next morning. Suddenly I started reading the papers and watching television for news on Vietnam. The next day I saw excerpts from an interview President Kennedy had with Walter Cronkite about Vietnam. Kennedy said we could not withdraw from Vietnam and that the president of South Vietnam, Ngo Dinh Diem, was out of touch with the people. Over the next few days I began a search of the recent history in Vietnam and found that Army was one of the four hundred original Green Berets sent to help the South Vietnamese in the spring of 1961. Kennedy had inherited a warning from the Eisenhower administration that troops might be needed in Vietnam to counter Khrushchev's belligerent support for the North Vietnamese and the "wars of liberation."

Up to this point only "advisers" were in Vietnam. I'm sure this was our buddy Army's role and that he was privy to knowledge about a pending big increase in combat troops from the United States.

My life seemed to shift right after these few days. It shifted back to my college days, the ROTC, the Four Horsemen, and my childhood days of playing war. It shifted from the mind and heart of creativity and my present state to the days of my fascination with war.

In my heart I think I knew I was just in a temporary phase here in New York City. I knew my life would change. I had forgotten or at least placed on a back burner my military thoughts, but they certainly came forward fast.

At the beginning of November I was following stories about the fragility of the Diem regime, and from reading the news I could tell that everyone in the Kennedy administration wanted to get control of the politics in South Vietnam so we would be able to get combat troops there. I believe that with hidden support from the United States there was a coup, and Diem was reported to have been killed on November 2, 1963. Over the next few weeks there was a power vacuum.

November 22, 1963.

"Amie ... my honey ... did you hear the news? He's dead. They shot him! He was such a young man—God in heaven ... How bad ... how sad."

Mom was the person who told me on the telephone that John F. Kennedy had been shot to death in a motorcade in Dallas that morning. I, like everyone of that era, remember the moment as if it was today.

Life changed for many young people and probably everyone in America that day. Innocence was gone—a youthful American consciousness was snuffed out. But I had known that America was changing from the moment I read Army's letter two months before. The conflict that would become Vietnam and the polarization that would strain America was going to happen whether or not a young President Kennedy was shot. American political administrations and the military industrial complex that supported it were headed in the direction of deliberate military confrontations with the rest of the world. That was the nature of our free market and capitalistic society, and that is what we struggle with to this day.

My two years in the Village and Manhattan were carefree and filled with learning. I further bonded my relationship with Ben and Zelda and my new friends Manny and Fanny. I met many people, well known and not, and I wrote poetry and music. Army's letter and Kennedy's death threw me back to hidden places within my being. It threw me back to the days when I was obsessed with my family's secret, thinking about nothing else. But I was not surprised; I knew that growth through change was the norm for Amos Boris Lardowitz.

Apparently, neither Donny nor I ever mentioned Hitch in our conversation about Army's first letter. He must have received it, but neither of us got a call from him, nor did we try to make any contact.

The second letter from Army came one cold and damp February day. Army was quite clear. He was of course still in Vietnam, and he used the words *order you* as if we were being called to duty. Donny called me as soon as he got the letter. He was concerned that there was "no real war" yet. I thought it was a strange remark, but he was "Turk" and not Donny anymore, and I felt that I had to accept who he was.

It was kind of a strange spring in 1964. News was coming out of Vietnam daily. There were still only about twenty thousand American troops there during that year. A draft was in place, but there was no buzz among people I talked to. My mind was on it, though, and the regular calls from Turk only reinforced my concentration.

"I don't want to be drafted, man—I don't want to be drafted. I want to enlist, man."

What Turk said to me during one of our telephone conversations that late spring kept being repeated in my head day after day and night after night. I knew what he meant. The military was drafting single men between the ages of eighteen and twenty-six, and it was only a matter of time before it was going to be increased many-fold to fight an overt war in Vietnam.

Well, in August 1964, the Gulf of Tonkin incident happened in Vietnam. An American destroyer, the USS *Maddox* was attacked off the coast of North Vietnam. This was the provocation President Johnson needed to justify the massive escalation of the war and, believe it or not, more than 80 percent of the American people were behind him. Later on, the attack would prove to be probably a fabrication, as the incident was really provoked by the *Maddox*. At any rate, America was war bound.

I really didn't anguish over my decision to enlist. Although I knew I was prime meat for the draft, I felt that it was time for me to go to war—time for the Four Horsemen.

Turk had called Hitch twice, but Hitch had kind of cut him off and said he would call back but never did. Turk and I talked about who should pursue the issue with Hitch, and we decided I should.

"I tried, Ammo … They listed me as 4F … I can't go."

Literally moments after I initiated the call to Hitch, he blurted out the above. He rattled off something about two pierced eardrums and difficult vision and two hernias and on and on. I really wasn't pushing him. He seemed to be defensive and justifying all the reasons why he'd never make it in the military. I didn't want to be judgmental, and I wasn't. I finished our call by telling him when Turk and I would enlist and to keep in touch.

OK … now for Mrs. Lardowitz. I had never prepared my parents for an eventual military escapade. I probably never thought there would be a war soon after my graduation. But this situation was serious, and most everyone was talking about it, including my folks.

"Mom, Donny and I are enlisting in the army," I said over the telephone one early September evening without any warning.

"So … how is your job?"

"Mom … Donny and I are going into the army."

"So … did you hear Ed Sullivan announce that the Beatles are going to be on his show? You must be interested in that."

"Mom … I would probably have a good chance of being drafted anyway."

"Jemima had another grandchild … a little girl … Gotteniu… so cute."

"So anyway … how are *your* grandchildren?"

And that was how it went, for I finally knew how to deal, as an adult, with the stonewalling Mrs. Lardowitz. This was round one.

I was really getting excited about the change in my life. I told Ben and Zelda one night at the Underwear over drinks. I didn't editorialize and neither did they. I just said I was going into the army. Everyone knew guys who were being drafted. They were cool because they knew the seriousness of the day, and I think they wanted to give me an even keel.

I wrote the letter to Army for Turk and me. It was short and to the point and included something like "reporting for duty, sir" and "ready and able." I didn't mention Hitch at all.

"So … can't you stick a pencil through your ear or drool a lot?" said Mom immediately after I picked up the phone and without any hello about a week later.

"Mom … you have to be kidding." End of round two.

Round three: "Jewish boys don't go into the army. They don't fight wars." *I knew this was coming.*

"Yeah, they do everything in their power to run away," I blurted out.

"My Amie … you're so different … my Amie."

Knockout.

I talked to Turk probably twice a week for the next month. I needed to list my studio for rent. Fortunately the book I was working on was just about starting, and telling my boss I was going into the armed services was a layup, considering the times we were in.

I was fully caught up in the moment. Turk's excitement and fervor helped drive my enthusiasm for our enlistment—and at this point I felt there was no turning back.

We decided we would enlist right after the new year of 1965. It was a compromise that honored both Turk's mom and my mom. My mom wanted me to celebrate one more Hanukkah and my twenty-fifth birthday, and Turk's mom wanted one more Christmas.

Shipping Out

It was mostly a rainy and dingy two weeks after the New Year and my birthday. I was living at home since I had moved out of my studio in early December. I don't think I had pleased either Mom or Jemima at all. They were quieter and more reflective than I had ever seen them. Dad seemed all right, but of course he always seemed all right. I myself seemed to have plenty of time for reflection. Sydney, my niece, was six years old, and Morris was three, and Clara was just walking at one year. I knew I would miss them, especially Sydney. She loved me very much and was tuned to whatever I was thinking. I spent quite a bit of time with her before I left.

I tried to make somewhat of a break with Ben and Zelda and Manny and Fanny and the Underwear. I knew the memory of the last few years in the Village would stay with me as a sweet joy.

Turk and I spoke often. He really was a good friend even though he seemed to be two people: Donny and Turk. He was vulnerable and impressionable, which only mirrored my own duality. We would be an OK pair, I thought—taking a monumental journey together to unknown and exotic places.

Turk and I made a pact to enlist the second week of February and to do it in a city that neither of us had been to. We decided we would just walk into an army recruiting center, and that would be it.

I picked Trenton, New Jersey, the state between my state and Turk's state. Trenton was the historic city that General George Washington engaged at the end of December 1776. The famous painting of Washington crossing the Delaware by Emanuel Leutz depicts this event. As well, Washington wrote a letter to General McDougal about this battle, and I have seen the original in my dealings. I thought this city would be a fitting start for our new adventures.

Turk asked me to pick an auspicious date that we should enlist—one from the Civil War. I decided February 9 was important because that was the date in 1861 that Jefferson Davis was elected to the newly formed Confederate States of America in Montgomery, Alabama, and it essentially split the Union apart and set up the War Between the States. Fortunately February 9 was a Tuesday, so the Army Recruiting Center would be open. We agreed to each take a bus to Trenton and meet there and then proceed to the center with only duffel bags in arm.

The fateful day arrived. Someone had sublet my studio with all the furniture, and I had brought all my personal belongings home. My most prized possession, my Martin guitar, I decided to leave with my folks. I knew it would be safe. I picked out a complete change of clothes and my toiletries, and they fit in one duffel bag. I was ready. Mom and Jemima shed a few tears and I was off.

As I walked to a seat way back in the Greyhound bus, I started to have the feeling I had had when Ben and I started our Delta trip. I felt as if I was a small speck on the surface of the world and was being transported to adventures unknown.

Turk was waiting for me at the terminal. We bear-hugged each other with bright, sincere smiles.

"Ready, soldier?" he said.

"Ready and able, sir," I replied.

"We are here to enlist," I said in a weaker voice than I expected.

"You're kidding," said the recruiting sergeant sitting with his feet up on the desk.

"We want to go to Vietnam," blurted Turk.

"So take a bus," laughed the sergeant.

"Seriously, Sergeant ...," I said.

"OK, guys ... I sit here all day with nothing to do, and I occasionally get some ninny who wants to play games with me ... so I play games. I never had two jerks before who walked in together to enlist."

There was a palpable silence as Turk and I turned to look at each other as if to say, "This wasn't a great start."

"You're on, guys," said the sergeant, breaking the ice as he pulled two folders of papers out of his desk drawer.

And that was it. He told us this would be a preliminary enlistment and that we would be sent to Fort Jackson, South Carolina, for evaluation, medical exams, questionnaires, and other things to be sure we were fit for service. He asked us if we wanted transportation or would provide our own, since Fort Jackson was about seven hundred miles away. He told us that although there were no army buses going with tons of recruits from Trenton, he could give us vouchers for the Greyhound bus.

Once more we were specks on the planet, like ants zigzagging across terrain to a distant unknown destination. We'd be going through Maryland, Delaware, Virginia, and then North Carolina and into South Carolina. Once more I would be traveling through the historic South, and at a tenuous time in our country's history. By this time in 1965, there was a growing, more combative movement among black America, and its leader was Malcolm X.

There is something to be said about a long bus trip where you have left all your belongings and friends and home and job in a kind of suspended state of animation. It enables you to reflect on your being, and you can examine your life as individual freeze-frame incidents. I was doing that during this trip with Turk. I think Turk was different. I don't think he questioned or analyzed himself at all except for those rare moments when he broke down and seemed to become a pleading child. Even though we were different I was extremely comfortable with Turk, and ultimately I knew I could trust him with my life, as he could trust me with his.

I was prepared for the South since I had had my experience in Mississippi, but I knew Turk was not. Lyndon Johnson had signed the Civil Rights Act of 1964 the year before and things surely were changing, but there seemed to be more belligerence and defiance than I had witnessed earlier. Of course, my memory included the wonderful spiritual time I had had with a Negro community in Mississippi. I think that I was able to help Turk focus on our own quest and separate ourselves from this turmoil.

"Welcome to the U.S. Army," blared the loudspeaker as we joined about thirty or so other disheveled-looking young civilian men.

Everything was a line. We were in a line more hours of the day the first week than we weren't: a line to the heart doctor exam, a line to the eye doctor exam, a line to the testicle doctor exam (cough), a line to the barber (or was he a sheep shearer?), a line to measure our pant leg—and always a line to eat.

Turk and I were fortunate that we got into the same concrete building and the same open barrack room since our last names, Koslowski and Lardowitz, were close together in the alphabet. Life sure became simple. *Help me! I'm in prison.*

Both Turk and I took to the discipline pretty well the first few weeks. Recruits were taught to act collectively, to lose our individuality, and to take orders and perform to the exact millimeter of accuracy required by our drill sergeants. We marched and marched and did tons of sit-ups and push-ups. The first eight weeks or so I felt as if I was becoming a better person, more focused and astute and a stronger soldier.

I had thought that basic training was going to be about eight weeks long and possibly twelve weeks. But it seemed that our relatively small group was being held up at Fort Jackson without placement or assignment. I then realized that there were changes going on at the camp, and the buzz was around that new combat training and hand-to-hand combat procedures were being implemented as well as a more rigorous program of individualized physical indoctrination.

I began to realize that our country truly was preparing for war. Turk and I had timed our enlistment just right and ended up in boot camp preparing for the jungles of Vietnam. Both of us were singled out for the new, much more rigorous training camps. We had new drill sergeants and they were really harsh. It seemed that almost weekly we were being joined by a greater and greater number of new recruits, many of them draftees.

A strange transformation seemed to be occurring—young scared boys and men joining us who did not want to be in the army and did not want to fight a war. The drill sergeants became verbally abusive to most every recruit, insulting everyone and practically spitting in our faces. I realized they were preparing the unprepared to travel to a godforsaken but beautiful and exotic place to be exposed to constant death and fear of death and to not know who their enemy was.

We were being trained in the new Counter Guerrilla Warfare program. There was talk of ambushes and booby traps and a new way of warfare.

I saw many recruits break down and cry incessantly. I saw verbal abuse to the point of torture, and I saw recruits physically unable to perform what the army wanted them to.

Turk was a natural. He was in his element. The harder he was trained, the stronger and more focused he became. I think I got my strength from my identification with the soldiers of the Civil War as well as their plaintive letters that I took as my own. Without that I would have cracked.

I became transformed—I became a soldier. I was trained and retrained to fire weapons accurately—weapons that kill or maim. I think that many other recruits who were successful lost their own thoughts and their own mind and had it replaced by the indoctrination of warfare. I think I needed more. I needed to know that what I was doing was right. At this impressionable time in my life I must have rationalized the need to protect my country, my family, and my democracy. Just as Abraham Lincoln, ultimately a man of peace, made a decision in April 1861 to pit American brothers against brothers and friends against friends and go to war, which destroyed America as he knew it at that time and killed thousands of Americans, I knew I had to make the same decision.

Turk needed no thoughts. He never analyzed. Something in his early life almost genetically transformed him into a soldier of war, almost a machine capable of taking orders and removing any doubt from his mind.

There was much activity at Fort Jackson at this time. It was a buildup, a buildup to war—a place that Turk and I were dropped into that suited our quest.

I remember being tested to the point of breaking; I think I was singled out for my name and for being Jewish. *Lardowitz* was an easy target for slurring. I was yelled at within a half inch of my face: "Lard Ass" and "Lard Hog" and so on. I don't know what kept me going, but I do feel that my closeness with Turk and the bond of the Four Horsemen strengthened me. Strangely enough, even though the four were three, I don't think it mattered.

We must have been about nine or ten weeks into training when the company was ordered to the field and our company commander as well as our personal drill sergeant was present. It seemed that they were about to make an announcement. There was some spiel about how proud the army was of us, and then the commander announced that a select few exemplary soldiers were going to be recommended for airborne training with the 101st Infantry Airborne, which was taking shape in Fort Campbell, Kentucky. He started to reel off names; the first was Donald Koslowski. He said Private Koslowski was the best soldier in the class and called Turk up to the front of the company. I felt an excitement that I could not have imagined. I was tingling with emotion for Turk. As the names were read I realized that I desperately wanted to be included in this group. I wanted to be one of them—I wanted to be with Turk.

"And the last of you men to be selected is … Amos Boris Lardowitz."

I beamed and my body felt flushed all over as I walked forward and caught the eye of Turk, my buddy, and his half smile.

Twenty of us … only 20 out of 120 men … I felt so proud and high. The next few days were glorious for Turk and me. Weeks of tortuous training had changed us. I seemed to have metamorphosed into a completely different being. I was leaving behind who I was before, and that previous incarnation was becoming a fuzzy memory.

I had written three letters to my family midway through our training: one to Mom, one to Ben and Zelda, and one to Sydney, Morris, and Clara. I was kind of nonspecific and conversational about the weather and emphasized the lighter side of training. I knew at this point that I would need to call Mom and give her the real news about my move to Fort Campbell and then my eventual destination. I knew she would be beside herself with worry.

Turk and I wrote a letter together to Army in Vietnam. We didn't know what he was doing but we knew he was probably in a very dangerous situation. We thought he would be very proud of our achievements.

We were scheduled to fly by troop transport to Fort Campbell after a five-day R-and-R leave, a trip of five hundred miles. Both Turk and I really didn't want to go home. Even though we didn't actually say it, I think we both felt somewhat afraid to break our persona of training—so we both decided just to call our moms and give them the news over the phone. It would at least be softer interim news, although obviously at some later point we would have to call again when we finished our training and got our final orders.

I think Mom and the rest of my family had developed a more fatalistic approach to my venture at this point, for my phone conversation went pretty well.

Our group was called together just before the five-day rest and surprised by our collective promotion to private first class and a special ribbon for exemplary training.

"You were selected because you stood out as strong and smart soldiers," said the sergeant as about a hundred of us sat in an auditorium facing him on the first day at Fort Campbell. "Vietnam … Vietnam … totally different from any other place on this earth—and engaging and destroying the enemy is totally different from any war the army has fought."

He then proceeded to tell us about the new Airmobile Division, which consisted of dropping infantry into difficult terrain by helicopter not normally accessible by other means.

"You will be assigned to squads of eight to ten men. You will be dropped into enemy terrain. You will have one of three missions—search-and-destroy, clearing, or securing."

The sergeant then explained the meaning of each. Search-and-destroy consisted of finding the North Vietnamese Army, the NVA, at their remote base camps and attacking the small individual camps. Clearing was more hairy and consisted of driving the enemy away from the local population areas and interacting with the local people. Securing was the most difficult and consisted of squad-size ambushes among the remote villages to flush out the Vietcong fighters who were farmers by day and insurgents by night, and then establishing relationships with the villages. He said we could be on a patrol for days until our missions were complete and that it would all be in the Highlands of Vietnam. He also said this tactic had been used since 1964 in Vietnam but that we would be the soldiers to perfect it—and without it the war could not be won.

Our bird was the Huey UH-1 helicopter capable of carrying eight to ten of us, deploying us in the most remote and difficult terrain, and getting us out fast. Of course we needed it to pick us up again after our mission was complete.

Man, we worked hard. There were about ten of these Hueys and we played war games until we thought it was real, often jumping out of a Huey at ten feet above the ground on rolling terrain and then heading off to "enemy" war camps. A number of guys dropped out or were injured but Turk and I excelled, feeding off our commitment to and admiration for each other.

While we were training, I often felt that even our superiors were flying by the seat of their pants when it came to the tactics of jungle war—but so be it, for we had made the mental and physical commitment.

At the end of May 1965 there were only about eighty of us left. We were all called to a meeting late one Sunday night in one of the tactical classrooms.

"I am proud of this group. You are very focused and strong," said our company commander. "Gentlemen, in one week you will be situated in the

Highlands of South Vietnam—you are leaving tomorrow at 2300 hours for Okinawa. Make your phone calls."

That was it—short and sweet. There was a scramble for the four phone lines we were allowed to use. Excitement was abounding.

I called Mom and kept it very short. She told me she loved me.

From the moment we piled into the troop transport my mind was not my own anymore. From that moment on I felt as if I could step outside myself at any time and observe who I was and what I was doing. I was a soldier—an anonymous soldier traveling through surreal events I had never seen or imagined before. In Okinawa I bought a small notebook and two pencils. I vowed to myself that I would write a diary if I was out in the field and to write as often as I could. I was about to become what had enthralled me my whole life: a soldier in the field describing his horror. I would have to write small and not use a lot of words, for I couldn't carry a larger notebook.

We entered Vietnam through Cam Ranh Bay and then were transported by a small troop carrier to a forward camp from there. Turk was still with me, but I knew we would be split up, for our commander had told us that each squad would consist of eight men, and we would "have no buddies" among us.

5 Jun 65. I can smell the rain forest. We are situated on a field with small rolling hills around us. There are clumps of dense vegetation, which are the rain forests. They are a distance away. It is threatening to rain. The air is moist and warm.

7 Jun 65. This post has about 300 men. I have just been chosen to a squad. Apparently there are 10 squads going out. I hope that Turk is in one. I haven't talked to him yet.

8 Jun 65. 0600 hours. I can hear the whomp whomp of the Huey blades. I can't see them. But I know they are coming.

They're here. I feel like they are alive. They seem like fairy-tale small flying dinosaurs ready to transport us to the world of make-believe.

0830 hours. We are in the air—eight of us. Our faces look the same: I think filled with uncertainty on our first mission.

0935 hours. Flying low over thatched villages interspersed with fields of crops surrounded by hills and forests.

1240 hours. An empty, recently vacated Vietcong camp. Beaming smiles I see on all our faces—almost giddiness. I puff the first cigarette I have ever smoked right down to the butt.

1440 hours. Amid the whomp whomp sound and the bumping bodies I see the relief in us all. Huey pilot announces base camp in 15 minutes.

Euphoria. That is the only word I can use to describe the mood of the enlisted men who had made their first airmobile mission. We were walking on air and giving high fives to all. I caught sight of Turk, who had a broad and happy smile as he said, "Scared those VC good, huh, Ammo?"

Well, this mood didn't last long, for late in the day one of the PFCs overheard a conversation between the company commander and one of the platoon leaders. In essence he heard, "Who the hell screwed up? What a freakin' waste of men and materiel. You didn't engage anyone?"

Oh well, trial run—but probably thank God, for I don't think any one of us was ready to fight.

We made two additional missions in the next week, both announced as search-and-destroy. We were told we had Huey Cobras or Hueys with rockets as backup to soften the enemy. On the first of these two missions we could actually see the surprised troops scurry away in twenty different directions while we were in the air. We could also see the fire from the sky. We landed and jumped out, firing our automatic weapons in the direction of the fleeing VC. I didn't see any hits, and I never saw anyone go down. My heart was pounding heavily as we were ordered to freeze and then regroup. I collapsed into a small hunched figure and pulled out my notebook.

15 Jun 65. 0915 hours. My heart and the whomp of the Huey blades are pounding through my being—they are one. Excitement or fear or both—no matter.

Well, the rains came … monsoon rains in June, on one morning. Wet and warm and bored for a few days, my tentmates and I played a lot of cards. We cleaned and recleaned our firearms and polished and waterproofed everything we could possibly waterproof. The rains were steady but relatively light. I wrote one letter home describing base camp but not the missions we went on.

About seven days into on-and-off-again rains our platoon leader announced a mission coming up. We would be part of a bigger operation farther up the Highlands toward the Drang River. Our mission once more would be search-and-destroy, with no contact with the local villagers, although other teams would be doing search-and-clear and still others search-and-secure, with the idea of establishing small but permanent posts within and close to small communities of locals by the river.

We were told that at least two other companies would be involved, with possibly thirty or forty Hueys and backup firepower support. Each squad had a squad leader and a radioman, and we would always be in touch with the platoon leader, who in turn would be in touch with the company commander, who obviously would be situated with the guys directing the operation.

The rains were incessant. It was tough for all of us to be upbeat because of the weather. It seemed like we waited for eons for orders to move out. Each day was a mixture of contrasting emotions. I remember the excitement of waking up in the morning to the steady beat of rain off our canvas tents, usually at four. I could feel my heart beating strongly through my whole body—and then as the day wore on and we either drilled or cleaned, the weariness started to set in. *Tired, man … I'm tired of this shit.* From dinner on and closer to bedtime I could feel anxiety setting in—nervousness. And once again I could feel the beat of my heart through my fatigues getting stronger and stronger. *I want to jump through the tent and outta here. I can't stand it.*

"OUT OF BED … OUT OF BED!!!!! NOW!"

What the shit … what's happening? I jumped up and out of my cot in an instant to the screaming voice of the platoon sergeant's voice six inches from my skull.

Excitement was mounting. I could see the relief and giddiness in the faces and expressions of my tentmates. *Man … we're moving out!*

There was a frenzy of activity everywhere. You could not help but be swept up by the emotional aura around the camp. In every soldier's face I could see the same bright expression of excitement I felt within my own being.

I could feel the immensity of this operation. I could hear and see in the air more Hueys than I had ever seen together. We were up and out in one hour, dressed, and loaded with ammo and rations. Suddenly moments away from staging on the big field I realized I hadn't seen Turk. I wanted to at least make momentary eye contact, but it seemed futile with hundreds of grunts running in all directions and all looking the same, so I just said under my breath, "See ya, buddy."

I remember vividly my first reintroduction to consciousness. My whole body jerked. My eyes were very sensitive, and I could not keep them open. I felt a nagging pain deep within my back, and I couldn't sit up from my bed. *Where am I?*

Turk! I remember saying out loud once.

Above me, looking down, I could barely see a large man's face through my squinting eyes, and I heard something like, "Easy, soldier … You'll be OK …"

"What happened? My back hurts …"

"You're recovering from body trauma, son."

"I can't remember … What happened?"

And that's how it seemed for I don't know how long. I think I remember the same scene being repeated more than a few times and with a different face above me each time.

I was told first only that I was in the Third Field Hospital in Saigon. Then I was told I was not paralyzed but should not move too much. Then I was told I had suffered total body concussion that caused momentary and short paralysis, and that it was probably from a fall and a blast, and that I had one small bullet wound through the muscle of my left arm.

I remember vividly the moment I noticed a small calendar on the far wall of the room that housed me and a dozen other guys in beds. *October?*

Thinking back on this period I still am unsure how long it took me to catch up on time. I really could not remember much detail about anything. I asked nurses, aides, and doctors numerous times about Turk. *Where's Turk?* The answer was the same: "It's OK …"

I was a patient, and my usually active and inquisitive mind seemed to just narrow down to basic thoughts. My back hurt. I was hungry. I wanted to get up. I was not hungry. I didn't want to get up … and so on.

I seemed to have had moments when I connected to my life. The first one I can remember was the thought that Mom didn't know where I was or that I was injured. I was told by a wandering liaison sergeant that my parents knew I was in a hospital in Saigon and that I was recuperating. I remember having a really clear moment when I asked how long I had been in the hospital. I was told I had been there only two weeks. *October?*

I opened my eyes one morning and said out loud, "... June?" About a week later I realized I had lost a summer in my mind. During this same time, I was making good progress toward walking on my own. Yet obviously, I was not aware of how I was injured or where the time had gone.

Where's my personal stuff. Where's my personal stuff? Where is it? It was a revelation. I wanted my stuff. I knew I'd been writing. I knew I'd been keeping a log or diary of sorts, or at least notes.

A young, pretty nurse said to me, "Amos, we have your clothes and boots and helmet and other things in our locker area. What do you want?"

"I want what's in the deep pockets of my fatigues. I want a notebook." I felt so clear about this—the clearest moment in the three-plus weeks I had been there.

I saw what she was carrying from the distant part of the large ward where she entered. I could see that it was a small but thick notebook. I felt my heart pounding with excitement.

My notebook! I was momentarily extremely excited. And then, as I began to open the notebook, I felt trepidation ... almost fear. I realized then that this could have been witness to my missing four months. What a strange feeling. I felt as if I was opening up someone else's life—someone else's nightmare, someone else's trauma. My mind was immediately thrown back to my letter-reading days. I felt like I was in a surreal moment, one I could never have made up or planned on my own. As I sat up in bed with the notebook in my lap, my mind returned. I became Amos Boris Lardowitz all at once. I forgot I was in the hospital or in Vietnam. My life had become that notebook and what could be in there—a soldier's notebook, a soldier's life. Countless times I had read a soldier's personal horrors—but this was mine.

I could not skim the pages. I could not get beyond the first page at first. I could not look to the back of the book—and that was what the next two weeks were like.

I'm not sure why I did what I did. Maybe it related to my experiences with Ben and what I had learned about the Cosmos ... Maybe it was who I was anyway, with my almost obsessive attraction to the written word and war. At any rate, I would not go beyond reading anything that I could not relate to chronologically or that I could not believe happened to me. And I would not look at the last page until I had read and felt my life unfold in front of me.

I was lucky. My wardmates had varying levels of injury. We were all there because we had been in a firefight and gotten injured. I do not know why, but I could stand a distance from my trauma, emotional and otherwise, and bring it to myself in measured, safe doses of reality at a pace that ideally would keep me sane. Not Billy—he screamed in the night spontaneously. Billy had lost a leg and had a severely injured and bandaged hand.

15 Jul 65 0900 We scrambled—smell of bombs ... I saw the medic giving a guy an IV ... He was over a hundred yards away—all this happening and a small bird lands on my shoulder. What does he know?

And so it went over the next week. More than thirty small pages, written in tinier and tinier handwriting, probably because I'd thought I was going to run out of writing room and that would be a disaster.

I only really remembered the moment I'd said to myself, "See ya, buddy" when we headed out on June 23, 1965. That was the last reality for me. The readings after that I had to bring down from the Cosmos. I felt the moments, but it was in a sort of detached way—I was reading another soldier's letters.

I was told that I was getting out of the Third and would head to the Sixth Convalescent Hospital in Cam Ranh Bay soon for continued rehabilitation. Then it was hoped that I could get back to my unit, but I probably would not see combat, for I had suffered spinal trauma and the docs could not be sure I wouldn't get paralyzed again.

Billy's scream that night was monstrous. I felt bad for him, and the nurses never came in. He had many of these, but this one was big.

"Billy, man, listen to me," I said as I hovered over his bed within inches of his face. "Tell me ... describe what you see. It's not happening to you ... It's happening to someone else. You're above the pain, man ... You're looking down on it. Billy—listen to me ..."

He fell asleep. I had a fitful sleep that night, but I also had a surreal dream. It was of Ben in a white robe coming toward me and saying, "Kid ... Kid ... stream of consciousness surrounds you, Kid," and then he softly disappeared.

At about ten the next morning Billy yelled across the room to me, "Amos, come here."

He told me I had helped him. He told me he had seen himself as someone else and had followed that guy and lived his horror of bullets, bombs, and pain.

"Thanks, man," he said softly.

Ben's dream prompted me to do what I did right after he said that. I grabbed my notebook and ripped out a blank page at the back and said, "Billy, I don't care if it's in the middle of the night ... Write ... Write what's in your mind like it's someone else. Describe it—write whatever you can."

Billy screamed in the middle of the night a few nights later. I jumped up and saw him grab the pen and paper. He wrote, damn it—he wrote. I didn't let him know that I saw him write.

The next morning I saw him reading what he had written. He told me, "I had the weirdest sensation. I felt as if I could get beyond myself ... outside of myself. My pain was not my own, Amos. It really helped."

I felt a strange strength within me that day. My body was even stronger. Alice the day nurse told me I looked better than normal in every way.

Meanwhile I had my own demons. *Where's Turk?* No one wanted to talk to me about it.

I must have been especially nervous one day, for I got a visit from a captain, and I could see from his medal that he was a chaplain.

"Hi, Amos. How are you today?"

"Fine, sir."

"Can I be of help to you?"

"I don't know. I'm Jewish, sir."

"So am I."

"Are you here to make me kosher?" I said strangely without even thinking.

"I don't think so ... unless you want to."

"Do you know something that I don't?"

"No ... I don't think so."

And that's how it went. I felt kind of comforted by him. He told me he was a rabbi and that there were few Jewish chaplains in the army—and obviously not many Jews on the fighting field.

I was told that night that I was going to be transferred to the Sixth Convalescent soon. I became anxious, for I wanted to get up to speed on my life, so during all my waking solo time I dived into my journal. I was becoming aware of my summer in the field. There had been many days of boredom and a few days of combat missions. I started to remember things. The short notes triggered the real memories.

I was really becoming nervous, for I realized by the number of pages left and my notes that I must have written pretty close to my injury time and possibly that very day.

What had happened to Turk? No one wanted to tell me. At this point, though, I decided it was more important for me to discover my missing life and that through this I would find my buddy. I felt I needed to get up to speed before I left the hospital.

1 Oct 1965 2200 Finally another mission. It promises to be big. I feel hardened and purposed. I know no other life. Jenkins. Smith. Simpson. McCabe. They are gone. Taken away by the winds of war. I cannot imagine a life other than where I am. The world does not exist except for the commands of superiors. Turk is OK and I can still hear the birds. I guess that beyond our hell there is some sanctity, for these soft little beautiful things can still escape to green fields far away.

2 Oct 1965 0300 Whoa! Only time for a short scribble. This is it, man. I'm awake and dressed and momentarily waiting for Sgt. Vernon to scramble our asses outta here.

That was my last entry. Oh boy, I thought, I still had no feeling for what had happened. The only time left unaccounted for in my life were the days October 2–4, for I was admitted to the field hospital on the 5th.

Eagle base … this is Carrot Head … Eagle base … taking some fire … Not sure if I can stabilize … what the shit? Got to pull up, damn it … Hey, you guys … Brace yourselves, man—hold on to anything—shit!

I felt my body jerk violently as I awoke in a sweat. *Oh God, I'm falling.*

I screamed out loud, awakening Billy. "Amos—what's happening?" he yelled.

I remember! I remember what happened! That voice in my dream was our Huey pilot. Our chopper must have got hit. He couldn't stabilize. I was falling out the open door to the ground.

I could not remember more at that moment, and the next morning and into the next day I became increasingly despondent. I just lost any feelings that I had. Poor Billy, even with his own severe injuries, was very worried for me. I was not doing well.

It must have been about one week after my realization when an aide approached me and said, "Specialist Lardowitz, there is someone to see you in the rec room." I did not feel like myself and was even reluctant to go.

"Ammo … how are you, guy?"

"Oh my God … Army … Army …," I cried. I never had seen Army or heard from him in 'Nam to this point. I think that I must have collapsed, for I fell into his arms and just cried, and we stood there in an extended bear hug. It must have been quite a sight, for I was an enlisted man and he was a captain.

"Ammo, they tell me you're having a tough time remembering …"

"You came just for me … to see me?"

"Yeah, soldier, just for you and me … and the Four Horsemen."

"Where's Turk? Where's Turk, Army?" I was shaking all over.

"Ammo … Turk saved your life, man … He saved your life. He's being considered for a medal."

"What do you mean, medal?" I was so nervous.

"Honor … Ammo … honor."

"Oh God … Army—he's dead, isn't he? He's dead?"

"I'm sorry, my buddy … I'm sorry."

Oh Donny … oh Donny—my friend. Why? Why did we do this? Why? Why?

They delayed my transfer for about a week. I sobbed the whole time. I was just a well of releasing emotion with no thoughts at all. I had no memory of anything beyond my fall. I do remember hitting the ground and a loud noise and a sharp pain in my back—and that was it.

I numbed my being at this time. I could have had thoughts about home and Ben and Mom and Dad and my dear Sydney. But I had nothing but a deep sense of loss and grief. In a way, though, it was almost a satisfying feeling, for I was just one-pointed. I was mourning. I was not thinking of war and horror, just a release of my emotions, and they were deep and strong. In between spontaneous out-loud weeping, I felt a strange sense of peace. Maybe it was that Turk had become Donny to me again. Maybe I thought he was at peace finally. Maybe I felt that the only reality in life was the finality of death and the acceptance of its place in our insignificant lives. I had never lost anyone before. I remember fearing Mom's death, but it hadn't materialized. Those five days were purely my own, and I was responsible to no one but my inner emotional feelings.

But of course, there was more to this than Donny's spirit. Obviously, he died as Turk—as the warrior Turk. And frighteningly, I could not remember the probably horrific moment we must have had together. Army told me Turk had saved my life. We must have been together after my fall to the ground, yet he was not in my squad. He was always in another Huey. He was never with me. What was the circumstance? What had happened?

I would eventually need to know, but my emotions were not ready to find that place in my psyche where I witnessed one dear friend's life and possibly others' who were sacrificed in a micro-moment of eternity.

Army didn't spend much time with me when he told me about Turk. In his wisdom, he decided he would be the letter bearer, the telegram, the telephone call announcing the death of a soldier. And in all the wars that humankind has contributed to, it is the micro-moment of death and the micro-moment of notification of the loved ones who are left behind that their son, daughter, husband, or wife has died that is the essence. In the reality of death, the circumstances can remain unknown, for war itself is the cause of death, and it is futile for the living who are left behind to experience more than the shock of death itself.

I thought of Donny's mom and his sister, Patricia, and the moment of their notification. I felt a deep hopelessness in my heart at the thought.

In a separate reality, my reality, I could not accept Turk's death as it stood—a known fact in an unknown circumstance. After all, I was his buddy—he was mine.

Why is there no vision? Why can't I see? I felt as if I were a blind person feeling his way across a street he desperately wants to cross but can't.

And that was how it was when I left for the Sixth Convalescent Hospital in Cam Ranh Bay.

The Sixth Convalescent Hospital sat above a beautiful beach at Cam Ranh Bay right on the South China Sea. The water was warm and clear, and the sand was a pristine white. This was being developed for an R-and-R center: rest and relaxation or rest and rehabilitation. Eventually there would be room for about fifteen hundred soldiers. It was in its early stages at the time I arrived.

I guessed that everyone I saw would be broken in some way or another. I was broken in spirit as well as needing some physical time. If you lost an eye or a limb, or were disfigured or paralyzed, you wouldn't be here; you'd be on a large bird heading for an unforgiving place—our America, our home, a place that at this time could not separate the soldier from the war. Everyone else was waiting and looking at the sea coming ashore serenely yet purposefully, in undulating waves—waiting to heal, to return to the hell that had sent them here in the first place.

They wanted us to wear blue pajamas, maybe to feel like we were home on a long holiday weekend lounging around with friends and family, kind of doing nothing.

That was the image, but not the reality. The demons were within—within all of us in different degrees and for different reasons. I knew mine, and initially the guys I met must have known theirs—but we didn't know each other's.

I met a lot of people there. All the residents were guys. Some cried a lot and some laughed a lot. I met guys I would not normally have hung around with. But of course, we had a lot in common; someone had decided we needed to rest our minds or bodies or both.

Being who I was, I was attracted to the lame, the injured of mind and spirit. I had plenty of time to think in the first ten days or so. I actually was wondering why I seemed to feel everyone's pain and why I wanted to. It was here on this tiny spit of an oasis on an alluring white beach, facing the colorful and peaceful undulating waves of the South China Sea, that I realized finally that Amos Boris Lardowitz had no choice but to feel the pain of others. It seemed that empathy was what I had been looking for up to this point in my young life. I was twenty-five years old, and here I was in the middle of a war—a war I wanted to participate in—a war I needed to go to personally to feel the pain, the pain of the world—the pain of the soldier.

I didn't think of my own demons initially at the Sixth. I was spending a lot of time with guys who were mentally in tough shape. Once more, I became kind of their coach, helping them relieve or resolve nightmares that were raging or hidden within. I started to console a few guys with the words *stream of consciousness*. Feel it, get it out, I said. I encouraged them to see the words come out in a stream—a stream of consciousness. Write it, yell it, and say it. And deeper within my own psyche, I hoped this would get them in touch with the Cosmos. The all-knowing Cosmos, creativity and otherwise, that exists to share all life's experiences and is able to heal in mysterious ways—the Cosmos that could suddenly descend and make you understand the unforgiving world we live in.

One day while I was walking on the beach alone, I heard Nick from behind, yelling to get my attention, "Hey, Stream—Stream." I turned my head and we started to walk together. And that was the moment I became known as Stream to everyone there at the Sixth. Doctors and nurses called me Stream; orderlies and native Vietnamese called me Stream. I was Stream.

Stream could not help Ammo. Right then, I was blocked. My own consciousness had a pile-up, a freeway jam, an obstacle that prevented me from seeing my own vision—the vision I needed to move on in life, to become one again with myself.

The last peaceful snapshot of the Sixth in my mind's eye was the day everyone followed me down to the beach. I felt like a pied piper of sorts. There we were, many with paper in hand, writing and spouting words leading into words that awakened the sleeping inner demons and summoned them to the outside so they could "get the hell outta there."

I was due to leave for my unit in the field the next day. I wasn't going to be in combat as an airmobile, I was going to be support. My own demons never returned during this respite—they lay dormant. I still had no memory beyond my fall.

I was ready for transport and felt rested but uneasy on the day of departure. At the headquarters building were some guys coming in. I saw one guy look down on my insignia and say, "Screaming Eagles, One Hundred First, great, man ..." Then he looked up as if he were thinking and said, "Hey—were you involved with that fiasco, the village thing?"

I looked inquisitively at him but we had no more time. I turned and he was gone.

And that was that. But his words were the ones that began to unblock the jam. Maybe because it triggered thoughts in me—it triggered a return to my own need to unravel the mystery of my injury and Turk's death.

I returned to my unit more subdued in spirit, a quieter person. I saw changes in our company—we lost 15 percent to casualties: injuries and death. The commanders were the same, although my platoon leaders changed.

While getting a routine review by a company officer, he looked down at my transfer record and then up again and said, "Stream ... Stream. OK, Stream it is. Welcome back."

I was no longer Ammo. In my evaluation someone must have been enough impressed positively or negatively with my nickname to put it in my permanent record.

I believed I was transformed. I did not feel like a combat soldier anymore. Circumstances had taken my bravado away—circumstances that even I could not put my finger on. In my heart and mind I knew that only time stood in the way of the discovery of the missing moments in my life.

I spent the next few months in the relative safety of the camp, writing often to Mom, Ben and Zelda, and Sydney. I also wrote a letter to Donny's mom and Patricia. I told them I was going to visit them when I got home.

Consistent with who I was, I would not ask anyone about the incidents that had occurred at the time I was injured and Turk was killed in airmobile. I couldn't. All my life, my secrets were truly my own. And as with my question to Dad about his sister, I needed to find the answer.

Toward the end of my tour in Vietnam, approaching February '66, I got anxious. I knew that if I left this place without discovery, I would possibly leave the clues to a deep memory permanently buried in the Highlands of 'Nam.

I asked to be taken out on combat Cobra Huey missions just to accompany the guys deployed and to keep the pilot company, but I also wanted to get closer to my hidden memories. On the night of the second mission I was allowed to go on, I suddenly awoke in a startled sweat with a fuzzy picture of a combat firefight in my mind. I always kept my notebook at my bed, and I started to write.

I see sky above me and hear the deafening sounds of whomp whomp ... the blades of the Cobra ... I can hear small-arms fire ... I hear panic in voices around me ... I hear the horrible "medic ... medic" ... strained and scared voices crying for help ... Whose life is about to be taken? I am on my back and it hurts so much, but I try to turn my head to look where tracers are going ... The pain is so bad that I can't feel fear ... It has gone to others. A fuzzy scene almost like a serene impressionistic painting facing me ... beautiful faces ... childlike—then all is gone in what seems to be a magician's puff of smoke—gone ...

My writing hand was shaking after I finished. I had to hold it with my other hand for a few moments. I felt uncomfortable and incomplete.

I found myself taking long walks, especially in the quiet of the night. We were on a field base that was heavily guarded on the perimeter. It was hard to find a secure place where I could be alone.

I sneaked out one sleepless night. I used my stealth training to move unseen past a few sentries and into the dark, moonless fall landscape. I could not really see anything but black-on-black shadows. I felt strangely secure in this self-imposed loneliness. I knew in my deepest heart that I wanted to shock my inner demons to let the Cosmos descend and open them up.

I remember walking very slowly and looking straight ahead at virtually nothing when suddenly I felt energy in my body that seemed to vibrate. I felt weak and kind of woozy, and my knees started to buckle. At the same time, in the blackness of this place, I saw a bright light descend from above my head into my vision in front of me. I collapsed to the ground, my lower legs under my knees. There I sat with straight back, my legs under me, with the brightest of light almost causing a halo effect in front of me. And it was at this moment that I envisioned initially what I thought was a dream, but in a split second I knew was my reality: my missing moments, my missing life—my missing horrors. The Cosmos had descended.

Turk, Turk … you're here—help me … I can't move. I think I've been hit.

I'll save you, Ammo—I'll save you …

What's in front of us? … A village … people. Children—my God—what are they doing?

Oh, what a beautiful mother holding a beautiful child!—STOP! You're destroying the beauty of the world—STOP! Shit … man …

I heard a voice yelling, "Kill the suckers …" and then I heard another say, "Motherfucker—you're shooting at one of our guys. Man—you killed him—you killed him!"

More explosions and fire … and I remembered being lifted. It must have been a stretcher and into a duster, the medic evacuation copter.

Tears rolled down my face as I sat motionless, watching the bright light recede to the horizon in front of me until it seemed to be just a speck.

My God … why?

The worst things in war had happened to me. If I had died, the loss would have been to my family and friends. If I had been maimed and physically broken, I would have had to gather my inner strength to heal and repair myself. But those things did not happen. What happened was the ultimate thing that I would not have control over. We killed the innocent and beautiful. And specifically, to save my life, my buddy did the shooting. In turn, in the fog of war, he was killed by our guys, in what is called "friendly fire"—a disgusting euphemism, for there is nothing friendly about it. Turk had died in war. War had killed the spirit of life for me at that micro-moment. And I knew that this event must have taken place countless times, with many horrible variations, leaving the beautiful and innocent maimed and scarred for eternity. It would also leave the participants, the trained, with deep holes in their being for the rest of their life—holes that would not and could not be repaired by prayers or psychoanalysis.

I found out through my own discovery that only a few knew of this "village fiasco," as one guy had put it. The report was that Turk was a hero, charging the enemy and firing his automatic weapon until he dropped in a hail of enemy bullets.

In reality, this was the wrong place, the wrong camp. This was a quiet village of women and children, and Turk was dropped by weapons of his own comrades, his own buddies.

And worst of all, he thought he was saving my life.

I became someone other than myself after this realization. Maybe I was becoming myself, actually. Before this, I had been a soldier. I cherished my training and our deployment. I cherished the camaraderie of my buddies and my dear friend Turk in particular. I cherished the power of our mission and what I thought of as its purity. I cherished my country and what it stood for, and our purpose.

My life as a soldier was over as of the micro-moment of this discovery. I was still there. I was still in 'Nam. I was still with comrades and superiors and the frightening machines of war—but I was no longer a participant. I was alone in spirit. I was a lonely boy named Amos who longed for the days when I played baseball as a kid on the field next to the Bronx River Parkway—and I was angry.

I was two weeks away from the end of my tour in 'Nam. I felt isolated and dejected most of the time, and the rest of the time I had no feelings. I remember thinking of the word *redemption*. Initially I did not know why

I thought of that word, but I soon discovered that my total being was looking for a way out—redemption for the horror I had witnessed and redemption for the misdirected and misguided follies of those who wage war.

In those short weeks I started to find what redemption meant to me.

I was attracted to a guy who had witnessed his squadmate explode in pieces all over him. He seemed to be a walking ghost and was scheduled for R-and-R at the Sixth. For three days I stuck to him. And when he found out that I was nicknamed Stream, he told me that guys were talking about me.

I encouraged him to write his thoughts and fears. Initially he could not put pen to paper, but then he tried. He could not put a coherent sentence together. I told him to write a word that described his feelings ... then another word.

On the day that I left for Germany and then eventually the States, he was on his way to Cam Ranh Bay.

As I sat in the large and noisy troop transport, at thirty thousand feet and surrounded by other soldiers heading out, I felt a tiny sense of redemption. Maybe this shell-shocked young guy who was headed to the beaches along the South China Sea could experience a moment of peace—a moment when the Cosmos would descend and take a few of his demons away.

Home Again

BEFORE BEING SHIPPED back to the States, I had time during my short stay in Germany to reflect.

I kept thinking of Ben and the Cosmos. Ben truly helped me understand that the Cosmos housed all of humankind's creativity and that this creativity really belonged to no one individual, but to all. So any reference to creation cannot be claimed by anyone, even the most accomplished painter, novelist, and musician, for he just snared it out of the communal Cosmos anyway—it was not his to begin with.

I learned from my own letter-reading experience, and then from my most recent horrific life experience, that the Cosmos also housed *all* of life's experiences, creative, destructive, or otherwise. Humankind's suffering is universal and within all of us, I thought.

My attempt to escape my demons or face them was really an attempt to just throw them up to the universal experience of pain and suffering and horror and just hope that they would meld into the universal Cosmos.

I began to feel that we could bring the Cosmos down and it would heal or reveal or we could throw our horrors up and they would be shared with the universal suffering and be diluted.

My attempts at sharing this kind of ethereal concept with my buddies in Vietnam, who suffered so much, was to hope that their inner demons could be relieved. I felt the same deep sadness over the horrible losses of the innocent. Maybe, I thought, if we could release the horrors of the war experience, we could heal the souls of those we had destroyed by our actions as well.

These were the thoughts that consumed me and probably got me through this transition, and they probably kept me from becoming insane. I knew that I soon had to face the world I had come from and that it still existed at home.

I spent about a week in Germany. I was given a leave of two and a half weeks before my duty assignment in the States. I had not yet been given orders for my next post.

Obviously, away from Vietnam and the horrors of war I was beginning to feel more disconnected from the stark reality of the past. It was both a good and a bad thing, for to see normal life so abruptly was to flirt with the schizophrenia of this bizarre world that we live in.

I certainly felt excited about seeing Mom and Dad and the rest of my family. I couldn't wait to see Ben and Zelda. Zel was like a soft, beautiful dream in my mind. And I knew that during this time, I had to see Donny's mom and sister if I could. This was the hardest thing for me to face on coming home, for our whole connection would be complicated by the lies of war.

My God, I never realized until I got to Germany that there was an enormous buildup of troops and materiel. The war was really getting bigger.

In my zest to participate, I had never really noticed that from the beginning, there was resistance to this war. In my changed state, I began to notice the buzz.

Once more, I felt a momentary peace way up in the sky, looking down on the clouds and distant land and ocean on my flight to America. I know this was an aberration—for the beauty of our planet tries to hide the reality of its horrors.

"Oh, my Amie … my Amie … God in heaven … you're home …"

Mom saw me first as I walked down to the tarmac from our large transport. She ran to me and hugged me and wouldn't let go for many minutes. Her tears flowed down the shoulder of my uniform. I cried as well.

I almost felt as if I had just awakened from a deep coma because my senses had to renew what had been so familiar to me before I left on this adventure. I remember my initial thought at the smell of American air. I breathed deeply, probably in a futile attempt to cleanse myself of the experiences I had been through.

We drove to Susan and Alvin's for a coming-home party that day, a day that would prove to be among the most joyful of my life. I returned to my family. There were no agendas, no expectations—just the utter happiness at seeing me alive and well. And the children had changed so much in this seemingly short year. Syd was going to be eight. She was so pretty. And Morris and Clara were like little monkeys, all over me.

As we headed home to the "sububs," where I was going to stay during my leave, I felt like a little boy again. I thought of my Martin guitar. Mom had propped it up next to my bed as if I had just placed it there. The next few days were like bliss. I had two handmaidens all over me, Mom and Jemima.

I got my needed rest and left for the city to stay with Ben and Zelda for a number of days. I took my Martin, a few clothes, and my belly bloated with pancakes made by Mom and then pancakes made by Jemima, the two always competing for my affection.

I arrived in the city right smack in the middle of an anti-war demonstration. In fact, it was a large one of about thirty thousand people and included placards that said VETERANS AND RESERVISTS FOR PEACE. I really felt uncomfortable. I was in civilian clothes. I did not have to wear a uniform during my leave. What a strange feeling I had. I almost felt compelled to run straight into the center of the march. I had this weird excitement. I had the feeling that if someone had a mike, I would grab it out of their hand and protest war. I don't think I had ever had such a strong feeling of rebellion in my life. It was kind of a satisfying feeling. I knew then that it also reflected a deep need to cleanse myself.

What a sight Ben and Zelda were. My God, they were still the same people I had left. Initially I did not know why I thought they would change, but soon afterward, I realized I had gone through a horrendous transformation, and that maybe I expected to see change in others, especially the people who helped form who I had become.

Man, I loved my Manhattan. That part of me I had not lost; that part of me no war or tragedy could take away.

Ben and Zelda put me up for as many days as I wanted to stay. I wanted to see Ben's store. I wanted to smell the old manuscripts and the cigarette smoke wafting in and around. I wanted to hear the action on the street—the loud screech of the garbage trucks and the rude yelling of the cabbies impatient with traffic. I wanted to slyly sneak my peeks at Zel just to reinforce in the physical world what I had carried with me across the whole planet—and had held on to tightly in my imagined world. It was going to be sweet times at least for a few days. At night, it was off to

Manny's for some "needed libation and talk." I even sat in on a blues band and played some sweet licks on my Martin.

Ben and Zelda never talked to me about Vietnam during this short stay. They mostly led the conversation, and it was all about what was going on in Manhattan and the music and literary world.

After a great two days and nights, I got a call from Mom at Ben's apartment.

"Amie, honey … you just got a telegram today. You are going to San Francisco … the Presido or President or something like the Present … you have to report on the fourth."

What she was trying to say was the Presidio of San Francisco, a sprawling large army base that was a staging point for troops shipping out to 'Nam. God, I didn't have enough days left. I really wanted to at least spend one night with Donny's mom and sister.

Ben offered Rita, the car.

"Come on, Kid, take her. She's getting old but loves to travel …"

My plan was to spend my last night with Mom and Dad and the night before that with Donny's family.

Ben and Zelda and Manny and Fanny wanted to have a small get-together for me on the night before I was to leave.

I felt protected and comfortable with my friends. I knew they would be there for me forever. I remember the smiles and laughs and jokes. Manny was his usual cutup, and Zel and Fanny were their usual mischievous selves. And of course Ben was always aware and appropriate.

"Hey, guys … Jack is in town. He said he'd pop in," said Ben halfway through the evening.

"What's Kerouac up to?" replied Manny.

"I don't know … floatin' around somewhere," said Ben.

"OK … Jack baby …," said Ben as he eyed Jack Kerouac when he saw our table.

After the usual benign gender-bending verbal banter, Jack looked over to me and said, "What's up with you, Kid?"

"I'm on leave."

"From what—the world?" Jack said almost sarcastically.

"No. I'm in the army."

"Wow … really. Good for you, Kid. Those asses out on the street. Why don't they protest the garbage or something," Kerouac growled. "Hey, you goin' overseas?"

"Been there ... heading to San Francisco."

"Were you in Vietnam?"

"Yeah ...," I said almost apologetically.

"There you go ... Good for you ... a patriot ... a soldier. Hey, want to hitch a ride with me cross country?"

"I was going to take a transport in New Jersey."

"Hey, I'll get you there on time. I'm off to California, man—nothing better than to deliver a soldier to his post."

And that was that. With all my friends in agreement, Jack was going to meet me in Manhattan after my short trip to Donny's house, and we'd head off to California together.

I was dreading my trip to see Turk's family. In my mind, I alternated thinking of him as Turk and then Donny. I realized that he was both to me, and I felt that his spirit probably felt the same.

I called Mary and Patricia and was off very early in the morning, heading to Pennsylvania coal country and the town of Cokeburg. It would prove to be a long and arduous nine-hour, 365-mile hilly ride. I was really kind to Rita because she was kind to me.

I stopped for gas just before Cokeburg, where my eye caught a flyer on the building outside the general store. It said HARDY COUNTY FAIR, MOOREFIELD, WEST VIRGINIA. *Hardy? My God ... Hardy ... Moorefield? Something familiar ...* I ripped the flyer off and folded it neatly into my pants pocket.

I arrived in town toward dusk on this dreary March day. Turk's dad, Donald Koslowski, had come to this area to work in the mines and then enlisted in the infantry at the start of World War II. Cokeburg was a coal town and that was all of it. These towns were set up by the mining companies and were called patch towns. The homes were all uniform and often attached two-family units. It was not uplifting. Cokeburg had lost its mine in the fifties and pretty much had no direction. I knew that Patricia, who was three years older than Donny, worked as a beautician. She was married once and divorced, and had no children. Their mother, Mary, never remarried. She worked at the one general store as a part-time bookkeeper and counterperson.

From the outside, their house was pretty plain and small. It sat in the middle of a row of the same company-built houses.

I really felt trepidation as I walked up the steps and approached the door. I almost felt as if I was here to notify the family of the death of their son.

"Amos … poor boy … Amos. Donny really loved and trusted you," Mary said as she hugged me.

Mary was a slight, pale woman who seemed to have lost her spirit. Patricia seemed older than her years and somewhat caustic and sharp in her conversation.

The inside of the one-story home was simple. The Koslowskis were Catholic, and there were many crosses on the walls of the living room, some with Jesus attached. All the furniture seemed old and cheap except for one beautiful secretary desk that I noticed right away. I could tell it was a real American antique.

Mary had dinner ready the moment I came in. I think it was her attempt to initially avoid the painful questions about her son Donny's death. We had pretty small and benign conversation as we ate. I also knew I could not be anything but grateful for the sacrifice Turk had made to save my life, even though I knew there was no enemy and he was killed by his friends—and that my life did not need to be saved.

"What good is a medal of honor when war takes away your loved ones?" Mary finally said as we drank tea.

"Oh, Mother … we fight to protect our freedom … our way of life—the American way," said Patricia almost scoldingly.

At this point I could see the difference between the two. Mary was a mother and a wife who had lost both of her men. She could only see the losses produced by war and the emptiness left—the emptiness that rejects the nurturing spirit. Patricia, on the other hand, solved her unhappiness by accepting the fate of humankind and the perceived good of her country. She saw no gray—only black and white, good and evil.

Mary kept the conversation about her son, Donny, to more endearing memories. We sat around quietly for the next hour, and suddenly Mary turned her head toward the beautiful desk and said, "Amos … I keep all of the world's good and bad memories in here. This desk was the only thing I have ever received from the material world. It was my grandmother's. It has such history. It is the only thing I own of value, and I keep the memories locked up here to be softened by time." Then she opened the center drawer and pulled out a key. "This beautiful key to the lock on top is in the center drawer."

She said this as she looked straight into my eyes—she seemed to have such beautiful and sad eyes.

Only fifteen minutes later Mary said, "Amos, we are going to sleep. If you like, you can sit up until you want to retire. Good night, son."

After Mary closed her bedroom door, I immediately felt a silence I had never felt before. It was so quiet. There was no noise outside and none inside. I felt as if I were in a cocoon or some sort of inner space. In the dim light, my eyes drifted to the beautiful secretary desk. In my heart I knew Mary had meant for me to open her memories. By the look in her eyes I knew she had given me permission to take the beautiful old key and unlock the top.

I opened the center drawer and unlocked the secretary desk. There was a well-worn soft leather desktop and neatly laid-out cubbyholes and small drawers with the most beautiful carved wooden scrollwork. There must have been a few dozen old photos in one large cubby. There were neatly bundled letters in another. I could see now what Mary had meant; she had sneaked away her memories to a safe place—away from harm and away from her emotional pain. But there were bad memories here also—equally hidden and also away from Mary's emotion.

It seemed to happen almost like the experience I had had most recently in 'Nam, during my dark and lone walk. I felt this darkness and quietness, and my eyes seemed to have a fuzzy tunnel vision. My right hand spontaneously reached for the farthest cubby, and I pulled out what appeared to be a medal and what looked like a folded old telegram. Just above my head, at the same moment, I began to notice a bright white light. It began to encompass me in warmth. I opened the telegram at the same time I was caressing the round, raised medal.

I'm not even sure if I really read the telegram at first. I think I received the message from the Cosmos, for I started to fall to my knees and hear the voice reading. It was Mary's voice as I sat crunched and low to the ground.

Oh, no … no … God … no. My Don … you're dead … What is this? The Young Turks … My Don is not a Turk, he's not Turk …

I felt myself becoming a child. Sobs all around me—a heavy, deep pain—a feeling of deep loss. Tears … small baby tears running down my cheeks. I felt myself holding on to Mary's leg as I sobbed … and she sobbed.

My God, I had become Donny! Three-year-old Donny, sitting on the floor and holding on to his mother's leg as she cried.

Minutes later I could feel the light recede in front of me toward an unreal horizon—and then it was gone.

From this moment, at the early age of three, Donny was imprinted. He was imprinted with the death of his dad and the deep emotional loss of his mother—and it was such a profound life experience that it came to me because I was open to it right from the Cosmos. I became Donny—just like I became myself again to find my lost moments, and just like I became Vincent Van Gogh at the moment of his creativity.

Apparently Donny's dad was in a combat squad that nicknamed themselves the Young Turks after a movement during the late 1800s in Turkey. Initially the Young Turks were a progressive and forward-thinking group of people, but later they would be accused of participation in the Armenian genocide.

I sat in the dark for the next two hours fingering the medal Mary had received for her husband's bravery. I must have dozed off, for I awoke suddenly to the sound of a truck passing on the street in the very early morning.

I felt drained but peaceful as Mary made breakfast for the three of us. I was leaving shortly to go home. I had been able to stay only this one night. What I had experienced I could not have predicted. Patricia really wanted me to see the town's honor roll of dead soldiers before I left. Donny's dad was listed with his medal, and that was where Donny's name would be also, she said proudly. Mary turned her head away from us as Patricia told me about it. We had a momentary tearful good-bye.

I stood silent for several minutes in the foggy early morning in front of this small monument of stone with a bronze placard of names. Revolutionary War. Civil War. World War I. World War II. Korean War. Beneath each war was listed the names of the dead. The grass beneath was dead, and if there had been flowers, they were gone. There was no flagpole, but a small plastic American flag was stuck into the ground alongside. Bicycle ruts crisscrossed close to the monument, and I could see chips of stone gouged out—probably from kids careening into it on their way to having fun. I stood there looking at it for a few minutes and then closed my eyes. I could still see it with my eyes closed—vividly, I thought. That is what I wanted—and then I left.

My nine-hour return trip was filled with spontaneous, uncontrollable tears flowing down my face, drying almost immediately from the wind of the road. I had the top down, and it was a freeing feeling—a feeling of cleansing.

Kerouac and Lardowitz On the Road

April 1, 1966 Friday 9:30 A.M. Somewhere outside East Stroudsburg, Pennsylvania

"Ole smelly New Jersey, we really miss your stank … don't you shower or somethin' …," sang Jack as he held the wheel with just one hand and kind of hung his other out the window. We were about three hours into our trip across America to deliver me to my duty station and him to … I wasn't sure where yet, but I was sure to find out.

"Does all of New Jersey smell like that, Jack?" I asked, respecting the fact that he was umpteen years older than me and maybe should know this.

"I dunno—and I don't care. I prefer to picture New Jersey as a smelly place because then I can cruise into Manhattan and feel like, man, I'm in the Garden of Eden—get what I mean?" I nodded kind of to say yes and also opened my window and hung my arm out. I was feeling good right then. Here I was with Jack Kerouac … the Jack Kerouac … the *On the Road* Jack Kerouac—and we were on the road.

We were going 823.3 miles and it would take us twelve hours and fourteen minutes. That's what Jack had told me would be the total time it would take us to get to Chicago, where we'd stay our first night with a friend on the South Side. Then it was off to Route 66 all the way to Santa

Monica and then up the coast for a breezy and great final ride to San Fran and my drop-off.

Jack was driving a '57 Chevy Bel Air Sport Coupe. It had two doors and no divider between the front seat and the back seat. "I love this car, Amos—Georgiana's old enough for me to afford and pretty enough for me to love. And man, you want to open those windows and feel the air comin' in around and through you. And man, the best of all is when you ride with your friends ... They have to get into the backseat through the front ... kind of personal ... It reduces everyone to humble contorted critters bending and folding in the most ridiculous positions ... but once they're in, man, you just want to go forever, for you owe nobody ... You answer to nobody but freedom."

I knew what he meant. Taking Rita for a ride was like going out on a date with myself, I thought. I was starting to feel really comfortable with Jack and realized why. He would always say what he was thinking and his mind was filled with thoughts. And when he didn't have anyone to talk it to, he'd write. He was profoundly and verbally prolific. On the other hand, I had tons of thoughts also, but my persona was to dwell on them in intricate ways while they floated around in my psyche, often never coming out.

"O beautiful for spacious skies, for amber waves of grain ...

America ... America ... God shed His grace on thee ...," sang Jack spontaneously an hour later. He had a soft, low singing voice, but he was really in tune. I was beginning to relax on the beginning of this trip as we sped at 70 mph toward Chicago. "Chicago ... great city ... bootleg city, man ..." said Jack.

April 2, 1966 Saturday 8:33 A.M. Just outside Chicago, Illinois, on the beginning of Route 66

"Oh, thank God we're outta here. These people were so boring. But it's so good to have ersatz relatives to stay with. Man, you need something to sleep on other than a crab-infested couch or floor with nails and a cat-piss smell—don't you think so, Amos?" said Jack as we finally got on to Route 66.

"Yeah, Jack," I said in agreement.

"Man ... Route 66. America's highway ... and man, it's all the way to California and the coast. I can feel the surf. We're going to drive Georgiana right into the ocean and bathe till the smell comes off."

"Yeah, Jack," I said.

"What's that rattling in the trunk, Jack?" I said about two hours later into our trip.

"I got a Thunderbird in the back and a Chevy in front, man."

"What do you mean?"

"You'll see when we stop, soldier. Hey, you see the beautiful flowers on this trip?"

"What flowers?"

"See, man ... you got to notice the rare beauties before they get their heads cut off and they're off to the netherland."

"Where are they?"

"Lookee ... lookee along the divider there. Quckly ... see the little sweet blue flowers? Oh, look ... the tire ruts ran one over," said Jack with a half smile.

"Yeah, poor things," I said and then proceeded to burst out laughing for no reason at all, as did Jack. I'm not sure if it was Jack or just the kind of free-spirited trip we were on that was starting to make me giddy—and giddy I needed, for my mind had certainly been in overdrive during the last few months.

"Trapped by glass, their faces speed by," Jack said and then looked over to me as he drove. "Your turn, my boy."

He meant for me to improvise some spontaneous short prose. "Surrounded by Georgiana's warmth, they munched peanuts," I said.

Laughing, Jack said, "She caressed their aching bottoms."

"The sun, shining, asks for a ride," I said.

"The moon asks for a divorce."

"Baby clouds frolic over the mountaintop."

"Thunder scares the magnificent eagle."

"God looks down: this is not my planet."

"The planet looks up: this is not my God."

"The road, a painting unfinished."

"Run over several times, the chicken looks for another job," Jack said, and then burst into a hearty guffaw.

Jack continued, "Man—don't you see why the road is great? You can observe everyone by just getting an overlook of their life without getting involved. But make no mistake, there exists behind all those closed doors and tight little towns and big cities the pimps and derelicts, the doctors and lawyers, the teachers and the snot-nosed little kids who want to be like their older brother or father or some other half-successful half man. And then there is the finer sex. Man, it would be a travesty if there were no finer sex. What would you have to live for? Everybody has got to have a woman. And if you don't have a woman, you need a car or boat or fishing rod that you can name Giselle or Freda or Georgiana."

"Yeah, Jack." Here he was—not able to write, but writing in his head. I was thinking how opposite we were, but really the same. The same crap floated around in my head, around and around. But if I had talked like this to Mom or Dad, they'd have sent me to a shrink.

"Hey, Amos, you were drafted?"

"No, I enlisted."

"Unbelievable … You're a good kid … fighting the commies …"

"Yeah, I guess so."

Jack suddenly changed the subject and said, "Hey, we're going to stop in one of my favorite places: Carthage, Missouri, at the Blue Moon Cottages. They're dirt cheap, but private and nice. Amos, that's what's great about America. Look at where we've been and where we are. Illinois, Chicago … urban and big … steel buildings and steel people. Suddenly we're in Missouri. Man, the name even sounds like another country. Slow and drawly like you stuffed your face with cotton balls and tried to make a coherent conversation."

"Yeah, Jack."

The next 450 miles were like a breeze. We didn't eat much at all. At the gas stops we'd pick up bags of goodies, snacks. Popcorn was our favorite. It was fun eating popcorn with the windows open, letting the errant balls fly out the window in a kind of mad swirl, only to be crushed under the wheels of the twelve-wheeler behind us.

We pulled into the small rural town of Carthage about seven thirty in the evening. Most of these small towns had one coffee shop or truck rest stop where they made some hot food. So at our overnight stops Jack said we'd eat enough to lose only a little weight.

Jack opened the trunk and pulled out a large bottle that looked like wine. He said, "Thunderbird, where you been, my friend? Amos, meet Thunderbird, my friend and backseat companion—always there to sweeten the night." And he took the biggest swig I had ever seen from a bottle—almost like he'd been in the desert for years and this was the first water he'd drunk the whole time.

Well, Jack was buzzed. I could hear it in his speech, and I could see it in his walk. He was the same guy but loaded with the dumbing effects of cheap alcohol. Oh well, I thought, it's the same guy—just a little tipsy.

"OK, soldier," said Jack as we both sat on the steps of the small cottage after dinner about ten o'clock. "My job is to get you to your base so that you can protect our country. That's my job. Protector of the protectors—that's me."

He was drunk but kind of sweet and blabbing at the mouth even more than usual. I had this urge to drink with him. I'd been drunk before, of course—all American boys get drunk—but I had never really gone on an extended binge, the one I expected to see from this moment with Jack right up until we jumped into the Pacific Ocean. And boy, I could have used an extended drunk, so I said, "Give me a swig, Jack."

"No, soldier—soldiers can't drink. How can you protect our country if you're drunk?"

"What do you mean? How can I protect my country if I'm *not* drunk, Jack?" And Jack burst out laughing in kind of a flood of hee-haws, like I was tickling him and he was begging me to stop, but the more he cried the more I tickled. And as we sat on the steps close to each other, his laughter made me laugh more, and before you knew it we couldn't stop. In the middle of all this he passed the bottle to me, and I took a swig and passed it back to him, and he took a swig, and so it went until we both just sat there looking up to the sky. I remember seeing more stars than I had ever seen in my life in the sky—but I think many of them were the same star just moving around in my fuzzy head that night.

"Where's your uniform, Amos?"

"In my rucksack."

"How come you're not wearing it?"

"I'm on leave, Jack. I don't need to wear it."

"Yes you do. You're protecting our country."

"Oh shit, Jack, you're drunk and so am I."

"I'm taking out your uniform and putting it on you."

"No you aren't."

Jack proceeded to run to the trunk of the car, pull open my rucksack, and take out my uniform. I ran over to him and we both started to pull at it. Before I knew it we were tugging at it like we were on opposite sides of a tug-of-war—but man, with my uniform. He was yelling and I was yelling, and from the next cottage over was more yelling: "Cut that crap out, you jerks."

We both fell to the ground, exhausted. "Look at my uniform, Jack. It's a mess. What the hell." And we both rolled over onto our backs and stared quietly up into the night sky. Just before I fell into a deep sleep I heard him say, "Sorry, man."

April 3, 1966 Sunday 6:30 A.M. Carthage, Missouri

Oh boy—my head felt like a basketball after an overtime game. We had to get up early every day to make the trip on time. And one thing Jack was good at was getting up early. I lay in bed and rubbed my eyes and tried to get into focus what I thought was a strange dream. Jack was on the other bed straightening out my uniform, brushing it and cleaning the metal insignias with a cloth. "What are you doin', Jack?" I said in a semi-sleep.

"I'm getting it ready for you to wear."

"What do you mean, getting it ready?"

"To wear today in Elk City, man."

"What's Elk City and why do I have to wear my uniform?"

"Elk City, Oklahoma ... my favorite diner and the most patriotic people you'll ever meet."

"Who cares?"

"I care," Jack said as he continued to clean my uniform. "We're stopping for the greatest hamburgers in the country. And if Flo is there, the hamburgers are going to be even better," he said, saliva dripping from his lip.

"Who am I to argue with you—you almost tore my uniform in half. I'm afraid of what you'd do if I refused you. But let me tell you, Jack ... that's the last place I wear my uniform until I get to my duty station—deal?"

"Deal."

And we were off. Jack said Elk City was about 350 miles away. We'd arrive for a great late lunch that would satisfy our stomachs for the day.

"Hey, Amos, did you see where we just came through?" Jack said, awaking me from my early morning nap on the road.

"No, Jack."

"Dorothy country."

"What's Dorothy country?"

"The Wizard of Oz, man. Kansas. Tornado country."

"Oh yeah."

"Man. I was in love with that Dorothy chick when I saw that film."

"In love with her?" I said incongruously.

"Yeah. I was seventeen in 1939. Don't ask me why—maybe because she was so innocent and could sing so well."

"I wasn't even born yet," I mumbled.

I couldn't believe I was doing this on the road—but I was. I changed into my uniform about fifty miles from Elk City. Boy, I thought, Jack looked so pleased, almost like he was a proud dad or something.

"Hey, boys ... well, well. Jack," said the brown-eyed beauty as she looked down on us sitting in a booth.

"Flo ... Flo ...," said Jack.

"And who do we have here?" said Flo, looking at me.

"Flo, meet Specialist Amos."

"Hi, soldier."

"Flo's dad, uncle, and brother are all army men," Jack said kind of proudly.

And that's how it went for the largest and juiciest hamburger I had ever seen or eaten. I needed four napkins tucked into every crease of my upper chest to prevent my uniform from melting away into one gigantic grease ball.

"Can I change now?" I said a few miles out of Elk City.

"No. Not until we pass through Amarillo."

"Amarillo?"

"Yeah, Amarillo, Texas. Texas, man, the home of the real patriots. Texas—where the Alamo is."

At this point I was feeling strange. Here I was, a real Americana buff rejecting all this patriotic shit, and here Jack was—a beatnik, I thought. My God—he was purported to have invented the word. Was this a role reversal or something?

Jack said we were going to lay over in Santa Rosa, New Mexico, on our next stop. We'd arrive about nine or ten.

I wanted to drink that night. I wanted to swig Thunderbird with Jack. I even wanted to keep up with him. Once more, sitting on the stoop of our cottage—Jack liked cottages—he said it was like his home away from home, a little house all alone so that he could do anything he wanted to. We started to talk. I was drunk and Jack was drunk.

"Jack … I didn't know you respected the military like you do," I said awkwardly.

"I don't think most people know who I am," Jack said. He put his arm over my shoulder and continued, "This stuff is bullshit. By the time you get all the stuff out of you and on to paper and after many crappy years of rejection and searching, suddenly someone decides that what you did was important and the world wants to know you and own you and label you and screw you and make you reproduce your genius again. It's all bullshit. Man, I'm just trying to keep up with myself." There was a moment of quiet, and I was thinking of saying something, although I wasn't sure what, when Jack continued, "Amos, I'm a born Catholic. I tried to be a Buddhist. I'm a football player. I was in the Merchant Marine. But most of all I'm a writer. I chronicle life, man. It's just the life ordinary people live. There's a lot of underbelly in this capitalistic country, but the forces that be want to box it and place it up for sale and make movies out of it and big-selling books. Hey, I'm not like Ginsberg. He's a radical man. He'll demonstrate against anything in society that he feels is inequitable. I'm a chronicler. I live. I tell stories, real stories, about people doing things—many times not pretty things—but not everyone is successful in life. Not everyone can grow up and get a law degree and have a successful business and a house with picket fences and kids with smart grades."

We sat quietly after he finished this discourse. I remember thinking that his stories were just people talking and thinking out loud and being themselves. I remembered the start of our trip and the free and open feeling I got from Jack being on the road. Yeah, I thought, maybe the hungry world is just looking for the next "One," as Ben would put it, only to chew up a creative guy who doesn't know how to handle fame or the world's scrutiny or adoration.

In those quiet moments I also thought about myself and my life. In my own impressionable way my life grew by absorbing Jack Kerouac's spontaneous prose lifestyle. Through him and Ben, I learned to cope with life by exploring the stream of consciousness. And here I was, sitting with Jack Kerouac—the somewhat tortured Kerouac—who seemed to not cope with who he was and his own genius.

Jack seemed to continue his stream after the few moments of quiet. "You know, man, I remember back in '59 I was really sought after because of *On the Road*, and I was invited to the Steve Allen TV show. What a setup, man. Here was Steve, suit and tie, in a lounge, playing on the piano what he thought would go with the 'Beat generation' and asking me these contrived questions about myself and the 'generation'—like I really wrote the book on this, know what I mean? Like there really was an organization with regular meetings." And at this point Jack produced a hearty laugh.

"Jack, I saw that program. He also asked you what the word *Beat* meant. I remember you said it meant 'sympathetic.' I didn't understand then, and I don't now. It's described that Beat means 'down and out' or like 'offbeat.'"

"Hey, there you go. Yeah, he called me the embodiment of the Beat generation, and yet nobody knows what the hell it means. Sympathetic, man—like understanding someone's feelings—empathy and compassion. Maybe it just means ordinary people sharing their lives together and opening up to each other."

"Yeah," I said introspectively. And it was that simple, I thought. If only we could all express ourselves simply and honestly. But then I thought that life could be really cruel, something I had realized in 'Nam. Many poor souls can't handle the horrors of the world. Many poor souls can't handle the expectations and daily demands of the normal world either. Maybe Jack was one of them. Why had I been so lucky so far? It seemed that I was kind of deflecting the demons from myself for the moment. Who knows, I thought, maybe I too would succumb to the craziness of this world.

April 4, 1966 Monday 7:10 A.M. Leaving Santa Rosa, New Mexico

"OK, passengers. All aboard for the final days before we arrive on the beaches of Santa Monica—teeming with the riffraff looking for quarters dropped by the pretties in their pink two-piece eye poppers—and eyed by muscle-bound muscle heads who couldn't spell their mother's maiden name—and broken-hearted anorexic lads with bottled-up dreams hoping that the mighty California sunset will bless upon them the true art of acting …"

Wow, it felt so good to hear Jack just be himself without introspection and my probing questions. We were off. "Long day today, Amos. We're going to lay over in the Joshua Tree desert about eight hundred miles from here. Then the next morning a christening dip in the Pacific and straight up to Big Sur … man, my Shangri La. And I deliver you in one piece with uniform the next morning, soldier."

"Yes, Jack."

Jack let me drive about half the time from here on—what a feeling. I don't think there could be a better young man's ritual than to drive, windows open, in a Chevy coupe through the vast and open scenery that is America out here. Vast desert colored by the impressionists of old and the sun, dotted by the monuments of nature. No thoughts could be evil out here. This drive time would prove to be cleansing for me, and I think for Jack also.

There really was nothing around but the infrequent gas station with a smattering of goodies for us to munch on and the occasional Native American selling pottery and trinkets by the road. I tried to keep my thoughts about the culture of the "Indians" out of my mind. Certainly I was brought up on the cowboy-and-Indian mentality, but I momentarily dismissed my misgivings about the anachronism that I knew was my America.

Stupefied by our long and almost surreal drive we arrived at Joshua Tree National Park well after ten. It was dark, but there was a pastel glow to the sky and you could see the Joshua cactuses silhouetted like sculptures on the horizon. "Where we staying?" I asked Jack.

"Right here, my boy … right here," he said with a sweeping gesture toward the seemingly empty place.

"Right here?"

"Yep, laid out on nature's pad to soak up the energy of the land."

And laid out we would be. Jack picked what he said was the oldest and wisest Joshua tree. He looked up at it and said, "Beneath your majestic body we lie, to receive the blessings of the world. Scrape the crusts of ignorance from our souls and let us awaken with new spirit and life."

"What was that?" I said.

"I dunno—I made it up," Jack said with a shrug.

We lay down on a bed made up of all the clothes we wore on the trip except my uniform, our heads abutting the base of the cactus. Jack pulled a marijuana joint out of his pocket and lit it. He offered me a puff. I sucked it in while looking up to the sky, which seemed to still have a soft, almost sunsetlike glow. And back and forth we went: a drag for Jack and a drag for me—until the weed just burned itself out and Jack flicked it away. I watched the ember fly through the air and tumble a few inches and die out—silence, of noise, of thought, and even of who I was.

April 5, 1966 Tuesday 6:30 A.M. On Route 66, 30 miles outside Santa Monica

The California sunrise at our backs warming the car, cruising comfortably, I felt a kid's excitement in my blood. Jack had sufficiently built up the goal of jumping into the Pacific so that I couldn't wait to do it.

"Three blocks from the ocean, man. I'm goin' to hit the brakes at the curb along the beach road, and we're goin' to race to the surf. It's a race, man ... First one in gets an ice cream sundae at Pearl's diner above Malibu." We both bolted forward as Jack careened Georgiana into the curb. He suddenly jumped out of the car, screaming gibberish and leaving the doors open. He had an unexpected edge on me as I followed suit, leaving my door wide open. Jack flailed his arms widely, and we both stumbled into the morning surf. "Shit—it's ice cold," I yelled.

"What did you expect, soldier?" yelled Jack above the crashing surf. We sprayed ocean surf on each other for the next few minutes, and then we both started laughing hysterically, soaking wet at the edge of the beach. We started to walk toward the car, and I noticed a police car adjacent to Georgiana and a cop standing outside writing a ticket. "What's up, officer?" Jack said as we walked, soaking, to the car.

"Illegal parking, sir," he said without a crack in his voice or an expression on his face. "New Yorker, huh?" he then said, me not sure if he meant it as a slur or something else.

"No, sir ... Actually I'm from the great state of Massachusetts," Jack said to him. "And I'm delivering Specialist Amos to his duty station at the Presidio of San Francisco."

"In the service, young man?" he said, looking at me.

"Yes sir, army."

"Well ... I guess on account of your duty to our country, I'll let you guys have your fun for now," he said as if he were my fourth-grade teacher Mrs. Krause.

"Thank you, my good man," said Jack.

"Kerouac, you're a wimp," I said, looking at the cop pulling away.

"No, my boy ... I'm actually a pimp. I'm a pimp dressed up in a chameleon's suit so I could be whatever I want to be—be it a salesman, a professor, a drug addict, or a laborer. All so I can get into the cracks and crevices of society and stir up the activity we call human ... and all for a story woven together as a chronicle of human folly." Pretty hefty stuff, I thought, for a simple excuse not to get a ticket from a cop.

Off again, up Pacific Coast Highway 1, hugging the beaches and adjacent rolling hills, we cruised toward Frisco.

What a beautiful trip it was from here on. We could see the surf hitting the beaches at almost every turn, and if we couldn't see it, we could hear it crash to the shore. The weather was gorgeous, and the sun played peekaboo with us on every twist and turn. Jack and I were quiet for hours—but this quiet was true serenity. I remember thinking that both of us needed this extended moment of peace away from the world, moving through its beauty at our pace and with no obstacles.

"We're close, Amos. Your last stop before your duty, soldier, will be my most favorite place in the world." Jack slowed the car as if looking for a place to turn. He then made a sharp left into what I thought was a clump of trees and brush. It was amazing, because they just seemed to part and give Georgiana enough room to pass through. It was like a magic trick, for they closed right behind us, like a secret passage in a fantasy castle. There we were, driving over what appeared to be only a bumpy path surrounded by trees scraping their leaves across the car. It felt as if we were passing through a dense jungle. The bumpy road twisted in many directions as Jack slowed Georgiana almost to a crawl—and suddenly without notice the scene opened to the beach strewn with large boulders and rocks, and the surf crashing its many shades of blue mightily onto the shore.

"Holy moly, Jack ... it's beautiful."

"My place, man—my place. My thinking pad."

I felt as if we were in a 3D picture inside a child's book of fantasy places. It was complete in all directions. Nothing seemed out of place. It was all a neatly arranged and flowing beauty, complete with the natural sounds of the world.

"Big Sur's little hideout. That's what I call it," said Jack wistfully.

And there we just sat on the beach, looking at each wave hit the shore. We watched the sun dip itself into the ocean's horizon and the afterglow it produced. We continued to sit quietly for another fifteen minutes or so as the features of this beautiful place became dimmer.

"OK, soldier … back to the real world."

At this point I really felt that I was being protected—protected by Jack. I now understood that he wanted to deliver me intact to where I needed to go because I was a soldier and protecting my country. With all of Jack's complex narrative floating around in his head, he needed to be simple and single-minded also—and to be just an American with American values.

"I got a spot outside of Frisco where we can lay over as road vagabonds and watch the glorious Golden Gate awaken and stretch her bones till she stands tall in the morning sun. Then we can watch the salesmen and laborers rumble across her painful belly without even knowing who she really is—till nighttime, when her loneliness sets in."

And there we went—a cool and half-hidden spot that gave us a picture-book view of the Golden Gate Bridge. We slept in the car that night, snoozing intermittently to the various sounds of the bridge road produced by the trucks and cars passing.

April 6, 1966 Wednesday at the break of dawn, overlooking the Golden Gate Bridge

"Wake up, you sleepyheads … I ain't goin' to shine on you if you ain't got nothin' to do my lovelies …," Jack woke me up with his singing. "OK, soldier … fun is over. I promised delivery, and I produce delivery. Man, it's the one decent thing I can do in life right about now."

"Yes, Jack." We were both preparing for the end of our free-spirited ride across country. It was fun for me, and it lifted at least momentarily the burdens I had recently been carrying.

At the curb and adjacent to the Presidio army base Jack said, "I'm giving you my new address in St. Petersburg, Florida, Amos. I don't know when I'm going back, but you can reach me. Also, here's Ginsberg's number … He's in Frisco."

"Thanks for everything," I said sincerely to Jack as I left the car with my guitar and rucksack and other bags. I remember my wave as I disappeared into the mass of people dressed in army fatigues and uniforms. As I turned away from the car, I could still see Jack in my mind's eye, sitting at the curb in Georgiana, waiting until I was completely gone.

Allen, Amos, and Janis

I reported to the duty station listed on my papers. It was in one of the buildings on the Presidio.

"Amos Boris Lardowitz, Specialist First Class, Active U.S. Army reporting for duty, sir."

"Welcome, Lardowitz," said the desk sergeant. "I see that you recently came back from a tour of Vietnam. Welcome to San Francisco and the Presidio. Oh boy, I see you are to serve under Captain Awfull. Lardowitz, you may want to opt for another tour to 'Nam—and I'll deny that I ever said that, by the way."

"Yes, sir."

Well, I learned the same thing on the same day from another guy of equal rank to mine who was working under the command of Captain Awfull— that his name was an accurate description of who he was. I was told that he did the first sit-down meeting with all his new charges and treated everyone like it was a dress down—namely he had nothing nice to say to you and made you feel like shit.

I met a private named Joey who was going to work with me. "He's got a nameplate on his desk as large as they could possibly make. It says Orinn B. Awfull, Captain, USAR. It's a going thing with that nameplate as to who can come up with a new way to humiliate him."

"I don't understand."

"Like you have to sneak into his office and tape new letters or words to the plate. You know ... Orinn *is* Awfull ... or Orinn *is* Awfully *smelly* ... or Orinn *is* Awfully *stupid* ... Get it?"

"Yeah."

"And one thing—the new guy's got to do it."

Oh, great, I thought. I really needed this in my life. "But what happens when he finds it?" I said.

"He goes into a tirade."

"I see where you have come from, soldier. But make no bones about it, Jewish boy—this is hell too," said Captain Awfull, sitting at his desk opposite me.

He was a short muscular man with a round head and closely cropped hair with a prominent bald spot on the top. He had a somewhat bulbous nose and a very thin pencil moustache typical of the thirties. His ears were kind of crunched like he may have been a boxer, and the left seemed to be leaning to the right and the right seemed to be leaning to the left. Not one feature on his face matched another. He looked like the potato-head toys I used to play with when I was younger—the ones you tried to make the funniest features with.

"Yes, sir," I said as I tried to catch glimpses of his nameplate when he momentarily took his eyes off of me.

Orinn the Awfull ... Orinn, you are Awfully ugly ... Boring B. Awfull.

They just kept going through my head as I tried to listen to his lecture about the importance of counting bolts that fit onto the desks that were to be shipped over to 'Nam.

"Polish them, sir? Did you say polish them?"

"I say what I mean. Do not ever ask me a second time what I said, soldier," he said with an angry growl.

"Yes, sir." Oh, what an asshole, I thought.

My duty station at the Presidio also housed the Letterman Army Hospital. This hospital had received wounded from World War II and the Korean War as well. And now it was a receiving center and inpatient and outpatient treatment center for the injured from 'Nam. In my walk from the barracks to my duty post I would pass through the courtyards of the hospital. I immediately became affected by the sights of the walking and wheelchaired wounded that I passed. It brought me back to my own injury and the injuries of my comrades. And here I was, I thought, trudging to the mundane and useless job that some moron decided to order me to do just because he had rank over me. What a useless waste of personnel and a gross lack of compassion for the people who gave their lives to their country.

I seemed to have only one thought in the first week of my new duty, and that was how I could top any of the other guys' maceration of Awfull's name. It kept me going and at least momentarily kept my mind off the inequities and immoralities to which I had been a witness.

I wanted to do something completely different, but I was having a hard time figuring out what to do. Then on a morning walk about ten days into my job, it came to me. It would be great if I could change the nametag he was wearing on his uniform to something absurd, and there he would be, facing others as the hilarious buffoon he was. Changing his nametag, I fantasized, would be like climbing to the top of the evil mountain where the evil dragon from hell lived and stealing the amulet that hung around his neck that gave him his powers—while he slept, no less.

I could do this, I began to think. I could do this. I would need to know when he changed uniforms. I already knew where he lived. He lived in the senior officer quarters by himself. Of course no one would live with an evil dragon, I thought. I already knew where the dry cleaners were on base. Additionally, I knew that once weekly a hired maid cleaned each officer's apartment. I could make up a new nametag. All I needed to do was find the store that handled these things. And this nametag would not be just glued or Scotch-taped letters on paper. This would be the real thing—embossed, like a brand, right into his forehead for all to see.

I also needed to see if he dressed in civvies so that I could sneak into his apartment and replace his tag with the new one when he was away.

Everything would have to work out perfectly and be timed just right. It was worth it, I thought. I felt that if I could pull this off, it would be retribution for his ignorance and possibly the ignorance and insensitivity of countless others in the military—I was a warrior once more.

Initially I thought I would have to jimmy my way into his apartment through a window. But then I decided the easiest thing would be to sneak the new tags in when the maid did her cleaning. I realized that I needed to change all his nametags and replace each one with a new one. Of course, I couldn't change the one he was wearing, but I figured it was only a matter of time before he changed his uniform for a newly pressed one. I also thought I needed to change his name so that he really wouldn't notice it. It would be sort of an illusion, especially if I kept the letters and spacing about the same. And then, it would be great to see how long it took for the first person to notice and then for him to notice. Boy, was I having fun with this devious plan!

I Am Awfull ... Oh, I Am Awfull ... and variations would go on in my head when I closed my eyes and hit the bed. It really should be close to his real nameplate, Orinn B. Awfull. I needed him to not see the change, for it would immediately stop the trick dead in its tracks. So I decided to work on just his first name since "B. Awfull" was bad enough and it could appear to be the same tag. After three days of nothing but word games in my head I came upon *Urine* as the word of choice. It had three of his first name's letters and had the same number of letters. Even though it would not make a sentence, it would be a real shocker.

I was getting bolder and bolder, for I thought I wanted him to have his new nametag for the base commander's inspection of our unit, which was coming up in three weeks. The inspection was in honor of a new regional three-star general. It was like school, for there would be spit and polish and everything cleaned up like it had never been before—and only to impress someone higher up in rank.

Getting the tags made up was easy. The store that made them was owned by the same Chinese American who ran the cleaners. The guy who handled the order was a young Chinese man who didn't even look at the name closely. I made it my business to walk past the officers' quarters on the day the maid cleaned. The officers never stayed in their apartments on that day. I walked up to the maid and told her Captain Awfull wanted something from his apartment and had asked me to get it for him. I scoped out the place and saw how many tags I needed and where his uniforms were. I knew I was going to pull this off. I also realized he would wear a newly pressed uniform for the inspection.

I decided to time the change to be as close to the inspection as possible. He would be wearing a newly pressed uniform, and his whole unit of thirty men would be there, including me.

Fortunately the inspection for our unit was on a Monday and the maid would be cleaning the Friday before. Generally the officers in these units took the weekends off and often wore civvies then. I decided to pull the final switch on the Friday before. The only thing that would break the plan would be if he noticed the change. But I was counting on his lack of curiosity and his attention to doing everything exactly the same way and with no imagination. I really felt that he wouldn't even notice the difference.

Five new nametags in hand, I headed toward the officers' quad on cleaning day. Consuela, one of the base's maids, seemed to have as much affection for young soldiers as I did, so it was a breeze to just walk in to Awfull's apartment and sidle toward his bedroom and begin my dirty deed.

Consuela was cleaning the living room, head immersed in the vacuum cleaner, while I was in the bedroom quickly doing the switch. I changed all the tags to the three uniforms hanging up in the closet and placed the two additional on the bureau. Done. I could do no more, I thought.

Well, "D Day" came. Colonel Stark, Captain Awfull's superior, walked into the large open supply room with Captain Awfull. He looked around and smiled at the roughly thirty of Awfull's underlings, including myself, spiffily dressed up in the army's finest dress uniforms.

"Men, I'm proud to bring General Sutton to this unit," he said almost at the moment three men entered behind him. One was General Sutton, a real general-looking general, I thought. He was accompanied by two neatly dressed, handsome younger captains—his attachés.

The big five initially stood in kind of a semicircle, shaking hands. Then Captain Awfull, walking two steps behind General Sutton, introduced all his men as if he really liked us. This whole scene took about ten minutes and was well planned time-wise since the general had to repeat this probably twenty times the same day.

We all stood in an "at ease" stance facing the officers as General Sutton looking at Captain Awfull's chest and apparently at his nametag, for he said in kind of a Texas drawl, "Good crew, YOUR ... INE." My God, I thought; he's actually reading Awfull's name from his nametag and doesn't know how to pronounce it. Instead of saying URINE, he drawled a kind of variation—YOUR ... INE—as if in an attempt to make sense out of what he read.

I could feel the hidden chuckles of my fellow enlisted guys as the scene seemed to unfold slowly and painfully.

I swear to this day that I saw a sly smile appear on Colonel Stark's face through this ordeal. I'm really not sure, but I think General Sutton caught Colonel Stark's momentary joy, because he looked down once more at Captain Awfull's chest and said very clearly, facing all of us, "Good crew, URINE ... good crew," and walked out.

I could not believe what I had heard. The general had actually called Awfull "Urine."

The proverbial pin could have dropped as Colonel Stark looked at us and Awfull and said, "Thanks, men ... Good job. Let's go, Captain," and escorted the captain out.

Unbelievable ... unbelievable. It could not have gone better. There we stood, the bunch of us, laughing and guffawing. Guys were saying they had seen the look on the colonel's face and that he really must have enjoyed it. And we all swore that General Sutton had to be the coolest general in the army, for he had picked up on the stunt. We also all decided that Colonel Stark was praising us and probably protecting us when he said "Good job," which would probably save our lives from the evil Captain Awfull.

Obviously the talk of the unit was who could have done this unique and dangerous deed. I was told when I arrived that when the nameplate on his desk was changed, nobody would fess up. It was kind of a club, I was told—a secret club—and it was an honor to collectively stay quiet. But the talk was incessant about how brazen this had been, and how innovative.

Captain Awfull never said a word about it. I was also told that this was absolutely the first time he didn't take the unit to task. The talk of the unit was that it was a masterpiece of skulduggery.

Lying in bed on my back late that night, arms behind my head, I felt a real satisfaction, something I hadn't felt in a while. I realized I needed to rebel against the powers that were. I realized then that I was hurt myself and disappointed by the world and also especially by my own America—my America—the country I adored.

What amazed me about myself was that I seemed to be emboldened, and because of this I didn't even think of the consequences of my actions.

Was this the new Amos Boris Lardowitz? I thought. I peacefully dozed off.

My boring, useless job took me through the hospital quad. I continued to be emotionally affected by the broken spirits I passed. I could not help but stop each time and talk to one of the guys, at least to give them some encouragement. I realized I was returning to the person I had become in 'Nam. I really felt a deep spiritual satisfaction in giving back to the injured of mind and body.

One warm, early May morning the sweet smell of lilacs floated through the air. I was walking through the hospital area when I heard a voice behind me saying, "Hey, Amos—hey, guy!" I turned my head and saw a guy sitting in a wheelchair. My God, it was Billy! He was the kid next to me in the field hospital before I went to Cam Ranh Bay.

"Billy. How are you, man?"

"OK, Amos ... Hey, Stream—you're Stream, man!" he said as his eyes lit up.

He called me Stream. But I had gotten that nickname after I left Billy and went to the Sixth Convalescent.

"Stream?" I said.

"Yeah, man … You're a legend, man. What are you doing here?"

"My duty station in the States."

"Yeah … mine also," he said with what I thought was sarcasm. He was paralyzed.

"Hey, Stream … I want you to meet some of my buddies. They need you, man," he said with a sincere smile.

Oh boy, I thought; my rep had followed me. In my attempt to share the pain and suffering we all had to go through, I had become a "legend" to guys who had been injured.

This moment was a small epiphany for me—a way out or a way in, so to speak, of my inner being. I'd been spiraling downward emotionally and needed an uplift.

"Hey, Stream … get together with a few of my roommates. They've all got their own transportation, man." He was of course referring to their wheelchair status.

I told Billy I would meet with "the guys" the next time I had a day off.

On the following Sunday five guys, including Billy and me, met in a corner of the quad where the guys would wheel themselves out. What a shame, I initially thought. They were so hungry for any interaction that would uplift their psyches. They seemed so neglected, and tortured with the dreams of the past—their war experience. They all had different injuries but common paralysis. They wanted me to "Stream them" like Billy told them I had done with him—encouraging their consciousness to explore whichever way it wanted to go.

"Let your mind go … Float above yourself. You can experience anything you want to. Talk it out. If you can't say it, then write it. Just connect any words you can think of to describe anything you want to feel and let it go, man … let it go." And on it went.

Billy said these guys had no animation in them before I sat down with them. They smiled and laughed and in some instances cried. Individually they had witnessed horrors beyond description. At least one of them had witnessed "fragging," which was becoming more and more prevalent. Fragging, which referred to the use of a grenade or fragmentation device, was the expression used for enlisted men killing their own platoon leader officer in the field—their own guy, deliberately, so as not to go into a hopeless dead-end where they could easily get killed. This war seemed already to make no sense, and the buildups were yet to come.

I felt a real satisfaction in sharing my life with these guys. We had all been through hell and back, and it seemed that the only ones who cared were the buddies who had been to 'Nam and experienced the same hell. There was a void. Very few people who hadn't experienced war wanted to know us.

My base life in the States over the next few months got into a kind of groove. I really enjoyed my free time with the guys, most of them seriously injured in 'Nam and all of them with no place to turn for help. The army had not provided any support for any of us after our tours. Billy was in for the near long term since he had a real pain issue and paralysis. He would bring new guys to our meetings all the time. It reached a point where from a distance I could see this wheelchair caravan approaching me—new faces with notebooks and pens in their laps—and I hadn't even met them yet!

My only off-base excursions were to a safe enlisted bar in a working-class area of San Francisco where army personnel were welcomed. Anti-war fervor was pretty active in the area, and Haight-Ashbury, the developing hippie enclave, was becoming a breeding ground for discontent.

Sometime in June, a really nice month in the Bay Area, I found Billy parked in his favorite spot with the most dejected look on his face.

"What's up, man?" I asked.

"My army is shipping me out."

"What do you mean?"

"Getting rid of me ... rid of me—like in discharge. I was told there is no more room here. They don't have enough doctors or anything here to help me."

Billy came from Iowa. He was going to be a lifer, he'd once told me. But not only did they not want him in uniform anymore, but they wanted to subcontract his care. He knew that in going home he would have a hell of a time getting care through the veterans service since there were few options where his family was.

Once more I felt as if we were being let down. This war was snowballing into territory that sucked up every decent American. That night I dreamt I was being chased by a tornado that got larger and larger, and I was only a half step in front of it. As I ran, alongside of me were a small girl and a dog running with me. I heard her yelling something to me, but I couldn't hear her because of the enormous sound of the tornado.

"What did you say?" I yelled.

"Which way is it to Kansas?" she yelled back.

"Kansas?"

"Yes … Kansas … Toto and I want to go home."

And then I awakened in a major sweat. *Kansas?* What's in Kansas? I thought—just as Mom would ask. Then I realized that Jack and I had gone through Kansas and he had made it a point to tell me about it. Thinking of Jack, I began to think of Ben and Zelda. I felt that I needed to touch base with someone I trusted and knew. Suddenly I realized that Jack had given me the telephone number of Allen Ginsberg, who lived in San Francisco. I liked Ginsberg, and I think he liked me. I decided I would call him the next day after hours.

There I stood, enclosed in one of the base's public telephone booths just for us enlisted men.

"Hello, this is Amos Lardowitz. Is Allen Ginsberg there?"

"Yeah, man … hold on."

"Ginsberg here."

"Hello, Allen, this is Amos … Amos Lardowitz … you rememb— …"

"Hey … Amos, my boy. Where are you?"

"Here in San Francisco."

"I just got back from a trip to Kansas. You're lucky to get me."

"Kansas? I just thought of you because of a dream I had about Kansas."

"You on anything, Amos? … By the way, what you doin' here?"

"I'm in the army, Allen, did you know? Stationed at the Presidio."

"Hey, you want me to spring you? Great—I got it. We could scale the walls. But first we'll call the local news … no, the national news services. Hey, I got it. We'll scale the walls with naked young girls. You know how many girls in the Haight would get naked in a minute? … Actually for any reason, my boy, but for this cause we could get hundreds. We'll get you out. You'll be a cause celebre." I could see the headlines: POETS AND JUNKIES AND NAKED YOUNG GIRLS FREE SOLDIER TRAPPED IN TOWER.

I could not help but burst out laughing as I listened. I felt immediate and comforting relief over my previous angst.

"Hey, Amos … what are you doing tomorrow night? We got a group of us at my place. I'm having a reading of my new work that I wrote driving through Kansas. Hey … bring your uniform and we'll burn it after the reading."

"Come on, Allen …"

"Only kidding."

"I'd love to come."

I got directions to Allen's Fell Street apartment. I wasn't supposed to be off base that night, but I had a very strong vibration pulling me off. I felt strongly compelled to go. So off I went, kind of surreptitiously, kind of not, by multiple buses.

Knocking on the door, I felt almost the same way I had when I was waiting to enter Baba's Olatunji's apartment—excited and nervous at the same time.

There were more than ten people in the apartment. Man, it reeked from weed. But so be it—coming from 'Nam, anything went—and everybody smoked if they could.

Allen saw me and with a great smile gave me a hug. He was smoking a joint and thrust it toward me with a friendly hand. I hesitated for a moment and then took a toke. I felt comfortable from then on.

"Hey, Neal … come meet Amos," yelled Allen across the room.

"Neal Cassady," he said as he extended his hand to mine.

"Hi … Amos Lardowitz. Jack Kerouac was just talking about you."

"Where is the sucker?"

"We drove out to the coast together from New York a few months back."

"What? Is he writing about you?"

"No … I don't think so."

"Amos, Neal is the character Dean Moriarty in *On the Road*."

"Come on, Ginsberg, give me a break," scowled Neal.

Neal was a rough-and-tumble guy with chiseled tough features who was a good friend of Allen and had an abrasive relationship with Jack.

"Amos," Allen said, extending his hand to one corner of the room, "here's the peyote and weed corner. It's OK for you to try those." Moving his hand to a small bedroom he said, "Over there is the LSD den. Don't be brave, my boy. Stay out if you want to stay in the armed services." Then he chuckled and his mouth opened in a wide grin and he belly-laughed out loud.

I smiled but said nothing. Allen's apartment was like a messy college student's. Dirty dishes were everywhere except in the small sink where they should have been. There were doughnuts, and there was cold coffee and some very hard and I guessed very old pizza. Everyone was in some sort of intellectual conversation that seemed to be like a contest or something. There were two women and the rest were men. I was pretty comfortable just observing. Neal engaged me a couple of times with what Allen said was his "convict tough guy talk." Allen whispered to me to just say "Yeah, man" after every couple of sentences.

About an hour into the evening Allen stood up on a chair and said, "Come with me to the Vortex, my friends. Come with me to the Wichita Vortex."

Everyone stopped talking, and they all sat down on the floor in front of Allen in a lotus position (I didn't know what it was then) as if they were ready for a meditation.

Allen began reading from a manuscript. As he read, he would emphasize words and sentences with a broad sweep of his left hand.

Napalm and black clouds emerging in newsprint
Flesh soft as a Kansas girl's
ripped open by metal explosion
three five zero zero
on the other side of the planet
caught in barbed wire, fire ball
bullet shock, bayonet electricity
bomb blast terrific in skull and belly, shrapneled throbbing meat

While this American nation argues war:
conflicting language language
proliferating in airwaves
filling the farmhouse ear, filling
the City Manager's head in his oaken office
the professor's head in his bed at midnight
the pupil's head at the movies
blonde haired, his heart throbbing with desire
for the girlish image bodied on the screen:
or smoking cigarettes
and watching Captain Kangaroo
that fabled damned of nations
prophecy come true ...

I sat, at first dumbfounded, and numb, but then gradually I felt my skin start to crawl from my feet up with tiny pricks, like there were tiny little spiders biting and crawling, biting and crawling up every inch of my skin. I felt my face start to get flushed—and I had a strange feeling that everyone was looking at me. Then I felt wetness on my cheeks and realized that tears were flowing uncontrollably down my face in a continuous and relentless stream. I began to shake, and in my head I thought there was an earthquake. Silently I screamed, "Get out! Get to free ground! Out! Save yourself!!" Then a sudden numbness again pervaded my whole being. I felt as if I was no longer in my own body. I was sitting behind myself and looking at my own back—and then the being in front of me just seemed to get smaller and smaller. I thought I was moving away in front of myself—but then I realized I was moving backward. I floated away and through the open window behind me. The air felt cool and comforting. I heard birds singing. I looked up and there were clouds amid a dull blue sky. I felt myself enveloped by these clouds, and they just picked me up and carried me away until I felt as if I was no longer part of the earth. I then felt nothing.

"Amos … Amos … you OK, man? You OK?"

I must have returned to earth with the touch of Allen's hand on my shoulder as I sat on the floor.

"Oh boy …" is all I said.

As I was leaving to catch the last bus back to the base, Allen put his hand on my shoulder, as he did when I was on the floor, and said, "Amos, I want to take a walk with you at Golden Gate Park for a few hours—during the day. Can you get off?"

"Yes, Allen," I said softly. "I'll call you."

I slept that night without any dreams. My psyche was spent. About midday I started to think about the evening before. I knew I needed to understand what had taken place with me before I saw Allen again. But I really wanted to see him as soon as possible.

I let the thoughts come on their own as I performed my boring duties. My whole consciousness had met its individual parts like an atom being bombarded by multiple electrons from every direction—and then a big bang and a bright light—and awareness.

My whole life I had been fascinated by my America and war. I could not help but feel the excitement and fear of the soldier through his own handwriting. The curiosity of being carried me to far places within

America, out of America, and within my own mind. I then lived the childhood fantasy I had always wanted to experience firsthand. I became every soldier. I became the war. I became the fear and pain—and seemed to be able to experience every other person's pain as well. I didn't need to read the letters anymore—I was every person writing his horrors.

All of my experiences have come without drugs. In fact, they have just come to me—as my awareness came to me in 'Nam, as well as at Donny's home, all from the Cosmos.

I think what happened as Allen Ginsberg was reading his poem was that the conflicts inside of me over my country and myself just exploded into a clear picture of who I was and where I was going. I flew out the window—my old life was over. I wanted to fly within the clouds and with the birds and among all the natural things. I had experienced Allen's abrupt and horrific descriptions for myself and wanted no more of this—no more. I wanted to be free. I wanted to free myself of the contradictions that were my country and the contradictions that were myself—I wanted out. I truly was emboldened—emboldened to trust myself when I saw inequity. Be myself, I thought. Be myself.

I arranged to meet Allen on Sunday morning at the entrance to Golden Gate Park. I felt cleansed and open to new experiences.

As soon as I saw Allen, I thought he looked very soft and caring. And he continued to be that way throughout our morning walk in the beautiful, soft sunny light.

"Amos ... I know you. I know who you are. You were a teenager when I met you with Ben. Ben Fink is the keeper of the Cosmos. He is my inspiration as much as yours. He knows all and doesn't have to experience anything. He separates the bullshit from the real. He thinks you are a shining light—a light up in the Cosmos that will never dim and will eventually point the way for others."

We continued walking, our steps almost in unison with Allen's speaking cadence.

"Amos, I'm a provocateur. My whole life has consisted of shaking up society. I revel in shocking the powers that be. I also love my country. If my country will change because of me, it will be because I stuck my tongue out when the president of the United States offered me his hand—or possibly maybe pulled my pants down and exposed myself." We both spontaneously laughed out loud. He continued, "Amos, you're more subtle. You search and explore and analyze and make sure you are righteous in your thoughts and deeds. You can't change yourself. You're on a path of self-discovery just as I am. Our paths will cross, but we never will merge. But the important thing is that I learn from my brazenness and my confrontational attitude—and I also learn from the already learned. I have been around the world. I have smoked and taken every drug known to exist. I embrace all faiths and religions, and I challenge all authority. But I also learn from those that are basically good. Amos, you are a basically good human being. And if I leave this earth knowing one good person, I'm fine."

We sat down on a bench overlooking the bay.

"Allen, I am so conflicted sometimes. I then doubt myself."

"Amos, it's OK for you to explore. You will never stray from the reality that is you. You live within deep conflicts that you work out eventually. But only good comes of it. Be you, man—whoever you are at the moment."

I knew I would continue to have conflicts and doubts. I knew I would continue to search for who I was through the mystery of my family. But I think I understood Ginsberg.

"Hey, man," Allen said, breaking the somber talk. "Hey ... You need to hear some music. Can you break away Saturday night and meet some musicians?"

"I'll certainly try."

I felt energized Monday morning. I felt as if I was on my own mission—a clear one. I finished my boring duties deliberately early so that I could spend time with my wheelchair buddies. I also wanted to see Billy as much as possible since he was leaving soon. I felt that I could do no better good in the army than to help my war buddies through their horrors. Our country owed it to them—and I was fortunate enough to be able to share myself with them.

I knew that people in my unit knew what I was doing. I also knew that Captain Awfull would eventually get wind of it. But my recent experience and talk with Allen Ginsberg had transformed me. I trusted my disobedience, whatever the consequence, for I felt that it was the right thing to do.

I met Allen at his place and we headed by bus to the Avalon Ballroom, where Allen told me we'd see a concert by his friend Janis Joplin and her new band, Big Brother and the Holding Company. We got a great seat at the front of the stage and watched this young woman and band belt out heavy blues-based rock and roll. I had smoked a joint with Allen just before and was really stoned. I intensely enjoyed the music.

After the concert, Allen signaled me to walk backstage, and we walked right into Janis Joplin filled with sweat.

"Hey, my Beat poet and premiere anti-war hero—Allen Ginsberg," said Janis.

"Hey, girl. You are the coolest chick this side of Austin."

"Who's your sidekick?" Janis said, looking at me.

"Amos, my New York friend."

"Hey, Amos, you like the concert?"

"It's my favorite music," I said, meaning it. I felt her raw and honest energy.

"Cool. Hey, Ginsberg, come on over to where we're staying and party with us … OK?"

"Yes, my love."

We landed in an apartment in the Haight area filled with the band members, roadies, and friends. There was liquor and dope. It was a relaxed scene, and I didn't feel that anyone was abusing anything. I was surprised at how comfortable I was. In the middle of the night, sitting on the floor and sharing a joint with one of the band members, I started to feel as if I had become a different person. I almost had a mini–panic attack when I realized I was still in the army. I began to think that this was the start of a temporary dual life. The panic left me fast when I realized how much I was enjoying myself. Looking over at Janis, I was thinking that I really liked her. She seemed very sincere.

What a free-spirited time I had in the Haight-Ashbury area that night. As well as feeling my own spirit soar I had landed right in the middle of an emotional revolution. People by the hundreds and then thousands were converging on this area of San Francisco to experience the birth of the hippie movement. They were nearly all young people disenfranchised from something: family, society, friends. The revolt against the Vietnam War was growing larger and became a catalyst for this brewing monumental movement.

My duty time was filled with the mundane, but I took more and more risks to be with the injured soldiers I was meeting through Billy. I wasn't sure why I was not being brought to task by my superiors, especially Captain Awfull, but I really didn't care, and maybe that's why I wasn't bothered. Maybe I had become untouchable or something—and it suited me fine.

In the papers, I could see that Janis and her band were playing many dates during June and July 1966. I went to Allen's place for a number of his poetry readings during that time.

It was a cool Sunday afternoon at the end of June when Allen invited me for a walk in Golden Gate. I caught a bus to his place and was pleasantly surprised to see Janis there. She told Allen she had needed a break from the heavy schedule. We were all going to take the walk, but Allen got a call from someone and begged out at the last moment and suggested that the two of us go it alone. I shyly smiled and agreed, and Janis coolly approved.

Janis had a naturally warm, personal way about her, although her stage presence infused her with energy that gave her a bigger-than-life persona. She was really easy to talk to.

"Janis, you have a feel for the blues like you've lived them."

"With all the heavy rock and roll, you still feel the blues in my songs, Amos?"

"I've had a lifelong fascination with the blues. There's something about its roots that make it authentic to living."

"You know, Amos, I was brought up in rural Texas, and man, you'd have to be stupid not to see the suffering we've caused our black neighbors. I don't think I've suffered, though."

"Neither have I … Jewish boy from the Bronx," I said, kind of trailing off the last few words.

"What did you say?" Janis turned to me and said.

"Never mind … but I feel the same way. I think I've been searching my whole life for some connection to the America I want to exist in my head and the America that really is."

"Blues baby … Blues."

"Yeah …," I said with a smile. "Yeah … there is no other music that is played with the same musical progression all the time. There's no change … It's just the emotion that's changed … the expression of suffering … the throwback to the slaves' chants in the fields."

"You'd better believe, baby. You're right on, Amos."

Janis and I shared something that didn't need explaining. We came from very different upbringings but had similar feelings about life. Once more, on this walk, I had a fleeting thought about my family and its history and my search for something I could not yet put my finger on.

A couple of Saturdays later, Allen invited me over. He told me Janis had the only free Saturday night she would have in a month and would love to spend it with Allen and me.

Allen had gotten pizza and spaghetti from a local restaurant. We were drinking, although not heavily, and Allen went to the kitchen cupboard and took out two sugar cubes. He handed one to Janis and said, "Here, I owe you some acid."

"What's that, Allen?" I said.

"The feared aliens—who will take over America and make people so happy they won't want to fight wars and take over other countries and oil fields."

"What?"

"LSD, man. I told you. Stay away or the army will lock you up so that you don't give it to anyone else."

"OK, I want some," I said brazenly, buzzed by Southern Comfort.

"What do you say, my female friend from Texas? Do I give the soldier some acid?"

"Hey … far be it from me to pass judgment. If he wants it, give it to him."

The next thing I remember is that we were all lying on our backs with my head on Janis's stomach and her head on Allen's and his head on his cat Petunia's body. I felt as if we were all up in the sky just floating around. I heard Allen say, "America … America" as he waved his hand in a broad sweep.

America when will we end the human war?
Go fuck yourself with your atom bomb
I don't feel good don't bother me
I won't write my poem till I'm in my right mind
America when will you be angelic?
When will you take off your clothes?
When will you look at yourself through the grave?

I felt my whole being spin slowly. I felt as if the three of us were lying on a large relief map of the country. I could see from the periphery of my eyes every border of every state and that every state was a completely different color. Colorful clouds above us came down and almost touched our faces in a sweet tease. I felt as if I my body was touching every mountain and valley and tree and flower, and that my toes were bathing in every brook and stream and river of our country. As I lay there, I heard a soft refrain. It seemed to come from a distance and then become louder.

O beautiful for spacious skies,
For amber waves of grain,
For purple mountain majesties
Above the fruited plain!
America! America!
God shed his grace on thee,
And crown thy good with brotherhood
From sea to shining sea! ...

It was so beautiful and sweet, and the voice was clear and loving ... and I realized that it was Janis singing. And then I heard distant drumbeats that seemed to get closer and closer. I wasn't sure where they were coming from, because they seemed to be all around me. I heard myself scream out loud, "Incoming—incoming—scramble—cover ..." I felt rain on my face, and the clouds became gray as I squinted to try to see. Above me I saw a smiling face with a voluminous beard, and I remember saying, "God ... it's you ..." The face looked down on me and said, "I wish," and I opened my eyes and rubbed them like a child as I felt an arm lift me up and through the gray clouds into the blue stratosphere above, where I could see the bright sun and feel its warm rays on and within my body.

"It's cool, Amos ... it's cool," the voice of God said to me, and then I felt really comfortable. The voice of God continued, "I'm not sure if I should create woman or a zebra next ... What do you think, Amos?" I opened my eyes and there I was, face-to-face with a laughing Allen Ginsberg and a smiling Janis Joplin. I started laughing, and Janis started to laugh, and Allen laughed even louder until I could see tears roll down both their cheeks and feel tears roll down mine.

Allen, Janis, and I were bonded permanently and forever after that moment.

Lysergic acid diethylamide became a part of me. I had never been attracted to drugs, and my whole life of curiosity and discovery had been a pure inner quest. But now I was morphing—though in reality I was only changing directions in my life. My physical being was in the army, but my mental and spiritual being was on the streets of Haight-Ashbury—the streets of spiritual revolution, the streets that attracted those who were possibly only unsure of themselves and needed to experience an opening of their psyche.

At any rate, I had landed.

The three of us spent as much time together as possible. Allen was involved with many things—poetry, music, and his anti-war life. Janis was a growing legend pulled on by the thousands. Allen and I would attend her concerts, and many times I would focus only on the people looking at her. The young girls seemed to be mesmerized. I could actually hear their thoughts of admiration and almost envy—of really only wanting to be able to express themselves and relieve their suffering by wailing out loud straight up to the heavens just like Janis. These were white middle-class young girls wanting to express the suffering within them as if they were black slaves in the fields wanting to sing the trials of the lives. I realized that within all us humans there is universal suffering that needs to be relieved—opened and let go, recognized and accepted by the relentlessly oppressive world.

Even though our lives were pulling on all of us, Allen, Janis, and I tried to get together at Allen's apartment once weekly. There we would sit, in yoga position, facing each other in a circle. We dropped acid—and then we all became one, a unity of three.

I remember the first night we did this. Looking at Janis and Allen I felt as if we were beings of the same mind. Allen said just one word or short expression and expected me to follow and then Janis.

"Sweetly born"

"Of hope"

"The child"

"Carries"

"The world's"

"Weight"

"Growing"

"Shrinking"

"Laughing"

"Crying"

"Until the weight"

"Of the mind"

"Closes"

"The door"

It was simple, and each word or expression became a three-dimensional and psychedelic figure that seemed to attach itself to the previous and the next and then dance around our heads in front of us. I believe that for this moment of eternity we shared the thoughts of one mind.

I remember how we "streamed" our consciousness together.

"The river flows"
"from the pure mountaintop"
"to the valley below"
"Expecting sweetness"
"and kindness"
"Unexpectedly flowing"
"through factory walls"
"returning abused and tainted"
"with poisons of corporate greed"
"As the child bathes"
"the mother drinks"
"The world becomes smaller"

I realized that our catalyst was Allen. Allen Ginsberg was able to express the positive and negative without angst and guilt. And for the first time in *my* life I was allowing myself to experience the real world—good and bad, black and white, beautiful and ugly—and the acceptance of the evil juxtaposed with the divine. Letting it go. Letting it out. Saying it. Feeling it. Caressing it, and then throwing it all away right up to the Cosmos where it came from so that only the purity of spirit remains.

I was already helping others on my own before I met Allen and Janis, but now it was like I was able to see inside this complex world and expose its inner core—its electrons and the most micro-particles of its being.

I wrote incessantly during this time. Words and sentences and thoughts just flowed out onto paper. It finally didn't matter that there was contradiction between good and evil or the beautiful and the ugly—I was able to express it all. My America, the country of my fascination, was the epitome of paradox. She wooed me with her beauty and potential and aspirations—and she tried to destroy me with her prejudices and discrimination and greed. It all flowed through my heart and into my mind and onto paper as I wrote poems and spontaneous prose and streams of unconnected thoughts that were really connected. And it was all momentarily freed like a sudden unexpected dam burst, causing massive destruction in its path but creating the beauty of its flows of water, meandering seemingly aimlessly but really with purpose, forming streams and brooks and rivers.

I had been freed. I had been freed. I felt within me the excitement of a slave's unexpected release and how he now could softly caress a sweet rose and bring it close to his face and smell its fragrance without a whip lashing. I felt his subsequent harsh disappointment and physical attack by people of limited mind and heart who tried to destroy the only thing he cherished: the freedom to breathe. They became one within me—both sides of the world, both sides of all humans who struggle with their own demons, some destroying by their sheer power like the wall of water from the dam, some creating beauty and sustenance by birthing a brook or stream by their flow, and all within each of us.

And this is how it went for weeks and weeks and weeks. Endless words composed of individual letters forming sentences that connected thoughts that became realizations. After being written they just seemed to merge with the giant Cosmos to be stored somewhere before being brought down again by someone else in need.

"The death of beauty"
"The beauty of death"

These conjure up extreme opposites, yet they are mirror images—always connected, always related, always the same.

For months, I felt opened up. I continued to help my wheelchair buddies through free expression. I managed to do fewer and fewer of the duties I was ordered to do. I also felt empowered to spend more time with Allen and Janis.

I attended the "Human Be-In" with Allen in January 1967. It was a mixture of faiths and music and free expression. The anti-war movement was building even more, and I felt compelled to walk with Allen at the Spring Mobilization to End the War in April 1967 in San Francisco. There was a similar march in New York City. We walked to Golden Gate Park, where Janis and her band played.

I had no feeling of guilt or remorse during that spring. I remember walking through the hospital quad right after I had counseled my wheelchair buddies on a day in May 1967. I was heading toward my duty for the day. I felt a push from behind that almost knocked me down. I heard this mean, gruff voice from behind say, "Up against the wall! Hands over your head—spread them!" I tried to look back, but I couldn't. I was being manhandled. I was frisked really hard as my face was pushed up against a brick wall. Then it was "Hands behind your back!" and then the harsh, painful feel of handcuffs closing on my hands. "Turn around!" There I was, face-to-face with two burly, muscular military police officers. This took place within sight of my wheelchair guys. Out of the corner of my eye I could see the horror on their faces as I was dragged away.

"Where have you gone with Allen Ginsberg?" said the lieutenant loudly, within inches of my face. There I was, in a small dark interrogation room with two MPs and the interrogator.

And on it went. Obviously the army had finally decided it would not tolerate my behavior. Obviously, Allen was on the watch list for his outrageous behavior, and now so was I.

I found out that I was to be detained—they didn't call it jailed—for an undetermined time, to be questioned and probed until I 'fessed up my conspiratorial and un-American and subversive activity.

I answered every question honestly. The attack had only strengthened the feeling that I had done nothing wrong—and indeed I had done nothing wrong. I was a patriotic American with the feelings that came from the patriotic concerns I harbored within me. My ambivalence had disappeared as well as my Jewish guilt. I was an American as much as any American. Ginsberg had opened me up. He was born of Jews. He looked like the Jew who tailored my dad's suit. He looked like my rabbi. He looked like an ordinary person—and he didn't owe anything to anyone. He expressed himself where he wanted to and whenever he wanted to. He didn't have to guess if he was right. He was righteous, and he knew it—unlike Kerouac, who ultimately bought into the image of what an American should be.

After my relatively short interrogation I was led to an area of the Presidio I had never been to. It was obviously the military police and brig section. My living space was a locked room about ten by ten feet with a small window out to an inner courtyard. The room consisted of a small hard army cot, a small sink attached to a wall, and a separate commode. There was one light and it was one of those gooseneck things that hung on the metal headboard of the bed. I was told I could write anyone I wanted to and receive or make one call a day for no longer than three minutes. I was also told I would have an interrogation at least once in the morning and possibly another one in the afternoon. I would also have all my meals brought to my room.

Strangely, I thought they didn't have much respect for me as a real subversive; I thought military prison was harsher than this. I began to realize that they wanted me to reveal myself by writing letters that they would then read, and that by speaking to people they could connect me with subversive activity. I didn't have any subversive connections and could not imagine anything they would want to do to me. I had already lived the hell of 'Nam—so what, I thought.

OK, creeps … I'm outta here. There isn't a military prison in the world I can't get out of … Algiers … Casablanca … You shoulda seen the one in Siberia. You'd better watch me close!

I awoke suddenly my first night still spouting Cagney-like phrases from a dream I was having. Strangely, I chuckled at the thought of my face and Cagney's voice.

The first two days were the same. I was interviewed for only about forty-five minutes each morning, and the questions were the same. "Who have you spent time with off base? Where have you gone?" I told them the truth, except for my acid trips.

On the beginning of the third day I started to feel some angst when I realized I should call Mom. It was my first call.

"Hi, Mom."

"Amie … my sweet."

"How are you and Dad and Susan and the kids?"

"Fine, honey … How are you?"

"Fine, Mom."

"You sure, Amie?"

"Well …, I've been detained really."

"What? Retrained for what?"

"No … actually detained … like locked up …"

"By who? Can't you get out?"

"Actually, by the army."

"Amie … how can they lock you up? For what?"

"For spending time with Allen Ginsberg."

"Ginsberg? Do I know his family?"

"No, Mom … I'll call you in a couple of days … OK?"

I think I was a relatively low-profile case for the army at this point, because I didn't seem to appear in the news or nosy Mom would have known.

On the fourth day I was having something for breakfast when I glanced out the tiny window on to the courtyard. I saw in the distance first a few guys in wheelchairs coming closer from around a corner; then a few turned in to more—and there must have been about twenty-five chairs rolling closer to my window. As they approached I could see that each was carrying a placard of sorts. They got close enough for me to be able to read them. WHEELCHAIR BRIGADE, said one. FREE LARDOWITZ, GIVE US STREAM, LET AMOS OUT, WHEELIES FOR AMOS, and TAKE ME INSTEAD, read others. I could see the guys raising their hands in the air and hooting and making all sorts of noises. I got my face as close to the window as possible and could see that they saw me. There was an instant roar and the roar became a unified chant: "Streeeeeeam … Streeeeeeam." This must have gone on for about five minutes, and then I could see three MPs walking toward the group, which was in a kind of semicircle facing my window. It was an amazing sight. The burly, tough-looking MPs were trying to herd the wheelies away from my window. What a hilarious sight this was. I'm sure the MPs had no training in this kind of demonstration, for the wheelies were outmaneuvering them like rabbits darting across a field. Some actually ran over the boots of the guys, and others did one-wheel turns to get away. They all were scattering in different directions still hooting and chanting "Streeeeeam" as they wheeled. This must have gone on for about a half hour, and I could see more MPs coming. I think the MPs didn't know how to handle these guys, like they thought they were fragile eggs and would crack if they caught them. Meanwhile the wheelies were tough as nails and seemed to be having a ton of fun.

I was called out of my room as the last wheelie was caught. I was brought to what looked like a hearing room. There were only two MPs there. At a desk in front were three chairs. I was told to sit on a chair directly facing this desk. About two minutes later from a door on the side came three uniformed officers—colonels. They had the insignia of the judicial branch.

The lead officer asked me the same questions about my activity as I'd been asked before. I looked him straight in the eyes and told him the same thing. He then asked me if I had anything to say. What followed was the longest moment of my life. I had a vision of two roads diverging from each other—going in completely different directions. In my mind, in this brief moment, I knew I needed to choose one. I said, "Yes, sir.

"Sir, I feel the army has neglected the very dedicated people it has asked, many without their consent, to risk and often give their lives for their country."

"What do you mean, soldier?"

"War is horrible. It is unpredictable and often has no meaning. Altruistic reasons for war end up as muddled, horrific quagmires with no way out."

"Are you opposing this war, soldier?"

"Sir, with respect, I have volunteered for this war. My hurt comes from the consequences of war. My buddies, who have served and come back with broken bodies and broken spirits, deserve more. Wars end the physical pain, but spiritual anguish remains for a lifetime. The army owes them, sir. The army owes the very people it has asked to give the ultimate sacrifice for their country. Give them counseling. Respect them. Care for them."

"Thank you, Specialist Lardowitz."

I thought I had seen a flash of concern in one of the officer's eyes when I finished. I was not sure of the other two. I had told them the truth—and that was it.

Two days went by and I had no interviews. I didn't feel like calling anyone or writing. I felt spent. I had opened my heart to these officers and had no more emotion in me.

On the third day after the hearing I was called to the same room. This time only the lead officer was there.

"Specialist Lardowitz, we have recommended a discharge from the army for you."

I was shocked at the way he said this. I wasn't expecting it. I felt instantly hurt, as if someone had just slapped me in the face.

"But sir ..."

"You will be discharged immediately and ordered off the base. You will not serve in the Reserve after discharge."

I don't think they could have hurt me more. Maybe that was their intent—to punish me for honestly bringing to their attention the needs of their wounded. What a crock, I thought. I could only think of my buddies and how I would miss our get-togethers and the sharing of our trials. Who would help them? Where would my guys get help? I couldn't sleep at all that night.

Unbelievable, I thought—I had to leave the base in two days. I was being booted out—expelled, discarded, thrown away. I could think only of the guys—the wheelies. I made a concerted effort to see each one of them before I left. I wanted them to know how much I cared and that I would always be thinking of them. I made each of them promise to pursue the group meetings and the techniques we had developed. They all promised that it would have a life of its own no matter who left. That at least gave me some satisfaction, but I was saddened by the abrupt ending to my military life.

I decided not to call Mom or Dad or Ben at the moment. I walked out of the Presidio in civvies with my guitar, rucksack, and close-cropped military haircut. I wanted to walk—and walk I did, straight toward Haight-Ashbury.

Hippie Hill

I WALKED AND WALKED, getting satisfaction only from the cadence of my steps. I felt as if I was an obsessive-compulsive with no vision of anything but aimless direction to anywhere. The San Francisco day was crisp and clear. I felt anonymous—I felt alone—I felt nothing.

Suddenly and without even knowing how I got there, I found myself at the foot of Allen Ginsberg's apartment. I wasn't sure what I would say to him. "Hey, man … I've been booted out of the army."

And Allen's response? "Hey, Amos … Cool. Join the revolution, my boy" or "Hey, cool … Let's drop some acid, my friend." Neither response, I thought, would satisfy me.

Then I thought of what Mom would say. "Oh, my poor Amie …" Maybe she wouldn't say that. Maybe she would say, "God in heaven. Thank you. You didn't need that army anyway. I'm so happy you are home, my Amie."

Nothing I made up in my head, sitting on the steps to Allen's apartment, I thought, could satisfy me. I was dejected and empty.

I decided I needed to bite the bullet and at least see Allen, even though I hadn't the foggiest what to tell him. Climbing the steps I felt trepidation in every move. I knocked on the door and almost immediately it opened. I was face-to-face with someone I didn't know. I tried to at least be cool. "Hey … is Allen in?"

"No … he's out of town for two weeks."

And that was that. I really felt alone at that moment. Whatever I did or whoever I would call was nowhere in my brain.

I walked again, and once more without a conscious thought. Just the walking itself was satisfying. I'm not sure how I got there, but I walked to Golden Gate Park. Probably because of fond memories of my walks with Allen and Janis, I gravitated there. Of course it was a pretty place with beautiful old trees and ponds and grassy knolls—all overlooking the Pacific Ocean.

I stopped on a lovely grassy hill and just plopped down on my back, my guitar next to me like a pet dog, and looked up to the sky. Exhausted, I was void of all thoughts.

"Hey, buddy … got a joint?" the face said, looking straight down on me.

"Uh … no."

"OK, man … Mind if I sit down here?"

"No."

"Where ya from, guy?"

"Oh, I'm not sure …," I said, actually reflecting the state of my being at that moment.

"Hey … I know what ya mean. I'm from nowhere, too, wit' actually nothin' to call mine. I ain't got a job. I ain't got nothin', man. Hey, where's the hippies?"

"I dunno."

"I came to see the hippies. I wanna be a hippie. I hear they dropped out of life to be hippies. I wanna learn to be a hippie. Problem is, I never had a life. I couldn't keep a job. My dad is a drunk and beats my mom. My brother was killed in a accident at the furniture plant. My sister ran away wit' the mechanic that was married to her best friend—I wanna be somethin'."

While he was talking I had a flashback to my own life. I could tell him I was a Jewish boy from the Bronx whose dad was a doctor. Or I could tell him I had just been booted out of the army. Or I could tell him I almost got killed in 'Nam. I don't know why I continued the conversation, but I said, "Will being a hippie make you something?"

"I hope so," he said as I looked closer at this poor guy. My God, he was a derelict, I thought. He had rotten teeth and a pasty complexion and reeked of alcohol and dirty clothes. I started to wonder if that was what I was going to look like soon. I had lost my identity at this point, for I could not imagine another life for myself. He finally got up and left as I just stared far out to the horizon.

I must have slept all night on the lawn. I awoke to the laughs of three people sitting alongside of me.

"Hi … I'm Agnes from Minneapolis. This is Joe from Peoria, and that's Patty from Canton … and you?" They all looked a bit younger than me and like normal suburban kids.

"Hi," I said kind of sincerely. "I'm Amos."

"Where you from, Amos?"

"New York."

"Groovy," said Patty from Canton.

"Great, Amos. You're Amos from New York."

"Hey, Amos from New York … want to catch some breakfast?"

"OK."

I spent all day with the three of them. They constantly referred to themselves as Patty from Canton, Joe from Peoria, and Agnes from Minneapolis, and they constantly called me Amos from New York.

They had a real ritual for survival, meeting up with different small groups of other kids. They walked everywhere and ate as they could, depending on how much money they could gather either from panhandling or doing card tricks, or asking for odd jobs with a cute smile. They slept either outside or in a number of different apartments that were shared intermittently by other kids. There seemed to be a network of contacts, either friends or sympathetic businesspeople, who helped them live off the street. They hardly talked about anything substantial except where they would meet up with other friends or how they would catch the Grateful Dead concert for free. They seemed to be pretty nice kids. They all smoked weed. And when they got stoned later in the day at another park, they talked of eating the biggest hot dog they could ever imagine with the most sauerkraut and mustard. They never asked me why I was in Frisco or what I did before I got there—I was only Amos from New York.

I had landed in hippie land, I thought. These kids were just happy to try something new and didn't like where their lives were going. I had already been involved with the "movement," consisting of the people who had thoughts and concerns and would take action like marching for peace or justice. I realized that the change taking place had many layers, like a seven-layer cake. You could cut into it and taste each individual layer—and they all tasted different.

As my day wound down with these nice kids, I began to think, So who am I? They certainly didn't care who I was. But I had abruptly lost my life.

I thought I should care who I was. I had been searching for who I was my whole life. I had discovered something in the attic that pursued me and wouldn't let me go. I never rested. I was always thinking. But now, my life had come to a stop.

I slept once more on the grassy knoll and had a dream in which I was the last passenger on a train going through the flat landscape of the Midwest with only scrubland on either side. The train pulled in to the last stop, where there was a small, dilapidated shack and a sign that said RAILROAD CROSSING. There was nothing but flat land to the horizon. But on closer examination, I could see what appeared to be gravel roads leading from the station. I looked closer as I got off the train and they seemed to multiply before my eyes, becoming hundreds of gravel roads. I stood there stupefied as I watched the conductor wave to signal the train's departure. I didn't know which road to take.

I decided the next day to catch Janis if I could. I knew she was playing that night. I knew most of the roadies, so getting backstage was not a problem.

I waited backstage for Janis after the concert. She was excited to see me.

"Hey, Amos. You catch the show?"

"Yeah, Janis. "

"What you doin'? Want to come over later?"

"Yep."

I dropped acid with Janis that night at her apartment. She seemed to be getting worn out, I thought. She was also mixing drugs and drinking Southern Comfort like it was water.

"You sure you're OK, Janis?" I said, slurring my words from my high.

"Cool, Amos … My fans own me, man. I'm driven. What else is there?"

I didn't answer her. I couldn't answer her. I could see right then and there that she was slipping—sliding into a danger zone—but what did I know? I couldn't even figure out what I was right now.

Somewhere in the middle of night as we were falling asleep I thought I heard her say, "Hey … take these cubes, man."

I walked a lot the next day. Janis reminded me that her place was my place, and told me where the key to her Ashbury apartment was hidden; if I ever wanted to crash there, I could whether she was there or not.

I remember lying on the grass and once more looking up into the night sky. I put my left hand in my pocket as I lay there and felt about a dozen LSD cubes.

And so it went. I became something instead of being nothing. I became high, and during those times by myself I wrote. My body floated to the farthest and most remote places on earth. I felt as if I was above everything at times, and at other times I felt as if I was inside of everything. I remember writing about every feeling I had.

I saw images of my life everywhere—and I wrote it all in a disconnected stream.

Mother, child, Vietnamese sunrise
Floating through marsh
Carrying fragrances
of life
Caressing then exploding
into dust
Becoming one
With the Cosmos

Darkness
take me
Away to
places unseen
unheard unspoken

Monuments
of stone
Breaking into
writhing tortured
contorted confused convoluted
slivers of shale

Freeways on pavement carrying the politicians to plutonium-laden bombs begging for destruction

My mind got deeper and darker as I lived for days and then weeks on what would be known as Hippie Hill. I became one of thousands who lost themselves or possibly found themselves on Hippie Hill.

I know that I lost time itself. I can't remember if I ate or not. I can't remember if I slept or not. I do remember that I dropped acid—my life then truly disappeared.

I know I spent some time at Janis's apartment, for I remember seeing myself in a mirror and wondering who I was. I didn't shave or cut my hair. I had become a long-haired hippie without consciously making the effort. I always carried my guitar and do vaguely remember jamming with other musicians.

I remember bad trips. I had night sweats, and I remember crying out spontaneously for no reason. I was feeling myself slip away as a human being—and I was not sure where I was going.

I don't think I called anyone on the telephone. I do remember wandering throughout all of San Francisco.

I have this vague recollection of being turned away at the gates of the Presidio and some MP saying, "Get away, you hippie bum."

My God … Oh, you are so lovely … and soft … and your eyes are so beautiful … Zel.

"Is that really you, my Amos?"

"And in my fantasy you talk to me … Cool."

"OK, my lovely … stand up."

"Hey, Zel … stay with me a bit."

"Amos … I'm here—really here."

Oh boy! I awoke from one of my night trips out on Hippie Hill to the beautiful face of Zel in my view. Of course I thought it was one of my good trips—and there were fewer and fewer of them—but she insisted she was really there. I went along with this hallucination, for I really wanted to see her.

"Oh, Zel … stay with me."

"Amos … I'm here. Ben and I decided that your prose was getting darker and darker. You need help, Amos."

"You read my stuff?"

"We receive letters from you once a week like clockwork."

"Cool."

"Really cool—and it's time to heal our little Amos."

As this foggy fantasy continued, I felt the gentle tug of Zel's arm as she pulled me up. Standing in the morning sun, I looked at her. She was my Zel. She looked beautiful and soft. She wore a skimpy pastel dress that hugged the beautiful contours of her body. Her blue eyes twinkled in the morning light. She wore a touch of lipstick but no other makeup. I could smell her fragrance. "Hey, Zel … I love you. Kiss me," I said.

"I love you too, Amos, but not until you shave and shower."

And that was it. A sudden burst of reality went through my body and up to the top of my head—she *was* really there.

"Zel … it's you."

"Yes, Amos. It's me."

Oh my God, I thought. I must have sent many letters to Ben and Zel. What did I write? Quite embarrassing, I think—probably a whole shitload of stream of whatever. And here Zel had come to San Francisco to save me from myself.

"Is Ben here?" I said, still not quite believing she was real.

"No, my honey … *I'm* here."

Quite definitive, I thought.

"OK … now what?"

"First and foremost we clean you up. I didn't come all the way to the West Coast to smell you like this."

"Yes, Zel," I said, either finally believing she was really there or at least willing to go along with my weird hallucination.

I'm not sure what I remember next, but I think it was after I awakened from what probably was a nap. We must have gone to an apartment, for I walked into the bathroom to see a shaven Amos. I still had long hair, but it looked combed and smelled of shampoo.

"Oh, Zel … you didn't bathe me like a baby. Did you?"

"Actually, Amos, you were quite permissive."

Oh no …

It's hard to believe, but the woman of my dreams and the love of my life was taking care of me like my mother would. As I became more sober, I couldn't decide if I was happy about that or not. I remember consciously accepting this—after all she was *my* Zel, and whatever she wanted to do to and for me was A-OK with me.

The first thing Zel told me was that drugs were off limits. "I'm not on drugs … just LSD," I said.

She said, "Listen here, Kid. You listen to me and do what I say, OK?"

My God, I thought, she never called me Kid. Only Ben called me Kid. I didn't want her to call me Kid, so I decided I had better listen.

She then said I had to eat breakfast, lunch, and dinner.

"Are you making us food, Zel?" I asked, still probably in my stupid state.

"No, my lovely, we go out to eat at a natural and organic restaurant."

She told me that the place where we were staying belonged to a dear friend of Ben and hers and that he was out of town for six months. She said she was going to whip little Amos into a normal man within that time. "Yes, Zel," I said like a passive and compliant puppy dog.

Zel wanted me to play my Martin and play often. She also wanted me to sing the songs I had written earlier. She told me she didn't want me to write yet but that I would start as soon as I regained some normalcy.

We went for long walks during the day and Zel made sure we hit the nice parks with flowers and cute little paths. She said she wanted me to return to a sweeter time in my life or at least one that was not as crazed.

I started to play my Martin and sing some of the songs I had written. I heard Zel first hum and then actually sing the lyrics in harmony with me, or in a duet. She had a great soft, clear voice that fit with mine.

I was starting to feel more normal and obviously protected with Zel around. I had been off LSD for about two weeks and had drunk no alcohol.

I felt inspired and wrote a song. I knew it was attributed to Zel when the lyrics and music came spontaneously to me.

Even if my sun hasn't shined
And my life does unwind
I will always love you
forever

And when my dreaming is through
And I've got nothing to do
It will always be me and you
forever

And if the flowers lose their bloom
And my mind runs out of room
It will always be me and you
forever

I will always love you
Even if the sky sheds its blue
I will always love you
forever

I guess that was my love song for Zel—one I had been writing in my head for years anyway and finally really wrote. I was surprised that I was not embarrassed. And what was really amazing was that she started to sing it with me in a kind of duet—a lovers' duet.

In my own special way, I had Zel as my own, I thought. She was not my physical love—she was my love in a deeper way, and because of that it would last longer than the physical ever could.

Zel nurtured me for weeks. She returned me to a place I had been before—the more centered place of my life. She knew who I was and gave me back myself.

During our long walks I was tempted many times to ask Zel about her life. She never talked about herself, only about Ben and either literature or music. One soft, sunny afternoon we found ourselves in a quiet spot overlooking the Pacific.

"Zel … what about you? Where are you from?"

"I was brought up in New England."

"Do you have brothers and sisters?"

"Yes … I have a younger and older sister and one brother."

"Wow … two other girls like you?"

"No, Amos …," she smiled and continued. "No one is like me."

"I know," I think I said, exposing my infatuation. "You went to college—you told me."

"I went to a small college in Rhode Island and the school closed just after my graduating class of '54."

"Ben told me your father was a professor there."

"He lost his job that year. My father is a brilliant poet and writer—still unpublished."

"And your mother?"

"Amos, my mother died when I was fourteen. She was sick a long time, and for some reason I became the caregiver for our family even though I was the second youngest."

"What happened to your dad?"

"My father is a sweet and brilliant man, much older than my mother, who functions only in the world of words. He is incapable of being what the world expects."

I could not help asking Zel about her being Jewish. I felt my heart beat in my throat as I asked, "Zel … you're Jewish?"

"Yes."

"Where did your family come from?"

"My mother emigrated from Romania to Canada and then to the U.S. My father's family was all intellectuals and socialists. They taught or wrote."

"Both were Jewish?"

"Yes. The most vivid memories I have as a child are of my mother reciting Friday night prayers in Hebrew, shawl on her head, lighting the Sabbath candle."

In my mind's eye I could see Zel looking up to her mother as she lit the candle. "Zel … why were you different?" I said, probably trying to understand how she seemed not to fit my stereotype of a Jewish girl.

"Amos … we lived in an old farmhouse, and we had many barn cats. The females always got pregnant, and I raised the kittens and gave them away to classmates, townspeople, and strangers. What I discovered is that each kitten, even in litters of seven or eight, had a distinct personality that had nothing to do with upbringing. They were who they were at birth. Some were hopelessly shy … Others were bold and brash, and it had nothing to do with their sex. Early on in life I realized that you can be whatever you think you are and that life is a series of choices. I made sure I would travel down paths I wanted to and not what was laid out for me by society or others."

In my mind, my parallel thoughts were about my discovery in the attic and my search for something in my family. Here was Zel, confident and secure and not doubting who she was or where she came from. She was really just like Ben.

"Ben's family is Jewish also?" I said.

"Yes. Ben is an only child. I adore Ben's mother. She put him out in the world and wherever he landed, she let him experience it. Ben walks a straight line to anywhere. He takes no side roads for the scenery. He decides where he wants to go and he goes."

"Ben's dad?"

"He died when Ben was ten. He was a carpet salesman."

"Aha!" I laughed. "So that is where Ben gets his moves!"

Zel laughed also.

We had a great time that day. I felt so good about the easy conversation. I had landed back on earth again, being just curious Amos.

I knew that Zel wrote. She was very private about it. I know she was writing out in Frisco. I also know she wrote prose. I think she was satisfied with who she was and did not want to expose herself to the critical world. I felt as if I had known her forever and really didn't need to "read" her as well.

After my conversation with Zel we seemed to laugh a lot. Zel decided we would "write" spontaneous poems as we walked—each completing the other's thoughts.

Zel said, "Happy feet"

"can cross the street," I continued.

"with steps so big," she said.

"they seem to dig"

"big trenches

"by the benches" … and we couldn't finish and would just burst out laughing.

My life with Zel during this month and a half was like that of two children just experiencing the fantasies of life. She helped me by keeping everything fun. There were no heavy thoughts, and we didn't include other people. We eventually cooked meals together at the apartment. I knew in my heart that she was watching my every move to be sure I healed and returned to sanity from the deep holes I had dug with drugs and the horrible experiences I had witnessed. I would be forever grateful.

I was feeling quite comfortable when one morning Zel said, "Amos … I forgot to tell you, but about a week ago I found this in the back pocket of your pants." She handed me a folded flyer. I opened it up and saw that it was the flyer mentioning Hardy County that I had quickly grabbed from a wall just before I went to see Donny's family in Pennsylvania.

"My God … I put that in my pocket and forgot about it," I said.

"Well, here it is. What is it?"

"Oh boy … Zel … my Achilles heel, I suppose. My quest … my search … my doubts … all rolled into one."

"OK, Amos …"

I knew I would have to be more up front with Zel. We were so close.

"You know, Zel ... since I was fifteen I have wondered about my family. I found an old photo in the attic that was a mystery ... a mystery about my dad's family history ... and it's my quixotic search, I suppose."

"Why? Do you doubt something?"

"I don't know. I think I need to form a circle or something with all the loose ends. I think I need this to understand myself and my country for some reason."

"You know, Amos, I once had a kitten that had a personality like no other before or after him. He was a little boy. Before I gave him away I noticed that he was very shy and kept all to himself. I remember giving him to someone who lived three miles away. Well ... believe it or not, two weeks after I gave this ten-week-old kitten away, I found him curled up next to a bale of hay in the barn where he was born. I picked him up and gave him back once more. Once again, I found him a week later, curled up to his birthplace. This happened three more times, and finally the family I gave him to told me to just keep him. Amos, he slept next to his birthplace his whole life. He was just where he wanted to be. I never questioned it."

"So ... should I curl up next to something?"

"You keep coming back to something you want to curl up against. So why question it? Just do it."

"But what's going to happen?"

"Amos—what's going to happen will happen. Thinking about it won't make it happen sooner. Look at the flyer. You found it. You put it away. You forgot about it ... and it came back again when it was supposed to. Your discovery is already yours. You will complete the circle when *you* are ready."

What Zel said sounded right to me. I had never opened myself up like this before and it sounded right.

My life continued to be like a love story in San Francisco over the next month. I realized that as I became more normal and my outlook on life became more productive, it would only be a short time before Zel left—a bittersweet but satisfying ending.

I was truly at a turning point at this time, and I left my heart open for the next adventure in my life. But as well, I had become so relaxed that I wasn't sure if I was ready to chase rainbows or climb mountains.

On the night before Zel left I awoke from a dream and wrote:

Gentle breeze
carry me to soft mountains
On roads
paved by those ahead of me

Once more, my past seemed to just appear and almost pull me to places I did not know but felt were within me. Something was stirring within me—something from the faded photo of Henrietta.

The Quest Begins

I ARRIVED HOME TUESDAY, November 14, 1967.

Mom and Dad and Jemima were well. It was strange, but their lives had continued over the last year and a half with seemingly no changes. The world was changing, and we were embedded in this monstrous war, but Dad's daily life of doctoring remained the same. Mom had adjusted magnificently with the residual effects of the stroke, and Jemima—well, Jemima was a permanent part of our family who chuckled along with everyone and gave her motherly advice freely.

Susan had matured into a busy kosher mother of three. Alvin continued to climb up the banking ladder, seemingly taking no risks if he could avoid them. Sydney was nine and Morris was seven and Clara was five. I had missed the kids the most. And I especially had missed my Syd. She still seemed attuned to me. I was worried for Susan though. I thought her drive was too intense, and she was certainly not as capable as Mom of handling either motherhood or the stresses of marriage.

Zel had left Frisco and come to New York about a week before I left. I think she knew I could use a transition—a kind of settling and quiet time for myself before I came back. I also think it was her way of saying to me, "Amos, I trust you …," in essence to know that I had returned to myself and would not fall again into the deep, drug-induced abyss.

I stayed home for a few days with Mom and Jemima and Dad. I think we all realized that Amos had grown up. My family had not shared the most horrific parts of my life—and they shouldn't have. I became an adult because of and in spite of my obsessive mind, and I was beginning to accept who I was.

I headed off to Manhattan feeling almost like a free spirit with just a hint of the quest inside of me. Ben and Zel offered to let me stay at their place until I decided what I was going to do with my life. Of course, I had already felt the compelling urge to travel somewhere, but I left myself an open time to gather my thoughts.

Ben and Zel had a small get-together for me at Manny's Underwear with Manny and Fanny. We had a ball. We talked about old times, and Manny had plenty of jokes. He turned to me abruptly and said, "Hey, Amos … how's the Wheelchair Brigade?" Whoa, I thought. Who told him? I knew Zel didn't speak of anything that occurred with me.

"Hey, I caught the quick blurb on TV," Manny then said.

"Oh boy …," I said reluctantly.

"Hey, Stream … we're proud of you, man," Manny said.

Ben just sat there and gave me a really satisfied look—almost like he was proud of me also.

Sitting there with my true friends I realized that I had truly arrived. I was who I was right at this moment. Looking back at myself when Ben had first introduced me as "Kid," I knew I had become part of the group. It was amazing that Zelda and Ben had grabbed me out of the depths of my misery, and how Zel spent all that time with me a coast away and gone from Ben. Boy, these were my true buddies.

It was a great night, that first return to Manny's Underwear.

I felt compelled to get in contact with my other friends. Allen had returned to San Francisco and was really busy with his anti-war stuff and his speeches and writings. We had a warm talk on the telephone, and my mind went back to the day we walked in Golden Gate, where Allen told me that our lives would cross but never merge. And so it happened for now.

I tried to call Janis many times over the next week. All I got were people I didn't know, and they wouldn't let me talk to her. I knew she was really flying high, for she was already becoming a legend. But once more, I worried for her, thinking she had let herself buy into the downward spiral of drugs and alcohol.

And Jack … I'd had a great time with Jack. At Manny's everyone had talked about Jack and the direction his life was taking him. They all adored him but felt that he was losing his essence—his spirit. I tried a number of times to reach Jack but failed.

I desperately wanted to hear the voice of my buddy Babatunde. I knew he was still in Nigeria. After many tries, I connected with him by phone.

"Hey, A-Moes," he said like we had just seen each other yesterday.

"Hey, Babatunde."

"What's up, man?"

"Well … water under the bridge …"

"Know what you mean." And so it went. We talked for an hour about Babatunde's life in Nigeria and his family and the political situation there. We also talked about the Vietnam War and the civil rights turmoil in America. Babatunde remained the most clear international friend I had. He was my window on the rest of the world. In a moment, he could open me up to a different view of my America and the rest of the planet.

I came back home for the Jewish holidays and the New Year, and in January of '68 I was able to get a month-to-month furnished sublet in Manhattan. I felt as if my friends understood my need to just "hang," for I truly was in recovery from the deepest hole I had ever been in.

For the next three months I worked with Ben during the day and played at night with our circle of friends, mostly at Manny's. It was a sweet time—a time for my Manhattan to caress me and for me to cozy up to the excitement of my city.

About every two weeks I would come home and sleep in my old room. This also was comforting, returning me to the place of my upbringing and nurturing.

"General Grant, I don't think that we have enough men to overtake the Rebs' right flank. The river is swollen from the spring rains."

"Listen here, Lardy … horseshit! If we don't do it now, we will never defeat them."

"I'm not Lardy, sir … I'm Lardowitz."

"Listen here, Lardy, don't give me that horseshit. I want Lardy. Goddamn it, man, Lincoln wants Lardy and I'm gonna give him Lardy … no bullshit."

"Sir, we don't have enough men."

"Horseshit. Where's the Hardy Brigade?"

"The Hardy Brigade?"

"The Hardy Brigade! Bullshit! Horseshit! Goddamn it!"

"We have a Hardy Brigade?"

"Horseshit, Lardy. Don't you know we have a Hardy Brigade? We got three hundred men in that brigade. They're all named Hardy. Don't you know that, Lardy? Horseshit, damn it! They're all named Hardy ... Lardy ... they're all named Hardy—Lardy!"

I awoke in a sweat. I looked around and saw that I was in my bed at home. It was obvious to me that my quest had begun. I could not put it off any more.

I pulled out the flyer I had kept from my visit to Donny's home. I lay back down in my bed and held the flyer up, reading it again and again. It was like a magnet to me. What attracted me to it were the words *Hardy County.* I tried to analyze why I thought this was a sign but couldn't come up with a rational reason. I thought back on what I had written just before I left Frisco. *Soft mountains ... on roads paved ...*

West Virginia ... West Virginia ...

I lay in my childhood bed that morning and envisioned myself once more as a tiny speck traversing the landscape of my America ... the American landscape ... overturning every rock and peering into every crevice ... knowing that if my distant past existed, I would find it—I would find it.

Finding Wordie

I BOUGHT A USED '63 Chevy and took off from New York on Tuesday, April 16, 1968, just days after Martin Luther King was assassinated and President Johnson signed the Civil Rights Act. I brought a road map of the United States, my Martin guitar, and a suitcase. I brought a thousand dollars all in twenties and stuffed the bills all over the car. I decided to drive in the direction of Donny's home in Pennsylvania and then just feel my way through the coal country and Appalachians toward West Virginia. Maybe I felt that the Cosmos would be good to me. I was determined to find one person named Lardy. The phone books did not have any. I slept in my car at night. I decided to start in the small towns and work my way to Moorefield, all in Hardy County. My routine consisted of breakfast in a local coffee shop and conversation with the locals.

Two weeks of schmoozing and eating bacon and eggs had passed, and in a small town fifteen miles from Moorefield a little old guy with a hillbilly twang said, "Lardy … Shurre … He's in Moorefield, fella."

I stopped at what looked like the local town government building and asked if anyone knew a Lardy. I was told that he got a lot of visitors and given directions to his home.

I felt excitement all over as I wound my way through the country town and to its outskirts.

And there it was—a small clapboard one-story house somewhat similar to the Brooks home in Mound Bayou. It had a small covered porch in the front. Two rocking chairs sat side by side to the right of the door. There was a screen door, which was closed, but the inside front door was open, and I could see into the house somewhat.

I knocked on the wood part of the screen door. It kind of vibrated and didn't make much noise. My heart was pounding. I could feel my pulse everywhere in my body as I waited.

I heard a distant sound that must have come from a room behind the room I could see into.

"Hallo." The voice had a strange enunciation and the accent was on the "Ha" so it sounded like "Há … low."

"Hallo … hallo." It was a man's voice and he kept saying "hallo" like it was sonar or something. I heard it louder and louder until he appeared right behind the screen door and said one last "Hallo."

"Well, hallo," he said.

"Mr. Lardy?" I said, afraid he was going to say "No" or that Mr. Lardy was dead or something.

"Yep, what can I do for you, young fella?"

"Do you think I can talk to you, Mr. Lardy?" I said, not knowing how to begin.

"Yep … everybody does … What is it, young fella? Do you need to store something, or did you lose something? … Or do you need a book at the library? Tell me, young fella."

I was stunned. I didn't know what he meant by the weird questions. They all took place through the screen door, so I could not really see the guy I was talking to well.

"Do you mind, Mr. Lardy, if I open the screen door?"

"Oh, yep … I forgot … you need to see," he said, and again I was confused by what he meant.

He opened the screen door, and I saw standing in front of me a tall man in dark blue overalls and a light blue denim shirt. He had short gray curly hair, and his eyelids were half closed, and I couldn't see his eyes.

He also had the very short stubble of a beard, like he hadn't shaved in a few days. He stepped out onto the porch and extended his right hand to the two rocking chairs.

"Sit down, young man."

I sat in the nearest chair and he sat in the other one and gently rocked back and forth as he said, "Tell me what's on your mind."

"Mr. Lardy … I …"

"Wordie …," he interrupted.

"Mr. Wordie," I said nervously.

He laughed a broad laugh and said, "Wordie, son, Wordie."

"Wordie … do you … or did you … or anyone—actually, are you related to a Henrietta Lardy or maybe a Hardy Lardy?" I said.

It seemed like an eternity that I had kept the words "Hardy Lardy" within my lips and not uttered them out loud to another person.

"And who are you, my friend?" he said.

"Amos … Amos Lardowitz."

"Well, well … Amos … little Amos. I'll be darned … Amos," he said. A cheerful smile came across his whole face, although his eyes still stayed somewhat closed. "Little Amos …" and he seemed to look away and somewhat up into the sky.

"You know me?" I said nervously.

"Know you, my boy—you're my nephew. How did you find me?"

"What—you're my uncle? Oh my God … Who? What … No … You're not my dad's brother—are you?"

"Hardy Boy?" he said, and suddenly his face seemed to change. "Is he all right, Amos? He's all right, isn't he?"

"Oh, yes … He's fine."

"Well, how did you find me? Did he send you here?" he continued.

"No … oh my God … I found you through an old picture of Henrietta."

He almost cut me off, and started to lift his hands as if he were going to touch my face. He then cupped his hands around my forehead and down my nose and cheeks, feeling my face, and said, "Let me see you, my boy … My goodness, you look like your dad."

I realized right then and there that he was blind. I was shocked. I became flushed and thought I was going to faint but caught myself.

"Oh … you didn't know that I see differently from you, Amos. You don't know about me, do you? I guess Hardy Boy has honored his brother's wishes … those of a stubborn man who wanted to lead his life as it was and not interfere with others' happiness."

"You mean you didn't want to be his brother?" I said.

"No, Amos, it's not like that at all. It's an old story, my nephew … an old story."

As he was about to say something else, a car pulled right in front of the house. Wordie turned toward the open window of the driver's side and said, "Gilbert, what can I do for you?"

"Wordie, I need to get James Fenimore Cooper's *Last of the Mohicans* for my students in English class. Do you have it in the library?"

"Gilbert, it's in … it was returned on May 15. It's in stack B, second shelf … I believe three books from the left. I'll be there tomorrow. You can get it then."

"Thanks, Wordie …" and he drove off without ever getting out of the car.

Wordie then looked at me and said, "Where were we, Amos?"

"Wordie, please tell me everything … everything. I've been waiting so long for this moment." I sounded like a child.

"Little Amos … so's you don't get scared about everything I'm sayin', please understand that I remember everything I've ever been told since I've been an itty thing. I guess God did have a purpose for this little blind boy after all. And just in case you feel sorry for me, don't, for I see more than you could ever see without my eyes. You can tell that I see, 'cause I see Gilbert, who just left. I know the sound of his car for a hundred yards. There are 134 cars, 23 pickup trucks, and 3 motorcycles in Moorefield, and I know all of them and who drives them—and as far as the library goes, I'm the main librarian. Thirty years ago I got the job and was walked through the whole collection step by step. There are now 1,343 volumes in 23 stacks with 125 shelves, and I know where every one of them is. I also know the titles, author, date of publication, and if the book is in or out and when it's due. I got to admit I get help now twice a week, since I'm gettin' a little older, but only a little help … not much, I tell you. I got my job and I do it. I also know everyone's family history since they tell it to me so's they don't have to remember it for themselves. For instance, Harriet Foss was born on March 4, 1919, at three thirty in the morning. It was a Tuesday. She got her firstborn on May 3, 1941, named Calvin, her secondborn on March 1, 1942, named Nancy—and I could go on through the child number three and four and a list of nine grandchilds … of course only if Harriet wants me to know, and it so happens she does, just like 98 percent of everyone living in Moorefield wants me to know about 95 percent of what they know so's they don't have to remember it for themselves. Now that's trust, my Amos … that's trust—and that's my job, Amos."

He had picked up the pace of his talking to rapid fire. The sentences were barely finished before another began. Just then, another car pulled up in exactly the same spot as Gilbert's and the driver, a middle-aged woman, rolled down the window and leaned her head out and said, "Wordie, that key to the safe deposit box—where did I put it?"

She then looked at me with a puzzled look and Wordie said, "You can trust him, Ruthie. It's in the extra bedroom in the brown bureau … last drawer—under the underwear on the right side way back."

She waved and drove away and Wordie looked at me and said, "That's what she told me where it was to be three years ago," and he then raised both hands almost like saying he was sorry he seemed to know everything about everything.

"So's I continue, Amos—since I been a teeny thing I had a mouth on me that wouldn't stop. Hardy Boy and Ready Etta sometime couldn't take it and just walked out of the room as I rambled on."

"Ready Etta? Who is that?" I said.

"Oh, boy—I guess you know nothin'. Hardy Boy didn't tell you nothin', I suppose."

I interrupted him and said that my dad had never mentioned his family down here. I said I'd always thought his family was from Europe like Mom's.

"OK, Amos, Ready Etta was Hardy Boy, your daddy's, and my sister. She was born first on November 11, 1900. She was christened Etta. She was a slowpoke and never ready, so's Daddy and Mommy would always yell out, 'Ready Etta?' when she needed to do chores or go to school or do anythin'. And they just kept callin' her Ready Etta because it was easier to get her ready since she was always late—and she became Ready Etta."

"So who's Henrietta?" I asked, confused.

"That's Ready Etta, but that'll have to wait a couple of sentences or more since I'm just beginnin' my story on your family, Amos."

"Laizie gave birth to Hardy Boy, who was born on June 12, 1902, and named after your gran'pappy, who was also called Hardy. Laizie is my mommy and your daddy's mommy, and Hardy is my daddy and your daddy's daddy." At that point I realized that he needed to use the most words to describe anything. He continued:

"Laizie was christened Elizabeth and was generally called Lizzie but she was pretty slow and she was called Laizie by her folk. After your daddy was born, then I came and that was the last. I was born on December 4, 1912, and unfortunately Laizie died in delivery of me. A shame 'cause Laizie wasn't really lazy, I'm told; she was a sickly little thing all along and just darn gave in when I was bein' born. Daddy told me that I almost wanted to go back to the Lord also with Mommy, but I decided, he said, to be strong and stay here on earth. Right off the bat, I had trouble seein' things, but I could see almost till I was six, and then mostly my eyes just gave way, and I got blind almost for good at eight exactly. Ready Etta was twelve years when I was born and she lost her mommy and just became the woman of the house since Daddy was all alone and had to work the farm and sell the crops and milk. She took care of us boys and made the house a home for the three of us, and she was barely a kid herself. I was a talker, Amos. I guess not seein' I just used a lot of words, and my mouth never stopped movin' … so's Daddy and Etta says, and I remember the day February 12, 1917, on a Monday when I was four years old that I talks so much and use so many words everyone is now goin' to call me Wordie forever—by the way, I was christened Peter up to that point, Amos—and Wordie after that point and forever.

"We had a farm in the county probably 'bout thirty miles from here, and we all chipped in and helped, with Ready Etta doin' all the woman work, and we all went to school also. I found out especially that I remembered everything I was ever told if you told me only once. I remember the day Friday, October 5, 1917, the teacher, Mrs. Homer visited us at home and said to me that I have a memory like a photograph just taken and I put it away in my head and I always know where it is. And she said I must have a million pictures and I know where each one is and what they looks like and what everything is in detail in the picture."

I was absolutely mesmerized, sitting directly opposite Wordie as he talked, both of us in our rockers. I noticed that late afternoon had turned to dusk, but he continued.

"So's I guess I should move fast forward"—You've got to be kidding, I thought. What was his speed now?—"and fill in the pieces later. Hardy Boy was a good boy, and Daddy seemed always to be concerned 'bout him and his happiness, since he seemed lost most of the time. I know I was always a burden and had to be taken take of by Daddy and Etta, and that left no time for Hardy Boy to have anything given to him. Daddy never did remarry, and he worked hard to feed us and send us for schooling. We all got good schoolin', though—Daddy made sure of that.

"You know, Amos—Hardy Boy as he grew up was gettin' concerned 'bout Etta havin' a good life for herself. As Ready Etta's eighteenth birthday was comin' round, Hardy Boy came to me—and I was almost six, mind you, but I still understood everything. He told me he wanted her to change, and she should be more of a woman so's she could have a more normal life. He told me he wanted her to change her name since Ready Etta was not a normal name, and that Etta wouldn't do 'cause he wanted her to have a completely new life for herself. He decided he wanted her to call herself Henrietta, and it was a pretty name and new, and it was close to her name of Ready Etta and sounded like it so's people wouldn't mind much when they called her, and maybe someone would fall in love with her, and she'd be happy forever. Hardy Boy was sixteen at this time. He said he had a special eighteenth-birthday present for her, a real special one that would go along with her new name. He went all the way to Moorefield, 'bout thirty miles away, and he ordered a beautiful dress for Ready Etta's eighteenth birthday. He planned that on November 11, 1918, on Monday, exactly on her eighteenth birthday, he was goin' to take Ready Etta in our wagon with Samuel the draft horse leadin' and drive her to Moorefield with him and get the dress from Mademoiselle Sweeny's dress salon and make her put it on—and then waitin' would be the traveling photographer Randolph Photographers and tell her 'bout her new name and have her picture taken and wait for the picture card and write on it 'My sister, Henrietta Lardy.' This way she'd be beautiful, and you could see it on the picture card, and she'd see her new name and then have a new life."

I could not believe this moment. I had waited fourteen years for this exact second and had that mystery floating around in my head all that time—my life seeming to exist only for these revelations I dreamed about night and day. That photograph and its inscription in the attic had controlled everything that I had become during this time. The picture shaped my maturity into a grown man. It shaped my thoughts, my desires, and my consciousness—and now it was starting to become completely revealed to me. Wordie continued:

"Hardy Boy left with Etta at six thirty in the mornin' that day and said he should be back about ten thirty in the night. I was so excited. I couldn't wait all day and all night and kept tryin' to look at the only clock we had in the house. You know, Amos, I was still seein' somewhat, bein' I lost my whole sight two years later. I couldn't eat, I was so excited. Daddy said I should calm down, but I see he's also excited and nervous. Come ten thirty Amos and Etta were not back. All the next minutes seem like hours. I remember the time—it was eleven fourteen, and I heard the clomping of Samuel's feet as he approached from the north road. Daddy had fell asleep, and I yelled to him to wake—he jumped up like the devil had tickled him in his back, I tell you. I ran out of the house bare feet up the road about a hundred yards and sees Hardy Boy and Etta. I ran alongside Samuel—boy, did he seem tired. I could see that Hardy Boy had a big smile on his face, and I also saw that Etta was beamin' with pleasure and looked so fine in her new dress. They tied up Samuel and came into the house and immediately Hardy Boy opened his arm in the direction of Etta and said, 'Mademoiselle Henrietta, meet my dad and my brother', and she curtsied and said with a shy smile, 'How do you do?' and we all burst out into the biggest laugh out loud. What a joy, Amos—what a joy, I tell you.

"I then feel her soft and beautiful dress up and down. It was rich and thick and beautiful with all sorts of ribbons and curls. I can see it now real clear, Amos. And Hardy Boy pulls out the photograph and we all get really close to it under the light—including newly named Henrietta, and everybody is oohin' and aahin' over the beauty in the picture—namely Henrietta.

"Well, Amos I can still just see that beautiful photograph in my mind right now, and I could see that it is the one thing that sent you all the way here to find your West Virginia family. See, Amos, Henrietta still lives within us—thank the Lord—and her beauty is alive and here with us."

"So what happened to Henrietta?" I asked.

"A terrible thing happened, Amos. Henrietta was just about six months over her eighteen years and her new name when she got the scarlet fever and just died, Amos—June 12, 1919—she just went to the Lord."

"Oh no," I said, caught up in this most beautiful story about Henrietta.

"Daddy was devastated and cried for a month, I tell you. I was so sad. Hardy Boy promised to care for me forever and take care of me and make me happy. He also said he would become a doctor and make me see again, for we all knew that my sight was goin' completely away soon.

"The next year was so difficult for us, Amos—so difficult. Hardy Boy became like Henrietta and did all the house chores. He cooked and prepared all the food and did all our laundry, and he did continue to go to school and help Daddy way into the late night. He sure made me do all my schoolin' also.

"It was goin' on to a year and a half later, and Daddy started to tell Hardy Boy that he had to have his own life. I was gettin' bigger and stronger, and I was used to my not seein' much also. Right after my eighth birthday on December 12, 1920, when Hardy Boy was eighteen, Daddy insisted that

Hardy Boy had to go to school and away from here. He wanted him to go and become a doctor. I told him I wanted him to go also and become a doctor in a big city and have children. Finally Hardy Boy said he would go only if he could come back and cure me of my blindness. Mind you, Amos, I was gettin' stronger and stronger and knew where everything was, and you know my memory—it was gettin' good. I really wanted Hardy Boy to go. Daddy saved five hundred dollars and just gave it to Hardy Boy. You know how much five hundred dollars was in 1920, Amos? It was a lot of money, I tell you.

"I remember the day and exact time that we took Hardy Boy to the train—January 4, 1921, on a Tuesday. It was really cold and damp. We put Samuel's rigging on, and all of us went to the train station cryin', but inside I was happy, for I wanted Hardy Boy to have his own life, Amos."

He then stopped for about thirty seconds and turned his face up to the sky like he was seeing and said, "Wow, it's gettin' late—work tomorrow. Amos, you travelin' through? I want you to stay here as long as you want."

"Uncle Wordie—I came here only to find Dad's family," I said strongly emphasizing the *uncle*.

"Oh, boy … that's really fine, Amos—I'll show you your room, nephew," he said, emphasizing the *nephew*.

Uncle Wordie took me inside his home, a neat two-bedroom house all on one floor and very simple, I guessed so that he could traverse it well with his limitations. I took the spare bedroom, which he said he never really used. It had a cotlike bed and an old bureau with nothing in the drawers, and there was one small lamp on a table by the bed.

Both of us forgot that we hadn't eaten dinner, and Wordie opened the refrigerator and pulled out an apple pie with a thick crust and said, "My belly thinks my throat is cut, Amos" (Appalachian for "I'm hungry"). "Amos, you know how many pies I get a week?" he continued.

"No, Wordie."

"A dozen, nephew—all from my friends who appreciate my memory. Mind you, I don't eat all of them, I share them."

And we both finished off the whole pie piece by piece and by hand and went to sleep.

As I lay in bed on my back, with both my arms over my head, I felt comfort in my heart. I don't know if I was dreaming, but I think I heard Wordie pass my room and say under his breath, "I knew I'd see my kin again." Maybe it was a dream, maybe not.

The sun woke me up about six thirty in the morning as well as the sound of Wordie singing:

In the sweet by and by

We shall meet on that beautiful shore

In the sweet by and by ...

The lilting and melodious song came out of Wordie as he puttered around in the kitchen.

He was singing a hymn with an Appalachian gospel style. It seemed different from the Negro hymns in that it had more of a country feeling. He had a beautiful soft voice.

"Uncle Wordie, good morning. That's a beautiful song."

"Hallo, my nephew ... a good mornin'. I think 'In the Sweet By and By' is my favorite hymn. You know, Amos, I sing in our church on Sunday," he said proudly. "I do believe I know by heart fifty-two hymns. I sing one a week on the Lord's Day, and Pastor Johnson asks me to add one more favorite, and I seem to always sing 'In the Sweet By and By.' Nobody has ever said they didn't like it, Amos—nobody. I 'company myself on the organ also."

"You really play the organ and piano too, Wordie?"

"Yep, one thing Henrietta and Daddy and Hardy Boy wanted was for me to have somethin' artistic of my own, Amos. I took lessons from Pastor Smith's wife, Beatrice. She was taught piano by her folk. I see you brought a guitar, Amos."

"Yeah, I play and also write songs."

"Well, well ... we now have a combo of two. You're goin' play with me, won't you? I only play at church. There's an organ up on the dais and a piano in the community room. This Sunday, nephew—is it a deal?"

Even in his blindness, Wordie could tell that I had this broad sweet smile on my face. I said, "Yes, Uncle."

Wordie told me that he worked from ten in the morning to three in the afternoon at the library, and he invited me to watch him "do his moves," as he said. He also told me to "mosey" around town and meet the "folk," 'cause as soon as he mentioned that his nephew had come to visit, everybody would know it and want to meet his "kin."

I had these fantasies all day telling people Wordie and I were kin. I thought of introducing Wordie to Cantor Krickstein and saying, "Meet my kin from West Virginia, Cantor Krickstein." I couldn't get that word out of my mind.

Actually everybody I met did say almost the same thing—"Glad to meet you, Amos. I hear you're Wordie's kin—he's a good man, that Wordie."

I must have spent about two hours in the Moorefield library. It served quite an area since it was the only one around for many miles. Wordie would stand behind the long counter that was directly opposite the entrance of the library. Behind him were the stacks. When someone asked him if a certain book was in the library, he would tell them immediately, and within the blink of an eye he went to get it. Wordie's walk was kind of different—almost like he had thousands of preprogrammed routes he was following. And with his phenomenal memory, I'm sure he did. Only once did he call Edna, a diminutive little lady with reading glasses hanging from her neck.

"Edna, please help me a minute. Check this shelf. Am I right near *Moby-Dick*?"

"OK, dearie ...," she said, and she went to the stack where Wordie was and continued, "You're right on, Wordie. That's the book."

"Thanks, Edna."

I felt quite comfortable all day in Moorefield. I was feeling that my journey was complete and my mind was at rest. As the day wore on, though, and I knew Wordie's work day was ending, unanswered and unasked questions crept into my mind—questions about why Dad and Wordie had never gotten together all these years and why my grandfather and Dad had the same first name as the county they lived in. I needed to search for more answers about my family.

Wordie made soup for us early that night so we could "continue a-talkin' family."

He told me he ate a lot of soup and just threw "vegee-tables" in the pot and let nature take its course. He told me I was lucky that butcher Norman had run out of "hog's eyes" so he hadn't "put the lil' buggers in"—and then said, "Jus' kiddin', nephew."

After dinner we sat on the porch in the rocking chairs. It was a very comfortable night, and I sure was looking forward to continuing my "learnin'" about my Appalachian roots.

"Uncle Wordie ... I still don't understand—did Dad come back? Have you seen him?"

"Amos, first of all, we Appalachians, and I include your dad, are a very stubborn bunch. But we also are very committed and we persevere through the darn toughest stuff. My daddy and I really wanted Hardy Boy to have a life without us—and if that meant never seein' us agin, so be it.

"He was eighteen years old and headed up north. We didn't know where at first … and I don't think he knew where he was goin' and where he'd end up settlin' his roots. But he ended up in New York City. He was a smart one, I tell you—his schoolin' down here was real good.

"Amos, he didn't write right away, and we were worried off the bat. But we had faith in the Lord to keep him safe, for certainly our itty family suffered too much, and Daddy and I knew God would take care of us and Hardy Boy. We think he wandered like the Israelites in the desert until he found his home."

I noticed a number of things about Wordie. He was well educated and knew very complex words and phrases, but he would intersperse southern Appalachian dialect at times and then switch back to a more traditional and formal way of speaking. I also noticed that he would often refer to the Bible and metaphors associated with the scriptures and life. I realized that this was the way of the Appalachian people—and now these people were my people. Wordie continued:

"It was nigh on a year, Amos … a year … and we get this letter from New York City. Daddy is so excited, for we never get anything by the mail. We have to take Samuel to Bradley's General Store where the post is to see who it is from. I remember the day as if it was today, Amos—Monday, October 9, 1922. It's from Hardy Boy! Daddy is sweatin' and all red and so happy. Right on the spot, on the wagon in front of Bradley's while Samuel is just restin', Daddy reads Hardy Boy's first letter to me. He writes that he got a place in the city with a bunch of other young men like himself. It was a roomin' house, and he bunked with four boys in a room the size of our outhouse. When Daddy reads this to me we both burst out into a laugh, for we know that Hardy Boy is only kiddin', since Daddy barely fits in our outhouse. He says it costs him a dollar a week, and the owner, a nice lady, gives the boys biscuits and coffee for free every mornin'. He also writes that the biscuits are not fit to eat and the boys generally throw them at each other for fun. He says he is looking for permanent work so he can really save money and go to school. He is so happy that Daddy gave him the five hundred dollars. He writes that he still has two hundred dollars and it's in a big bank. Daddy and I are amazed. We never saw a big bank—actually we never saw a bank—so we don't know what it could look like. Hardy

Boy writes in that first letter that he is doin' odd jobs just to pay the rent and he'll write again as soon as he has a real job.

"Daddy and I know not to worry now. Hardy Boy will write again, and we just should wait patiently for his letter. The next one came on a Monday afternoon, March 5, 1923. We were so excited again. Hardy Boy writes that he got his real job. He writes that he is a electricity helper, which is he helps the man who puts in electric lights and wires. We learn later that what that person is called properly is an electrician—but we never would understand that from the beginning. Hardy Boy writes that we should see New York City. It is a bustlin' and hustlin' place with all kinds of motorcars and trucks. He says they are puttin' together buildings that go so high up in the sky, they scrape it. There's talk that New York City is goin' to have more people in it than any city in the world soon. They say that London had the most people and soon New York is goin' to pass it. He says he works a lot, for electricity is needed by everyone and everything. He saw his first movie in a real theater. He saw Rudolph Valentino. He wites also that nobody can drink liquor anymore. Daddy and I laugh since we know down here everybody makes and drinks their own stuff—so we wonder what the fuss is about."

"Dad wrote to you and used his name, Hardy Lardy?" I asked as Wordie finally took a breath.

"Yep … that last letter he told us he'd write a letter every two months and keep us up to date on his doin's. In that letter he asked Daddy to write him back and let him know we were well. Some of the other boys were gettin' letters at the roomin' house, and he wrote the address for us to send. Daddy was well schooled also, and he read me a nice letter he composed to Hardy Boy tellin' him we are well and want him to do well to encourage him.

"Amos, you can see that we'd never ask him to come back here. Life here is so different from the city life. Daddy and I knew we couldn't take city life and Hardy Boy couldn't return to Appalachian life—you see what I mean, Amos?"

I nodded in agreement and began to see a more complete picture of the relationship between Wordie, my granddad, and Dad.

"Hardy Boy writes like clockwork every two months, and it was one and a half years, and he's workin' as a electrician in many tall buildin's that touch the sky. Finally, he writes in the summer of '24 that he has saved enough money and he's goin' to City College in the fall. Daddy and

I are whoopin' it up when we get that letter. We thank the Lord and take Samuel out for a long ride into town and tell everybody we see at Bradley's General Store.

"The next few letters he tells us that he needs to work about twenty-five hours a week as an electrician to make up for the money it costs him to live and pay for schoolin'. Boy, Daddy and I think that Hardy Boy is real committed to schoolin', and we are so proud of him."

"When did Dad meet Mom?"

"Well … well … now there is a love affair brewin' for a long time. It's like one of my special soups with all kinds of root vegee-tables … You know it's goin' be good … It smells good from the beginnin' … but it's goin' to need a lot of time to get to be soup, Amos.

"So, Hardy Boy gets this here job in '26 at Moscovitch Furriers, where they are makin' a new store out of the old one in New York City. They are makin' a fur storage vault and it's electrified to keep it a proper temperature. Everybody is buyin' furs—they all have so much money in New York. Well, Hardy Boy gets in real close to the whole family, since he is workin' there for about thirty hours a week. He makes friends with all the young boys workin' at the store and even the owners. They become real close and like Hardy Boy a lot. You know, it's like they became family … and Daddy and me were so happy because he sure needed family since he didn't have us.

"Well, one day in '26, Hardy Boy is workin' in the new fur vault fixin' some electric problem, and he writes he got scared out of his wits. You see, there's furs hangin' like people all over the place, and you can't see through them. Hardy Boy writes that he was movin' the furs with his hands to cross the room, and right in front of his face he was confronted with another face, and he jumped up and grabbed a fur coat, and he fell to the floor only to have your future mom lookin' down at him and laughin'. He writes that he looked up and saw the prettiest face and teeth he'd ever seen. She helped him get up, and they started talkin', and he found out she's one of the Moscovitches' daughters.

"Amos, I think they both were in love right away in the fur vault, and she was only fifteen. Your daddy was right respectful so he kept his distance, he writes. But I tell you, for the next year he writes only about the Moscovitch family and Helen.

"You know Amos, he keeps writin' about the Moscovitch family bein' Jewish, and the first time he writes *bein' Jewish* we have to ask Preacher

Jenkins if there are really Jews now other than in the scriptures. Of course, he tells us there are. Hardy Boy is writin' about how the family honors the scriptures. He says their holy day is Saturday. He writes that they are a real nice family and they like him a lot. He also says they don't know his last name, since he works for the electrician company. They are a large family, and everybody laughs a lot, and he's in love with Helen, and he truly believes she's in love with him. But he's right respectful, since she's only fifteen and still in public school and he's twenty-four and in college school."

As Uncle Wordie finally took a breath and we sat for the moment contemplating our family, I saw where this was all going. It became obvious to me that Dad became Jewish. As I thought about this, I could hardly stifle the chuckle that came out of my mouth. Fortunately, Wordie wasn't tuned in to my absurd mind. Certainly he had to clue me in on how this transformation occurred.

"OK, continue, Uncle Wordie ..."

"Well, the whole next year your daddy did well in school and worked only at the Moscovitch Furriers. I remember the letter from Hardy Boy we get on Tuesday, December 11, 1928, sayin' he's applyin' to the Flower Fifth Avenue Medical School. Wow, Daddy and I say. What a fancy name for a school. He's really gonna be a doctor. We both dance around arm in arm doin' the Appalachian jig, we're so happy. But then he writes in the next sentence that he kissed Helen. That's all he said about it. He just kissed her. Daddy and I don't know what to think. He writes in the next sentence that Helen is graduatin' high school while he's graduatin' City College and that she applied to City College when he applied to medical college. Daddy and I think somethin's brewin'—a deeply rich soup, Amos ... somethin' cookin' together, Amos—cookin' together.

"Well—the next letter has a return name on it that sure shocks us, Amos. It says 'Har Lardowitz' with the same address and handwritin' as Hardy Boy's. And in that letter, Amos, Hardy Boy writes that he got into medical college and he's gonna marry Helen when he graduates medical college and they'll have a family together. But he says that he'll never be able to marry her if he isn't Jewish since her family wouldn't approve, so he's plannin' to change his name and become Jewish, and he did some studying and found that a lot of Jewish names have a 'witz' on the end. He also says that Helen knows where he comes from and that he's not Jewish. He also says that while he's at it, he'll change Hardy, since up in New York he'd never met a Jewish Hardy or for that matter any Hardy. And he says it's gonna be real nice because it's a nice religion and they read the scriptures like we do. He wanted to write us with his new name to see how we liked it. He says he needs to file papers at the courthouse, and it will take time, but they say he could have his new name in two more months. Daddy and I are happy for him. We really don't care if he changes his name, for we want him to be happy. And for bein' Jewish, they read the scriptures, so's it's fine with us."

So there I sat—and there Uncle Wordie sat—for the moment quiet, quieter than he'd been in the short time I had known him. This was the answer to my quest for the moment. My secret picture in the attic had yielded itself to me, but I hadn't had time to process it yet, and I had a gut feeling there was more to discover and more to learn about my family.

I thought Uncle Wordie was unusually contemplative after he completed the history of his brother, Hardy Boy.

"Uncle Wordie ... what more occurred?" I asked, kind of leading him.

"Oh, Amos ... life is filled with hardships in the Appalachians and we certainly get used to it, but poor Daddy got sick just weeks before Hardy Boy said he was gonna come home just before he was to start medical college. On July 12, 1929, Friday, Daddy fell ill with a fever. Doc Roberts came to see him. Daddy wouldn't go to the city to a hospital. He wanted to stay home. Doc came by every day. Hardy Boy rushed down here only to find Daddy very sick in bed. We hugged and hugged when we saw each other, Amos—and we were so sad. Daddy was happy when he saw us together from his bed, though. He was just so weak, Amos, and he died on July 31 at one thirty in the afternoon, with Hardy Boy and me by his side. We buried him in the old Lost City cemetery on Sunday, August 4, 1929, Amos—and he was gone."

It seemed so abrupt, what Wordie had just told me. I was shocked, and there were tears flowing down my cheeks, and Wordie just seemed to be contemplative and quiet with a distant look on his face. He continued:

"Amos ... somehow it seemed normal, this suffering. We'd always hear of folk in town with the same losses. And we'd comfort our neighbors by bein' there for them. Our life was of the land and very simple. We believed in the Lord and accepted all what occurred. I believed that my handicap was a blessing in disguise, for it made me special. It made me focus on who I was and what I could do for others and myself. Amos, I still believe that the more you have in material goods the more unfortunate you are, for you lose yourself to your possessions. And for my blindness, Amos … I know that you have not heard a robin sing like I have, and I know that you have not smelled and heard the comin' of a thunderstorm from ten miles away. And you can see, Amos, that my life is a happy life of giving and caring and knowin' all who are important to me. Amos, I believe your daddy is exactly like me. He is strong and secure, and he never wavers from his responsibility and commitment to his family and his patients."

Wow, I thought as he stopped for a breath. His voice was soft and clear, and his expression was serene and calm. Uncle Wordie had just shocked me with this personal sermon that seemed to come out of nowhere—but really came from the roots of my family way down in the West Virginia mountains, in the middle of Appalachia.

Wordie told me that Dad stayed another week, and they had talked "forever," he said. They decided together as brothers, and as the last of their family, to be strong and independent. Wordie insisted that he would not want to be anywhere else but in the West Virginia mountains and that he wanted Hardy Boy to have his new life in New York. Wordie told Dad that he was fine with his blindness and did not want Dad to feel responsible for him. They made a pact to respect each other and always love each other even if they never saw each other again.

That was it for our evening as I heard all the wild sounds that were coming out of the dusk. Uncle Wordie seemed tired but peaceful, and we went to bed early.

I spent the next few days thinking about Wordie and his life from seventeen on, when he was suddenly thrust into being a blind orphan and all alone. I thought about how strong he was and how he insisted on living the life he knew already was right for him. How did he do it?

I learned in that week that Wordie was quite a guy, and mostly I learned it not from Wordie—for I felt that he wasn't a braggart but a storyteller of true stories. Wordie never showed me the plaque I discovered in the library honoring him for founding the library forty years before. He never told me about the first program in the South that taught blind rural children how to cope in life and read Braille, and his role in founding it. I found out about his goodness through the people he touched with his personality, and his commitment to giving.

I also thought of Dad a lot in those next few days. It was interesting, I thought, that when I'd first discovered the mysterious picture of Aunt

Henrietta in the attic, I hadn't thought of why Dad was who he was. I always respected him as a caring father and doctor with the abilities to bend to any crisis or problem, a loving man. At that moment I felt his conversion and commitment to Judaism was just part of who Dad was, a dedicated person. In reality, then, Dad and Wordie were the same, born out of the same stock. They were strong and sure and of course stubborn.

I obviously thought of Amos Boris Lardowitz and my long meander through discovery after discovery to find out who I was. In thinking about myself, though, I don't believe my quest was a narcissistic one. I think that my quest has always been related to who I am in relation to the world and its people and how I can live better for all humanity.

Wordie took me to his Harmony Baptist Church on Sunday. Actually, I drove him. He told me he rode with a different friend every Sunday to "share the gospel" and "be their memory bank in case they need one on the ride over."

Pastor Johnson greeted me with a broad smile and open hand as we entered the church. Everybody, about fifty people, wore all-knowing smiles about "Wordie's kin bein' here." Pastor Johnson read selected portions of scripture and then gave a sermon on tolerance, which I thought was quite apropos. He then told Deacon Lardy to "do your thing," which I thought was a funny expression. Wordie hadn't told me he was a deacon. I found out later that a deacon in this small church was a trusted and valued member who was the first assistant to the pastor—quite a compliment for Wordie, I thought.

Wordie sat down at the organ in plain sight of us all and with a sweet smile began to sing:

Once like a bird … in prison I dwelt …
No freedom from… my sorrow I felt …
But Jesus came and listened to me …
And glory to God … He set me free …

He set me free … He set me free …
I was blind … but hallelujah, now I see …
I shall ne'er forget the day …
When He washed my sins away …
And He set … He set me free …

It was of course beautiful. He had so much joy in his voice, and I thought the phrase *I was blind, but hallelujah, now I see* was quite poignant.

The service was about over when I noticed Pastor Johnson about to address me.

"Amos, please be so kind as to accompany your uncle Wordie on your guitar while he plays and sings 'In the Sweet By and By.'" I looked up at Wordie and said to both of them, quite embarrassed, "I didn't bring my guitar, Pastor."

Wordie jumped in right away and said, "Pastor, I'll get it—it's in the trunk of the car."

That sneak—he had put it in the trunk without my knowing. Also, he must have heard me fingerpicking the melody the other night—and I thought I played really quietly! His senses are definitely superhuman, I thought.

Well, the whole congregation was chuckling with joy as I attempted to accompany Wordie while he sang and played the ending hymn. It sure was fun, though, and when it was over, there was a lot of clapping.

I savored the new relationship I had discovered with my uncle over the next few days. Spring had arrived in Appalachia, and my mind, on its own, felt like it had come home. It was both a strange and beautiful feeling, and I seemed eons away from my Jewish life in the Bronx and "sububs." The Vietnam War and my horrifying experience with Donny were finding their distant place in my heart, thank God.

I felt as if I were finally heading in a direction that I must have been searching for all my life. Obviously, I could not picture my destination yet, but I felt I was where I was supposed to be right then.

Wordie told me he had insisted that Dad go back to New York City and go right to medical school and not worry about him, or he would not be able to study and become a doctor. Wordie said he left the farm and went to live with Edna and her husband, Woodrow, and their two children in Moorefield—and in Moorefield he remained until this day, leaving his birth home for good.

Dad continued to write, and he actually sent Wordie money every month, as much as he could afford.

I thought that theirs was an amazing bond, one that tragedy and separation could not destroy. And through the years, I began to think, the two brothers, once very similar, became completely different people living in completely different cultures. Yet the bond remained, and their love and commitment to each other stayed strong even without physical contact.

Wordie told me a funny thing about a letter he received from Dad on November 29, 1929.

"Hardy Boy … Har … told me that the stock market crashed in that letter, and I went around town tellin' everybody that I hoped no one was killed when it collapsed. Finally, after a week I understood what he meant and all the townsfolk laughed like heck."

Well, this must have been a tough time for Dad and Mom and her family, for the Moscovitch Fur Company lost 75 percent of its business. Interestingly, Dad was able to continue to work as an electrician while he went to medical school and was putting in about a twenty-hour day between school, studying, and working.

Dad became engaged to Mom in the summer of 1932 between his third and fourth year of medical school. They were married August 27, 1933, just after Dad graduated medical college and the same year that Mom graduated City College. Of course, his Jewish transformation had been complete from 1929 on.

I guess Uncle Wordie was the brother who insisted that there be no knowledge of his life in Appalachia for fear of Dad losing his family and life in New York City. Dad had to honor Wordie's wishes since they had made that pact. Once I knew, I realized that I could not question their decisions. I realized that their roots and upbringing were what gave them their persona, and it came with the gutsy determination and stubbornness born of Appalachia.

Dad's early life was complete, I thought, and I was satisfied.

My interest in my American heritage began to take me further from my dad's birth. Here I was, related to people of American birth deep within my country's history. It was at this spot that I felt the undiscovered nagging at me. I thought about my American grandfather and how I had discovered him by seeing a flyer for a fair in a county that had the same name as his first name. I was prepared to stay the course and to put the rest of my life on hold until I found what I was looking for.

"Uncle Wordie, tell me about your dad. When was he born?" I said on a warm spring evening as Wordie and I sat on the rockers on the porch.

"I'm afraid, Amos, that there's not much to tell … Daddy was an orphan, although he did tell me he was born in 1863."

My mind went back to the Civil War as I heard the words. My grandfather was born during the conflict that had possessed me, starting as a child and into my adult years. If only I could go further into my American past.

"But who told him he was born in 1863 if he was an orphan, Wordie?"

"I knew you'd get to the rest of your kin, Amos. Your persistent Appalachian roots are showin'," he said with a sly smile, and I smiled softly when I saw that. "Rebecca told Daddy."

"All right, Wordie—move that mouth of yours," I said fondly in a way that could be used only with a close relative.

"Rebecca—Daddy's nanny. Daddy came to my gran'parents' farm by horseback ... that is, to Laizie's parents' place ... understand, nephew? They were young'uns, your great-gran'parents, Amos ... young'uns. They hadn't children yet. In fact, they had only one child and that was Laizie, and she wasn't born till 1878. Daddy tells it like Rebecca tells him, Amos. Rebecca brings Daddy in 1864 on Old Ivory with a long beautiful mane and tail blowin' in the wind, and with the sweetest disposition. She comes to the farm out of the blue with little Daddy sittin' on her lap in front of her on Old Ivory."

"What do you mean, his nanny?"

"His black-as-coal nanny, Amos—his black-as-coal nanny."

"Do you mean she was a Negro?"

"If she was black, nephew, she'd be a Negro, I guess."

"A slave, Wordie?"

"If she was a Negro in 1864, Amos, I suspect she'd be a slave."

Oh my God, I thought. I began to picture this black woman on a white horse carrying a white child through the wilderness to a new home during the turmoil that was the Civil War.

"Wordie, what do you know about Rebecca?"

"She died in 1880, as Daddy told it. Jonathan and Elizabeth and Daddy were there at her deathbed. Your great-gran'parents on my mommy Laizie's side were Jonathan and Elizabeth Lardy. Daddy was seventeen years old, and little Laizie was only two years old, and she was Daddy's future wife, of course. Daddy says nobody knew exactly how old Rebecca was; she was a young'un when she rode into the farm, but Daddy said he thought she was about forty when she died. "

"She lived with your grandparents on their farm until she died?"

"Yep … She worked in the field, growin' things … and she sang beautiful field songs and hymns all the time. Daddy tells us that she taught everybody lots of schoolin'. That's why we are all so schooled, Amos—it was Rebecca who taught us—it was Rebecca. Daddy says Rebecca was a wonderful and exciting person, Amos. He always said she was the light in his eyes. She was the one who gave him hope and faith. He always said that, Amos— always."

"He told Dad this?" I said in disbelief.

"One thing our daddy always did, Amos, was to sit us down together, Etta, Hardy Boy, and me, and tell us Rebecca stories. Daddy would tell us from his memory bedtime poems and stories that Rebecca made up for him when he was a young'un.

"I remember always sayin', 'Tell us Rebecca stories, Daddy—tell us Rebecca stories.' Your daddy said the same, Amos."

I found this unbelievable—my dad sitting as a child, listening to stories from his dad that came directly from the Civil War through the heart of his father's black nanny.

"Did she live in the same house as Laizie's parents?"

"Yep, she lived in the attic above Jonathan and Elizabeth. That's the farmhouse I was brought to the world in—and your daddy … and Henrietta, poor soul. That's the farm our family inherited, Amos, and that's the house my poor daddy left this earth to go to heaven in—and that's the home I left at seventeen years old, seven days after Daddy died—I left for good."

"Wordie, please share Rebecca stories with me," I said as if I were my dad as a child.

Wordie closed his eyes, only for the second time that I had seen, and seemed to return to the days of his early youth.

He kept his eyes closed as he recited from memory:

Go to sleep, my chillun
Do not weep, my chillun
For the sky will bring
The soft and fuzzy thing.

"And then Daddy would bring from behind his back a rough ball of wool from one of our sheep and tickle us in the belly and we'd all laugh so hard. It didn't matter how many nights in a row he recited that poem, for we'd all sit there anticipatin' him ticklin' us. He'd recite Rebecca's poems like these:

Dream a real dream
And come true it will

Do not be afraid
For the fragrance of the flowers
Will protect you

The light from my love
Shines brighter than the brightest star
And it's inside your heart
"And then he'd touch our hearts with his hand."

Do you know how to make your heart smile?
You can sing a while

Amazing, I thought—a little child listening to poetry and prose from a Negro woman who was possibly an African slave, and then he passes it on to his own Appalachian children.

I dreamt very vividly of Rebecca that night. I saw her as a young and beautiful woman with a sweet, engaging smile. It surely seemed that Rebecca had had a serendipitous influence on my Appalachian family's upbringing.

The next day I could hardly wait to pursue my questions about Rebecca—who she was and where she came from, bringing along my grandfather.

I lay awake early the next morning at about five, thinking of the farmhouse that my family lived in and whether it was still standing or not. If it was, I desperately wanted to see it.

"Uncle Wordie—your birth home—where is it?" I asked as Wordie was cooking some eggs.

"Amos, my boy … I can't tell you if it is still standin'. I never went back to my early life, but it was outside Lost River, deep within Appalachia, my nephew—deep within, bordering the dense forest up against Great North Mountain."

"You all lived off the land?"

"Everybody lived off the land, Amos. It went way back to when the Indians lived here. Everybody was subsistence farmers … We grew what we ate and ate what we grew, except for the occasional bull we'd take to town and sell after we grew it for over a year, since it was a twin of a milkin' heifer. Same goes for the sheep and goats. Lost River was the town we'd go to— the one with the general store and post office. It's no longer there, Amos—must be like lookin' for a needle in a haystack … the farm thirty miles from here, more or less. So many farms and a poor, poor existence but one I'd go back to in a heartbeat, although too tough for many folk. But loggin' and state roads have taken a lot of the farms. Boy, we must have had 150 acres to grow."

I thought Wordie could actually see what I was thinking. I'm sure my face had a look of fierce determination to find this farm, and even though he had no sight, I knew he could really see me.

"Amos, my boy … you're goin' to ask me if I'd know it now, considerin' I'm blind. You know the answer to that. I'd know it by the smell of the wood in the house, I'd know it by the feel of the grain on the front door, I'd know it by the warmth of the sun that comes through the windows and touches my face and my blind but sensitive eyes. Yep, Amos, I'd know it—I'd know it. And I suppose you'd want me to go with you, nephew. I will. You'll find it, Amos—you'll find it if it's still standin', my boy. You've got Appalachia in you, my boy. You've got the grittiness to do it … if it's still standin'."

Wordie and I talked about where my grandfather was buried, as well as Henrietta. He thought that possibly his mother was buried there also. He called it the old Lost City cemetery. I started to think how I would narrow down the radius of our search for my family's farmhouse. Obviously, we would need a starting point. Wordie's library sure came in handy, and I spent all of the next day looking for clues. I discovered that it was going to be impossible to pinpoint exactly the old Lost City cemetery. There were many small cemeteries in the 1800s, and many were family ones that had been abandoned and had grown over. I could not find reference to a Lost City cemetery, but there was an unincorporated town called Lost City. The one thing I hoped was that it would be there, since many communities and historic associations might want to protect these small pieces of revered land, although most were not named. The idea, I thought, would be to find some point of reference for distance so that I could draw a radius on a map and begin to search that way. The smaller the better, I thought, since this area was very rural and mountainous and mostly inaccessible. My idea to find the cemetery first was that it was closest to the farm, according to Wordie, and that would hopefully make our search easier. The small town of Lost River was farther away, and the old buildings were long gone. Either way, using Wordie's phenomenal memory would certainly be the key, since he remembered everything forever. The key would be to get an approximate distance to the cemetary somehow, and in discussing it together we came to the conclusion that Samuel the draft horse would be the answer. All we needed to do was figure out how fast Samuel walked—and he only walked, at the same lazy speed, as Wordie would say. Then Wordie's memory would come into play. We'd pick his mind until we came up with an exact time he'd remember for any trip Samuel took. And as heard before, Wordie would spout off the hours and minutes it took for such-and-such to happen—or for such-and-such a trip. The one incident I thought of was when my dad took Samuel and Etta to Moorefield for the picture. Wordie was so excited that he was on top of the whole itinerary. He remembered that Dad had said having the picture made took exactly three hours. Dad had said that Mr. Randolph had told him that if it took more than three hours to take the picture and develop and print it, it would cost more. Dad had said he'd finished just on time, and it hadn't cost him any more. He'd also told Wordie that they came right home and had no time to eat or do anything else. Wordie had already told me that Dad had left with Etta at exactly six thirty in the morning. He remembered that the time was exactly eleven fourteen in the evening when they returned. So we were dealing with sixteen hours and forty-four minutes that they were away. Wordie said that it was common knowledge of those who traveled to Moorefield, and some lucky enough to go by automobile, that it was about thirty miles away. If their actual travel time was thirteen hours and forty-six minutes (three hours was subtracted for the photo) and the toal round trip was approximately sixty miles, Samuel had gone just a little over four miles an hour. That seemed like a good starting point. I could draw a thirty-mile circle around Moorefield and look for the farm and cemetery only along the eastern periphery, but Wordie and I thought we could do better. Wordie figured that the average trip to town took about two and a half hours. It was somewhat harder to figure the exact mileage to town since his dad would always make a side trip just to "please the kids." Wordie also remembered that the one cemetery trip was one and a half hours. I figured the mileage on each by Samuel's walking speed.

At the library the next day, I sat down with graph paper and pencil and a compass. I made three circles, one with Moorefield as the center and the other two on the periphery of the outside radius on the eastern side, including the town of Lost City and and a pure guess where the town of Lost River was. At first it seemed like an unintelligible mess, but after looking at it from a distance and drawing more concentric rings to allow for error, I saw a pattern that looked good enough to consider mapping for travel. What the heck, I said to Wordie, and he laughed a deep belly laugh and agreed. "The more rings you draw the better—good logic, nephew."

But smart as he was, Wordie noticed a flaw in my calculations.

"Nephew—do you really think Samuel walked like the crow flies? Even the automobile doesn't fly like a crow—get it, Amos?"

"Oh yeah, dumb me—thirty miles is certainly not a straight line," I said, embarrassed.

I decided to spend a day trying to correct what could be a large error in calculation.

I got myself a compass from one of Wordie's friends and drove my car slightly southeast toward the Great North Mountain. I was going to find any landmark that I could map at about thirty miles. This way I would be able to reduce the circle's diameter to a more reasonable distance. After a tedious time finding some marker, since the area was so rural, I found one that appeared on a map of the county. The radius was actually reduced to twenty-three and a half miles—which certainly meant there were a lot of twists and turns.

After correcting my error, I sat with Wordie and described what I was seeing. I also got a topographical map from the Forest Service and compared them side by side.

"Wordie, I can see that part of the radius on the eastern and southeastern side away from Moorefield goes right up to and into the forest of Great North Mountain."

"Yep—our land kind of bordered the forest and included part of it also," he said.

The other small circles centered on Lost River and Lost City seemed to be helpful. I was interested in the intersections of all three of them with one another. I thought I could start at that point and work out.

Wordie told me the farmstead was close to what everyone called the Lost River. Obviously, he said, "you can't live where there isn't water."

On my map, the Lost River meandered in and out of my seemingly schizophrenic circles.

Because Wordie didn't want to take off from the library, we decided that on the next Saturday, we would start out at five thirty in the morning and spend as long as we could possibly tolerate finding the farm. We also decided that this would be our first exploratory trip and that we should not be disappointed if we got nowhere.

Wordie cooked for three hours Friday night. He insisted on bringing the victuals," as he said, since it was "no use getting hungry and then stupid." I laughed when he said that.

I could not sleep that Friday night. I lay awake, once more on my back with my hands behind my head, looking up through the ceiling and into the imaginary sky above.

I pictured Wordie and me as Lewis and Clark on the night before they left for their long discovery of untamed America. What would we find? Could we actually find my family's farmhouse? Would there be people living in it? Would it be abandoned—or simply not there? In my mind, I could not accept the latter. I thought I would will it to be there.

As I was eating a piece of toast with jelly at five in the morning, I saw Wordie kind of sniff the air.

"What's up?"

"Fog comin' ..."

"What?"

"Fog—low clouds and mist ... and fog—in and around the highlands and mountains ... Makes it more difficult."

"Should we have listened to the radio for the weather, Wordie?"

"With my nose, nephew, you don't need no radio weather."

I laughed and he laughed and we were off. It was almost like the start of my Delta trip, but then I had felt like I was a passenger. Now I felt like the pilot—but I certainly had my navigator along to guide me, and a good one at that.

As we drove east in the quiet morning, the sky became brighter, but gray and white billowy clouds blanketed us. And then, as Wordie predicted, as I drove along the undulating rural roads through gently sloping hills and valleys, I could see fingers of fog hugging the low areas. As we started to drive through the stuff, I realized how dense it was. Wordie announced, without my saying anything, "Through the clouds, nephew." I began to think it was going to be really difficult to map anything on this trip, but it sure was beautiful—the Potomac Highlands were beginning to fascinate me like nothing else in my life before.

As we continued what would end up being just a dry run, I daydreamed as I was driving about the beauty and stillness that is now, and the history that once was.

Well, we lasted about four hours. Wordie and I both felt that this just would not be our day, but we were excited about returning.

The next day I began to worry that Wordie would not take off from his library job frequently enough for me to satisfy my yearnings. But Edna came to the rescue. She knew we had gone, and she wanted me to find the Lardy family farm. She said to me at the library that Monday that she had always felt guilty about taking Wordie away from the home he loved so dearly. Unfortunately, she said, she could never find the farm on her own and would not remember it anyway, since it was such a sad experience for her. Edna said she had blocked that day out of her mind. Poor Woodrow was long gone, and her two children had moved from the Highlands of no opportunity to the West Coast. Interestingly, she used the word *quest* to describe our coming journey.

Edna insisted to Wordie that he go with me and be at my disposal and do it for her. She told Wordie her mind would be at peace about the abrupt displacement she had caused in his life if we found the family farm. She said the right things to Wordie, for he would give up his responsibilities only for another's needs, and he felt Edna needed this closure.

In my heart, I knew that Wordie needed this also. He would never seek to return to the past on his own. And I believe that I was his catalyst in discovery, as he was mine.

The old farmsteads deep within the Potomac Highlands were log homes, and the outside boards had the log bark exposed. This would probably make a house more difficult to spot because of the camouflage effect. But then I thought it might have a better chance of still standing because it could sit undisturbed and unnoticed for many years while new forest growth reclaimed it. There was also little development to this point in those backwoods areas. Most people had moved away to the cities or just died and disappeared.

I remember the exact day, June 22, 1968. It was a Saturday, and it must have been the fourth trip we had taken. Up to this day we had had no luck. I don't think we were discouraged, but I could see that Wordie was more tired on each trip.

"A beautiful and clear and sunny Appalachian mornin' to you, nephew," Wordie said, serving me eggs in the early morning.

"A beautiful mornin' to you, uncle," I replied.

And we were off. It was beautiful, and the forecast was for a comfortably warm, bright day.

The last time we had gone, it was raining steadily, and my mind unfortunately had drifted back to the Highlands of Vietnam from the Potomac Highlands. I never told Wordie about any experiences in the war, so my thoughts had to remain my own. Interestingly, I seemed to identify with the similar beauty of the two lands. For only a brief moment, my mind returned to the horrors and tragedies I had witnessed—but my lifelong quest was too strong to allow the past to enter and take me over.

"I feel good about today, Amos."

"So do I, Wordie."

We meandered up and down rolling hills and through meadows of grass. Above the horizon the lazy soft, billowy clouds were moving fast amid the developing blue sky. It was the kind of day that you could smell the terrain changing. It seemed that every flower and tree and rock and meadow had a distinct olfactory sense as we drove through.

Wordie and I were just enjoying the scenery, each other's company, and the trip when we decided to stop for our prepared lunch on the side of a road that had a lookout to Great North Mountain in the distance.

We sat on some large boulders, and Wordie started to sing:

Sun of my soul, Thou Savior dear,
It is not night if Thou be near;
O may no earthborn cloud arise
To hide Thee from Thy servant's eyes.
When the soft dews of kindly sleep
My wearied eyelids gently steep,
Be my last thought, how sweet to rest
Forever on my Savior's breast.
Come near and bless us when we wake,
Ere through the world our way we take,
Till in the ocean of Thy love
We lose ourselves in Heaven above.

I closed my eyes and began to sing with Wordie as he repeated the last phrase. I felt the warmth of the sun on my face and could feel and smell the essence of the Highlands—all without sight, and with deep identification with my dear uncle.

We ate Wordie's lunch and then sat quietly for some time. Then both of us got up and turned our faces away from the Great North Mountain and toward my car. I knew in my heart at that moment that we would find Wordie's home. There was no conversation between us as my '63 Chevy meandered almost at her own will through the ups and downs of the gently rolling country roads of the Highlands. I felt peace for Wordie and me and could see his face as he seemed to smell the beauty of the land.

"Amos … turn back … about a half mile, my boy."

"What, Wordie? What do you mean?"

"The smell of the river—the Lost River."

"What do you mean?"

"Daddy used to describe the scenery to me as we traveled with Samuel. The Lost River is named because it goes underground and disappears at some point. I know that place, Amos—I know that place. In my mind and soul I feel and smell the change, Amos. It is a fifteen minute Samuel walk from my home, Amos—fifteen minutes, I tell you. That's a mile or so, my boy—a mile."

My heart began to pound as Wordie completed his thought. *My God, we are near.*

There didn't seem to be any houses or development along this stretch of road. I began to look very carefully for any path, or even a trail that seemed to cut into the woods from this road we were on.

"I smell home, Amos, I smell home—right here, my boy, right here," Wordie blurted out, startling me.

I stopped the car right then and pulled off to the edge of a woody area. Wordie opened his door and walked out and began sniffing and seemingly looking up and out into the deep woods beyond.

"What's up, Wordie?"

"Follow me, my boy."

There was nothing but woods, although it appeared to be secondary growth, the growth that occurs after a forest returns from abandoned farming. Wordie was actually feeling his way through the woods without sight. I didn't see any path or clearing up ahead. The weather was warm, and the early afternoon sun was filtering through the delicate leaf cover and onto the ground. It was a beautiful, soft feeling I had. The only sound was the delicate and soft-paced crunch of Wordie's shoes as they touched the forest floor. I followed about ten feet behind Wordie and was completely quiet. We must have walked about a quarter mile into the woods when Wordie just stopped and looked straight ahead even though I knew he could not see. I turned my head to follow the direction he was "seeing."

"Wordie—a house—a house!!" I first saw horizontal logs and realized it was a log home. It was about two hundred feet ahead, and there seemed to be a small clearing adjacent to it.

"Yes, I know."

He continued to walk directly toward the house with deliberate slow steps as he cleared occasional tree branches with his arms. He stopped about fifty feet from the log home surrounded by new forest growth and bent over to touch the ground. Wordie dug his hand into the earth below his feet and pulled up a handful of shale.

"The road Daddy and I made from Lawton Quarry."

Wordie continued to walk toward the house. It was an old log home with a front porch flimsily held up by three posts. It was about fifty feet by thirty feet with a small addition to the side with an overhang roof. The windows were large, but all were broken. Along the short side I could see one window on the second floor.

Wordie stepped up onto the porch. The sun was still high in the early summer sky, and it filtered through the trees onto the home. He raised his right hand and began gently rubbing the molding on the house that was directly adjacent to the door.

"My gracious … my gracious."

I could see through the mottled light that reflected off Wordie's face a small tear sliding out of his right eye and onto his cheek. I walked up onto the porch and put my arm over his left shoulder and gently hugged him.

"We found it, uncle …"

"Amos, my boy, you gave me a gift … a real gift," he said sincerely.

It was an amazing few hours—Wordie seemed to actually see. He knew how to take every step within the house. Inside on the first floor we found just one straight-back chair and the original cast-iron woodstove that had served for heat and cooking. Outside we found, covered in brambles, the iron plow that Samuel had pulled his whole life. It was deeply rusted. Wordie didn't say much. He just walked slowly, stopping to touch and feel surfaces and smell the air. Occasionally he would say quietly to himself, "Etta" and "Hardy Boy" and then maybe chuckle. I could see that he was transporting himself back to his childhood and family. I just followed him like a shadow, and I believe he was not even aware for a while that anyone was with him. Wordie had traveled to a distant time and place, and I was happy for him.

I wanted Wordie to take everything in at his own pace. We'd been there more than an hour, and Wordie had been walking around the house when he sat down on the front porch steps and said, "Amos, my boy … sit with me."

There we both sat quietly for another twenty minutes or so. Wordie then stood straight up and said, "Let's go, Amos."

Our trip back to Moorefield was quiet except for Wordie's soft humming of Appalachian gospel hymns.

The next day, Sunday, I attended services with Wordie. He seemed serene and happy, and his voice was clear when he sang. I could hear whispers about the "Lardy family farm" being found. Pastor Johnson's sermon began with the "birth of the family through toil of the land," and I knew he was referring to our family's home. At the end of the service the pastor announced that a "celebration of joy" would happen at the Willows' barn on Thursday.

I let my mind enjoy the sweet fruits of our discovery without thoughts over the next few days. I think Wordie did the same—it was truly a serene feeling.

Well, Wednesday certainly started auspiciously. About seven thirty in the morning, before Wordie was heading off to the library, Clarence Abbott beeped his horn in front of Wordie's house and yelled, "June 27th will be Lardy Family Farm Day! Come one, come all—four o'clock in the afternoon, tomorrow, at the Willows' barn at the bend!"

Wordie was told the library was closing early Thursday, and sure enough, the town just closed shop at three in the afternoon. Wordie came home and told me that it seemed like a "stink bomb" was set off and everyone had left town. Of course he knew the celebration was for him. I drove Wordie to the Willows' barn about three twenty. There must have been a hundred cars, and there were even a few horses and buggies. Colorful banners were hanging outside from the rafters to the adjacent tall trees. We heard music inside.

"Well, I'll be! Frederick, Jesse, and Chester with their fiddles! And Margaret on her dulcimer! And who is that on the drums? Is that Cecil? No—it's Cecil's son Clifford! Well, I'll be darned! Hey—those clogging feet I'd know anywhere! Stella and Blanche … the clogging twins—boy, are they good! Theodore on the bass—great! And who is banging on that piano? Is that little John Boy?"

Wordie was unbelievable. As soon as he entered the barn, he knew everyone by the sound of their instruments.

"And what do I smell … fried okra and cracklin' corn bread? Pickled crab apples—yummy. OK—who burned the walnut cookies?" Wordie was really funny.

There must have been two hundred people packed in the barn, with music and food everywhere. Little kids with clogs were falling all over the place trying to keep up with the clogging twins Stella and Blanche. Wordie was ushered to his piano, which had been transported from the church. He sat down and started to play rapidly an Appalachian country rhythm, and the clogging twins tried to keep up with him. It was hilarious as almost everyone started to join in clapping and clogging and falling all over the place. This must have gone on for about forty minutes, and then everyone, including Wordie, seemed to collapse in one heap in the center of the barn floor—and then we ate. I ate everything, although I stayed far away from the stuffed possum. The country ham with red-eye gravy was great, though.

After dinner there was more music. I had brought my guitar and joined in on the tunes of West Virginia country music. The fiddlers played off each other in an improvisational jam that tore the house down. The party wound down about nine thirty in the evening as Mayor Floyd made an announcement amid happy but tired faces that every June 27 in Moorefield would now become the "Lardy Family Farm Day" and that all businesses would close at three o'clock for the community barn party.

As I was driving Wordie home about ten thirty, he turned to me and said, "Dear Amos … thank you, my boy … thank you."

I remember lying down to sleep completely relaxed and satisfied that June 27 evening. I awakened about three in the morning and felt the urge to sit on the porch. Wordie was sleeping. It was a clear and warm early summer evening. The stars were very bright and the quarter moon was low. I sat on the steps of the porch and looked up into the sky. And then suddenly, I broke down in tears—uncontrollable tears. At first, I wasn't sure what I was crying about, but then I realized I had put myself completely aside during this successful quest for my dad's family home. I had only shadowed Wordie and thought of his feelings as we walked through the house, and I had bathed only in his joy during the celebration—and now it had hit me. It was my family also, I thought—my family ... my dad's childhood home and his dad's childhood home. And there it was, deep within America, deep within early Appalachia, undisturbed—and with my heritage within it.

A Jewish boy from the Bronx ... that's all I am ... and here sits my history ... here sits my family's roots—I'm only a Jewish boy from the Bronx. And the tears continued to flow.

I think Wordie was very smart and intuitive, for he seemed to know I would be the one to delve deeper into our common heritage.

"Amos, are you going to the farm today?" he said when I visited him at the library the next day. He knew I had deeper thoughts and unfinished family business. I think, though, that Wordie was completely satisfied for himself.

My drive to the farm was somewhat strange without Wordie. I felt a little trepidation at being alone with my own thoughts and without him. I parked the car once more just off the road and walked slowly to our hidden treasure within the woods.

Sitting on the steps of the porch, I began to think of my dad. My God, I thought, Dad is eons away from this place—a Jewish doctor in New York City. I began to think of Dad as a child growing up in the culture of pure Appalachia, strengthened by hard times and his family's faith in religion. But then maybe his life was no different now—family, service, hard work, and faith. Once more Dad and Wordie melded together, becoming inseparable and truly brothers in my mind, although I felt that this would not be the place for Dad to return to at this point.

I must have spent about four hours walking through the house and then outside where the fields were. I let myself feel the place as the farm and home it had been.

Rebecca's Legacy

YOU'RE BEAUTIFUL—YOUR SMILE, *your laugh—you smell so sweet—a sweet wonderful fragrance of flowers ...*

I remember saying this out loud as I awoke in a sweat a few nights later. *It's Rebecca—Rebecca.* I saw Rebecca's face over me as if she were looking down on a sleeping child to make sure everything was all right. My God—she was real, I thought, with bright brown eyes and beautiful white teeth.

I could not remove Rebecca's face from my mind the next morning. I didn't say anything to Wordie. I just felt compelled to go back to the farm that day. I think I must have separated Dad, Henrietta, and Wordie's upbringing from the deeper past of Rebecca on my initial discovery of the family home. It must have been an unconscious will—but now she appeared to me in a vivid vision as if beckoning me back to my deeper family roots. Interestingly, Wordie and I hadn't walked upstairs to the unfinished attic that once was a hayloft and then became Rebecca's room.

There was no door at the bottom of the stairs that led to the attic on the second floor. At the top of the stairs was a closed door. I climbed the stairs deliberately and slowly, each step producing a creaking sound seemingly from the past. As I opened the door, my face covered in spiderwebs, I started to feel very different—as if I was entering a sanctuary.

The afternoon sun was coming in and cast a large swath across the center of the floor. This was an empty attic space about twenty feet by fifteen feet with the one window on the south side. I felt very distant from the present. There was a quietness I cannot describe to this day. I stood motionless and thoughtless for about ten minutes and then suddenly collapsed to the floor in the center of the room. I could feel Rebecca's presence in and around me. I was on my knees and felt compelled to touch the floorboards—old oak boards worn and wide and unpainted. My hands seemed to be sliding over the floorboards of their own will. Suddenly I saw a bright light throughout the whole room. It was similar to the experience I had had in Vietnam and in Donny's home. Initially I thought the sun had become brighter, but it hadn't. Then I felt as if I was beginning to float in space above the room, and a sweet flowery fragrance surrounded me. My left hand brushed against a large crack between two of the floorboards. I could tell it was loose. I lifted the board, and underneath it, above the first-floor ceiling, my hand brushed against a pile of papers neatly tucked in the space between the beams.

My God—handwritten letters—manuscripts ...

There I gently pulled from its long-standing resting place a stack of papers about an inch and a half thick, neatly wrapped with what I thought initially was twine, but on closer inspection was tightly wound flower stems. There was one delicate dried flower in the center. I lifted the stack very carefully since one breath would have scattered the flower. And then I caught the fragrance—the fragrance I had smelled during my vivid dream of Rebecca. My God, I thought—this flower was the fragrance. *It was sent to me in my dream. Rebecca—you sent me this flower—this fragrance!*

I knew these were Rebecca's own writings. I did not even have to look at it. I knew this was Rebecca's legacy—left for the ages—left behind to be found or not found. I placed the stack in my lap over my knees with my legs tucked behind me. I was sitting straight up on the floor. I placed both my hands over the letters, the sun coming in behind my back and casting my shadow on the floorboards in front of me. As I looked at my shadow, it seemed to become a perfect silhouette of Buddha—and then the tears flowed once more as I said out loud, *"Rebecca—Rebecca."*

I think the passing sun finally moved me, for I was no longer casting my shadow. I felt that I was holding antiquity—I felt that I had antiquity within me. I dared not even look at this treasure yet, for I felt its power and meaning and I was afraid to enter its historic space. I felt as if I were its steward, its protector. I will enter this long-lost American time with deep respect and love, I thought. Carefully and slowly I returned the stack to its resting place.

For two days I walked in a dream. I said nothing to Wordie. I felt as if I had discovered the great American treasure, the treasure of the ages—not just a historic manuscript that a historian like myself searches for their whole life, but my own personal historic manuscript that related to who I am.

At this point in my professional life I was considered somewhat of an expert on authentication and interpretation of American historical manuscripts. I don't think anyone in this field would even dream of a personal discovery like this—yet my dream had truly led me to mine.

I had always become the ink and then the words and then the hand that produced the thoughts. And of course, this led to the person who put the thoughts to paper—and if I was successful, I became them. This type of scientific discovery is an inner one—"grabbed from the Cosmos" to become your own experience. And I think I was truly blessed to have the opportunity to become Rebecca—a living person deeply involved in American history, but also in my personal family history.

I decided that Rebecca's room would become my conservatory, my reading room. I thought her spirit would provide me with all that I needed. The letters had lasted on their own in this natural condition without heating and air-conditioning, and I decided to leave them in their original home under the floorboards between readings.

The stack consisted of more than a hundred neatly piled papers. I planned to read them consecutively so as not to tear any of them, and I'm sure she had a reason for their order.

It may sound strange to the readers of my memoirs, but I never even looked at the papers initially. In my heart I knew it was Rebecca's legacy. She had entered me in my dream, and the connection was made—her fragrance bonded me, and she lived again within me.

I also decided I would not tell Wordie about Rebecca's letters yet. He knew I would spend many days and many hours at our ancestral home anyway.

I prepared myself with notebook, portable light, magnifying glass, and instruments to carefully peel the pages from each other. I also brought my camera, which I had brought on my trip and was outfitted with lenses that could take a perfect picture of a page for reference.

I noticed that the papers at the beginning were the same size and of reasonable-quality rag content from the mid-nineteenth century. Farther on in the stack the papers seemed to be of poorer quality, and the last quarter of the stack appeared to be from pages of newspapers or pages ripped from books and cut neatly to the size of the stack, which was eight inches tall and six inches wide. These latter printed pages had writings in the margins and on any unprinted surface. What this told me, without even looking at any dates Rebecca may have notated, is that paper probably became scarce with time and that she had begun to write on anything she could get her hands on.

I decided I would not look ahead at the writings but would go page by page until I understood and felt her presence at the moment of creativity of each page. I knew in my heart that Rebecca's presence was within the organized narrative she had left for the ages.

The first page was blank as if it were a frontispiece. I turned it over with muted excitement. There was no date on the first written page. The exact reproduction of this first page follows, along with my spontaneous observations at the time. The writing was in faded ink and very deliberate and only in individual non-script letters:

B'ao ku ishe o tan   Iya Iya Baba Baba   Baba mi Iya mi
Dide dide lalafia! Dide dide laafia!
Tika tore, okanki I gbe
Wanderer Wanderer Wanderer
Bi a ko ba jiya to kun agb on a o kge oore to kun aha

My God—this must be African. I do recognize Baba and Iya as father *and* mother *from the Yoruba language of West Nigeria. Rebecca must have come from Nigeria as a slave—but when? The slave trade from Africa was curtailed because of the abolishment of trade in Great Britain and the United States in 1808 … Of course, owning and breeding and selling slaves in the U.S. was still legal …* Wanderer *appears to be an English word—the only English word on the first page …*

And so it went … slowly and methodically and with my heart's empathy for Rebecca. Even though each page from the first presented a historic mystery yet to be solved, I vowed to continue to look at one page at a time—for I knew in my deepest being that Rebecca's soul lay within the consecutive narrative, and that to know her was to feel her thought at the moment she had laid ink to paper.

This day I stopped at the first page. I felt I could not go on without sharing this family treasure with Wordie, even though initially I had thought I would go it alone.

"Wordie … I found something in Rebecca's room."

"I suspect you did, nephew," he said, as if leading me.

"You know?"

"Amos, my boy, I only know what I feel, and what I feel is always the truth, and once it is in me, it is there forever, even though it may lie dormant until it becomes realization." Boy, that was a mouthful, I thought.

"Uncle Wordie, I discovered handwritten letters of Rebecca."

"I suspected you would."

"You knew she wrote and hid the narrative of her life before she arrived in West Virginia?"

"What I knew, Amos, was that you would come here—I knew that my dear brother Hardy Boy would come back in spirit and share the beauty that was our family and help me complete my life in the highlands of Appalachia. It's really you who have been sent to open up secrets that I always knew were living within and around us—secrets that are very special."

I felt my eyes tear as Wordie finished and then lifted his hand to my face in a delicate caress. I will always remember that moment vividly. I felt my being become silent. For the rest of the day my thoughts were silent. I felt a strange peace in my heart until the next morning, when I once more awakened to Wordie's soft gospel hymn.

I was energized—my mind that morning was firing on all cylinders. I knew I needed to find a translator for the Yoruba language and to connect with possibly the New York Public Library in Manhattan for research as I went along here. I knew that I was to be entrenched here indefinitely.

I was able to reach Babatunde by phone in Lagos, but it took two days to get the call through. I made it as clear as possible without sharing the details of my personal discovery that I needed to translate some Yoruba to English with someone in the States if possible. Babatunde found a friend at Morehouse College whom I could reach by phone twice a week at a specified time. This would work well. Through my own connections in New York I found a researcher at the New York Public Library who could search for things I could not find in Moorefield. I had my team, Wordie was on board, and we were ready.

The first line on the first page translated as such:

When there is life, there is hope Mother Mother Father Father My Mother My Father

The second and third line:

Arise, Arise in peace

Wickedness and kindness will be rewarded unfailingly

The last line:

If one does not experience enough suffering to fill a basket, one cannot enjoy enough good to fill a cup

The only English word, *Wanderer,* was an enigma for many days into the next week. I glanced ahead a number of pages to see the first page that had a date, about twenty-five pages into the stack. The first date was February 3, 1860. More and more English was interspersed through each page until Yoruba words appeared only infrequently.

I wanted to discover the meaning of *Wanderer* on my own. I realized that at the time Rebecca started writing she probably knew how to speak English but could not write it, so this was a word she must have seen somewhere. I couldn't connect *Wanderer* with anything at first. I awoke one night suddenly to the realization that it was connected to her first entry into America. It could have been a first impression or something like that and then it hit me abruptly.

A ship—it has to be a ship … a slave ship …

I was right on. I could not find any reference in Moorefield, but my researcher in New York found the *Wanderer,* the last slave ship to America, in 1858. It was illegally outfitted as a slave ship and sailed to Africa and brought back about five hundred slaves to Jekyll Island, Georgia, on November 28, 1858. Many slaves died on this trip. It was then re-outfitted and used during the Civil War.

I felt certain that Rebecca had come to America on the *Wanderer.* She was probably under twenty years old and spoke and was able to write her native Yoruba language, which she would not have learned in Southern slavery. The first ten pages were Yoruba writings, which were almost all Yoruba proverbs similar to the first page. As I had learned on my trip to Nigeria, the social order of the villages was very structured and guided by complex ethical practices. Yoruba proverbs provided the rules for living, and many of them were metaphors. After the ten pages, Rebecca had started to write the English alphabet. She devoted two pages to this. It became apparent in a few more pages that she was mastering the art of writing English. The pages were dated at this point, and from March 1861 through November 1861 Rebecca was learning English, and progressing quite rapidly, I thought.

I deduced that Rebecca was a bright, articulate, well-learned person when she was snatched into slavery from her native Africa. From her Yoruba writings and from various expressions and words, I felt that she had come from a highly placed family in mid-nineteenth-century Africa. I discovered the word *oba* used frequently, meaning "king." I also found *omo-oba,* "prince" or "princess" or "royalty." From the early eighteenth century and into the mid-nineteenth century there were many wars among the kingdoms of Yoruba, and to the victors went the right to sell the vanquished to the slave traders and into the Americas. The slave trade was gradually slowed to a trickle by the naval blockades of the British in the early nineteenth century. But somehow, Rebecca's clan or royal family was invaded and unfortunate enough to be the last of the victims of the conquerors to be sold into the horrific life of slavery.

Over several weeks and before my eyes I could see Rebecca grow. I witnessed the first time she wrote her English name in December 1861—but what was her African name? I was not through with my complete translation of all the Yoruba words, but up to this point I hadn't discovered it. I began to think about this marvel in a different light. How is this young slave woman learning anything but the hard and cruel work of the cotton plantation? Who is teaching her? Who would teach her? This question began to nag at me as I continued through her narrative.

Beginning in early 1862 I could see a fantastic transformation in Rebecca's language. She was becoming fluent in written English. And what was most phenomenal, she was exploring poetry and prose, and when not doing that, she was writing in stream-of-consciousness style.

The individual pages did not contain a lot of words or phrases, and each page was about eight lines long. I believe that Rebecca was deliberately both sparse and concise in the portrait she was painting for posterity. She was truly developing into a literary artist—and she was a slave.

Initially, my approach to Rebecca's letters was a burst of inspiration mixed with professional analysis, but as I progressed along the path and into the next month, a change occurred in me. I stopped analysis and relied more on intuition and deep empathy. The Cosmos had visited me in a way I had never experienced before—I believed that I became Rebecca as I read her narratives. I understood her completely because I was her. It was a complete experience for me, no longer relying on my intellect.

I seemed to be able to fill in the spaces between the lines as if I were Rebecca. I could see and feel her hand move across the page as if it were my own. I became her as she ran her fingers through her hair upon finishing a poem and got up to look out the only small paneless window in her shack. I felt the cool, damp dirt beneath her bare feet as well as the warmth of the small wool throw that she had knitted as she covered her cold toes.

I awoke in the middle of the night softly saying her African birth name, Alika, which I had just discovered in her writings on my own.

Alika's poetry was mostly very explicit and occasionally ethereal to the point of mystical. Her stream of consciousness became mine as she rambled on in sentences describing loneliness and darkness and pain. I lingered on one page for days, filling in her life with my own being and empathizing with her deep feelings. I never questioned the authenticity of my observations or my ability—as sure as I was sitting cross-legged on the bare floor of her attic room, I was sure she was within me.

"Rain bring me water and wash my sorrows to the sea.
Take me to the fishes and taste freedom.
Salt water float me on a wave of happiness and carry me to the sun."

"Sun, why do you not stay with me? When you leave you bring darkness where I only turn to the four walls of rotted oak."

"Fingers of pain, each barb reminding me that suffering needs to fill my basket before the sweetness of my cup is tasted."

"I cannot wash my body of my difference my color God has given."

"Tell me what to learn? Why I am here? Are you near?"

"The sea that has given my family life carried me away."

"You can take my body—you can tire my mind. You cannot take the color of my soul."

"The magnolia is as sweet to me as it is to you. It is the only thing we share."

Rebecca was actually writing to someone now—someone she knew—someone in her life daily. She seemed to have fond words for this "friend."

"I look up at you. You look down at me. We caress the space between us."

"I see you through the blue sky and through the clouds. The sun cannot block your smile."

It was love!—I cannot believe it! Love!

All in prosaic style and in the most ethereal manner, I thought. How could she have developed this beautiful art?

"You touch me and take away the coldness and hopelessness of my damp existence."

This developing love story seemed to unfold from the second half of 1862 and on. Along with this sweet love there was turmoil developing in some of her narratives and poems—turmoil that seemed to be associated with the war that was starting to touch her life on this slave plantation.

"The sky darkens every day and our existence seems to be slipping away like the fallen leaf immersed in a raging brook."

I started to write what I was experiencing in my head—the moments between and during the actual time she put pen to paper. I was experiencing her thoughts, and I visualized her physical existence just as I was able to feel Vincent Van Gogh—and I started writing the narrative of her life as her poems unfolded.

"You take your hand and touch my arm with the fear that only love can bring. Softly the bond between us grows." *And her soft black skin melted like warm honey as the contrast between white and black melded into ribbons of muted earth tones.*

Oh my God! I had this perfect vision of her lover—he was a white man! It just came down to me from the Cosmos and through my being and onto the paper. I never even thought consciously about it. The vision just appeared, and it became one with the unfolding life of Rebecca.

I was writing a love story—one that was taking place in a reality far away that had returned to be lived again, one that took place within a time of war and upheaval, and one that was so unique, and that should never had occurred: the love of a black slave and a Southern white man within the horrors of the Civil War.

I never gave thought to what I was experiencing as I continued to read and see her life within my mind's vision. I was able to go back and just add the visions to paper, filling her narratives with the physical reality of her life. I never thought of whether I was experiencing reality or a vision—or hallucination.

"How could love be real within the horrors of this world? How could I see sweetness and unity within the dark clouds of destruction? Possibly, a tiny light will become a beacon of peace, spreading to the far corners of the globe." *As she put the word* globe *to paper, the vanishing daylight disappeared from the tiny window to close her heart momentarily and end her thoughts.*

Rebecca awoke in the black silence of the night only to hear distant cannon, sounding like ordinary thunder. She prayed to the Yoruba deities that peace would enter her. "I cannot sleep. I weep for the children and the old and sick. I weep for the ignorant and misguided. I even weep for myself," *she wrote in pitch darkness looking up to the heavens that did not exist.*

Her lover was a young man, probably a plantation owner's kin. As 1862 turned into 1863, Rebecca wrote of losing her love in very abstract terms. I believe he may have been heading off to war.

Rebecca's life was vivid to me. Every day that I returned to her attic and retrieved the letters, I felt as if she was with me—in fact, I felt as if I had become her. I stopped thinking about my family and just continued to live her life within mine. Wordie never questioned my quest. I continued to stay with him, and I felt he gave me silent strength without question or judgment. I didn't seem to eat much, and my sleep was short but restful at night—I'm sure exhaustion helped.

"The long road to the House is no longer—the magnificent Oaks bowing in defeat and crying for their existence. Fire has taken many, throwing lives into memories and memories into ashes. Embers do not exist, for life is ending for the magnificent kingdom. You are gone. The footprint of the hoof remains as my only memory of you. Freedom is myth and myth freedom. Arusha give me hope." *Rebecca looked down the long road to the plantation house only to see empty spaces where windows were.*

It was the spring of 1863, and I believe the large plantation in which Rebecca lived was under siege. I believe her beau was off to certain battle, probably close by, fighting to save his plantation and way of life.

"Can life begin where it ends? Can love sustain where none is? Do I have the right to carry new seed in time of destruction?" *Rebecca sat motionless on her bed of wood, only a wisp of her shadow casting itself on the mud walls as she placed her hand softly on her abdomen.*

My God, she is pregnant!!! It came to me through her writings and my visions of her. Over the next few pages and months Rebecca continued her love poetry, but it pertained to new life and birth. There was also a period of despair, possibly relating to the discomfort of her pregnancy as well as the war and losses of life.

"With you gone, I am alone with my people and my body and my seed. What right do I have to carry love? What right do we have to become one among enemies? Maybe we have a right to melt the horrors of prejudice by becoming one from the two poles of the world." *Rebecca walked through the woods as she tried to breathe freedom from the solitude.*

Rebecca carried her child within her womb as she worked in the fields. She promised herself and others who were less fortunate to keep smiling—for without her smile the world would cease to exist. "Sunlight cares not for evil. It will spread its warmth to all. It is both a good thing and bad thing. It just mirrors life itself."

"August 23, 1863 You are born—my Phillip."

I collapsed to the floor—my body limp from exhaustion after reading that entry. I felt I had carried Rebecca's baby with the same feelings and the same pain that she had. I lay on that attic floor, Rebecca's floor, on my back looking up to the bare exposed roof beams with nothing on my mind—finally at rest.

I really don't remember how long I lay there. It was the first time in the two months I had walked up the stairs to her room daily that my whole being felt complete.

Suddenly, looking up, focusing on nothing, my eyes widened. I felt suddenly flushed, and I could feel my pulse beating like a drum throughout my whole body. My body jerked in one abrupt earthquake-like moment. I bolted up, seemingly not in control of my movements. *What the ...?*

My hands shaking almost uncontrollably, I leafed through the last two pages of Rebecca's narrative. I skimmed rapidly and without thought through the entries relating to her little boy. Finally at the last page, my excitement to the point of explosion, I read the last entry.

"April 23, 1864—I will leave with you, Phillip. There is turmoil and confusion here. There has to be light somewhere. I owe you a life, Phillip, a life of joy and love, a chance to live. Our trip will be wrought with danger. If we don't try, we have no chance for life. Old Ivory will take us—he will guide us.

Without the roaring sea we cannot swim
Without the highest mountain we cannot climb
Without our wildest dreams we cannot fly
Without adversity we cannot be"

OH MY GOD!!! She's my great-grandmother! Her son is my dad's father! My dad has a black grandmother! I have a black great-grandmother! MY dad has a grandmother who was a slave! My dad's dad has a black slave mother and a white Southern plantation owner father! I have a Confederate Southern white great-grandfather! But my dad's a Jewish doctor and I'm just a Jewish boy! Holy ...

And on and on ... I collapsed to the floor once more—spent to exhaustion. As I lay there for what seemed an endless time, I felt a sudden jerk within my body again—but it culminated in kind of a belly laugh. I felt my face loosen up and a broad smile come across my mouth. I laughed again as I lay there—then again, and then again—until I seemed to be laughing as if I were at a comedy club. Maybe it was the laugh of relief or maybe it was the laugh of my seemingly lifelong quest achieved. But I think the laugh was mostly the absurdity of my findings and the absurdity of my reaction. My discovery was complete—it was complete.

As time in the attic that day passed and I came back to the reality of my find, I started to think once more of Rebecca's strength and determination and qualities. How did she ever get from where she set off from to West Virginia?

I kept my final find of Rebecca's to myself for the next few days. For the first time in sixty-three days I did not go to the farmhouse. I hung around Wordie's house while he worked. He knew I had completed my reading but didn't ask me about it. He was really intuitive to the core and would never confront me about anything. He had the ultimate patience of a saint.

I began to think of the long and dangerous ride, actually still during the war—slave and son—he a mulatto. Was she on a course predetermined? Knowing that she took her writings with her, and who she was ultimately, I felt she was on a mission for posterity as well as on an escape to freedom.

I had found my dad's ancestral home simply through the name Hardy, discovering Hardy County. Could the connection to Rebecca's original plantation home be here? I spent the next few days at the Moorefield Library researching "Hardy." I found out that there were a number of Hardy plantations in Virginia. I also discovered that West Virginia was still Virginia at the time Rebecca traveled. So it was certainly possible that she traveled within the state. I also discovered that Hardy County was named for Phillip Hardy, who lived in eighteenth-century Virginia and was an original signer of America's Declaration of Independence.

I felt intuitively that Rebecca had deliberately left clues for future posterity, for she decided not to divulge that Phillip was her son. I think she felt he would have a better life as a white man than a mulatto—and she was right. She had searched out Hardy County and decided that this is where she would settle. It was her subtle clue—the Hardy connection—the connection to her son's heritage. She found Laizie's parents, and they were kind enough to let her stay. And they obviously adopted her son, for that is where he got his surname, Lardy. She always must have thought of him as Phillip, but she made sure everyone called him Hardy, his nickname—eventually enabling a future descendant to unravel the threads of history and discover who she was. She buried her treasure—her legacy, her letters—within her room, knowing they would be found. What an amazing woman!

I was complete once more, although I felt that Wordie should know my secret, finally discovered and finally divulged—at least to my Appalachian uncle—that his dad's mother was a slave.

"Uncle Wordie, I found out all of what I was looking for," I said the next morning as Wordie was cooking up some breakfast.

"Yup … I suspect you did," he said as I'd suspected he would.

"Wordie, Rebecca is your grandmother," I said, getting directly to the point.

"Yup."

And that was that. Wordie kept scrambling those eggs, with his head down as if looking into the pan. The expression on his face was one of satisfaction—quiet satisfaction, I thought. And we never talked about it again.

The next two days were warm and easy. I felt no pressure, and Wordie seemed relaxed. The morning of the third day I started to feel antsy about my find. Here I was, I thought, sitting on the solving of my mystery of fifteen years—from adolescence to adulthood—the mystery of my American heritage that I had obsessed over without a break. It was an obsession that had squeezed its way into every space within my being. It drove me and consumed me. Now what?

Hey, Dad—I know about your childhood in Appalachia. I met your brother, Wordie … and by the way—your grandmother was a black slave.

Hey, Dad—did you know that your dad's mom was a slave?

Hey, Dad—what do you think of black people?

Hey, Mom—tonight would you tell Dad that his grandmother was black?

No way! I thought, no way! I could not come up with a scenario that could satisfy me concerning telling Dad. I became blocked. I had found my holy grail, and it was only mine. It has no way out, I thought.

I was going to call Ben, of course, but I felt compelled to share this with someone in the family. Impulsively, I called Susan. Looking back, I realize this would have created a major family disaster.

"Syd—my Syd … how are you?"

"OK, Amie. You still away?"

"Yep—you know, holy crusade …"

"I know you, Amie." And she did know me.

"Syd, is Susan there?"

"No."

"Oh …"

"Amie, tell me. It sounds really important."

And I told her everything—because she was Syd, and I felt as if she were part of me, even though she was barely ten years old.

"Amie, that is so cool and amazing, but you can't tell Mom. She'll have a cow and a stroke. You know she will. Her life is a controlled kosher machine. What do you want to do, destroy it?" Syd was so smart for her age—and for any age for that matter. She stopped me within a foot of the railroad crossing as a monster freight train passed in front of me.

"Yeah—OK, honey ... back to my drawing board. Love you." And that was it for my family now.

I had been living with Wordie for four months. Out of all my experiences, it was the most unusual and tender, and it led to my discovery. We did not say much to each other upon my leaving. We had become very close, and of course we were kin. I think Wordie knew I would be back. He knew something would happen in a positive way to our family.

The night before I left I had a dream. I was outside a huge barn. It was an old, beautiful wooden barn sitting in a field. The sky was blue with wispy clouds moving rapidly. I could smell the sweet aroma of the pastures and the wildflowers. I entered the barn. The inside was huge, and the sunlight came in rays through the many openings created by the fallen old wooden panels. They seemed to crisscross each other at random. In the center of the barn there was this huge, beautiful weaving loom. It seemed to be two stories high and was made out of wood that had a striking patina. There was a chair in front of the loom made out of the same wood. I approached the loom and sat down on the chair. I reached out with my left hand and put it on the worn wooden lever in front of me. As soon as I did this, I started to feel a soft breeze, and I could smell the sweet wildflowers mixed in with the hay smell in the barn. At the same time, from the many openings in the walls I could see strands of fabric or thread making their way from the outside. They were multicolored and seemed to be of different widths. They appeared to be wool and cotton and other natural fibers. They almost appeared to be dancing. There must have been thousands winding their way in a rhythmic fashion. They all met at the center of the loom and started to interweave with each other. At first I could see only what looked like a small square patch of multicolored fabric, but then it grew rapidly as the threads danced in to the center of the loom. And finally there it was—a monumentally large blanket of what appeared to be thousands of interwoven colors. It seemed to separate itself from the loom and dance in the wind almost like a sail. I needed to arch my head up to see the whole thing—it was phenomenally beautiful.

I drove to New York the next day, not quite sure what my discovery would lead to.

Home with My Roots

I ARRIVED HOME IN Manhattan with my American roots aboard. It was a strange feeling. I felt as if I wanted to drive up to Harlem and walk the streets and slap fives to anyone on the street and yell, "Yo, brother." Yet I felt almost embarrassed to tell Baba and Babatunde, and especially Jemima. "What? Give me a break—you Jews don't have enough troubles in your past? You want to be Negroes now? Huh!" I heard her say in my mind. Whatever—I still felt as if I had snared my American heritage and it was mine—all mine.

Obviously, it was more complex than just *my* roots; it was my dad's family—one he had abandoned for a new life and a new culture. And to boot, he had his Appalachian, gospel-spouting brother alive and well in his family's birthplace. Around and around the thoughts went, complicated by the thought of what Susan's reaction would be and also by the issue of black and white—the black and white love story, forbidden and scorned in my America.

I settled into my West Fourth Street apartment the first night and slept without thoughts seemingly for the first night in weeks. I knew I needed to talk and share everything with Ben first. He was my alter ego—he was what I could not be.

I sat alone across from Ben at one of the small café tables that Manny reserved for his private use, facing away from other patrons. I was fingering a cold draft, and Ben had just warmed his body with a Hennessey.

"I don't know what to do. It's done. I was so possessed by this for so long in my life. I don't know what to do with it."

"Kid, that's why you see only Italian archaeologists unearthing ancient pyramids in Egypt."

"What?"

"You unearthed your *own* story, your personal story. Of course you don't know what to do with it—you're too close."

"Then what would you do?"

"Hey, man—I wouldn't look under my own rugs. I'm an excavator also, but I unearth this world's secrets to shake the foundation of importance that we feeble humans create for ourselves."

"Yeah, I know you, Ben."

"Kid, this world is self-created by the famous and those who want to be famous. It is created by those who seek power and money, obviously to build their own feeble egos, for their real brains are too small. And you know, every once in awhile the Cosmos intervenes and places its own stamp on a person or a symphony, or a manuscript or an event, and the small people of this world then flock to it."

"But Ben, the Cosmos came to me, man—it came to me. I wouldn't have found it without the Cosmos."

"Yeah, but you broke the cardinal rule ... You made it a personal quest. You're not detached. That's why this world is riddled with war. Those who wage it feel the Cosmos came to them and them alone, and that it is their birthright to force it on others. You need only one religious experience delivered to some idiot from the Cosmos to start a holy war that lasts for centuries, Kid—to say nothing of the greedy son of a bitch politician or dictator who was personally visited."

"Yeah, man. But unfortunately this discovery is for the ages, Ben ... It's not only mine."

"OK, then expose it to the world just as it is and pay no attention to your personal consequences."

OK, I see ... a rock and a hard place."

"Amos, you know the world needs us. It needs me and it needs you. We were meant to peel the layers of bullshit away and expose the truth whatever the consequences. You snared it, Kid—you snared it. You got the prize—stuck away for posterity with all its emotion and reality. You not only uncovered it, but you were there. The Cosmos came to you and you alone, and you entered history's place and Rebecca's space and heart, and you not only lived her every moment in reality, but you became her. Man, you've done more in this quest than I have ever done. But you went searching for it for the wrong reason. You went for it for your personal story. I never searched for anything personal. I would end up in the same place—stuck.

"What would you do, publish just the letters? Or your observations also? And would you leave in your revelations on her reality and run the risk of ridicule, or would you just print the whole thing and let it be as is? And man, would you say she was your great-grandmother?"

"I know, Ben," I said, feeling as if I had returned to the first day I met him—sheepishly shy.

And there we sat—me with my life's discovery on the table, and Ben, my touchstone to reality.

The vivid dream of the loom and its myriad fabric was real to me. The experience did complete me, but it did not prepare me for the consequences of discovery. I was awash once more. My lifelong obsession with my America forced her to give up her secrets, but I learned a lot from my experiences. I learned that adolescent attachment to the power of war that is solely American is corrupt and faulted. I learned that my America lived with her flaws hidden just beneath the surface of her beauty—I suppose like all beautiful things. I also learned that everything is much more complex than it seems—unless you're Ben, of course—and I was convinced that there was only one Ben on this planet. I also learned about the power of the Cosmos. I would not have had the tiniest inkling about the Cosmos without knowing Ben. I wondered why I was so blessed.

All these thoughts consumed me over the next few weeks. My euphoria over my beautiful and ethereal discovery gave way to the complexity of the world and my life—albeit self-created, I suppose.

I walked my Manhattan daily, seemingly aimless in direction. It gave me comfort to be anonymous. I let my thoughts float freely, and gradually I gave way to any decisions about my find. The only family member who knew about it was Syd. She was quite comfortable with it, and we didn't have to talk. I visited home with Mom and Dad. It was a relatively easy few weeks, but ultimately I knew who I was and that I would need to consciously make a decision.

Before I had left for West Virginia, Ben and I had decided to incorporate a publishing company just for the purpose of the "snared literary find," and certainly this is what I had discovered. It was obvious to me that Ben wouldn't push me to publish Rebecca's papers, but I knew it was in both our psyches.

I also kept thinking about my fixation with the blues and gospel and the African-American experience even before my discovery. I seemed to have had a lifelong yearning to feel the soul and rhythm of Africa and how it pertained to our unique American life long before I found out about my black heritage. It gradually came to me that I felt almost preordained, so to speak—preordained to find my personal holy grail and my America's Achilles heel.

The year 1968 was one of turmoil for America, considering the killing of Martin Luther King, and I knew there was enormous resentment and violence toward blacks, even though they were not the ones who had created the problem of racial discrimination and hatred. This only added to my inability to decide on the continuing path of my discovery.

Time is a healer, and patience produces time, and there is a time for everything, so I'm not sure exactly what happened over the next seven or eight years, but I think I understand what was taking place. I guess my soup was "a-brewin'" just like Wordie would say—and it wouldn't be done for a while.

Ben and I did open our publishing house, called Lardowitz and Fink, in the winter of 1969, and our first book was a "snare" that Ben got from William Faulkner. I wrote some and Ben wrote some, and it was well received. We were on our way to becoming the avant-garde and edgy rebels of the literary world adored by the snobbish Hamptons crowd and the critics. It was cool and comfortable for me, something I could not do for myself without Ben and something Ben would not do without me, he said. Of course, I didn't believe him. I had this thought that he was also completing his life's purpose by uncovering as many of the world's superficial layers as he could to expose her vulnerable core, and I think he got great joy in mentoring me and observing my naiveté and excitement.

Of course, I placed my own narratives of Rebecca in a vault, and the original papers of Rebecca lay in their natural home—I felt safe and secure.

At the same time, I started a foundation called Donny's Fund. It was dedicated to teaching peace to children and to the consequences of the glorification of war. It was as close to my heart as Rebecca was. It was my tribute to my dear friend Donny and his dedication to his loved ones.

Interestingly enough, we were so well received that our admirers pumped money into Donny's Fund. My awareness of the folly of war was very acute, especially because of my deep experiences, and I became an avowed pacifist, although one active in alternative solutions.

I received an associate professorship of American history and taught at City College part time. My course, reading and interpreting original historical letters, was very popular as the Vietnam War began to wind down in the early seventies. My perspective, of course, included personal stories and experiences, and I encouraged my students to feel the reality of suffering and life and history through others' words and writings.

Lardowitz and Fink (Ben insisted my name be first) had an office on Twenty-eighth Street off Madison Avenue in Manhattan. We rented an adjacent small office on the same floor for Donny's Fund, which was a nonprofit. Ben was very gracious as he insisted that half our profits go to Donny's. The next few years were busy for me. I made plenty of money and enjoyed my New York City life with my friends, especially at Manny's. Ben and Zelda and I were constant companions, occasionally mixed with the oddball girlfriend I brought along. Obviously none could compare with my Zel. I'm not sure why I never connected to a lifelong female companion, but I never really gave it much thought. My life would have been different for sure, and maybe I just was always in love with Zel.

As the years peeled away, Syd was growing up, and she started to come into the city to spend her Saturdays with me. She loved Manhattan and the offices and was interested in everything I did. I thought she was the only person in my family who knew who I was at a deep level, and she certainly was the only person to know Rebecca's story and her relationship to our family. Before my very eyes I saw her becoming a woman.

Susan and Alvin and Clara and Morris lived a pretty normal and busy kosher life. I could always see the stress in Susan, but I decided it was her life and her choices alone. Dad and Mom were the same. Of course, he worked hard and was well respected. After my discovery of his brother, Wordie, I always had a behind-the-scenes smirk whenever I saw him place a letter he wrote in his inside coat pocket to be mailed. Could that letter contain his check to Wordie? He never gave up his persona during this time. And Mom, well, Mom was Mom, attached at the hip with Jemima, her dearest friend and kosher companion. I wondered sometimes about her choice of best friendship with Jemima. Did she know about Rebecca in our family, and if so, was this a sign to all of us that she knew? She obviously knew about Dad's previous life, but I would never say anything at this time. I had vowed to keep my secrets right after that phone call to the ten-year-old Syd.

I kept in touch with Wordie and called him probably every two months. I visited him four times in five years, and we just shared each other's comfortable space. I had not gone back to the farm, although each time I was in West Virginia, I drove past it to be sure it was still there and in the same condition. For some reason I was supremely confident that Rebecca's letters would be there forever.

It was Saturday, April 5, 1977, and I was in our publishing office, and Syd was next door doing paperwork for Donny's Fund. I heard a knock on the door. We never had much activity that early on a Saturday, so I could not understand who would be calling.

I opened the door to a handsome young black man.

"Mr. Lardowitz?"

"Yes … Amos."

"Hello," he said and he extended his hand to shake mine. Meanwhile I was looking only at his eyes. They were so familiar and warm and almost mischievous. "William Brooks," he said.

"William?"

"Well … Little Bo."

"Little Bo?"

"Little Bo."

"Little Bo!!!"

I grabbed him with a bear hug and pulled him into my arms. I must have hugged him for five minutes, squeezing the heck out of him.

He was Little Bo, Lucy Brooks's son. He had been four years old when I'd met him in the Delta at Mound Bayou that Thanksgiving of 1956. My God, that was twenty-one years ago, I thought.

"Little Bo …," I said warmly, my mind wildly going back to that Thanksgiving. "How's Lucy—and Big Bo?"

"Amos, Lucy died last year. Poor Mom. She worked so hard to keep up a life for us. You know there was nothing in Mound Bayou for us, and we had no confidence in our color, if you know what I mean. Big Bo, Robert, was dejected and angry and heard about Chicago and opportunity in the big city. He took off in '66. He was seventeen. I ran away with him and I was fifteen. We chased Elmore's buddies and anyone he knew in music, but that didn't work for us. It got rough, Amos—you know … the ghetto and drugs and turf wars. Robert really got caught up with it—he got shot and killed in a turf war, Amos. The only thing that saved me was my thoughts of a better life somewhere, and I always seemed to latch on to your image coming into Mound Bayou—excited and from New York City. I saw hope in your eyes, man, that first moment I looked at you—I saw light and happiness and excitement. I kept that image in my mind after Big Bo died. I went to school, Amos. I went to college and I went to law school. I needed to do that. You inspired me, and Lucy needed some light in her life. I've been working in the movement. I started with Mr. King and did law work for the movement. I wrangle the law to give the poor and disenfranchised a break, man. And you really were my inspiration to live a real life, Amos—a real life. I would have ended up like Big Bo. He never had anyone to look up to. I owed it to him. Mom was very proud. And I felt compelled to find you. I see your work. I needed to see you, man."

Just as he finished that sentence Syd turned the corner from the other office. Startled she said, "Oh, sorry, Amos—didn't know you were with someone."

I turned to Bo and said, "Oh, Bo—meet my niece Sydney. She works with me."

I'm sure that that intro and the consequences couldn't have lasted more than ten seconds, but I saw it in slow motion. I saw their eyes connect in a way I hadn't seen in two people. There seemed to be a glow in the room, and the morning sun cast its soft shadow of those two on the far wall—I felt the Cosmos descend.

Bo was ready for a move. I think he truly was connected to me and my work and especially Donny's Fund. Elmore James had died in 1963 when the boys were eleven and thirteen.

Bo settled into Manhattan. He was an easy and charming and bright young man of twenty-six. His specialty was civil rights cases, and he got plenty of work. He offered his services to Donny's Fund, and I spent a lot of time with him. Obviously Syd was around a lot, and there was a special chemistry among those two. She was barely twenty-two and he a few years older.

As 1977 turned into 1978 my circle of friends included Syd and Bo and Ben and Zelda and Manny and Fanny. We all spent some happy times in the Village at Manny's as well as out on the beaches of Long Island.

I remember the moment one Saturday evening at Manny's, all of us around Manny's private table, laughing and conversing, when I actually noticed that Bo was black and Syd was white and that they truly were lovers in their hearts. I'm not sure why it took this long for me to connect the two physically, but maybe it had to do with Rebecca and her love. Suddenly, that evening, Rebecca's life returned to me in a vivid way, a hundred-plus years compressed into a moment. Two love affairs, both black and white, more than a century apart, became one at that table that night. I had no thoughts of the consequences—I only had visions of unity and love.

Ten years had passed, ten years of placing Rebecca within my heart tucked away. She returned to me that night in a dream—as beautiful as ever.

Syd opened the door to my hibernating past and would become the catalyst to the completion of my American journey.

The Planning

Syd did not need to tell me anything. I knew her and she knew me. She was like me, but she harbored no guilt or remorse if she took something on. I knew she and Bo were in love. I knew they would be married—and on their own terms. I did think about Susan and her kosher life, and of Mom and Dad and what they would think, but I knew that Syd ultimately could and would do no wrong.

I remember the day. It was a cold Monday morning in January 1978 at our offices in Manhattan.

"Amie—Bo and I want to be married."

"I know, Syd."

"Amie—I want to be married on June 27 of this year and I want the ceremony to be at the farm."

"The farm?"

"Yes, the farm. Our family farm."

"In Appalachia?"

"Amie, you know where I mean."

Syd had picked June 27, she said, because it was the date of the annual Lardy Family Farm Day.

I really think that without Syd my life would have been different. It was the same with Syd as it was with Ben and all the other meaningful people who had influenced my direction. When she announced to me her intention, I had no thoughts but that it would happen. I knew she was moving me along, almost as if I were the carriage horse and she was the gentle whip: "OK, boy, let's move along a little faster now."

Obviously Susan would need to know about Dad's upbringing in West Virginia. I knew that Mom knew. I began to think about how Syd would handle this with her mother. To my understanding, whether to disclose Rebecca's relation to our family would remain my decision.

I decided it was not my place to announce our newly discovered heritage to Susan, and Syd only reinforced this by telling me to keep away and that she would handle her mother. Certainly I had moments of anxiety thinking of the consequences. Would Susan have a major fit and blame Mom and Dad for not telling her about Dad's heritage? Would she blame me? And how about Bo? Man—not only was he not Jewish …

Well, I remember the day.

"Amie, I told Mom."

"You told her you're getting married?"

"Yes, and I just told her that the ceremony will be in West Virginia."

"And Bo?"

"Yes—and Bo."

"And at our family farm?"

"Yes."

"What did she do?"

"She kept looking at me with no expression, and then when I was through, she turned away and got on the phone and called our rabbi."

"Then?"

"I left the room and went out."

"Yes?"

"She didn't say anything that night to me—anything."

"Yes?"

"The next morning she asked me if Bo was converting."

I laughed in relief—Jews are so practical. If they can't have everything they want, they at least try to get something they want. Maybe Susan was more like Mom than I thought. Obviously she didn't want to lose a Jewish daughter, so she tried to gain a convert son. Oh boy, I hoped it would remain this easy. But of course it was Syd's life, really, even though it was intertwined with my quest and discovery.

Syd and Bo decided they wanted to have me arrange who would be invited and the nature of the ceremony. I know it was their way of honoring my commitment to our ancestry. I was truly touched by this.

I didn't have to think deeply about the ceremony. Thoughts came to me spontaneously, and I felt they were right. I suggested to Syd that Allen Ginsberg perform the marriage ceremony. He was as Jewish as Jews come, and he looked more like a rabbi than any rabbi. He was also a very real American with no bullshit in him. He became ecstatic when I asked him. I really wanted Babatunde and Baba to be there, as well as Donny's mom, Mary, and Donny's sister. I thought of Jack Kerouac, who had died in 1969 during one of my visits to West Virginia. And of course Janis Joplin overdosed in 1970; I would keep her in my memory. I asked Syd if my college buddy Army could come. He was very close to Donny and had helped me when I was in need.

It was really amazing, for Syd knew exactly what she wanted on her wedding day. We would invite our select friends and family, and then we would all join in at the annual Lardy Family Farm Day in Moorefield.

I knew I had some work to do with Mom and Dad. I needed to connect to Dad in some way to understand why he hadn't told us about his family. I needed to speak to Mom as a start. I waited until about two weeks after Syd had talked to Susan. Syd had paved the way for me, and I knew Mom was Susan's ultimate therapist, so there probably was no downtime for Mom concerning this issue. I guessed that she'd be really primed when I approached her.

"Amie, a young girl in love would do anything to keep her boy. Dad was so dedicated, and he wanted to please me."

"But why is he so different from me? He was able to keep this secret, and he completely blocked it out of his life."

"Amie, the two of you are more alike than you imagine. He had a quest just as you have a quest in your life. He vowed to himself to care for his family, and he left West Virginia for places unknown to him. He vowed to care for and support his dad and blind brother. His quest has never wavered to this day. You know that he helps support Wordie?"

"I know," I said, thinking how my quest was still unfinished and unfulfilled in my mind as of that moment. I still had secrets untold. As I was talking to Mom, I kept seeing Rebecca's face. I didn't bring up my discovery of Rebecca's letters and the fact that she was Dad's grandmother. I never made a conscious decision to withhold our true ancestry from Mom, but it didn't come out at this point.

After talking to Mom, I began to think that maybe Dad and I were more alike than I'd thought. Certainly, I was still harboring secrets untold just as he was. The only difference was that I had not resolved the ending. But then again, I thought, maybe Dad had not resolved his ending, and one day he was going to sit down with his entire family and expose his life. My thoughts about Dad were blocked, and I felt that I could not approach him myself. Throughout my whole life I could not question Dad. Mom would just have to talk to him, and ultimately I knew that his person would not change regardless.

Mom did tell Dad about my quest and my finding Wordie. As usual, Dad never acknowledged anything to me and, as well, never showed any emotion. Obviously, I thought, we both showed our stoic Appalchian roots: keep your secrets to yourself and just plow ahead.

When I called Wordie to tell him the news about the wedding, I had this thought that it could turn out to be a culture clash of earthquake proportions. I had dreams of caravans of Jews descending on Moorefield and hearing the citizens chanting, "Here come the Jews, here come the Jews."

"My goodness … my goodness."

I knew Wordie would say that in response to my telling him that the whole family was descending to our farm for Syd's wedding. And I knew that he saw beauty and good in it. His mind started to work immediately, and he said, "Got to put them up. We'll get Edna started on this, and I'll call Pastor Johnson and the new mayor, Virgil Franklin. Oh, what joy! Oh, what joy!"

After Syd told me that she wanted to invite all of our relatives who would come, and obviously they were all from Mom's family, I told this to Wordie. He announced to me on the phone one evening that Edna had arranged with Gracie, Bertie, and Gertie to be in charge of "puttin' people up." He told me Edna had said that there was nothin' the "card crew" could not do over a deck of cards "sittin' around" their card table. Edna told him to ask us whether the guests were "young'uns or oldies, and could walk or not."

I offered to pay for a chartered bus to take whatever family wanted to go to the wedding. The trip was more than 550 miles, which I knew could discourage some. For my part, it was really important to me to be sure of the people in my life. Ginsberg was on, and I knew he'd be great at orchestrating the ceremony. My dearest Ben and Zelda and Manny and Fanny were going to "fly down, open air, in my horseless carriage," said Ben.

"Hello, Mrs. Rabinowitz. This is Mrs. Lardowitz."

I knew this was coming. Mom had arranged to have the Passover dinner and celebration, which was two months before the wedding, at our house. I knew this would be her kind of "kosher coup," like a mother hen gathering all her chicks and making sure they follow behind. I remember the dream I had. There Mom was, cane in hand—but it had turned into a sword. And there she was, skewering the family and in-laws as they tried to escape, piling them up on the sword like shish kebab.

Passover did arrive, and she presented her most kosher and fancy self. She seemed to invite only the doubters or those who needed to be skewered. Of course, Mr. and Mrs. Rabinowitz were Alvin's parents and Syd's grandparents and would be Bo's grandparents-in-law. Jemima was there and had a very conspicuous commanding seat. In fact, Mom asked her to say the opening prayer. And before my very ears Jemima started speaking in Hebrew. Man, I got a glimpse of Mrs. Rabinowitz's eyes. They went from narrow slits to large cat eyes in a split second. I'm sure this was Mom's way of getting and keeping control of her developing family—kind of like the flag with the snake on it that says, "Don't tread on me."

As the family was asked to read the Hagadah around the table, Mom deliberately said, "William, please read." Of course she was talking to Bo and I'm sure, as well, she was both introducing him and inducting him and indoctrinating him into our family. I had another dream that night and it was of Mom mixing a cake in an enormous bowl that towered over her. She was holding a wooden spoon. She had her sleeves rolled up, exposing powerful, pumped biceps. She started to mix a goopy mixture of black and white cake stuff, turning the brew harder and faster until it turned into a medium brown color—boy, this was an easy dream to understand.

Needless to say the evening went well—or at least according to Mom's plan.

Of my two remaining Four Horsemen buddies, Army was still in the active armed service as a colonel. He was delighted to come. I called Hitch at the last number I had for him. After a circuitous route I had found out he was in prison in upstate New York for corporate fraud. I was initially shocked, but then I wasn't. I felt that I wanted to see Hitch, since obviously he wouldn't get leave to come.

I took the short drive up from the city to Wallkill, where Hitch was "stationed." Wallkill was considered a minimum-security prison.

"Hey, man, I told you I'd enlist in the armed services. 'Armed services'—get it?"

"Got it, but how did you get here, man?"

"Come on, Ammo—it's the American way. Just every once in a while, a sacrificial lamb is sacrificed, and you're looking at him. Making money drives our world, buddy. I suppose I'll need to change when I get out, but they'll still be doing the same thing. It's our class. We make our moola on the backs of the have-nots. It won't change."

Hitch seemed resolved and more than a bit sarcastic, but I wasn't sure if I was reading him right. I'd had this same feeling about him in school. Was he really himself or playing a role? At any rate I wasn't surprised that he was where he was.

"Yup, like the four corners of the compass, we Four Horsemen all represent the parts," Hitch said almost philosophically

He was right. I was even thinking that as I sat with him. Our America was like the four of us. Army was the driving military arm of the political system. Without smart and educated military officers there could be no war. Then Turk, who feeds our patriotism for wars and more wars—the soldier willing to give his life for his country and comrades without thought, and to be a beacon for more young people willing to sacrifice themselves, his vision coming from his own heritage of war, the perceived memory of his beloved brave father. Hitch, the back half of the military-industrial complex and what America fights for and builds her dream on—or at least the dreams of the politicians. What about me? Was Hitch really including me as the fourth point of the compass? I always wondered if he knew I was different and ambivalent, or even cared if I was. I felt at the moment I was sitting with him that he did understand me. He did include me as a distinct and different point on the compass. But who was I? He knew I was the soldier, someone Hitch would not be. But I was also the self-questioning one—the one who looked at ethics and humanity and motives. At this moment, sitting in the prison day room, I knew that Hitch knew me and understood that America consisted of an amalgam of the four of us. I was who I was because America had at least given us the freedom to question and think and doubt and swim upstream if others were swimming downstream. But I also realized that it would always be a battle for true democracy and compassion in my America, for the forces of capitalism may be stronger than its people's will for equality.

My God—Hitch was one of us even though he didn't go to war. I guess he wasn't meant to. I hadn't ever thought about that before this moment, facing him in his humble prison overalls.

My mind jumped to the vision I'd had at Cornell in the Straight cafeteria—the four of us heading off into four different directions. This moment in prison was an epiphany for me.

I grabbed Hitch's arm, pulled it forward, and hugged him closely.

"I love you, man," I said spontaneously.

"You too, Ammo."

June 27 was falling on a Tuesday. The wedding and the Lardy Family Farm Day would be perfect together. The guest list was narrowing down. As I expected, only twenty or so people would be going by chartered bus. Mom's brothers and sisters would all come, as well as two of my cousins. At times during the planning it seemed some of Mom's family thought they were going on a safari from the way they talked. I guess you could have looked at it that way.

I felt very close to Mary, Donny's mom. I knew how fragile and isolated she was, and I told her I would drive to Pennsylvania and pick her up. I never did talk to Patricia, Donny's sister, but Mary told me she would not come.

Babatunde was in Nigeria working in the government, and Baba was traveling with his band. Both were coming. I felt as if it would not be the same without them. They were so dear to me as well as being mystically close to me through our common heritage. At times I felt as if I should tell both of them about my discovery of my African-American roots, but I could not seem to talk about it.

Two of the special people in Bo's life were coming: Anna Mae, whom I had met as the spiritual leader of Mound Bayou when I visited, and Homesick James, his dad Elmore's rhythm guitarist and dear friend, who was with Elmore when he died. Anna Mae was the maternal and spiritual force that his mother, Lucy, could not be all the time. Homesick was a Delta bluesman of enormous commitment and love.

By the end of May everything seemed to be shaping up. Edna and the girls had placed everybody in homes or rooming houses, and Syd and Bo were settled in fine and excited.

The Wedding

Syd and Ben were the only people who knew about Rebecca's letters and the love story within. I never did ask Syd if she had told Bo about our Rebecca heritage. It was her life, and I trusted her. Syd felt that our ancestral home was a spiritual sanctuary. She did not want to see it before her wedding. She told me she would see it when she was brought to the farm for the wedding ceremony.

I decided I would go to Moorefield three weeks before the wedding. Syd was to arrive three days before and stay with Edna. Bo would come two days before and stay with Gertie's son. I arranged for the bus to come on Sunday, June 25. I had to be sure there was no travel and there were no events on Saturday because of Syd and Mom and Susan and all the family who were Orthodox. The wedding was to be on Tuesday at eleven o'clock, followed by the Lardy Family Day bash at the Willows' barn at three o'clock.

I arrived on June 6 and moved in with Wordie. He knew I was planning the wedding events at the farm, but he didn't know I was going to transport his piano from the church. Music was important to me, and I wanted Wordie to play and sing. I had also asked Babatunde and Baba to bring their drums. I asked Bo to be sure Homesick James brought his guitar. Allen Ginsberg was to arrive alone on Saturday.

I knew that the last time Dad had seen Wordie and the farm was fifty years before, upon their father's death. I wanted to be there when Dad and

Wordie saw each other again, and I wanted to see him as he set foot on the farm. I'm not sure what I expected, but I wanted to feel what my dad felt inside of him. It seemed that my whole life's quest consisted of discovering the enigma of my dad's deep self.

I needed to be sure there was kosher food for my family at the Lardy family gathering. Boy, I thought, this was going to be a strange event. Initially I didn't need to worry about the catering of the after-wedding party since it was to be part of the family day. I had previously arranged to drive to Pittsburgh to an Orthodox Jewish catering firm before I arrived, but I was a bit worried that they couldn't produce. I did the trip in one day and was pleased. Wordie asked the principal of Moorefield High, Pompey Delafield, to enlist six strong senior boys to help schlep the food from Pittsburgh to the barn. They also would help with other chores and especially with moving Wordie's piano to our farm.

The chuppah, or traditional wedding canopy, that signifies the couple's new home and that Syd and Bo would stand under was going to be made from branches and twigs scattered around the farm. Syd asked me to design it and to use wildflowers to adorn it.

I went to the farm every day after I arrived. Many times I walked around the house, just listening to the crunch of fallen leaves and twigs and the near and distant sounds of birds through the forest. These excursions were spiritual experiences for me. I rarely went into the house. About five days before the wedding I decided I should clean the house well. I brought a broom, and that was it. I knew Syd wanted to experience the homestead as I had found it and in its last state. I did not go up to Rebecca's room until the day preceding the wedding. I walked slowly from wall to wall, feeling Rebecca's presence and breathing in the fragrance emanating from her flowers. It was a meditative experience.

I waited for my most anxious moments—that of Dad and Wordie's meeting. I felt a mixture of excitement and nervousness.

The day arrived. Only two hours after the bus had pulled into Moorefield on Sunday the 25th, I waited with Wordie at his house.

The phone rang and I was in the living room when I saw Wordie pick it up and say, "Hallo." His back was toward me and he said, "Yes, Phillip, I'll see you in fifteen minutes." As he said that, I could tell that the muscles of his strong upper back tensed. He hung up the phone and turned around.

"Hardy is comin'."

"I heard, Wordie."

"Hardy is comin'."

I had never seen Wordie in the state he was in during the short wait for his brother. He was like a nervous child, moving almost aimlessly between rooms as if looking for something. I imagined the excitement he was feeling. I felt my own excitement and nervousness, but in my heart I also felt warm joy.

Wordie ended up standing by the screen door with it open. He stood almost motionless for the last five minutes waiting. I stood behind him.

"I hear George's cab—he's comin'," said Wordie at least thirty seconds before I heard it.

The car pulled up and Dad was in the passenger seat facing the house. Mom was in the back. I saw Dad open the door and stand tall, dressed in his customary suit and tie. Without any expression he walked up the wooden porch steps. Wordie still stood half hidden behind the screen door. When Dad reached the landing, Wordie opened the screen door.

"Hello, Wordie."

"Hallo, Hardy."

Dad then reached up with both his arms and grabbed Wordie's shoulders and pulled Wordie toward him. I was fixated on Dad's face. I realized again that it seemed that throughout my whole life I had been transfixed by the deep emotion that existed behind my dad's face. I wanted to see and feel what he felt at this moment. What I experienced was not a realization of who Dad was but who these two brothers were together. They actually seemed to look like two of a pair even though Dad was in a suit and tall and thin and Wordie was in overalls, stockier but the same height. They were bookends—they seemed like sculptured Appalachian bookends, and they actually looked like each other, although I had never thought this before. I could see the tiny tears in Wordie's eyes, but in Dad's face as he smiled I saw satisfaction—satisfaction that his Wordie was alive and well. He never gave away an emotion at that moment other than satisfaction.

Mom had climbed the stairs behind Dad, softly placing her cane on the landing and staying on the porch while they hugged. Dad and Wordie didn't say anything more as they stood face to face, Wordie with his arms straight down and Dad holding Wordie's shoulders. They stood looking at each other, Wordie seeing Dad with the special and wonderful senses he possessed.

It must have been more than two minutes that they just stood face to face, and then Wordie lifted his arms. He ran his cupped hands down

Dad's face the same way he had when he'd met me. No word was said. Visually it was like Dad was being caressed. I heard Wordie utter a soft "Hardy." Then Wordie pulled Dad toward him and hugged him and said, "Hallo, Helen."

Mom opened the screen door and walked in.

"Well ... hello, my mishbukka," she said with a wide smile on her face. I laughed softly but out loud. Here was my mom. She had never met Wordie and here she was acting like another coup had taken place. She had snared another relative, another new member of the family—in this case another old member of the family.

Wordie seemed to tower over Mom as he walked over to her. He proceeded to feel Mom's face. As he dropped his arms, he said, "I can see where Amos gets his good looks" and smiled.

Mom said, "You charmer" and smiled also. Dad cracked a small smile bigger than any I had seen in my life.

And then we had pie and coffee with virtually nothing said for about an hour—just like we were all family.

Mom told me she and Dad would see the farm on the day of the wedding. I asked Mom why Dad would not want to go before.

"You know how your dad is. He is very strong and purposeful. It must be his Appalachian roots." She smiled as she said this.

Syd and Bo had not seen each other for the previous week. Syd had the mikveh, or ritual bath, performed by her mom, Susan, in a pond on the Willows' farm.

I arrived at the farm early in the morning on June 27. It was going to be a warm day, with some mist in the morning that would burn off by noon. I had finished the chuppa the day before. Folding chairs had been set up in a semicircular fashion in front of the chuppa by my high school crew.

I felt peace and impending joy. But as well, I could not stop thinking of Rebecca. I was possessed by my indecision about what to do with her letters. I wanted the world to know. As I slowly walked outside the house, I felt Rebecca's presence. I began to think of my conversation with Ben about what to do with her letters. Ben would have published them as is, acknowledging the literary coup that it was. We had discussed the narratives I had added, and whether to leave them in. Then there was the issue of my family, and especially Dad—and again it seemed that I hit a wall of indecision. As I walked that morning of the wedding, I felt all these thoughts floating around my being. I saw bursts of sunlight filtering through the trees, and with them there were swirls of wind catching up the butterflies and other flying insects. They seemed to fly with these gusts, and as the winds and sunlight caught me, I felt a warm burst of wind in my heart. It was the Cosmos at work, reawakening me to the deep layers of life that existed just beyond my conscious being. I knew I really had no control over what was happening. Ultimately, the playbook was written and all I needed to do was catch the ride—Rebecca was within me.

I waited for the wedding party and guests to arrive.

Allen Ginsburg was wearing a white kurta shirt and salwar pants representing East Indian culture. He was also wearing an embroidered yarmulke, or skullcap, representing the Orthodox Jewish culture. He had brought his father's tallis, or prayer shawl. It was richly embroidered and very old. His beard was full and rich and resplendent. He looked like a spiritual pilgrim, and in actuality he looked like who he really was.

All the men wore white skullcaps with Bo and Syd's name and the wedding date inside.

Wordie wore his overalls and a beautiful plaid shirt. He had shined his own shoes, and they were sparkling.

I could swear that my four uncles were wearing the same suits they had worn for my bar mitzvah twenty-five years before—and they probably were.

Mom wore a knee-length dress that looked really formal to me. It was blue and had sequins. She wore pumps. She had told me she and Jemima were going shopping together for their outfits at Bloomingdales.

Jemima wore a pink-and-blue dress that was less formal than Mom's.

Mrs. Rabinowitz wore a dress similar to Mom's, only it was pink and a tad longer at the knee.

Anna Mae wore a colorful floral full chiffon dress and a wide-brim hat to match.

Babatunde and Baba both wore traditional African robes with beautiful caps.

Susan was wearing a stunning dress. It was the most formal: black and close fitting. Around the collar were embroidered flowers. Susan looked trim and fit, and I know she had deliberately lost weight, as I'm sure many moms of the bride do for their daughter's wedding.

Dad wore a sharp black suit and tie.

I wore a white shirt and slacks.

Ben and Manny both wore loosely fitting casual clothes with sandals.

Zel wore a silky pale pink dress that hugged every part of her beautifully sensual body. She wore her hair up, with wisps of it falling over her face. She looked sexy as usual.

Bo wore a black tux. It looked fantastic on him. He was such a handsome guy. He had a permanent bright smile on his face.

Sydney looked like she had stepped out of a fairy tale—the princess vulnerable and fragile and beautiful beyond description. She wore a long and flowing ivory gown that accentuated her beautiful tall body. She was a stunner. She also had a permanent smile on her face.

As I stood among the trees and birds and forest around our ancestral American home, I could see the diversity of humanity amongst us. I felt that this was a coming together of my own personal Cosmos. I felt the spirit of Rebecca and even Donny. And then I had this thought that I was only a catalyst and no more than that. Maybe it was everyone's story and I was just a small distant star among the many.

Allen stood alone at the foot of the steps to the house with the chuppa in front of him.

There was a center aisle between the chairs, and Allen raised his arm and signaled for both sets of the bride's grandparents to come forth. Mom was beaming and Dad had a soft smile on his face. Mr. and Mrs. Rabinowitz had a quizzical look on their faces as they walked, as if they wondered what the heck was happening.

Next Wordie and I came, both sharing the role of best man. As I escorted Wordie, my arm in his, I could feel the nervous excitement in his body.

Next was Morris, all suited up and awkward at best.

Then Bo, arm in arm with Anna Mae. She walked with joy and the rhythm of her spiritual being.

Clara came alone next. She was maid of honor. She was a junior version of my mom, wearing almost the same dress.

And then the beautiful bride, veiled, and flanked by her parents, Susan and Alvin.

We flanked the couple, and Bo and Syd stood opposite Allen, facing each other. Both were smiling.

I remember the moments before Allen spoke. It was quiet except we all knew that we were in a reclaimed forest. You could hear the buzz of the dragonflies and the chirps of birds in the trees. And out of the corner of our eyes we occasionally would catch a butterfly flirting with the wind.

"Bless Adonai, the One who is blessed. Bar-re-chu et Adonai ha-me-vo-rach.

"Ba-ruch Adonai ha-me-vo-rach le-o-lam va-ed. Bless Adonai, the One who is blessed to eternity and forever."

Allen went on with the Shema in Hebrew and English. He was magnificent. I could see the culture in his eyes. I felt the stir of our family. I could feel their satisfaction. I thought I heard Uncle Irving say under his breath, "A *real* Rebbi."

"Blessed art thou You Adonai, King of the Universe, Creator of light ...," repeated Allen in Hebrew, finishing his opening prayer.

Allen was holding a beautiful old prayer book and looked down on it only intermittently. I was truly impressed with his knowledge and presence. Behind him and on the floor were two beautiful silver and gold goblets filled with wine. Next to them, and rolled up, was the ketubah, or marriage contract. And next to that was a wineglass wrapped in a white linen napkin.

After a number of other short prayers, and other invocations, Allen said with arms outstretched, "Blessed is He Who has come, Who is powerful above all. He who is great above all. He Who is supreme above all. May He bless the groom and bride."

He then reached down behind him and picked up one goblet. It was filled with wine. He gave it to Bo and signaled for him to sip. He then gave it to Syd and signaled for Clara to lift her veil. She sipped. He held the goblet up and signaled for me, holding the simple gold ring for the bride, to give it to Bo. Allen then reached for the ketubah and unrolled it and read the essence of the marriage contract, partially in Hebrew. The ketubah was beautiful, with colorful designs and calligraphy. It was hand done. Allen then signaled for Clara, who was holding a small bouquet of white flowers as well as Bo's ring, to give the ring to Syd. Bo placed Syd's ring on her finger. Syd placed Bo's ring on his. They were beaming with joy. Allen gave them each a sip of wine. He then raised his hands and said, "Behold you are consecrated to me by means of this ring, according to the ritual of Moses and Israel." He then announced that we would share the honor of reading the seven blessings. I read one. Allen had Wordie repeat after him. Alvin read one. Susan and Mom read one. Morris read one, and then Allen read the last. "Blessed are you, Hashem, Our God, King of the universe,

Who creates the fruit of the vine." And then he repeated that blessing in Hebrew. Then Allen held the two goblets of wine and poured one into the other and then poured the other into the other, and he held both out, and signaled the bride and the groom to each sip. He then passed each goblet to all of us standing under the chuppa and we sipped wine. He then lifted his arms and stretched them out and looked up to the sky. He looked like Moses ready to part the Red Sea. He rolled his arms in a circular motion. I was mesmerized by it all, and only now did my first thought come to mind. He looked like he was a helicopter preparing to lift straight up into the sky and disappear—and I almost expected this to happen, knowing Allen Ginsberg. But it did not happen. It must have been some sort of ritual. He must have been praying. I think it was related to his Hindu and Eastern philosophy background. His arms stopped moving, his face returned to earth, and he reached behind him and picked up the wineglass rolled up in a linen napkin. He kneeled and placed it on the ground between Bo and Syd. He then looked at Bo and said, "Smash this glass with your right foot and it will symbolize that until our Temple is rebuilt, we cannot have joy." Bo smashed the glass, and Allen signaled with his arms for Bo and Syd to come together to kiss. They did just that, like they were in an old movie from the 1920s with no sound. Their bodies seemed like one, intertwined with each other. There was not a sound from the rest of us. Even the insects and birds and the whole forest had stopped. There was no wind—just the bright vision of the combined lovers. Allen then signaled to the audience to clap and we all did. It then seemed that the birds started singing and the dragonflies buzzed and the Appalachian forest was alive with activity again. Allen reached into his shirt and brought out a rolled-up sheet of paper. He looked down, then up to the sky, and then down again, and he raised one arm and said in a stirring voice, "Wedding Odyssey."

He continued:

"Wedding Odyssey. Black and white. White and black.
Making love to the world. Kissing the birds. Caressing the bees.
Enveloping the trees. Monuments of sweetness flowing dark
chocolate over the faces of indifference. Lightening their being.
Until darkness begets lightness ..."

Uh oh, I thought—and behind me I heard Uncle Irving mutter an annoyed "What's he saying?" Here he was, Allen Ginsberg, the stream-of-consciousness Allen Ginsberg. What else should I expect? He was the monument of poetry—of free-stream poetry, the man who mingled with every culture on earth, the man who embraced every crevice of human experience. What else should I expect? I thought. I also thought, Holy shit.

He continued:

> "Ribbons of color sliding into an ocean of gray. Fish smiling. Mountains kneeling over. Rocks becoming bunnies. Clouds saying I do. The sun loving you forever until the moon has an affair with the lovely Venus. Beauty is you. You are beauty. Beauty becomes you. The world melting into your beauty. You melting into the world. Becoming one with the One. Glaciers melting into avenues of honey. Honey sweetening the world. Two becoming one—the One—the only one. You and love. Love is you. We love you."

He then smiled a broad Buddha-like smile as he looked down on Syd and Bo. There was a soft rumbling of murmurs and I heard one tentative clap—I'm not sure from who—and another, until someone yelled "Bravo" behind me; I think it was Uncle Irving.

I turned my head and looked around. Everyone had smiles on their faces.

I had planned to surprise Wordie like he had surprised me at his church, bringing my guitar. I knew he could not see the piano up on the porch. I turned to him and said, "Wordie—would you play 'In the Sweet By and By'"?

Wordie smiled and said, "I would if I had my piano."

I said, "You do, Wordie" as I escorted him up the steps to the piano.

"You trickster," he said with a broad smile.

As he started to play, Anna Mae began to sing the words. She had a magnificent spiritual voice that resonated through the forest.

> *In the sweet by and by*
> *We shall meet on that beautiful shore*
> *In the sweet by and by ...*

Homesick picked up his guitar and started to add solo notes. And Babatunde and Baba began to caress their drums softly at first and then with more and more rhythm until the whole arrangement started to sound like an orchestra. Then people started to clap in unison with the music. It was wonderful. Syd and Bo were thrilled. It was pure joy and must have gone on for fifteen minutes. I think this mixed bag of humanity that was our wedding party become one during that musical moment—black and white, Christian and Jew, the Himalayas and Appalachia—all became one.

As it wound down, Anna Mae became quiet, and then I could hear her hum musically but very softly.

O beautiful for spacious skies
For amber waves of grain
For purple mountain majesties
Above the fruited plain!
America! America!
God shed his grace on thee
And crown thy good with brotherhood
From sea to shining sea!

Everybody was quiet. The musicians did not play while she sang. I looked up and noticed that the birds had perched on branches quietly, as if they were in a concert hall in the balcony tier watching a performance.

When she finished, everyone started to hug each other. It was amazing. It seemed as if someone had said, "Hug your neighbor to your right," for everyone was hugging. I felt warmth all over. I'm sure everyone did.

And we were then off to the Willows' farm for an Appalachian party.

We started filtering into the Willows' barn about two thirty in the afternoon. The whole town was invited, of course. It was an annual event. They had placed the food in the far corner along the wall as we had planned. There were to be the two sections for food, kosher and nonkosher. I noticed that someone had put up a small placard on the tables of the kosher food. It said COSHA FOOD. I giggled a bit and didn't say anything to anyone.

What a party. Frederick and Jesse and Chester's band was set up on one side. We had brought Wordie's piano back. Stella and Blanche, the clogging twins, performed. Homesick James and Babatunde and Baba played as well. There was a mixture of gospel, Appalachian, blues, and African tribal music. Everybody danced. Bo and Syd were on the floor all the time. Syd threw her shoes off and danced with her long gown in bare feet. I saw the "young'uns" from town sneak over to the "Cosha" food and touch some as if they were going to get a shock. Finally one of them ate a piece and giggled.

Man—there was food and food and food. There was spicy cabbage salad, fried okra, pickled crab apples, corn bread, fried chicken, mountain bean salad, squash burgers, wild game, sweet potato pones, Brunswick stew, sawmill gravy, biscuits, syllabub, homemade sausage, sorghum syrup, and wild grapes.

On the "Cosha" side we had three different tables since you can't mix meat and dairy dishes. We had one for the neutral foods that had no meat or dairy. This was the pareve table. The *milchig* and *fleishig*, Yiddish for the milk and meat, were on two other tables. There was tzimmes, kugel, gefilte fish, challah bread, knishes, corned beef, pastrami, lox, kreplach, matzoh ball soup, brisket of beef, schmaltz, and blintzes. Many of the locals asked to try the kosher food and vice versa for the nonkoshers from New York. It was an eating free-for-all. It turned out to be a great party. Uncle Sam started to pick up Bo and called my other uncles to help him. He placed Bo in a chair. The same was done for Syd. Someone yelled out, "Play 'Hava Nagila.'" The musicians looked over to everybody with a quizzical look. Then the Jewish crowd started to spontaneously sing this wedding song, and everyone started clapping in unison to the rhythm as both Bo and Syd were hoisted in the air. They were then jolted up and down on their chairs to the beat of the traditional Jewish wedding ritual. The musicians picked up on the melody and beat and, we then got an improvised rendition of "Hava Negila" with drums, electric guitar, piano, fiddle, bass, and dulcimer. You could hear everybody singing, but Anna Mae was especially vibrant. Bo and Syd were laughing to the point of crying as they were bounced all over the place. It was a sight to be seen. The party wound down at about ten in the evening. I think everyone thoroughly enjoyed themselves.

The bus was leaving the next day for New York. Syd and Bo were heading out together in Bo's car to an unspecified honeymoon destination. I was staying on. I knew that I needed time to digest this event and had many thoughts about Rebecca that I wanted to sort out. I decided I would return to the farm and sleep in Rebecca's room with nothing but a candle. I guess I was looking for something from the Cosmos—although I wasn't sure what it was.

Notes after the Wedding

Late Tuesday night, June 27, 1978
By candlelight on the floor of Rebecca's room

"I THINK OF WHO I am. I am Amos and Amie and A-Moes and A.B. and Kid and Ammo and Stream. I am Jewish and from Europe, and I am Christian and from Appalachia. I am white and I am black. I am a soldier and I am a pacifist. I have been in love all my life, yet I never have given my love to anyone. I am relentless with my quest and sure of it, and I am always questioning everything I do. I revere life and see life as absurd—and above all I am given the Cosmos as a gift. The Cosmos has taken me for the rides of my life, from the barren and darkest experiences on earth to the loftiest and serene heavens above— and it has brought to me visions never seen on earth. It has infused my soul with the rhythms and music of our collective life. It has taken me within the hearts of those who have lived in our past through their written words—and all of it only through its own Cosmic will.

"But encompassing everything, I think I am an American—and America is me. America is filled with promise and unfulfilled because she cannot live up to her promise. She is powerful and powerless. She is tolerant, and she is intolerant. She is rich, and she is poor. She is an adolescent, and she is an adult. She is beauty, and she is flawed. She is ignorance personified, complacent and incapable, and she is filled with aspiration—striving to do well and to be good.

"America, my beautiful, when will you become what you strive to be?"

I felt compelled to reach under the floorboards and pick up Rebecca's letters and bring them close to my heart. I felt as if I needed her. Gently I lifted the stack, and as I lay on my back in the ever-decreasing glow of the flickering candle, I placed the letters on my chest, the fragrance permeating my whole being—and I fell asleep.

I must have slept through the night soundly. And then I awoke.

It was quiet, with only the sounds of early morning—the soft wind, the songbirds.

I heard a distant whinny, like a horse's. I slowly rose and peeked out the window to see what I thought was the tail of a horse passing my view and instantly out of sight. It appeared to be white. I stretched and walked downstairs with no thoughts but curiosity.

On opening the front screen door there stood before me, right in front of the house, a black woman standing next to a beautiful white horse.

"Hello, Amos."

"Hello," I said almost as if in a dream. "Rebecca?" I said without thinking.

"Yes, Amos."

"Rebecca, what are you doing here? Where did you come from?"

"I came from my walk, my walk in the woods. I always walk in the woods with Old Ivory."

"My God …," I said in disbelief.

"You called me back, Amos. You brought me back to my home."

I just stared at her, speechless. There she was, slim and beautiful. She was wearing a light white dress to the knees, and her hair was curly and black and shoulder length. Her skin was deep brown, and her lips were full and almost pinkish white. Her eyes were brown surrounded by a sea of white, and her teeth were just pearls, shining in the morning mist. Old Ivory seemed to tower above her, and he stood straight and quiet as if he were her protector.

"Rebecca … Rebecca."

"Amos, you brought life again to our family. You brought joy and beauty. I knew our heritage would not disappear. Your empathy for the sweetness in life carried me home. You carried me and Old Ivory home, Amos."

"Why am I filled with such ambivalence?" I said, almost to myself.

"Because of who you are. The world is not kind and never was. Kindness comes from the heart, and only from the heart. And the heart is very fragile like the butterfly in wind. And you are all heart, my Amos—you are all heart."

"I want the world to know you, Rebecca. I want the world to see you like I see you."

"I didn't write or leave my letters to become famous. What happened here yesterday was my gift to the world, and it was also the world's gift to me. America need not know more about my life now. It is not ready. The world is not ready. America is not ready."

"Are you saying that I should not publish your letters?"

"Yes. America is growing slowly and her growth will be only from the heart, not her power and strength. My life is living on in you and Sydney and Wordie and Phillip. You will tell the world, Amos, but not now. It will come from your heart. You will know when."

"Yes, Rebecca," I said softly.

"Amos, walk with me and Ivory through the woods."

She extended her hand to me. I descended the few steps to the ground and opened my hand, and she held it as if I were her child. She then turned and we both walked slowly with Old Ivory away from the house and into the thickening woods. She said nothing as we walked through the crunchy leaves brushing past the soft greens of early summer. Her hand was warm and comforting. I felt as if I was walking though a mist. After a few minutes, I turned to look at her. She was gone.

Slowly and without emotion, I retraced my steps and walked back up to Rebecca's room. There lay the stack of letters on the floor. I picked them up and brought them to my chest as if to hug them. Once more the fragrance of Rebecca infused me. I stood holding them closely and dearly for about five minutes. I then kneeled down and placed the letters in their original resting place under the floorboards. I got up and turned around, and without looking back I walked downstairs and out the screen door to the road and my car. I stayed with Wordie for a few days, and we both relived the joyous wedding together.

I left for New York the next week.

My Notes on the Cusp of January 1, 1980

I AM CELEBRATING MY fortieth birthday alone in my log cabin deep within the woods of the Adirondacks. It is snowing right now, and the time is 11:58 P.M. It will be 1980 in two minutes, and I will be forty. I wanted to be alone during this transformation. I wanted to be with myself and within myself.

Syd just gave birth to a daughter—Rebecca Alika Rabinowitz-Brooks.

The stroke Dad suffered at the beginning of December has left him unable to speak and use his arms well, and obviously unable to work. Two nights ago, Mom by his side, I watched as Dad, trying to rehabilitate himself by writing, wrote in an almost unintelligible chicken scratch "Rebecca stories." He then looked up at me, and making a contorted effort, he smiled.

Everything is so quiet with the falling snow blanketing my world. There is not a sound. There is not a being. I arise and walk to the window and look through the glass, seeing only what I think is the reflection of my own face in the dark. It is not my face; it is Rebecca's face, and she smiles. I turn and walk to my desk. It is Mary's desk. She gave it to me after the wedding. I cherish it. It is filled with magic.

I reach into a cubbyhole and pull out writing paper. At the top of the page I write the title word *Discovery.*

The first paragraph starts, "I think it was in the fall of 1955, maybe September …"

Post Script

I FINISHED MY MEMOIRS in 1982. After the last word was written, and without thought, I drove to our farm with the only copy and climbed the steps to Rebecca's room, placing my unpublished manuscript under the floorboards adjacent to Rebecca's letters.

Two years almost to the day, in 1984, I went to the farm again and retrieved only Rebecca's letters with my accompanying narrative, but not my memoirs. I published Rebecca's letters under the title *From African Princess to American Slave: A Love Story*. I felt in my heart that it was the right time. I did not even think it was me filling in the moments of Rebecca's life. I trusted the Cosmos. I trusted my gift; I was present with her as she lived. I never acknowledged that she was my paternal great-grandmother. Her story stood on its own.

Rebecca's story won almost every prestigious nonfiction literary award after publication, although it stirred enormous emotions among the narrow minded in America. I had become a worldwide literary celebrity. It was translated into twenty-three languages and has gone into its tenth printing. It has made the publishers, Lardowitz and Fink, very wealthy. Every penny of the profits has been given to Donny's Fund, to teach peace to children. Syd and Bo have shared the responsibility as co-executive directors.

In 1990, my dad died, on January 1, my fiftieth birthday. I was with him at home. Just minutes before he died, Mom walked out of the room for a moment. I was alone with Dad. He motioned with a soft grunt, barely lifting his right hand in a gesture for me to come closer to his face as he tried to speak.

"Amos," he said very slowly, his voice barely audible. "Amos ... thank you, son. Believe in yourself. Share your gift."

Dad had never talked to me like this—like he really knew me. I was so touched that he thanked me like that. He was the ultimate provider but he never really acknowledged me that way before. He was always there for me—always—but he had never deeply thanked me.

Four months later I published *My American Journey: The Memoirs of Amos Boris Lardowitz*. With this, my journey and the journey to Rebecca's discovery were complete.

A few revelations came to me just after I published my memoirs:

I don't believe Dad ever knew that his father's mother was an African slave.

I think Dad probably was more like me than I could imagine—on a quest to new and unknown places to help support the family he left in West Virginia, just as I was on a quest to rediscover what he had left—both of us completing the circle.

My dad was the touchstone to my discovery, but my story is really about humanity and our interconnected lives and spirits—it is about the Cosmos.

I discovered also that humankind is a quilt whose interwoven threads consist of all of us—and when you trace just one small thread at the frayed end, you will find that it winds in and out and through the whole quilt, only to come out in the place you discovered it to begin with.

I discovered that my America was really just like me—not quite sure of herself, and searching and probing and not perfect by any means.

And most of all, I discovered that my African great-grandmother, who was a slave, was my soul mate—who would know?

Amos Boris Lardowitz